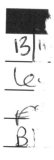

KT-449-085

THE ARCADE

The Arcade is set in Haisby, a small town on the North Norfolk coast, and tells the story of the townsfolk who work in its shopping arcade and of their fortunes during an eventful year.

It's an odd place, the Arcade. There is Sam, who runs the restaurant a good deal better than he managed to run his marriage. Caresse sells beauty aids and pontificates about diet whilst secretly gobbling chocolates. There is Miss Turner the tailoress in her wheelchair, and Marj who cooks and waits at table and loves a policeman. But most important, is Anthea, thirty-nine, the abused daughter of a sadistic cleric. Anthea is the catalyst who seems at first to have no place in the Arcade. Yet who can say that she is not the happiest of them all, in the end?

THE ARCADE

THE ARCADE

by
Judy Turner

MAGNA PRINT BOOKS
Long Preston, North Yorkshire,
England.

British Library Cataloguing in Publication Data.

Turner, Judy
  The Arcade.

  A catalogue record for this book is
  available from the British Library

  ISBN 0 7505 0181 2

First Published in Great Britain by New English Library Ltd., 1990.

Copyright © 1990 by Judy Turner.

Published in Large Print 1992 by arrangement with New English
Library Ltd., London and the copyright holder.

Printed and bound in Great Britain by
T.J. Press (Padstow) Ltd., Cornwall, PL28 8RW.

For all the girls who worked with me at the Coffee Pot Restaurant, Wrexham, but especially for Margaret Edwards whose boundless energy and enthusiasm, sense of humour and sweet nature made all our lives easier—to say nothing of her laugh! Thanks, Mags.

CHAPTER ONE

When Sam visited the Arcade for the first time the sun had been shining. It had picked out the subtle shades in the old paving stones, made the bow-fronted windows sparkle, and it had brought the brilliant May green of the churchyard at the far end of the Arcade into focus so that the covered way had seemed an enchanted place, a pathway to romance and sunshine after the grey and brown bustle of Lord Street.

That was why he had bought the wine bar. He had sent Martin down by himself a few days later to take a look and Martin, who had gone on a grey day, had been doubtful. But then they had visited Haisby together and the sun had been shining again. It had not seemed to matter that the Arcade led only to Cloister Row and the church, that Cloister Row itself had no fascinating shops but was a meandering little cobbled street with the churchyard railings on one side and flats and offices on the other. It was a dead-end, what was more, leading not to the sea, which would have been an attraction, but merely to a chest-high, white-painted cob wall which stopped the unwary from descending abruptly down a fifteen-foot cliff onto the pebbly beach beneath.

Today however, twelve months later, Sam turned onto Lord Street, enjoying a rare rush of optimism along with the warmth of the early sun on his back. He strode along the empty, six o'clock street, aware that he was in good time and ahead of the girls, suddenly filled with enthusiasm for the wine bar, the sandwich delivery service which he and Martin had started, and for life itself. It would all turn out all right, the wine bar would suddenly become the fashionable place to eat and drink, he and Martin would become millionaires and never have to worry again about paying the wages during January, or replacing staff, or selling off unpopular vintages.

The Arcade was bounded at either end by tall, wrought-iron gates. Sam unlocked them, swung them back, and then went down to the wine bar to open up for the girls.

The sandwich delivery service meant that in order to get the delivery girls away on time the sandwich-makers had to be in the kitchen by seven buttering, slicing, and slapping sandwiches into bags. No matter how the wine bar might falter, the delivery service throve. Three

10

bright, cheery girls left Sam's Place each week-day morning, baskets piled high with food, and returned at lunchtime, their bags bursting with cash.

So now, Sam unlocked the kitchen door and switched on the lights, then made for the cellar stairs. Marj would be in quite soon, she was always early, but until she arrived Sam would toil up and down the steps bringing up the sandwich fillings which were kept in the fridges downstairs.

As he worked, Sam reflected that if they had only got the delivery service and no restaurant, they would probably have been making a fortune, but the lease of the place was simply too heavy to support even a thriving business when a slow starter like the wine bar, was part of the deal. But still...Sam squared his shoulders and began to arrange the fillings along the back of the workbench...this was only their first year and in fact, though they had seen the wine bar for the first time twelve months ago, it had been September before they moved in. Plenty of time to make a name for ourselves, Sam consoled himself. Plenty of time.

A shout and a clatter at the Lord Street end of the Arcade told Sam that Tony, the baker, had delivered. The piles of loaves, baguettes and rolls were piled up on a table left out for

11

the purpose, but Sam always hurried along and got them in. You never knew, there were some pretty odd people about even at this hour, and dogs, too. Once, a baguette had rolled out of the wire tray and been christened by a leg-lifting dog. Sam had been wary ever since.

He was halfway back to the kitchen again when he remembered that sunny days, in fact, were not necessarily good for business. The punters did not want to leave the sunshine for the glassed-in Arcade, let alone for the darker interior of the wine bar. Martin, who was artistic as well as being an inspired cook, had done out the big upstairs functions room with paper seagulls suspended from the ceiling on fine thread so that they moved in every breeze, but even this eye-catching decor was not enough to lure the punters away from the Mac-Donalds and Wimpys and the various Hamburger Heavens which dotted the town. Few indeed, so far, were the holidaymakers who wanted an excellent meal in a quiet setting. They preferred to spend their money on greasy chips and burgers, on gassy beer or virulently coloured pop.

Sam minded all this more for Martin than himself. Martin was his twenty-seven-year-old nephew, the only son of his beloved elder brother, Edward. When Edward had known he was dying he had asked Sam to keep an eye on Martin, and with good reason, for Martin, though a genius, was also a hard drinker with the unreliable temper which sometimes seems to afflict gifted chefs. Consequently, within three years of his father's death, Martin had lost half-a-dozen excellent jobs. He had insulted a valued customer at the Savoy, thrown knives on board the *QE2*, lain on the kitchen floor of the Ritz in both a drunken stupor and the remains of his famous sherry trifle, tried to seduce a very rich, big-bosomed American lady...the list went on and on, with Martin repentant each time...until it happened again.

Sam had done his best but it had been difficult because his wife, Joanne, had hated Martin. It turned out she had not been all that fond of Sam, either, since she left him, bored by his addiction to gardening and birdwatching, deriding his steady but poorly paid job in the drawing office of an engineering firm. Joanne had ambition, and a strong sex drive. Sam had neither. He had quickly begun to view bed as a penance and had become adept at falling asleep as soon as his head touched the pillow. He knew he had been a bad husband and his chief emotion, when Joanne ran off with the man next door, had been relief. Now he could concentrate on doing his best for Martin. In fact, even buying the business had been a sort of escape, because the man next door had been married to the woman next door, and first she swamped Sam with reproaches and bitterness and then she began to insinuate that they could do a lot worse than to comfort each other. Sam, terrified, sold up and began to look for a restaurant even before Martin had slid under the kitchen table at his latest hotel. Within a month they had discovered Haisby-on-sea, found the Arcade, the wine bar, and the little house on Harbour Way.

Now, Sam staggered across the kitchen with the bread, laid the loaves in their appointed places, then made his way out into the Arcade once more, picking up the big yard broom as he went. Despite the fact that it was Monday morning and the Arcade did not open on a Sunday, the place was a mess. At the Lord Street end it was amazing how much litter gathered. The idlers and drunks who threw tins, chip papers and worse into the Arcade could not manage a really good hurl so they posted their unwanted packaging absently between the wrought-iron bars, as though in the honest belief that the Arcade had been built as an enormous waste-bin especially for their convenience. And convenience was the word, Sam thought resignedly, eyeing a large puddle.

Some enterprising soul had piddled in a fine arc through the gates; he would have to go back and fetch a mop and disinfectant. He didn't want his girls facing *that* first thing in the morning.

Sam fetched the mop and bucket and returned to his task. He tried not to remember the last Bank Holiday, May Day, which had dawned cold and overcast and had been a financial disaster. Even though it had come out quite nice after about eleven, no one had wanted a meal. They had set out late from their homes and on arrival in Haisby had bought takeaways; toffee apples, bags of popcorn, chips. The wine bar had only done fourteen meals all day, a disaster. Sam and Martin had cleaned down the kitchen in depressed silence, scarcely daring to catch each other's eyes; all their hopes had come to nought, the bright optimism of their fellow traders had proved false.

Clearing up that night, when Martin had stomped off home, Sam wielded his big brush on a sea of chip papers and lolly wrappers, for the eaters of takeaway food are prodigal with their rubbish, and wondered desperately if he and Martin should lower their standards, go for chips and mushy peas and brightly coloured drinks. But it would be the last straw for Martin's hopes of beating the twin demons of drink

15

and depression, to see the one thing he did excellently well brushed aside. No, they would struggle on for two years, as they had promised themselves when they first opened the place, and then see how things were.

Sam finished mopping and was about to make his way back down the Arcade when a bus screeched to a stop on Lord Street and a pair of long legs with a brief blue skirt above them descended onto the pavement. It was Marj, the morning manageress, getting off the bus with all the energy which Sandra, getting off the bus in her wake, lacked.

'Cheers, Fred, see you tomorrer,' Marj shouted, giving the bus driver the benefit of her wide smile and then turning her large, grey-green gaze on Sam. 'Hi, Sam! What a day, eh? Wish it was my holidays! Had a good mind not to come in, nearly phoned to say I'd broke me leg!'

Marj threw back her head and laughed, high and clear, a blackbird's shout. Behind her Sandra wobbled along on heels so high she looked thin as a rake.

'Morning, girls. You go and get started. I'm just clearing up.'

'Sure will, Sam.'

The two girls click-clicked past, high heels tapping, smelling of soap and talc, clad in summer dresses today instead of the usual jeans. They would want to go out in their coffee break and sit on the tombstones in the churchyard, stripping off as many of their garments as they dared—and that would be a good many —to soak up the sun.

Sam finished mopping and was following them along the paving when a bicycle's soft tick-tick made him draw prudently to one side. It was Poppy Bates, the third member of the team, who cycled in to work from the outskirts of town each day.

Sam, flattened against the wall, shook his head at her as she tore past.

'Go carefully, Poppy, there's a good girl.'

'Hi, Sam. Not late, am I?'

'Not yet.'

Poppy grinned and hurled herself off the bicycle. She was a small girl, just sixteen, on a youth training scheme, and Sam had a soft spot for her. She was always dropping things and burning things, but she was keen to right her mistakes and worked late when they were busy with never a word of complaint. Furthermore, so zealous was she in chasing non-payers to breathlessly point out their mistake that even Martin, who was harder on the girls than the soft-hearted Sam, could he heard to make excuses for Poppy.

'She's a good cook when she gets things right,' Martin said as Poppy took a perfect soufflé from the oven—and dropped it, excruciatingly, on her own sandalled feet. 'But until she get things right all the time she's a small disaster area.'

Marj was the efficient one. Smoothly, without a hiccup, she ran the sandwich side of the business, her voice breaking up into the raucous, unbelievable laugh which could be heard a mile out to sea in a gale. She lived a bus ride from work and went home when the sandwiches were made and the fillings for the next day prepared, then returned to help with lunches and to cook, so that Sam could have a bit of time to himself before they started evening meals—when they did evening meals, which was not often.

Sandy was a dreamer. She seemed to attract rotters and sometimes she made a batch of sandwiches all wrong, or tipped pepper into cake mix.

'Will you leave off a-dreaming, gal Sandy!' Marj would shout, putting things right at her usual speed. 'Come to your senses, my woman, and give that feller a knuckle sandwich, which he richly deserve!'

But Sam knew Sandy never would. She was made to be trodden on. A willowy blonde with big blue eyes and a soft mouth, Sam sometimes had to fight an urge to shout at her himself, and he was not a cruel man.

Now, Poppy abandoned her bike in the cellars and rushed up the stairs to take her place at the workbench. The girls moved into their routine, buttering, slicing, filling. And Sam began his own morning tasks which he could, he reflected, have done in his sleep. He slid chickens into the oven to roast and put forty eggs into a pan, then stood the pan on the stove and went into the restaurant to wipe down the tables. Then he heaved a sack of potatoes up from the vegetable room and began to chip them whilst around him the girls talked, shouted to him above the sound of the radio and commented, often rudely, on the news items which interspersed the music.

It was just another Monday morning, Sam reflected as he finished a pile of chips and put them in water. And next week was the Spring Bank Holiday when he would have to pay double time and pray the day started fine, with a sharp shower at around noon to drive the punters indoors for a meal.

But things could be worse. Martin had only been the worse for drink twice in the last eight months, and both had been high risk time. Christmas and New Year. And although

Martin had got rather furious a few times the girls had always managed to calm him down before he had damaged a customer, or the small but growing reputation of Sam's Place. If only more customers would come, Sam thought yearningly, plugging the kettle in for the girls' morning cuppa, then we'd be able to relax a bit.

'Kettle a-goin', Sam?' Marj shouted as he turned away from putting out the mugs. 'Right, then you git off home, kick that lazy Martin outer his pit! We'll be ready now when them sales girls arrive.'

Sam knew that Marj and her girls would manage equally well without him, that his presence was helpful but not essential, but he enjoyed the quiet of the early morning, the companionship, being ahead of himself with preparations for lunchtime. So now he made three mugs of tea, handed them round, and then went out into the Arcade and headed slowly down towards Cloister Row. He walked down to the sea-wall each morning, sometimes before his kitchen work and sometimes after, just to make sure...of what? He did not know, but it was a soothing ritual and one he would not have missed.

Cloister Row was quiet, only the pigeons, strutting and cooing on its cobbles, the offices shut, the flats above sleeping still. Sunshine spilled, golden, on the church, the gravestones, the long, unkept grass. It fell slowly, like honey through the emerald green of the new leaves on the trees which overhung the railings.

Sam strolled the length of the little street and then leaned against the wall, staring down. Below, the sea crept across the sand but the tide was well out today so no white-topped wavelets licked and creamed against the pebbles which mounded up into a ridge at the top of the shore. No one walked down there, either, not a foot-print disturbed the shining strand. Seagulls mewed against the blue though, dipping, glid-ing, then coming in to land, to squabble over cast-down crusts or the remainder of an ice-cream cone.

Sam watched for a moment, then turned and retraced his steps. He reached the Arcade and slowed once more, glancing in the win-dows of the other shops as he passed in a way which would be impossible, later, when the traders were in. Every morning he did this, trying to decide which shops were an asset to Sam's Place and which made life more dif-ficult.

Waves, the hairdresser, was always clean and pleasant and brought a lot of trade into the Ar-cade with its huge mirrors, comfortable chairs and bright young girls. Thank God for Emma and Jenny, bustling about with their scissors, cutting, blow-waving, perming, sending out for cups of tea and sandwiches. The two girls were both in their mid-twenties, capable and brisk. They came into the wine bar sometimes, ate interesting food and recommended friends and customers to try Sam's Place.

If only everywhere were like Waves, Sam thought wistfully, passing onto the Health Food shop next door. Run by Barry and Lana Johnson, it should have been a pleasant sight but wasn't. The window was full of bags of dried peas and beans, with a display of muesli bars and alternative chocolate. Sam counted three dead flies and sighed over the quantity of dust on the bags and boxes. It was a pity because the Johnsons were so enthusiastic, believing in their products, eating tofu and natural yoghurt and then sneaking over to the wine bar for a piece of Martin's famous Mississippi Mud Pie, or a crepe suzette.

The Johnsons were animal lovers and had a variety of tatty strays which came into the Arcade now and then, lifting a leg against someone's clean frontage or squeezing between the churchyard railings to defecate amongst the tombstones. Barry and Lana, a childless couple, loved the dogs the way they would have loved kids of their own, so it was more than one's life was worth to criticise a single one of the animals.

I wonder if a hint about the Johnson's window might bear fruit, Sam asked himself, moving on. But what was the point? Lana and Barry were doing their best, it would only hurt their feelings. Best let well alone.

Treat Yourself came next. Caresse Mortland leased and ran it and she was, as she kept telling everyone, a fashionable woman, but somehow the window was a let-down. Sam did not care for Caresse, a husky-voiced bottle-blonde, but he did think she could have made a better effort with her window. Today tall jars of soap jostled with a display of perfume, most of which was hidden by a paperchase of tissues and vari-coloured cottonwool, whilst a fan of combs and brushes completed the display.

Untidy, Sam thought dispassionately. Bitty, so that the eye drifted over the display, caught by nothing. He moved on, to the window which was right opposite his own so that customers, willy-nilly, looked out at it.

Bonner's, the old-fashioned gown-shop owned by Miss Violet and Miss Dulcie Bonner, whose faded, out-dated goods were scarcely ever bought, now came next. Sitting in the wine bar, Sam's customers must have shuddered at the sight of ancient pink corsets, loopy knickers and pairs of silk stockings which would have been a snip in the last War but which would never be bought now. It could not be good for trade, either his own or other people's, but Sam knew that the Miss Bonners were weary and wanted to retire. If they did perhaps someone would take over with modern, nineteen-nineties dress-sense, with the ability to pull the shop round, make it pay.

Cheeky little mini-skirts on a boyish model, Sam dreamed. Blouses and shirts, crisp white, mouth-tingling lemon, sweet strawberry, flirting, in the Bonner window, with lean blue jeans, baggy denim culottes.

But it wouldn't happen while the Bonner sisters were in charge so he might as well forget it. And besides, next to Bonner's was the antique shop, run by Archie Pinter, a retired army officer. Archie always did well because he knew his stuff, advertised in the places that mattered and had no staff worries. His window gleamed, his stock-lists were up to date, and because he was a widower he had plenty of time for the place.

Also, of course, Archie had that much envied attribute, a window on Lord Street. So he did not have to entice people into the Arcade, they could look at his display as they passed.

Having admired the antique shop, Sam crossed

the Arcade and looked into the only other shop on that side, for the wine bar took up all the rest of the space. Sam liked Elias, the tall, skinny man who owned and ran Glenarvon Antiquarian Books, and knew that the shop brought the wine bar a lot of custom, browsers who might buy a paperback or who spent a fortune on rare editions often came along to Sam's Place to read in comfort, sipping a coffee or having an early lunch.

Elias's window was beautiful, with rare books held open at their most enticing illustrations, books with beautiful covers closed, and many others displaying their titles. It always drew the eye, unlike some.

But Bonner's is bound to change hands one day, Sam told himself, stepping out into Lord Street and screwing his eyes up against the bright sunshine. And Lana and Barry will realise that a food shop must be clean. Even Caresse might pull her tights up and get a bit of order into the chaos of her window. And anyway, Sam added to himself, walking briskly along the pavement, you're off-duty now, so just enjoy yourself and look forward to summer.

At the end of Lord Street Sam turned right and then left and he was on Harbour Way. It was a pretty road with the houses all very individual, facing out across the water. Sam and Martin lived halfway along, three doors down from the Bonner sisters. Their narrow house was painted white with the front door, windows and shutters deep blue. Sam swung the wooden gate open, took two strides, and was at the front door. He unlocked it and went inside, closing it firmly behind him.

Immediately he forgot the wine bar, the Arcade, and his worries. He thought only about this dear little house which he had lovingly redecorated and furnished, and about Martin, snoring upstairs.

He and Martin were supposed to take turns to open up the Arcade in the mornings, but in practice it was always Sam. Why not? Sam was an early-bird, Martin a night-owl. Now, Sam made for the kitchen. Humming to himself, he got out the ingredients he would need for Martin's breakfast. He would do a grapefruit to start with in the beautiful cut-glass bowl which had once graced Archie's window. Then bacon, two eggs and fried tomatoes. He got the butter out of the fridge and put it on the table. By the time the food was cooked and the toast made the butter would have softened in the kitchen's warmth. Sam enjoyed spoiling Martin a bit, as he might have spoiled his own son had he had one, and it did Martin no harm.

Now, he lit the grill and slid four rounds of bread under it to toast, keeping a wary eye on it as he sliced tomatoes. Things were going well, he would start his own breakfast now. Martin was skinny despite working in kitchens, but Sam had to watch every calorie and anyway he did not have time to prepare two breakfasts with the loving care which he put into Martin's meal. Sam put an egg on to boil, setting the pinger so that he didn't forget it, and then cut himself a round of bread. No butter. Not for a five-foot-ten, fourteen-stone man in his early forties.

Breakfast prepared, Sam put the food into the oven to keep warm and went to wake Martin. He drew back the curtains and Martin mumbled a token protest as the sunlight fell across his face.

'Hey, Sam, I'm asleep,' he said, as he said most mornings, and then sat up, stretched and smiled.

He was a skinny, red-haired, freckled young man, a good deal stronger than he looked, with the light greenish eyes and fair lashes which went with his colouring. He blushed easily and blinked a lot but he could be charming when he chose, and he chose now.

'Oh, Sam, sunshine! It's my afternoon off, too.'

Sam grinned. Martin's afternoons off usually occurred when the sun shone but Sam didn't mind. He'd never been much of a one for lying on the beach, he was happier in the garden or down on the shore with a rod, and you could do both those things just as well in foul weather as fair, or Sam could, anyway.

'That's right,' he said good-naturedly. 'Here's your grapefruit; I'll bring your cooked food through in a moment.'

Martin grinned and dug his spoon into the neatly segmented fruit.

'It's lovely,' he said through the first mouthful. 'Oh, ground coffee!'

Sam went out, smiling. Martin had ground coffee every morning, but he always remarked on it. He was a good lad.

CHAPTER TWO

Diane Hopgood woke early, what with the sunshine and a certain amount of foreboding, but once she was properly awake the foreboding disappeared and nervous excitement took its place.

She had come to Haisby for a break, partly

because she needed one and partly at her mother's suggestion. Her mother had been Anne Bonner before her marriage and was very fond of her aunts, and worried about them, too.

'You need a rest, dear, and your great-aunts have quite a large house,' she had assured her doubting daughter. 'I'm not asking you to do anything, just to have a look around, see what you think. They're rather old to be running the shop, you see, but it seems they have no choice. I really am worried.'

So Diane had come down for a few days, moving into the spare room at 39 Harbour Way, helping a bit about the house, enjoying the beach and the town. And had seen her aunts' seedy, old-fashioned shop and immediately realised that her mother was right to worry.

The few days became a week, then two, but still Diane hesitated. What could she do? She wanted to help, she had no desire to go back to her well paid London job. She could spare them a week or two, perhaps even a month, to see if she could get them straight, but the great-aunts themselves were an obstacle, because they felt they were taking advantage of her.

'A lovely girl like you, with a wonderful career, trying to help in our place?' Aunt Violet marvelled. 'Oh, Diane, dear, trade is very poor, you'd be bored.'

'Poor? It's non-existent,' confirmed Aunt Dulcie. 'Indeed, there are days when we don't know which way to turn for...but we couldn't involve you, dear.'

But they had known they would, of course, as soon as Diane got to work on them, telling them she could straighten them out in a month or so, that she'd enjoy it, that she had been given leave of absence from her job as long as she cared to take it. And very soon the protests had faded to a proviso that she give up and go home the moment she wanted to do so.

So here she was, lying in bed in the sunshine, when today she was going into the shop for the first time, to take a long, hard look at it with a view to refurbishment.

Diane got out of bed and padded down to the bathroom. She took a chilly bath because the immersion heater had only been on half an hour, then dressed in her pink flying suit, a practical garment, tying back her mass of dark curls with pink ribbon. Then she slung her bag over her shoulder and pattered out of the room, across the landing and down the stairs. The aunts seldom left their rooms before nine, the shop was never opened before ten, often later. She reached the kitchen, made herself a cup

30

of tea and then looked at her watch. It said twenty to nine...she might as well go, get an early start.

Outside, the morning was fresh still, the sun warm. Gulls swooped over the harbour, their querulous cries making Diane think of childhood holidays by the sea, when her only preoccupation had been wondering whether it would rain or shine.

At this hour there were only a sprinkling of people on Harbour Way but Lord Street, when she reached it, was at its busiest. Buses, cars, delivery vans and people hurrying to work blocked the road and the pavement, with the smell of hot engines and exhausts cancelling out the earlier freshness.

Diane glanced down the Arcade and decided to nip over to the market first and get a few flowers. She found some blooms on the first stall, a handful of lilac, white scented narcissus and some deep pink tulips, and made her way back across Lord Street, dodging the traffic with a true Londoner's indifference to personal safety, looking forward, now, to this new challenge.

Aunt Violet was openly relieved that Diane was helping; she did her best to keep the books, she said plaintively, but people were so strange. The VAT man couldn't believe they neither charged nor took VAT and had worried her so much she hadn't slept for three nights.

Aunt Dulcie was different. Fiercely independent, at seventy-two she did not want to be a burden to anyone. She had taken care of Violet, a mere seventy, all their lives and would not give up now. But if Diane really wanted to help, could bring the shop back into profitability, then she would be grateful.

'I'll help with the books,' Aunt Violet had said the previous evening, gazing at Diane over the baize table-cover with its bobbled fringe, as out-of-date, as the Bonner shop itself. 'But there isn't much in them; trade has been so poor.'

'We muddle along,' Aunt Dulcie said. 'I keep telling the girl that VAT man was a crass young fool but I admit lately I've bitterly regretted Arthur never saw fit to talk about business to either of us. If he'd explained I feel sure we'd never have got into such a state.'

Arthur had been Great-uncle Arthur, an accountant and a man with considerable business acumen. But he had died fifteen years ago and since then the sisters had muddled along, as Aunt Dulcie put it, without any real understanding of what they were doing.

Diane gained the pavement and saw the antique dealer polishing his window. She smiled

32

but did not speak. Later, when she had more time, she would go along and introduce herself to all the traders, but for the time being a smile would have to suffice.

She reached Bonner's and unlocked. The door creaked open as reluctantly, one would think, as if it had heard about new brooms and wanted none of them. But Diane, undeterred, went inside and shut the door after her. Then she went round the counter, stood behind it, and stared.

It was appalling, there was no doubt of that. Dust lay wherever the aunts could not reach, in the curves and curlicues of the fancy banister rail which led to the upper floor and in the niches of the over-ornate mahogany counter. When Diane walked over to the rail of woollens she found dust had gathered inexplicably on the garments and was ridged inside the hangers as well. What was more the saggy woollens looked second-hand with the outside of the arms lighter than the rest. They were far from inspiring.

Diane moved to the second rail. There were a number of dresses, many with the hemlines fixed firmly in the sixties except where they were long and draggly, dating, Diane was horrified to realise, from a period so remote she could not put a name to it.

Impossible, Diane thought, mentally relegating woollens and dresses to some emporium in the sky where they could live out the rest of their lives in luxury, never being tried on, or indeed looked at, again.

The next rail held suits. Tweed suits, which she remembered having once been told did not date. It was a lie.

Moving on again, Diane noticed as she fingered the next offering—slacks with...heavens! ...bell-bottoms—that a musty sort of smell arose from the garments. It was not the smell of secondhand clothing exactly, though it was near it. Sniffing, Diane decided it was the faint smell of despair, compounded of tweed, silk stockings and damp carpeting. This lot will have to go, Diane told herself, and patted a horrible serge skirt consolingly. Faint dust arose. She went next to the window. Corsets! And long-sleeved woollen vests, in May! Who else would have silk stockings in this day and age?

The second window held hats, mostly made of felt or straw, in dark shades. They were unimaginatively clumped together on stands all set at the same height. Diane was reminded of a bed of toadstools in the dampest corner of a wood. And beneath them, lying in a dead-body attitude, was another tweed suit. It looked as though it had died running.

Diane took a deep breath, stooped, and gathered up as much of the window display as she could hold. She took the lot to the foot of the stairs, dumped it and returned for another load. Presently the window was empty, revealing the dun-coloured paintwork and the dirty glass panes.

Diane surveyed the shape of the windows, their depth, their backing, even the view of the wine bar outside. Her mind joyously embraced this part of the problem, for after gaining her fine arts degree she had trained as a window-dresser. Her 'wonderful career' had involved planning extravagant window displays and following the displays through in the store itself, so surely putting one small shop on the map would present no problem to Miss Hopgood of Barkworths!

But this, of course, was a very different challenge. Barkworths' windows were rightly famous and extremely large and the Barkworth budget was the envy of every shop in the West End. Here, the budget would be minuscule and the window equally tiny. What was more, she was going to have to tell the aunts that their entire stock was fit for nothing but the dustbin, not old enough to be sold to trendy students as antique wear, not fashionable enough for a nearly-new shop. Come to that, Diane could not see a jumble sale getting rid of her aunts' stuff. It would have to be the dustbin and she could anticipate, shudderingly, how hard it would be to persuade the aunts that what they probably thought of as a fortune in clothing must be immediately banished from Bonner's, if the new look she envisaged was to succeed.

But first things first. She must spend today clearing the place out and cleaning, but she could find no water supply, no kettle to heat the water, no gas ring on which to balance a kettle. She had never, until today, been given the opportunity of actually seeing just how bad things were and now, with her new knowledge, she was beginning to realise that this was more than a few weeks' work. Did she really want to have a go? Give up Barkworths and all that it stood for, very probably have to sell her half of the flat to keep herself solvent until such time as the place was open and selling once more?

She pulled out the little, spindly-legged chair and sat on it and thought. She knew in her heart that she would never go back to Barkworths, not whilst Tony was there, and the store was his livelihood as it had once been hers. Besides, there were other stores which would be delighted to employ Miss Hopgood of Barkworths.

Perhaps, in time then, she would go back to

London. But not now. Not for a while. So she would have a go here, see if she was capable of running a small business.

Having made up her mind, Diane stood up and headed for the door. She would go over to the restaurant opposite and beg a mop and bucket, get them to show her where her water supply was. And then she would get scrubbing!

'There's a girl at the kitchen door,' Sandy remarked. She was standing facing the glass-paned door, grating cheese for next day's sand-wiches. 'Let her in, gal Poppy.'

'Right,' Poppy said, abandoning the chipper, which she was feeding with sliced potatoes so that they would have a supply blanched ready for lunches. 'I wonder who she is? Customers go next door.'

'She's not a customer, she's the Bonner niece,' Sam said. He was putting a new till roll on in preparation for a coffee-time rush which would probably turn out to be a trickle. 'I saw her go into the shop a while back.'

'Wonder what she's doing there?' Poppy swung the door open. 'Morning. Can I help you?'

'Good morning. I'm Diane Hopgood, my great-aunts keep the shop opposite,' Diane said. 'I'm cleaning the place out today and I wondered if you could lend me a mop and bucket and a few other things? And could you tell me where my water supply is, please?'

'We'll lend you the cleaning things,' Sam said cheerfully. 'But there isn't a water supply, we'll have to lend you a bucket of water as well. Poppy, get the stuff from the cellar, there's a good girl. I'll run hot water.'

'We could fill an electric kettle for you, if you want,' Sandy volunteered. 'But your aunts always come here and order tea or coffee when they want it.'

'Tea or coffee? That sounds wonderful,' Diane said gratefully. 'Could I have a coffee and scone in about half an hour, please? I'll come and fetch it.'

'We deliver,' Sam said. 'I'm Sam, Diane, and my partner, Martin, will be in later, he's gone shopping with Marjory, our morning manageress. This is Sandy, and the little lass in the cellars is Poppy.'

'Hello,' Diane said, smiling at them. 'Nice to meet you. I expect you'll be seeing a good bit of me because I'm giving my aunts a hand in the shop, cleaning it up a bit.'

'They need someone,' Sam agreed. Poppy came panting up from the cellar with the cleaning materials as he finished running water into a bucket. 'Here, Diane, you open the doors and we'll bring the stuff across. Believe me, I'm happy to help in any way, if only because, forgive me, the wine bar overlooks the Bonner windows.'

'I see your point,' Diane sighed. 'Well, I'll do my best to improve your outlook.'

The small procession crossed the Arcade and went into Bonner's. Sam looked round speechlessly at the almost empty shop and the banister laden with clothing. Diane followed his gaze.

'I know...but what would *you* do? There's nothing I dare keep, the whole place has to change.'

'You're doing the right thing,' Sam said heavily. 'But we're all fond of the old ladies. I just hope you can do it without upsetting them.'

'I hope so too,' Diane admitted. 'Thanks for your help, and later, I'll pop over for a sandwich and bring it back for my lunch.'

'I'll send a girl over with a menu,' Sam promised. 'Good luck!'

He and Poppy made their way back to the kitchen, where Martin had just put in an appearance, his arms full of carrier bags. He grinned at Sam over the top of them.

'Special offer on mayonnaise,' he announced. 'Marj and I bought as much as I could carry. She's fetching butter and two big tubs of margarine.' He looked curiously at the older man. 'Where have you been?'

'Taking some cleaning things across for the Bonners' niece; her name's Diane,' Sam said. 'She seems a nice girl. She's trying to clean up for the old ladies.'

'She've got her work cut out,' Poppy remarked, taking some of the jars of mayonnaise from Martin. 'Did you see them racks, Sam? Stripped! She've tore that place to bits—what's she playing at, eh?'

'She told us, cleaning up for the old girls,' Sam said, but Poppy shook her head.

'No, she in't just cleaning, Sam, she's taking over.'

Martin pressed his nose against the glass and peered out, then turned to face them, looking knowing.

'She looks bossy, I thought so the other day when the old ladies brought her down here. Oh, she'll make some changes, mark my words!'

'If you're right, then I'm grateful,' Sam said, having given the matter some thought. 'What could be worse than loopy knickers and corsets?'

'Someone else selling sandwiches?' Martin said brightly. 'Don't shake your head at me, Sam, it's possible.'

'It in't,' Poppy said stoutly. 'She's got no water.'

'Hmm,' Martin said temporarily deflated. 'Well, how about an engineering works?'

'Oh, shut up,' Poppy chipped in. 'Do she look like an engineer?'

'Not a lot,' Martin agreed. He turned back to the window. 'She's kicking up an awful dust,' he announced. 'Now she's brushing all the muck out into the Arcade...she'll cop it if I see her!'

Poppy giggled but Sandy, who had been quietly getting on with her work, straightened.

'Whatever she do in that place, it'll make a world of difference to us if she get it right,' she declared.

Sam smiled. It was what they all said every time someone else opened a shop down here. It would make a world of difference. The last people to own the wine bar had let it slide, so he and Martin had made a difference but this time, with the summer coming, perhaps it really would mean improvements all round. If fashion-conscious young girls started coming down the Arcade to visit Bonner's, and popped in to the wine bar...if the young men from the offices on Lord Street came down in pursuit of the young girls...

Sam dreamed on. Outside, the sun still

41

shone, though you only caught the odd glimp-
se down here in the Arcade. They could do
with some luck, all of them. Diane could sell
the shop to someone else or run it herself, either
would be an improvement. But he did hope the
new owner wouldn't try to sell sandwiches...or
beauty products...or antiques...

Martin's afternoons off were, as Sam would
have been the first to admit, rather shorter than
most since they couldn't start until two and
usually ended at five, when he and Sam either
closed the wine bar and went home or started
preparing evening meals. But Martin liked to
lounge on the beach or sit on the promenade
and look at the girls and dream fantasies in
which he rescued maidens, got his just reward
and told Sam he was off to lord it at the
Waldorf Astoria, or to be kept in luxury by a
millionairess of great beauty and cushiony
bosoms.

Drink and temper had, however, forced him
to accede to Sam's eager suggestion that they
go into business together. Drink, temper and
a weakness for large women with plunging
necklines and enormous knockers. Sam did not
know and Martin did not intend to tell him,
but it had not merely been one woman who had
objected to a red-haired chef pawing her but

42

three, and they had only objected when he had tried to become a permanent part of their lives. In short, they had not minded a 'slam-bam thank you ma'am' in their rooms, but had not appreciated his assumption that the relationship would be more permanent.

Now, Martin strolled along the promenade in the hot sunshine and eyed the one really worthwhile hotel in the town and thought wistfuly that the place was probably crammed to the eyebrows with cushiony bosoms. The drink he could just about control, the temper he was working on, but his lust for cushions was boundless, so he simply disguised it as best he could and prayed for the day when he was rich and could give it full rein.

He had not told Sam he wanted to split as soon as the money was right because it would make life impossible. Sam, it was clear, loved the wine bar and was never happier than when toiling over a hot stove or being polite to customers. But he, Martin, was made for better things. The wine bar in Spain which Sam sometimes talked about was a nice idea, Martin grudgingly conceded that, but it really was a castle in Spain. Sam would never make enough money to move on and up, he would be lucky to be earning rent, because Martin knew that he himself would pull out, as soon as the time was ripe. First, though, the trade would have to forget the Martin Samuels who had got drunk, thrown knives and seduced valued customers. Martin would have changed his name, but red hair and freckles combined with extreme thinness are not all that common amongst chefs. What was more, his genius was allied to his name, so going incognito was not a good idea. Give it two years, though, he reckoned, and he could go back where he belonged. He would make it plain he was a reformed character of course, and if Martin ever felt pangs of guilt over his plans he soon stifled them. Sam and his breakfast in bed and his eagerness to take over any task that Martin did not fancy was all a ploy, really. A means of tying Martin to a mean little arcade in a one-horse town where he should, by right of his genius, be living it up in a five-star hotel.

Despite the fact that the season had not yet properly begun, the beach was quite crowded. Martin spotted a pair of melons crammed into a bikini top, dropped down onto the sand and slogged his way across it until he was level with the object of his desire. Only as an after-thought did he notice that the melon-owner was a woman of forty with a good pair of legs, a mass of gingery hair tied up on top of her head with a piece of ribbon, and the little bikini. She was oiled all over—gulp, went Martin, imagining oiled melons—and had sunglasses perched on her nose.

Martin shuffled nearer. He could have done with dark glasses himself and his blue jeans and long-sleeved shirt made him feel a trifle over-dressed, but he still shuffled closer. Suppose he could get into conversation with them... her...what then?

She was reading a paperback novel. Martin saw that her shoulders were very red, she would be sore, later. He was only six feet from her now, dared he speak?

'Good book, is it?'

The dark glasses turned towards him, then away again. She thought she must be mistaken, that he had addressed someone else.

'Good book? Your back's like rare steak, dear lady...want me to oil it for you?'

The dark glasses—and the melons—swung towards him. Martin swallowed. Oh, oh, ooh!

'Go and stuff yourself, you randy little runt.'

Martin blinked.

'Pardon? Were you addressing me?'

She did not deign to answer. Martin shuffled a bit nearer; he liked a woman with spirit. If she'd just let him oil her shoulders he was sure he could manage, somehow, to get a good look down her front, possibly he could even brush against her. The thought was enough to make him shuffle a few inches nearer...

The woman got to her feet, quite leisurely. She managed to do so without wobbling her melons much, which Martin thought a great pity, and he was still regretting it when her very large, sand-caked handbag swung round and caught him full in the face.

He landed flat on his back, spluttering, sand in his eyes and mouth, murder in his heart. She was saying she was sorry, laughing at him, moving away, calling to someone...

Martin rolled over onto his face and spat sand. His eyes ran water, tears plopped off the end of his nose and he longed to lose his temper, to run after the woman and scream that she was a prick-teasing whore, that she wasn't likely to get a chance like him again, not an old bag like her, not even with those big knockers.

But losing his temper was forbidden. If he lost his temper he'd never get to the Waldorf Astoria, he wouldn't even make the Grand Hotel, Haisby-on-Sea. He stayed where he was for ages, therefore, until the red mist had cleared from his eyes and the sand had been spat back onto the beach. Only then did he get to his feet and trudge wearily towards the town.

Never mind, he told himself as he walked. You've won a battle today, if not the war. You never lost your temper and so far, you've not gone hurrying off to drown your sorrows. Because just seeing those melons had reminded him of the good times which could be his once more if only he kept sober and cheerful. Sam thought he was saving Martin for the wine bar but really he was saving him for something far better. Two years, that's all I need. Martin told himself now, heading back towards the Arcade. Two sober, good-tempered years and I'll be off.

He reached the wine bar and went into the kitchen. Marj was cleaning down; she looked up and gave him her wide, innocent smile. If only she knew! Sam, collecting used dishes from the restaurant, asked him how his afternoon had gone. Martin replied that he'd sat on the beach and got quite a flush on his arms, really enjoyed the sunshine.

'I've put a menu out for this evening,' Marj said. 'It's steak and salad followed by those Brittany crepes you do so well.'

Flat as any crepe, poor girl, Martin mused as Marj said goodnight and made her way out of the kitchen. Still, it took all sorts. But you'd think Sam had a weakness for flat chests, looking round the staff. There was Marj for starters, and Sandy, with a couple of pimples where cushions should have flourished. And there was

Poppy, puppy-fat Poppy, all childish bulges.

Even the sales girls were small where they ought to be large. Sue had tiny ones, Dorothy had little apples, Maureen was practically concave.

Oh, well. And that Diane...another one. Only Caresse was well-endowed in the melon department and not only did she have a rich lover but she did not appeal to Martin. And the hairdressers were bustless to a man—or rather, to a woman.

'New potatoes with the steak, Mart,' Sam said. 'Want me to scrub 'em for you? And Marj made a deep apple pie before she left, she used your recipe.'

Martin graciously allowed Sam to scrub the new potatoes, and went to the fridge to make sure that the steaks were the ones he had ordered. He would cook a couple in wine, do one in puff pastry and two more in pepper sauce.

Quickly, neatly, Martin prepared his pans, got out the big one for the crepes, squeezed fresh lemons into a jug. Despite his adventure of the afternoon, despite the way he felt about the wine bar, he was happy.

CHAPTER THREE

Diane spent three whole days in the shop in the end, cleaning down and then redecorating in a pleasant shade of cream. She put a notice in the window announcing that Bonner's was closed for alterations, but apart from the odd person who glanced in as they passed she did not see any disappointed customers turn away.

The aunts themselves were quite happy that she should close for a week.

'A week's nothing,' Aunt Dulcie told her when she returned to the cottage. 'We often close for a week or two. People don't mind.'

Diane, choosing a piece of pink carpet and laying it herself, thought that any shop which could close for a week or two without finding business affected was either very successful or very unsuccessful, and there was no prize for guessing into which category Bonner's fell.

At the end of three days Diane brought the aunts in. She softened the shock by explaining she had cleared all the old stock out of the way and then invited them to a celebratory lunch at the wine bar. A consultation with Martin had provided the ideal menu for two old ladies, both with upper and lower sets to contend with. Grilled sole followed by lemon syllabub, coffee and mints.

The aunts took the news well. They were delighted with their newly decorated premises, and when they enquired after their stock Diane said vaguely that it was all 'upstairs, for now', led them over to the wine bar and sat them down with a medium dry sherry whilst she outlined her plans.

'Bonner's must start selling for the nineteen-nineties,' she explained earnestly as their first course arrived and was exclaimed over...

'Sole! Gracious, dear, how long is it since we ate sole?'

'Many a day, dear, many a day. In fact, if I recall, it was when dear Arthur took us to the Grand Hotel to celebrate his sixtieth birthday...that was a wonderful occasion, I remember...'

'The sole's delicious,' Diane agreed. 'But if we get the shop back into profitability you'll be able to enjoy sole once a week if you want— once a *day*, come to that. Only first we must get things sorted out.'

'Sort things out?' Aunt Violet said vaguely. She tasted a new carrot. 'These vegetables are cooked just as I like them. What a dear, clever boy Martin is...' She lowered her voice to a breathy whisper. 'Do you know, Diane, once upon a time I thought all red-haired men were bad-tempered, but Martin proves me wrong!'

'Yes, Aunty Vi,' Diane said wondering how on earth she was going to keep the pair of them to the point, but she had reckoned without Aunt Dulcie. The elder of the sisters was a woman of character. Now, she put down her knife and fork.

'Be quiet, Violet,' she said sharply. 'You've done marvels in the shop, Diane, dear. I gather when you mention the nineteen-nineties that you mean us to sell to a younger, more...more *with it* type of customer, but I cannot see such people buying our stock. What's more, I wouldn't know what to say to a gel with purple hair and a nail through her nose. It's not that I'm a snob, times change and manners with them, but I couldn't advise a gel like that, and we can't afford an assistant, you know.'

'You're right, of course,' Diane said, putting her own knife and fork down. 'But I've a proposition which I hope will help us all. I'd like to work in the shop and the very young aren't the customers I had in mind. I'd like to buy quality clothing, some of it expensive, some middle range. You see, you've got a small floor area and not a lot of rack space so you

51

can't afford to stock all the popular sizes in a wide range, you've got to specialise. And I've been in the business long enough to have a pretty good idea what to buy and how to attract the customers we'll need.'

'Buy for us? I don't know that our credit position would allow much buying,' Violet said. 'It's been a long time since we bought anything, we've been waiting for rack space, you see.'

'I realise that. But I'm selling my flat and I can raise a bank loan,' Diane said with a confidence she was far from feeling. 'And I've got a bit of ready cash which I'll use until the other money comes through.'

'But my dear, how can we possible repay you?' Aunt Violet wailed. 'And your wonderful job...you mean you'd give notice?'

'To tell you the truth, I'd decided to leave Barkworths before I came to Haisby,' Diane admitted. 'I like it here and I think we could make a go of Bonner's. I want to buy in so that the three of us have equal shares and if I ever want to move on, you'll be able to employ someone instead of me, because we'll succeed, I'm sure. Haisby needs a good boutique and I need the challenge.'

'Goodness!' Aunt Violet said. Clearly she had regarded Diane's job as even more wonderful than it was. But Aunt Dulcie, who had been eating steadily, finished the last scrap of sole, laid down her knife and fork and shook her head at her sister.

'My dear Violet, we cannot afford to persuade Diane hers is not the right course,' she said. 'We're in no position to turn down any offer of genuine help, we're sinking fast in water that's become too deep for us. If dear Di is good enough to throw us a lifebelt then we must clutch it and assure her we'll pay her back, one day. Furthermore, she must draw a salary.'

'Pay her back? Draw a salary? My dear Dulcie, with what shall we pay her?'

'Firstly, we'll take out a mortgage on the cottage. Secondly, we'll give her the cottage.'

'But we've nowhere else to go,' Violet pointed out. 'I don't think I could stand lodgings, not at my time of life.'

'That isn't what I meant, dear. We'll leave her the cottage in our wills. It's worth a shockingly large sum of money, Diane dear, because of the view across the harbour and all the rooms and so on. So she won't lose, Violet, not in the long run.'

'It's good of you to think of it, but the shop will do very well if it's brought up to date,' Diane said. 'As for a salary, I don't think that will be necessary, but if you could keep me for nothing it would help, at first.'

'Of course we'll keep you for nothing. And we must pay you what's fair.' Aunt Dulcie considered whilst Aunt Violet finished her meal. 'Would you say...seven pounds a week? I'm sure we could find that much.'

'We'll see,' Diane said, reflecting that her aunts were not just living in the past decade but the past century. 'At the moment I don't think you need worry about staffing or salaries, let's concentrate on stock. I thought I'd go to London at the beginning of next week and price things and find a summer theme. I'll spend the rest of this week bearding bank managers in their dens and arranging finance.'

Martin appeared at this point to a chorus of delighted approbation from the aunts.

'Diane ordered my lemon syllabubs for dessert,' Martin said now, smiling at them. 'A wise choice, you'll enjoy all that cream and sherry and lemon juice.'

'They do look delicious,' Aunt Dulcie said as the tall, frosted glasses were placed before them. 'Would it be very bad, Martin, to order some wine with them? I want to drink a little toast.'

'Wine? A Barsac might do...I'll see what I can find.'

'To our partnership,' Aunt Dulcie said when, with due ceremony, a bottle had been broached and poured. She raised her glass to her niece. 'To success for Bonner & Hopgood from two sleeping partners to the wakeful one!'

Diane drank, laughed, shook her head.

'No, Aunt Dulcie, we'll stick to Bonner, it's a well-known name. And we'll succeed...good luck to the boutique!'

And here Aunt Violet proved, once and for all, that she was not really in the nineteen-nineties at all. Raising her glass, glancing coyly round, she echoed, 'The boutique!' and then added, 'What's a boutique?'

'It's clean all right, but it's totally empty! She came in, decorated, put down new carpet, and now she's lunching the old ladies. They've sold out, I'm sure of it. The only question is, what'll it be? All that cream paintwork...I wondered about an optician? What do you think?'

Lana Johnson was in Treat Yourself, chatting to Caresse whilst Barry kept shop, which meant sitting behind the counter listening to the radio and stopping the current dog from raising a leg against the counter.

Now Lana and Caresse, whilst ostensibly standing in the doorway chatting, were peering into the wine bar where the aunts sat with their niece, raising their glasses whilst Martin hovered in the background, grinning from ear to ear.

'She's a relative, so if she's bought it she'll have paid them a fair price,' Caresse said thoughtfully. 'She's young, though, so she'll do something cheap. Nearly-new clothes, or antiques. That wouldn't please Archie.'

'It won't be antiques, not with pink carpet,' Lana said, mopping her nose. She was suffering from hay-fever, made worse by the fact that they had recently mown the long grass in the churchyard and it was lying beneath the sun turning to hay before their very eyes—and noses. Not an attractive woman at the best of times, with a smear of mucus across one puffin cheek Lana was enough to put most customers off. Caresse would have manoeuvred her out of her doorway except that the Arcade was empty and anyway, she was enjoying the conversation.

'No, you're right, not antiques.' Caresse pretended to consider. 'I wonder about a slimming centre? They sell health food and push the Birmingham diet and so on.'

'She wouldn't sell health food,' Lana protested. Even the red and shiny tip of her nose seemed to pale at the threat. 'Not with us right next door. Anyway, people on holiday don't diet. It could be a travel agent, I suppose.'

'Or a brothel,' Caresse said, hoping for an outraged reaction, but Lana merely smiled maliciously.

'It could be a beauty parlour; that would be one in the eye for you, dear.'

'It wouldn't worry me,' Caresse said promptly. 'It might even do me good. But it isn't big enough, the Bonner place. How about books? No, pink carpet doesn't talk books. A nice tea-room, now! Not that Sam or that awful Martin would be very pleased.'

'Not big enough; besides, they've got no water laid on,' Lana reminded her. 'It could be an optician. It looks just right.'

'I don't see,' Caresse began, and hastily withdrew into the shop as a commotion at the door and the sudden appearance of Martin, ushering customers out, heralded the arrival of Diane and the Miss Bonners in the Arcade. 'Come in or go out, Lana, don't just hover!'

Lana, rather to Caresse's regret came in, and together they watched the next part of the drama, only it turned out not to be dramatic at all. The three women disappeared into Bonner's shutting the door firmly behind them.

'They'll be settling the financial details,' Lana said knowingly. 'I've a good mind to go across and have a word with Martin.'

'Leave me out of it,' Caresse said. She began to rearrange the various bottles and jars on her counter. A smell sweet as hyacinths in the sun yet subtle as bean flowers reached her from some expensive talcum. Caresse jiggled the container and inhaled blissfully. It helped to hide the smell of Lana's uncured leather sandals and the odour of dog which always hung about her.

'You mean don't come back and tell you what he says?' Lana sniggered. 'Just because he pinched your bum once...'

'I was wearing my cream wool Hardy Amies,' Caresse said with controlled violence. 'He'd been carving a turkey, the grease marks never came out. He's a nasty little turd and I don't know how Sam stands him.'

'Or the girls,' Lana agreed, but Caresse shook her head.

'The girls are safe enough; that creep wants a real woman but he couldn't handle one. That's his trouble.'

'He handled you,' Lana observed, and giggled on a high, whinnying note, then sniffed.

Caresse winced. What a horribly juicy sniff the woman had, but she was simply liquifying with hay-fever and could not help herself.

'Well, Martin may be a creep but I bet he heard something. See you later.'

Alone in the shop, Caresse sat behind her

counter and wondered what Diane would really do with Bonner's. Not that it mattered, because anything would be an improvement. Presently Caresse looked cautiously around, then got out a paper bag, extracted a doughnut from its rustling depths and began, messily, to eat it. She was always on a diet of some description but allowed herself little treats, and this was one of them.

As she ate, she thought about Diane. It would be nice if Diane really did take the shop and came to work so near. She was a pretty girl, and what would be more natural than that a lively young woman like her should cast about in the Arcade for a friend and confidante? Someone a little older, like me, Caresse told herself, licking cream and jam off her fingers. We'll have a lot in common, more than I've got with the others.

Sam was all right, though. He was chunky and she had always gone for chunky men. Ronald, who had bought the shop for her and whose delightful, brand new mock-Georgian residence she shared, was chunky. But Sam was not the sort to start a nice little flirtation, which was a pity. Still.

Caresse licked the last of the jam from her long, scarlet-tipped fingers, then opened her handbag, fished out a mirror and examined her face for traces of sugar. She found a couple of grains on her upper lip and flicked them off, then stared accusingly at her reflection. Was her make-up running? Was her hair smooth, her shoulders dandruff free?

You look all right, she told her reflection at length. Not perfect, no one could look perfect after four hours in a shop, but she would do. She found a small box of cologne wipes in her bag and cleaned her fingers, then drew one luxuriously round her neck. Thank God for no wrinkles, she calculated her neck would go another five years, with care, before she had to think seriously about surgery. Although she had quite clearly seen, this morning before applying her make-up, some tiny lines round her eyes.

Through her window, Caresse saw Lana emerge from the wine bar. She was smirking. Caresse moved over to the door and opened it. She beckoned.

'Lana, could you sit here for five minutes. I want to go down to the church.'

This was Arcade-talk for the lavatory, and Lana agreed at once. She might need a shop-sitter herself one of these days and on this premise no one ever refused to watch over a till whilst a fellow-trader rushed to the loo.

Caresse, accordingly, walked briskly down

to the toilet. Once there, she got out her make-up and repaired the ravages of the day. Then she sat on the loo and had a tinkle, then she came out, washed her hands, dried them, applied handcream and returned to her shop as refreshed by her excursion as another woman might have been by a gin and tonic.

Lana, who had spent the interim examining Caresse's stock, cross-questioned her about the efficacy of oatmeal soap and the truth of a statement about a lipstick which purported to have been made without having recourse to animal experimentation. Caresse, who was a trifle vague about animals and lipstick—did the scientists make animals kiss each other whilst wearing frosted lip gloss?—bluffed her way through Lana's queries and managed to satisfy her by saying she would look into it. She always said that when a customer queried a statement by a manufacturer, for she had found that few people returned to discover whether a cream really did remove wrinkles, though shampoos which claimed to cure dandruff came in for quite a lot of stick.

Presently, she was able to take up her position behind the counter once more and mull over what she had seen, for she had not been idle on her trip down the Arcade. She had scrutinised the Bonner window and had decided Diane was going to open an Art shop, for she had seen that young person on her knees, spreading out an assortment of drift-wood, shells and dried seaweed, whilst the aunts arranged dried flowers in an olive-wood bowl.

Oh yes, it'll be an Art shop unless it's gifts and picture framing, Caresse told herself. She wondered whether to pop along and tell Lana, but decided against it. Lana was such a know-all, she would let her go on speculating about the possibility of an optician or a travel agent whilst she, Caresse, would hug to herself the secret that it was really arts and crafts.

She would tell Sam, if he asked, and possibly Jenny, at Waves, because everyone knew that you told your hairdresser everything, since they were like doctors and never passed things on. But as for the others...Caresse shrugged and picked up her magazine, opening it at the serial. Then she dug around in the bottom drawer of the counter and found a bag of fudge. In an hour she would ring Ronald and tell him she was ready to leave, and he would whisk her back to Compton House and listen whilst she told him how hard she worked. Then later, there would be martinis or something equally delicious, at the local, whilst Ronald boasted about his latest executive home—he was a building contractor—and told anyone who would listen that Caresse, bless her, was making a bomb in the beauty business.

It's not a bad life, Caresse concluded, biting into her first piece of fudge.

Marj blew in at two o'clock, as she always did except when she worked through and left at three, and saw that Martin had customers. It was the Miss Bonners and Diane so she waved to them, then got out the mixing bowl and began to measure flour.

Presently Martin came back into the kitchen with the dirty dishes and almost half a bottle of wine. He looked cross and hot. Marj had noticed that it often made him cross being nice to people but she was so pleased that he had been nice to the old dears that she forgave him his brusqueness with herself. Put that pastry away, he had said in his nastiest tone, and get out ingredients for three chocolate cakes and three maple and walnut. The buggers—he meant the delivery customers—the buggers ate all the cake today.

Marj didn't take any notice, of course. She continued quite placidly making her pastry because if she didn't Martin would be the one with a red face tomorrow when he tried to explain why there were no fruit pies or custard tarts. He heaved a sigh when he noticed but went out to clean the table down and came back easier, because he smiled at her and then went down to the cellars himself and came up with the cake ingredients.

'If I start them off, can you finish them?' Martin said. He had clearly calmed down. Marj, who had seen him slide the by-now-empty wine bottle into the bin, sighed to herself. Sam had told her when she first started to work for him that Martin had a drink problem, but frankly she thought if a couple of glasses of wine was a drink problem, then half the townspeople could be counted as raving alcoholics. No, what was really the matter with Martin was an overbearing nature which could turn violent. Plus the fact that he was absolutely dying to get his leg over, and didn't seem to have a hope in hell of persuading anyone to play.

If only he'd go for youngsters, Marj thought, wishing her pastry was bread dough so she could pound about a bit. Youngsters wouldn't have minded his bum-pinching, breast-nuzzling approach. The trouble was, Martin seemed to think he was some sort of a prize catch and went for mature women with lots of curves. They had to have a certain something though, Marj mused...he'd pinched Caresse that day, she could still remember the fuss over some old white skirt...a sort of stylish plumpness, was that it? But Martin had confided in her once that Caresse didn't really turn him on.

Still, Martin wasn't as black as he was painted. Not that Sam painted him black, quite the opposite. Sam thought the sun shone out of his nephew. He spoiled Martin, sang his praises, always undertook the dirty work, the unpopular tasks, so that Martin wouldn't be bothered.

No, it was others who didn't care for Martin. Past employers, of course, some of their customers, most of the staff. He had a chip on his shoulder of quite extraordinary dimensions when you considered how pleasant his life had become with Sam in charge of it. But the long, raw-looking face was often set in lines of discontent, the thin, knuckly hands plucked angrily at his white coat, whilst Martin waited for a chance to complain, to shout, to rub someone up the wrong way.

Sam, of course, hoped that his own kindness and having a business over which he had some control would turn Martin into a normal young man, but Marj couldn't see it. Perhaps Martin didn't want to be a normal young man, perhaps he preferred being angry and unloved. Perhaps there really is something different about a genius, Marj thought doubtfully, rolling out the first batch of pastry and fitting it into two giant custard-tart tins. Because he really does cook like an angel and he really can teach. She, Sandy and Poppy had all benefited from Martin's cookery lessons and she at least had sense enough to be grateful. The others, of course, pointed out that once Martin had taught them to cook certain dishes he was saved the job of doing it himself, but Marj did not think it was as simple as that. Many great chefs, she knew, would never pass their expertise on, but Martin was almost prodigal with his gift, as though he knew he would always be improving and inventing new dishes.

Or perhaps he really doesn't care, Marj thought now, watching out of the corner of her eye as Martin slopped ingredients apparently at random onto the big weighing pan and began to mix, using one hand instead of the electric whisk. Could it be that despite his ability, his heart was not really in cooking at all? That he longed to be a...ballet dancer, or a bull-fighter.

The thought of Martin in tights made Marj's mouth twitch; but the idea was still worth considering. She finished off the pastry cases she was making and rolled the paste into a ball, wrapped it in greaseproof paper and popped it into the fridge.

'Mart, what made you go in for cooking?'

You could never tell how Martin would react to a question; sometimes he was sarcastic or even rude. Marj waited hopefully, however. It seemed a harmless question, after all.

'Dunno. Yes I do, though. I was good at it and I enjoyed it. So why not get trained, I thought.'

'Were you good at it at school?'

'School! No, we didn't do it at school, only the girls cooked. I made the meals at home, my Dad and I took turns.' He paused, tipping something into his mixture and leaving a full set of greasy fingerprints on the jar. I must remember to clean it, Marj told herself, knowing full well that Martin's interest in ingredients ended when he finished with them. 'No, I wasn't taught, not at first. I read books, copied the telly, that sort of thing.'

'Wasn't your mum keen on cooking?'

Martin stirred vigorously, then reached for a tin and began to slop handfuls of mixture into it. He was sometimes a neat worker, sometimes not, depending on his mood. Today, Marj saw, was a messy day.

'May have been; don't know. She left when I was a few months old,' Martin said. 'Dad brought me up.'

'I'm sorry,' Marj said. 'I didn't know.'

'Why should you be sorry? I wasn't...I never knew her, did I, all I knew was that Dad and I managed great. He was a great cook, was Dad.'

'Then did he teach you?'

It was an unfortunate thing to say it seemed. Martin finished filling the cake tins and put them in the oven, which meant that Marj's custard tarts would have to wait their turn, damn Martin's eyes. Then he went and rinsed his hands under the tap in a very final sort of way.

'I said I taught myself,' he said nastily. 'Do the rest of the cakes, will you? I'm going to piss off whilst the sun's out. And I'll go to Lemworths, we're low on spices.'

'Oh. All right,' Marj said resignedly. She would take his blasted cakes out of the oven and put her custard tarts in just as soon as he was out of the kitchen and serve him bloody well right if the damned things never rose. Though his cakes always did rise—unfairly high, as well, when you remembered the evil mood he sometimes cooked in.

'Thanks,' Martin said, turning away from the sink. He grinned at her suddenly and a thin, hard hand rumpled her hair, slid for a second round her neck. 'Sorry I'm such a bugger. You're a gem, old Marj.'

It was the first time in living memory so far as Marj knew that Martin had apologised to anyone for anything. She sneaked a look at him, just to see if he was being sarcastic or had gone off his rocker at last. But he was shedding his apron, standing on one foot and rubbing his shoe, with its dusting of flour, clean on his trouser-leg. He seemed not to care that this left the trouser-leg all floury. Then he went over to the till, pinged 'No Sale' and took out a couple of notes, fanning them out for Marj to see.

'Taken a tenner, Marj, in two fives. Okay? See you later.'

Martin left, hurrying briskly past the window, heading for Lord Street. He'll go to the beach and see if he can pick up a woman, Marj thought, relaxing and reaching for the eggs. He was odd, and in a weird sort of way he had something going for him, after all. She could still feel his touch on the back of her neck, with a certain spiky sort of sexual attraction which she could neither understand nor explain but which she had been aware of as his fingers touched her skin.

Marj beat eggs and milk, added sugar, then poured the lot slowly through a hair sieve to avoid bubbles and filled her pastry cases. It took longer than she thought it would, and by the time the custard tarts were ready for baking Martin's chocolate cakes were cooked. As she drew them out of the oven Marj wondered what her Eric would think if she admitted that Martin's fingers on her neck had felt quite sexy. Eric was a policeman and thought a lot of Marj, but they weren't married or anything like that. No fear, Marj wanted some fun out of life before she found herself tied to a husband and kids.

At twenty-three, however, she no longer lived with her family but shared a small terraced house with three friends...except that mostly she lived with Eric, who had a nice flat in a converted mill five miles outside the town. She still kept up her share of the rent though so her friends didn't mind.

Life, Marj concluded, starting to mix cake filling, was a rum'un when you thought about it. There she was, all but living full time with Eric and deriding marriage as only for old fogeys who were tired of fun. She might just as well be married!

She worked hard, too. Eric didn't approve of her hours, thought she should get a proper job instead of fitting in with the hours which suited Sam and Martin. But he didn't know how hard it was to get a proper job in Haisby, out of season. He came from Norwich, where there were jobs to spare. And anyway, Marj loved her work. She didn't mind coming in at seven and leaving at two, or doing split shifts sometimes, seven till ten and two till five. It fitted in well with Eric's work and what was more, as she told him, if she did want to change her job now she would be able to boast a number of accomplishments which she had not had before. Now she could just about run a restaurant singlehanded, beside being able to whip up any number of fancy dishes.

Finishing the clearing up, Marj was about to start peeling apples when the bell on the restaurant door pinged and she had to abandon her task, grab for her pad and biro and make for the doorway which led through into the other room.

It was only one chap when she got there, too. A dark young man with curly hair and a mischievous face, wearing a combat jacket and jeans. He had made straight for the window table and was spreading out some papers on its surface. Come in to get his books writ up, Marj told herself as she approached. She liked customers like that; they were quiet and undemanding and allowed her to get on with her cooking.

'Hello,' Marj said, taking one of the green and gold menus off the trolley and handing it

71

to him. 'Can I get you something?'

'Cup of tea, please,' the young man said. 'Got any toasted teacakes?'

Because of its thickness, a teacake had to be constantly watched whilst in the toaster. It could not pop up of its own accord, like a slice of toast, so Marj knew she would have to keep her eye on it and release it manually as soon as it began to brown.

'Mm...but we've got some lovely scones,' Marj said enticingly. She wanted to keep an eye on her custards, not be glued to the toaster. 'Fresh today.'

'No teacakes?'

His eyes, very dark and slanted, twinkled at her. Marj grinned back at him. He was a wily one and knew what he wanted.

'We-ell, I might have one or two if you're set on the idea.'

'I am, rather. I'll have a cup of tea and a teacake then, please.'

'You wouldn't rather have a pot?' Marj wheedled. She didn't want to keep nipping to and fro getting refills. 'Why not have a whole pot?' she looked pointedly at his paperwork. 'I'm sure you'll get dry with that lot to work through, one cup will never satisfy you.'

'You ought to sell double-glazing,' the young

man said. 'What is it with pots? Twice the price?'

'No!' Marj said, affronted. As if she would go into overkill for the price of a pot of tea! 'A pot holds three cups and it cost ten pence more than a cup. Don't let me talk you into anything, do as you like.'

The young man grinned again.

'All right, you win. A pot of tea please, and a teacake. Toasted, of course. With butter. On a plate.'

'No need to be sarky,' Marj said. 'Coming up.'

It didn't take a moment to toast a teacake and make a pot of tea, and when it was all done she put it on a tray and carried it through. The young man was leaning over his work, a hand to his brow. Marj peered and thought it was names and addresses; probably a salesman of some sort, poor devil. But he looked up when she came level with the table and smiled again, quite cheerfully really.

'Thanks,' he said, taking the teacake. 'It looks good.'

'It is. We make our own,' Marj said. 'I've brought you the big water jug but if you want more, just holler.'

'I'll do that,' the young man said, but distractedly. His eyes were straying back to his

73

paperwork. Marj left him willingly though. The apples were unlikely to peel themselves and she knew how easy it was to leave a custard just that bit too long so that it set like concrete.

She was finishing off the apples when the bell from the restaurant pinged...not that doorbell, the one customers used to get attention. She wiped her hands on her apron and went to the doorway. Her customer was still seated, the teacake only half eaten.

'Yes?'

'I'm a stranger here, I only moved to Haisby ten days back. If you wanted to meet young people, where would you go?'

Marj considered, hand on hip.

'Like dancehalls, you mean? Or youth clubs?'

'That's it. Anywhere.'

Marj gave him the names of two discos, thought of two more, added the youth clubs she knew about and Reynards, the Health and Fitness Club on Lord Street. He nodded, jotting the details down on a small pad.

'Anywhere else? I'm on a scheme to help youngsters get work, I like to suss a place out first, make sure the need's there.'

'It's there all right,' Marj assured him. 'Go round the youth clubs—and there's clubs for the unemployed, too. Try them. You'll meet all sorts.'

'I will. Many thanks, Miss...er...'

'Marj. Want your bill now, do you?'

'Might as well. What's the damage? I don't need a receipt,' he added as Marj began to scribble. 'I'm not on expenses, unfortunately.'

'Nor VAT, I daresay,' Marj said, twinkling at him. 'See you again, maybe.'

'Sure.' The young man paid up, added a twenty pence tip and headed for the door. He was almost there when he turned round again.

'My name's Chris, by the way. See you!'

Marj returned to the kitchen and concentrated on clearing up. Youth schemes, eh? Pity Chris had come in the summer, when even the most useless kid would probably get a few weeks' work, but he'd realise he must stick around until winter set in and all the fly-by-night traders who serviced the holidaymakers had disappeared.

The kitchen door was open onto the Arcade as it was warm, so when Caresse said, 'Hi!' Marj jumped out of her skin.

Caresse giggled.

'Sorry, didn't mean to scare you. Any chance of tea and a scone? I'll have it at your outside table...better make it two of each, I can

75

see Lana hovering.'

'Coming up,' Marj said, trying to sound cheerful and not resigned. She had just realised that Sam didn't know Martin had run out on her, so he was unlikely to turn up a minute before five and she was behind already, from having to do Martin's work as well as her own. But if she really put her mind to it...

Marj began to hurry.

CHAPTER FOUR

Hold thou thy Cross before my closing eyes;
Shine through the gloom, and point me to the skies:
Heaven's morning breaks, and earth's vain
*   shadows flee;*
In life, in death O Lord, abide with me.

As the last verse of the hymn was sung the cross-bearer led the choir down the centre aisle, stopped and turned to face the coffin. The pall-bearers rose from their places and hoisted the coffin onto their black-clad shoulders. The cross-bearer led the procession out of the church. Anthea fell into place behind the coffin and heard the congregation creak and clatter out of the pews and begin to follow on behind.

The church was full to bursting, for until two years ago the deceased had been Vicar of this Parish and village solidarity and support for the new vicar had brought them to Albert Francis Todd's graveside.

One or two of them, Anthea thought, as they walked round to the freshly dug grave beneath the East window, might actually have come for my sake. After all, now that Father's dead I have no relatives that I know of, no one to take care of me. They might have come to support me, show me I'm not alone.

It was not so, though. After all, she had taken care of her father and the crumbling old house for more years than she cared to admit and a woman of...nearly forty...who stays at home with an invalid father is generally assumed to have chosen that course.

Anthea, of course, knew better. She had stayed because she had been too scared to go. Too frightened of her father's sharp tongue and quick, brutal hand. Her mother had died before she was twelve years old and since that day, Albert Todd had ruled her with a rod of iron, never letting her believe for one moment that she could exist without him, continually mocking her every effort, deriding her timid attempts to improve her appearance, denying her money, freedom, even a shred of self-esteem for any of these things might have led to her fleeing from his unrelenting tyranny.

So she had stayed, telling herself every month, every week, that she would go...soon she would go, get herself a job, make friends, leave the crumbling vicarage and its despotic incumbent far behind.

But she had known she would never do it; she was completely unskilled, almost un-educated, for her father had seldom let her attend school after her mother's death. He needed her at home, he was teaching her him-self, he was perfectly capable, thank you very much, of seeing that his only child got a good education.

The village schoolmaster, in awe of the knife-like intelligence of the vicar, had raised the mat-ter of Anthea's schooling a couple of times but had allowed himself to be fobbed off. Later, Anthea knew, her father told the authorities she was going to a private school. Heaven knew how he had managed to get away with this total fabrication, but he had. So that at the age of fifteen, when no one could any longer insist on her going to school, Anthea could read and write, add and subtract, and do very little else.

'Forasmuch as it hath pleased the Almighty of

his great mercy to take unto himself the soul of our dear brother here departed; we therefore commit his body to the ground; earth to earth, ashes to ashes, dust to dust; in sure and certain hope of the Resurrection...'

They were standing around the grave now, the coffin lowered into place and the vicar, nice, hobbledehoy Geoffrey Elgood (call me Geoff, everyone else does!) casting a handful of earth, catching her eye, giving her the sweet, un-worldly smile which had made Albert Todd so very cross. 'The man's a fool,' he had snarled when he had first met Geoffrey Elgood. 'No one but a fool or a two-year-old child smiles like that.'

But Anthea, returning the smile, knew that the vicar was no fool. He had tried very hard to like her father, but the Reverend Todd was not a likeable man. Geoffrey's quiet support, the way he came round to the old vicarage and spent a couple of hours being sneered at and despised just so that Anthea could get into the garden, were things she would never forget. It was the mark of a totally good man she told herself as, in her turn, she dropped a handful of soil onto the coffin.

'The grace of our Lord Jesus Christ and the love of God and the fellowship of the Holy Ghost, be with us all evermore. Amen.'

It was over. They were moving away from the grave, Geoffrey with a hand hovering to hold her elbow. People spoke to her, she answered, but it was not spontaneous. Many of the old vicar's parishioners had admired him but no one had been quite comfortable in his company, Anthea thought now. Least of all she.

She had not wanted a funeral tea but the Elgoods had assured her it was expected, so she had agreed to Elspeth Elgood making sandwiches and setting out a couple of tables in the old vicarage whilst they were at the funeral. Anthea had baked the day before and her contributions were also on the tables.

She walked along beside the vicar, listening to his gentle, amiable voice as she tried to bridge an uncomfortable moment. She wondered how she would feel, to see the big living room, empty for so long, thronged with people. Her father would have hated it, but he was in no position to complain about the oiks, as he called his parishioners, standing on his Turkey carpet in their muddy shoes, or gazing at his silver-framed photographs or the bookcase full of first editions.

He had gone from the vicarage at the moment of his death; Anthea knew it with a certainty which had almost shocked her. She had gone into his room and glanced at him, at the rise and fall of the thin chest, the movements of the throat. They were so slight as to be negligible but his malignancy hovered still, strong as the scent of the lilac by the back door but a good deal less pleasant. She had not believed he would die, though the doctor had told her days ago that only his will kept him alive. So she had glanced in, murmured that if he needed anything he had only to ring, and gone back down to the kitchen.

Ten minutes later she had mounted the stairs, in a hurry, almost running. She had heard nothing yet she had been dragged from her comfortable work in the kitchen up the dark stairs, across the landing and into the master bedroom.

There he lay, with nothing different about him, yet she had know that the instinct which had brought her here at a run had not been wrong. He was dead. And behind him he had left...nothing. No stir in the air, no sense of unrest, not even the faint breath of resentment he had shown so clearly that he was to die whilst she, so much less worthy, was to live. He had gone completely, leaving nothing behind.

She had spent her life in fear of him; even dying he had terrified her. Worst of all perhaps, in the last couple of weeks when every time his eyes opened they fixed on her face with such hatred, such greed for her life, that she had almost fainted. But now he had gone, leaving no trace of himself. She had dealt with the funeral arrangements, moving quietly about the house, forbidding herself the joys of the garden until she had seen him buried. She had entered the room suddenly, expecting a ghost, unable to believe that a spirit so full of vengeful feelings would not linger.

There had been no sightings, no feeling of an alien presence, only, sliding slowly and sweetly into her consciousness, the conviction that he had gone completely, would never worry her again. She was free. She was no longer bound by the inimical will, so much stronger than her own, which had preyed upon her for so long.

'Now, Anthea dear, we'll be very happy to have you at the new vicarage for as long as you want, you know that. But you'll have to go back home eventually. How do you feel about it? The house will be yours, I suppose, when the will's read?'

'I'll be fine. It was awfully kind of you and Elspeth to put me up last night, but I'll sleep at home tonight. As for the will, I don't even know if there is one. If there isn't, can't I have the house?'

For the first time since her father's death, Anthea felt a stab of fear. A will which left the house to someone else would leave her in a pitiable condition. No home, no means of earning a living, no money.

'It doesn't matter whether there's a will or not; I'm sure you'll have the house. Your father owned it, after all, the church merely saw to its upkeep whilst he was on their payroll, so even if there's not a will it goes to you.'

They were out of the churchyard now and turning into the old vicarage. The new, modern one where the Elgoods lived was a bit further down the road but it was not the sort of place for a large funeral tea. Albert Todd had despised Geoff for not insisting on a more imposing dwelling, but the Elgoods had central heating and preferred the modern house.

'I see,' Anthea said now. She looked down at her feet; they were small and neat, with straight toes. The doctor had once told her she had beautiful feet and she had treasured the remark, since her father had never noticed her feet. Every other part of her had been subjected, at one time or another, to his cruel tongue. Huge nose, little eyes, greasy hair, enormous hands, knobbly knees, sharp elbows, skinny shanks, spotty skin, loose lips...the catalogue had gone on and on, with the Reverend Todd thinking up newer and more cutting insults with every day that passed.

But now Anthea followed the vicar into the large, shabby living room and began, obediently, to circulate. She spoke to everyone, murmuring her thanks for their attendance, paying lip-service to the fact that they were so sorry ...she was sure they could not possibly be sorry, she was not, she was *glad*, but she appreciated the desire of everyone to get over to her that she had had a terrible life and they were sorry for that.

Some were quite frank. Mrs Gibson, who kept the post office, said encouragingly, 'We'll see changes at the old place now, my dear! You'll be wanting a job, wanting to get about a bit...', and Anthea had agreed that she did want a job, and her high heart sank just a little at the thought of the sheer impossibility of anyone wanting to employ someone as useless as herself. Only then she remembered her small and pretty feet and felt a tiny surge of what, in another person, might have been self-confidence. Her father had been wrong over most things, might he not have been wrong over her, as well? Except of course that she was fo...almost forty, and had never done so much as a day's paid work in her life.

'Summer's coming, you'll get a job in Haisby, easy,' Mrs Gibson reminded her. 'There's heaps of shops and offices, all wanting a nice young woman to work for them. I'm sure you'll get a job easily.'

She may have been sure but she sounded doubtful. Anthea thought that people in the village tended to forget how old she really was. They thought of her as the vicar's daughter, probably placing her somewhere in the late twenties, ten years too young. She was three years older than Elspeth Elgood, about the same age as Geoffrey. But in experience, she knew ruefully, she was only about as old as a newly born kitten.

'Anthea, do try my walnut shortbread,' Elspeth urged, holding out the plate and Anthea, who was not at all hungry, obediently took a piece. 'I should think everyone in the village must be here—it's a triumph, my dear, because it's you they've come for, not...' Elspeth broke off, clearly conscious of the tactlessness of finishing the sentence. 'Geoff says you're staying here after tea—are you sure you wouldn't like to spend a day or so with us? You're very welcome.'

'Thank you, but I'd rather be at home,' Anthea said. 'There's the cat to feed, and the garden...I don't want the garden to get out of hand. The raspberries at the far end will be ready in a few weeks and I want to bottle some and freeze the rest. I've decided to have that freezer Mrs Holroyd's selling, I hope there'll be enough money for that.'

'I'm sure there will,' Elspeth said, looking unhappy. No one knew the late vicar's circumstances but his meanness towards his only child had been proverbial. Anthea's clothing had always come from church jumble sales. Sometimes, particularly when her father became bed-bound, she had been tempted to take some of the housekeeping money and buy herself something new, but it had been too much of a risk. To be branded a thief was more than she could bear and besides, she had been tired all the time, exhausted as much by his malice as by the nursing of such a difficult patient.

'Then that's all right,' Anthea said now, having almost forgotten the topic of conversation but wanting to take the unease from Elspeth's face. 'I'll help you wash up and clear away but then, when everyone's gone, I'll mow the lawns. They need doing dreadfully badly.'

'Oh, Anthea, mow the lawns? Wouldn't you rather do something a bit more...' Once again the colour rushed up under Elspeth's fair skin. Anthea realised that the other woman had been about to suggest an orgy of pleasure and felt guilty because the Reverend Todd was barely underground. 'I'm sorry, of course you'll want to stay at home this evening. But tomorrow, why don't you have a day out? Try a bus ride to town and a wander round the shops...buy yourself something pretty...'

Murmuring that she would do so when she could spare the time, Anthea detached herself from the vicar's wife and set off once more on the round of her guests. Her first guests, and she was a woman of almost...

She cut the thought off short, offering cake, refilling teacups. Soon, she found herself thinking they would go and she could clear up and then, ah, how good it would be to go outside and get out the lawnmower and push it over the lawns and smell the sweet scent of new-mown grass and know that there would be no bell irritably jangling to demand her presence, no voice to shout peremptorily. No hand, either, to snatch at her hair, to bring his short cane whistling down across the backs of her legs. No fear. No Father.

Because of the sheer bliss of being able to garden for as long as she liked, eat what she liked and do as she liked, Anthea did not attempt to go out and see how wagged the great world for a whole week. In fact she might have continued quite happily at home had her father's solicitor not called. He came just as she emerged from a particularly jungly part of the garden, clippers in hand. She saw a spare, elderly man picking his way through the spring cabbage and went towards him, knowing her face was red.

'Miss Todd? Miss Anthea Todd?'

He called this as soon as he set eyes on her; Anthea blushed a shade deeper and hurried towards him, vigorously nodding, trying to hide the clippers and her scratched and bleeding hands behind her. She knew she looked a sight in a pair of her father's old trousers, a ragged jumper and elderly Wellingtons. Her hair was tied back with green gardening twine and her hands were filthy. No wonder she felt so hot and bothered and wished herself—and her visitor—miles away!

'Ah, Miss Todd, I'm Gerard Parkins, your father's solicitor. I came to have a word with you about his estate.' He gave her a small, tight smile. 'Can we go indoors?'

'Yes, o-of course,' stammered Anthea. 'I'll get you a cup of coffee, or a drink, whilst I clean up.'

'That would be kind.'

He was her father's generation, Anthea saw, but without the bitterness which had characterised the vicar. She saw him settled in the living room with a glass of sherry and some homemade biscuits and then scuttled for her bedroom.

It was a child's room still, but Anthea never thought about it one way or the other, she simply used it to sleep in. It had never been a real refuge from her father because it had no lock and on the one occasion when her fear had been so real that she had barricaded the door against him he had broken it down with the wood-axe. Since she had not the skill to mend it, it had remained free-swinging ever since, with one panel missing, which she had covered with a bit of curtain.

Now, she stripped off her jumper and the trousers, kicked the Wellington boots under the little bed and reached for her hair brush. A few vigorous swipes sent the hedge clippings flying, then she padded barefoot—delicious wickedness, her father would never have allow-ed her to behave like a savage—through into the old-fashioned bathroom, sluiced her arms and face with cold water, rubbed herself dry and returned to her bare little room.

Her clothes were all kept in an elderly chest of drawers, above which was her solitary pic-ture. It showed a rosy-cheeked Mary chatting familiarly to a stern, golden-haired angel. The angel hovered a couple of feet above the ground and directly beneath him a small red hen scratched the earth. It always looked, to Anthea, as though the angel had just laid, not an egg but a chicken, which made the picture homelier. But some wicked person had drawn big black spectacles round the angel's stern eyes, and that same person had given Mary's flat and sexless blue gown a couple of round breasts with nipples like organ stops. Though Anthea had done her best to rub out this artistic endeavour there were still faint marks. They had lasted, she mused now, tugging on a skirt, a good deal longer than the scars inflicted on her person by her father as a punishment for the drawing. Not that it had been Anthea's work, she still had no idea who had done it, but it had been she who had suffered. And he had not even thought it was she; as he had laid hold of her and begun the beating she had screamed that she would not have dreamed of doing such a wicked thing truly, Father, truly.

And he had said, breathlessly, for he never did things by halves, that he did not for one moment suppose she had the gumption to do such a thing. Her sin lay in allowing another to draw on a holy picture.

My sin lay in breathing, Anthea thought. He hated me, he never tried to hide it and any reason, or even no reason, was good enough to use his belt on me.

She buttoned her skirt and pulled on a blouse, fortunately she was still under-developed since the blouse was an old school one and barely met across her chest. Buttoning it with shaking fingers, she wondered just what Mr Parkins was going to say to her. Was he going to tell her that she must leave? She glanced round the room; cracked oilcloth on the floor, faded wallpaper, the bed with its thin blanket. It occurred to her, for the first time, that she could move out of this room now, into one of the better bedrooms. There was a spare room, overlooking the rose-garden, which had a carpet and a double bed. It would be nice to move into the spare room.

That was, if Mr Parkins was going to let her stay. Illogically, she found herself thinking that it was he she must now placate, he she must please. Presently, face shining with soap and water, heavy shoes rendering her small feet hideous, she went down the stairs.

Mr Parkins was standing in the living room looking out of the window. He turned as she entered.

'Ah, Miss Todd—may I pour you a drink?'

There had been drinks and glasses set out on a round silver tray in the living room for as long as Anthea could remember. She had never touched the drinks save to pour them for her father or his rare guests. Now she felt her face flame; should she accept his offer? Would that please him? Or should she refuse, because her father had always taken her refusal for granted.

'Er...er...'

'You don't drink? Very wise.' He was smiling, turning away from the tray. Anthea smiled back, uncertainly.

'I've never tried. But perhaps I could have a glass of orange squash?'

'Yes, indeed. After working so hard in the garden you deserve a long drink. I'll pour the squash into a glass if you'll bring some water, and I'll get myself another small one at the same time.'

Anthea hurried into the kitchen, filled a jug and returned. She had said the right thing, clearly—what a piece of luck! Perhaps now Mr Parkins would let her keep the house.

'Come and sit down, Miss Todd,' Mr Parkins said gently, when she had taken the orange squash. 'I'm afraid I've some rather mixed news for you about the estate.'

'I do have the house,' Anthea explained two hours later, sitting in the Elgood's toy-strewn front room. 'But there isn't much money, so

Mr Parkins doesn't think I'll be able to afford to keep the place going. I said I'd sell garden produce, but even that wouldn't be enough. Father had a thing called an annuity, but Mr Parkins says it died with him...' she gave a snuffly giggle '...a bit like an Indian widow.'

'Forgive me, but surely if you got a job you could keep the house?' Geoffrey said. 'Or you could sell it, it should bring in a good sum and you could build a modern house in the orchard.'

'Mr Parkins suggested selling,' Anthea admitted. 'I wouldn't mind, and I'd like a job, too. But what could I do?'

'Go into Haisby tomorrow, talk to an estate agent, buy yourself a new dress,' Geoffrey said. 'And then go to the Job Centre and see if anything appeals to you.'

'Oh yes, but...'

'It would be fun if you had someone to go with,' Elspeth said with swift understanding. 'But I'm *so involved* right now, what with exams and so on...'

Elspeth taught part-time at the local school. Anthea, who longed for company, shook her head.

'No, it's not that, I'm often alone. I'll catch a bus, spend the day in town. Mr Parkins said the same, actually. He gave me some money, from Father's estate, and told me to spend every penny and not to worry, because he would make sure I was all right.'

'And so will we,' Geoffrey said heartily, getting up to see her out. 'I don't want to hurry you, Anthea, but I've promised to go and see Miss Ridge and I know Elspeth's got to start our evening meal soon...'

'It's quite all right, I've got lots to do myself,' Anthea said. A small tide of Elgood young came flooding in from the garden, nearly bowling her over as she stood in the doorway. 'I'll come over tomorrow evening and tell you how I've got on.'

'You do that,' Geoff said kindly. 'Children, do be careful, are visitors invisible or did you *mean* to trample on Miss Todd's toes?'

Anthea waved and set off down the path. She was used to feeling in the way, kindly but impatiently greeted. It was infinitely better than being used yet despised.

Perhaps, she dreamed as she walked the short distance between the modern vicarage and her old home, perhaps it really would be fun to go to Haisby alone, to think and dawdle and look in shop windows, without having to hurry for someone else, choose what the other would like.

It would be a rare experience, anyway.

Getting into bed later that night—she had forgotten about changing her room until she was actually between the sheets—she felt once again the tingle of excitement, the rush of warmth to the cheeks, which denoted pleasurable anticipation of an event to come.

Even the bus ride would be an adventure and she would have a meal in a restaurant and buy some sandals. She might even buy a summer dress, though such things probably cost a great deal of money. Still, there was no harm in looking. She smiled to herself, seeing a mental picture of her mother, who had done her best, whilst she lived, to protect Anthea from the Reverend Todd. Her mother was nodding and smiling and Anthea could hear her voice as clearly as if she were still alive and near at hand.

'Half the pleasure's in looking,' she said. 'You have a good old look round, Anthea my dear. It's what I did when I was alive.'

I will, Anthea promised silently. She often talked to her mother because she knew very well that her mother had loved her and had suffered from Albert Todd as Anthea had suffered. She could tell her mother all sorts of things and receive only loving compassion, whereas if she told the vicar or Lily Betts, who was the nearest thing to a friend Anthea had ever possessed, they would be embarrassed.

They would not believe that a clever man like the Reverend Todd could possibly do and say the things he did.

Mother was the only safe confidante. Or she had been. But in future, Mother, Anthea said sleepily to her mother's gentle shade, in future I'll be able to talk about anything I please, because it can't get back to him and he can't beat me for it.

Not that the beatings were the worst part of it. Oh dear me no, the worst part, over the past two years, had been his cruel and hateful words. They had flayed a tenderer part of Anthea than her soft and shrinking flesh.

They had flayed her soul.

CHAPTER FIVE

'Mind the way, Poppy!'

Marj swung past the younger girl, glad to be going into the restaurant with an order just to get out of the oppressive heat in the kitchen. In the bay window, delivering four steak and kidney pies, she glanced across at Bonner's, opposite.

It was still empty, still closed. Martin, who

had the longest ears in the Arcade, said he'd heard Diane say she was going up to London to do some buying for the business but perhaps she had gone home, given up on them. After all, the Arcade had been slow for a while...trust it to perk up on a boiling hot day with Diane not around to see it! Everyone hoped that she would open Bonner's as a modern boutique, but no one dared to believe it until it happened. There were always rumours and so few of them came to anything. Arts and crafts someone had said, a jeweller's...but the shop remained closed, clean and mysterious.

Marj delivered the meals and flew back to the kitchen. She could feel sweat trickling down her neck but she was enjoying herself hugely. She loved being busy, loved the plaintive cries of 'Miss...I say, Miss...' which heralded an order for extra drinks or an unexpected pudding. All money, she told herself, all help for the wine bar.

'Two plaice and jackets,' Martin called from his post behind the bain-marie. He grinned at Marj. 'Hot enough for you? Mind you, you run so fast you cool yourself down as you go. Not like Poppy...Poppy, get up them stairs!'

'The stairs are killers,' Marj said fairmindedly, snatching tartare sauce off the sideboard. She could cope with the downstairs restaurant—twenty-seven covers—by herself, but it took Poppy and the part-timer, Alice, all their efforts to service the thirty covers laid in the functions room because of the steep, narrow stairs.

Poppy appeared at the top of the flight, leaning over the banister.

'Two mushroom omelettes, a ham salad and a seafood pancake,' she shouted. 'Can someone pass me up the bread rolls?'

'Come down for 'em,' Martin said cruelly. 'Let's see those legs moving for once.'

'Don't listen to him,' Marj said. She picked up the basket of rolls and stretched up until Poppy could take it from her. 'It's the heat getting to him.'

'He's a selfish pig,' Poppy said; too loudly. Marj turned in time to see Martin's thin skin flush scarlet and waited for the explosion but Sam, appearing from the cellars, chimed in.

'Here you are, another tray of Coke; who wanted it?'

'I want two,' Marj said, whilst Poppy scuttled back upstairs, 'Sam, I want an apple pie. Got any cream whipped?'

'All used,' Alice called, thumping down the stairs. 'God, there's a woman up there I'll swing for if she moans at me one more time.'

'Don't forget Archie's ham salad and Elias's

jacket spud,' a muffled voice from the fridge remarked. Martin, hunkered down, was finding more cream. 'Get Poppy back here.'

'I'll do it,' Marj said patiently. Poppy was not a bad kid, she would be down as soon as she had served her customers but not before, with Martin clearly in a mood. 'Do we still have strawberries or are we out?'

'Out,' Sam said briefly. 'The chicken in red wine walked out when I told him it would have to be raspberries or trifle.'

Marj was too hot to smile at the picture thus conjured up and besides, like everyone else in catering, she always referred to a customer by the food they ordered.

'Right. I'll do Archie's salad and Elias's spud and take them down, then nip over to the market and get some strawberries.'

'Worth her weight in gold,' Martin said, standing up triumphantly and waving a carton of double cream. 'Hey...pass me that.'

Someone had left almost a glass of wine at the bottom of a bottle. Martin drained it, wiped his mouth, then grinned at Sam.

'It's hot,' he said, sounding almost apologetic.

Marj passed him, threw a spud into the microwave, set it, then began to make a salad whilst Martin paused in his dishing up of hot food to carve the ham onto the plate.

The microwave pinged and even as Marj rescued her baked potato Martin was pushing past her to thrust more steak and kidney pies into the oven and a wail from the till announced that 'I need *change*...can anyone change twenty quid?'

Marj slid her plates onto a tray and held out a hand.

'Gimme,' she ordered. 'Not just one, several. I'll deliver these, go to the bank for change, and buy the strawberries; anything else whilst I'm out?'

'Get me a couple of new feet,' Alice said, nursing her toes with one hand. Sam, jumping back from the microwave and slopping milk onto his shoes, added that he could do with some asbestos fingertips. Marj laughed and left them to it, hurrying with her tray up the Arcade, first into the bookshop where Elias had to reach over the heads of several browsers to get his meal and then into Archie's place, where a young couple diligently compared two small rings.

Archie's old spaniel, Smiler, got to his feet as Marj entered and Archie, already standing, sketched a salute. He was retired Army, white-haired, white-moustached, with the upright bearing and neatness typical of his calling.

100

'Hello, here's my favourite girl with the best grub in the world,' he said, taking the plate. 'Cook it yourself? Eh?'

'Every radish,' Marj said, and was rewarded by his bark of laughter.

'Well done, well done.' Archie put his plate on the counter and patted Smiler, who was doing a neck-stretching trick as he smelt the ham. 'You busy?'

'Run off our feet,' Marj admitted. 'Do you want coffee later?'

'Please, my dear. But no hurry, no hurry.'

Marj left her tray with him and went on her way. First into the bank where she queued to have her notes changed by a Mr Tom Hetherington, a cheerful youth with horn-rimmed spectacles and a predilection for gossip which sometimes meant you were in his queue for ages. But he might know something about Bonner's and Marj, in common with the rest of the Arcade, was eager to get the latest score.

'Afternoon, Tom,' she said as she reached the head of the queue. 'Forty quid in fives, tens, fifties and ones, please. No notes and no copper.'

'No copper, and you a copper's moll?' Tom smirked, reaching for bags of ten-pence pieces to put on his little scale. 'How's Eric?'

'Fine thanks, And you?'

'Not so bad. I say, Marj, what about Bonner's, eh? A good thing it's all settled, don't you think?'

Marj nodded sagely.

'I like Diane,' Tom continued, weighing money. 'She's a friendly sort. Used to be a model, they say, I particulary admire her...'

'Tom, if you aren't busy perhaps you could give me a hand with checking this account,' the girl next to him said tartly. She was a brunette with fashion glasses which made her eyes look like great blue ponds.

'I'm busy, I'm busy,' Tom said hastily, reaching into his drawer for more cash. 'Sure you wouldn't like some notes? Just a couple of fivers?'

'Well, just a couple,' Marj conceded. She turned to the brunette, reading her name plate as she did so. 'I wonder if you know when Bonner's will reopen, Miss Agatar?'

'Next Monday,' Miss Agatar said promptly. 'That's why Miss Hopgood's gone to London this week, so she'll have some stock to show, really good stuff. She's selling her flat and she's raised a loan...the usual business.'

'Has she now?' Tom said, turning his head to stare at his neighbour. 'I knew she'd been in and out a lot of course, waggling her...'

'That's all you ever notice,' Miss Agatar

said, glancing contemptuously at Tom with her magnificently magnified eyes. 'Men!'

'At least I don't gossip about the bank's business,' Tom said untruthfully. 'I saw Diane heading for the station earlier and thought she'd probably changed her mind about buying a partnership with the wrinklies and was doing a moonlight.'

'This morning! No wonder no one in the Arcade knows about it yet, then,' Marj said. She gathered up her change and stuffed it into her apron pocket. 'Cheerio, both.'

'Goodbye,' Miss Agatar said. Tom, head down, was ostentatiously weighing money.

Back in the kitchen once more, Martin had reduced Poppy to tears and Alice to fury. Sam was looking worried and Martin, having vented his spleen, was looking pleased with life. Marj rushed to serve her strawberries, to enrich the till with change, and to pour oil.

'Poppy, the girl in the bank told me Diane's gone to London on a buying spree. I bet she'll get some real good gear.'

'Go on!' Poppy said, satisfyingly wide-eyed. 'Buying, eh? Wonder if she'll go for leather jackets and heavy metal?'

Poppy, a picture of respectability during the working day, could sometimes be seen on the streets at night in alarming T-shirts, tight jeans and long leather boots. Her favourite was a black shirt depicting a woman astride a gigantic snake. Martin had remarked on seeing the shirt that tastelessness amongst the young was clearly thriving and Marj knew what he meant. But Poppy was a nice kid; she had better disillusion her before she got too excited, for Marj was sure Diane wouldn't go in for bikers gear.

'It won't be that sort of stuff, Poppy,' she said as the two of them began to make banana splits, side by side at the long workbench. 'The shop's too small, it'll be classy clothes I bet.'

Martin hovered behind them. One of his many annoying traits was his conviction that he was the only person in the world who could turn out a really artistic banana split. Poppy and Marj, from long habit, tried to get so close he couldn't see what they were doing but he craned over Marj's shoulder, fingers itching to interfere.

'Call that a banana split? My God, Poppy, an *ape* could make a better one! It isn't as if I haven't shown you...'

Marj caught Poppy's hand. Together the two of them abandoned the banana splits.

'Sam, we're just going to take a break,' Marj said, above Martin's mutters that 'Yours was all right, Marj, not bad at all, it's just that Poppy won't...I can't seem to get it across to her...after all, I am supposed to be the chef...'

'Oh. Carry on then, Marj.'

Marj and Poppy walked slowly up the Arcade. It was still hot here, a stuffy sort of heat, but as soon as they emerged into Cloister Row the breeze off the sea met them, cooling brows and tempers.

'Marvellous to get some air,' Marj said prosaically. They walked into the churchyard and flopped down onto the grass. Poppy let out a long, whistling breath.

'Phew, that's better. How I stand Martin some days I just don't know. Wish I was Diane, gal Marj! All cool and sophisticated, lookin' at summer frocks!'

It was very hot in London, particularly in the narrow little street down which Diane was walking. The sun seemed trapped by the high buildings, the wind could not reach them, so the street sweltered in the rare sunshine.

Diane was wearing a sleeveless cotton dress with matching primrose sandals. Even so she sweltered with the rest because she had been working hard all day. In and out of shops examining, criticising, sometimes ordering, sometimes not. Chatting to one, making suggestions to a second, nodding approval to others.

She was tired out now, but she was nowhere near finished. Her friend Sadie, a buyer for Barkworths, had told her how easy it was to be jockeyed into buying something you didn't really want by saleswomen who knew your weakness. It could happen to a buyer for a big firm just as easily, as it could happen to a customer. But now, for Diane, it would not just be an unfortunate dress, it might mean three dresses, sizes twelve to sixteen, which none of your customers would want and which you would lose money on.

It was tricky, too, buying for summer when summer was upon you and everyone else was buying autumn stock. She had explained over and over but several of the drawling, hard-eyed women had told her bluntly that she should forget the summer and go for autumn, no point in taking what others had left.

But Diane intended to do no such thing and was buying with care and, she hoped, discretion. Not a single purchase had she made which she did not consider beautiful or striking. No use, with a tiny shop, to go for safe little numbers, quiet beige silk or conventional black. Other shops in Haisby sold that sort of thing, she must choose clothes which the punters would only be able to get at Bonner's.

Diane was on Great Portland Street now; familiar country. She tried to shut her mind to thoughts of Tony, but he kept sneaking back in; smiling, serious. She could even see the look of devastation which had crossed his face when he realised she was going.

Stop it, she ordered herself, crossing the road and peering down a likely side-street, only it wasn't the one, after all. Stop living in the past and think about your future, because you're already tired and there's a lot to do yet. Was she doomed to fail on all fronts, she asked herself? Emotional, physical, even commercial? She had to have the strength to put Tony behind her and to continue grimly buying until she had enough stock to open on Monday.

She crossed Great Portland Street again and felt sweat trickle between her breasts. She tried to remember just where she had gone the time she had wanted costumes for slave-girls in Barkworth's big *Golden Road to Samarkand* display. It had been a poky little shop down a tiny side-street and the rake-thin woman who smoked so much that her fringe was tinged orange with nicotine had gazed at Diane with hollow, black-rimmed eyes, nodding from time to time. Then she had produced a material so lovely that Diane had actually gasped...and within an hour she had slashed down on paper three ideas for slave costumes which had had Diane almost drooling.

'I do me own making up,' she had said, when Diane wondered aloud who could do the work in time. 'It'll cost you, mind.'

It had. But now, Diane came to a corner, turned it and knew she was on the right track. She dived down the alley, her memory telling her that it was here she had been last year, past these dingy shops, into the first doorway on the left...

It was the same. Dark and stuffy, smelling of material, cigarettes and perfume. It was also empty. Diane glanced round. There was material on a table at the back, half hand-printed with a bold, slashed-on design in a variety of different blues. The printer lay in a tray of paint: whoever had been using it had only just left the shop. Even as she looked a voice she remembered called from the back, 'Shan't be a mo, just takin' an order,' and she relaxed. The voice was hoarse, the accent that indefinable East End cockney which verges on a foreign accent without ever quite getting there. So she had found the right shop and soon, with luck, her *Pièce de résistance*, the garment around which she intended to create her first window display, would be hers.

'Sit down...chair by the window,' the voice shouted presently. Diane called back her thanks and seated herself in the creaky cane-chair. She leaned back, crossed her ankles and prepared for a long wait.

After a moment she took out her notebook to examine the details of the stock she had purchased so far, but it was only a desperate attempt to stop herself from remembering the time, almost a year ago, when she had first entered this shop.

It had been just the same, though the pro-prietress had actually been doing her hand-printing. But Diane had been a good deal younger, a good deal more hopeful, because a year ago she had been deep in Tony's thrall, with no idea that the future ahead could be anything but rosy.

She had been fascinated by the shop and had told Tony about it in bed that night. She could remember it so clearly! The outline of his pro-file against the faint light from the bedside lamp, the way he had nodded, drawing deeply on a cigarette as he listened so that the tip glowed, faded, glowed again.

'She does her own printing? And you think she's a gifted designer? It'll cost you,' Tony said just as the woman herself had done ear-lier. 'If she's as good as you say why's she not working for one of the big houses?'

'I don't know, but I know she's good,' that so-much-younger Diane had replied. 'Perhaps she just likes being her own boss, Tony.'

Tony had shrugged, then put his cigarette out by pinching it between his fingers, a trick which always made Diane wince, and turned to gather her into his arms.

'Sweetie, if you've found a genius sure and won't I be the first to cheer? If she's as good as you say she might like to do me an original to work an autumn display around.'

An original like that could earn the designer many thousands of pounds, Diane knew, and she guessed, from the size of the shop and paucity of equipment, that her new discovery could do with the money. Yet she hesitated to encourage Tony, suddenly certain that he would get nowhere with the designer. Despite his sexy Irish accent, blue-black hair and navy-blue eyes, she did not think that Tony would charm a special design out of Mona. If Mona was her name. Certainly above the shop front was a sign which read Mona's Modes, but Diane imagined it had been there a good deal longer than the proprietress.

'Well, see what you think of the stuff she's doing for me,' she had said tactfully. 'It's being delivered in five days.'

He had kissed the side of her neck and then they had made love and the subject of Mona had been allowed to lapse. When the costumes arrived Tony had enthused over them but to the best of her knowledge he had never actually got round to finding the shop.

Probably the one place in London I won't meet Tony is right here, Diane was telling herself, as the woman came back into the shop. She had a man with her...Diane's heart gave a great leap before she reminded herself how many times she had seen Tony, only to have him turn into a perfect stranger the moment he got close. This time she turned away, bent her head to study her notebook, just in case, this time...

'It's grateful I am, indeed.' That warm, dark-brown voice was engraved in her memory, neither could she have confused his *presence*, she could think of no other word for it. Every atom of her knew him, longed to welcome him, but she remained silent, her eyes on the book in her lap.

'And you'll let me have the material in a week?'

That adorable lilt, that altogether delightful blurring of consonants, sent a thrill along her spine. But she sat still, head bent so that her long hair hid him from her—and her from him.

Except that she would have known him any-where, in any pose, under any conditions.

'I'll be on me way, then, seeing as you've another customer.' The little laugh in his voice, meant to bring her head up, she remembered it well but ignored it—and him—completely, sat and waited whilst he said his farewells, left the shop. Only when several minutes had elaps-ed did she glance quickly up, to find the place deserted save for the designer who was quietly stirring her paint, picking up her lino printer, her eyes on her material, seemingly oblivious of her customer.

Diane stood up. She found she was shaking, no longer interested in designs, wanting to wonder aloud why he had not known her. She could catch him up if she hurried, but there was no point in that. They had parted for ever, it was not the sort of parting to turn into a fancy-meeting-you after the hell of three months apart. Only it was hard to have met by chance, and to have let him walk away, un-knowing.

'Yes?' It was the designer, rolling her printer carefully in the dark and streaky paint. 'You been 'ere before; right?'

'Yes, that's right.' Diane swallowed and tried to take a hold of herself. 'That man...the one who's just gone out...I used to work with him.

I was…I was quite surprised to see him here.'

'Yeah?' The woman put a long, rather grubby finger into the paint tray and flicked drops of paint at her material. It should have looked messy, but the paint flew from her finger in a perfect arc and landed with tiny dots and larger dots of paint looking as though each one had been carefully placed on the gleaming material. 'That feller wanted some stuff off of me.'

'So do I,' Diane said, keeping her gazed fixed on the woman's hands, trying to hide the pain which must be clearly visible in her eyes. 'Umm, I don't work for Barkworths any more, I'm on my own so I can't afford much. But I thought, if you'd do me just one special dress, perhaps I could pay you in instalments? It's for my first window-design.'

When you are asking for the moon it's as well to put some supplication into your glance. Diane looked up, to find the other woman giving her customer a slow, calculating look before bringing the printer down, quickly and carefully, on the material and then moving it to blur the outline. Deep blue paling, dawn breaking.

'Yeah? What sorta fing?'

Diane had been thinking about it for days now, but with the dark eyes on her she took a deep breath and said what she really meant.

'Anything. You choose.'

113

'Aah.' The woman abandoned her work and stood back, moving round the counter to stand in front of Diane. 'You'll give me a free 'and, like? I won't bankrupt you.'

'That's wonderful. I'll credit you, of course.'

'Good.' The woman looked Diane over carefully. 'You modellin' it?'

'Well, no. It's a very small shop, it belongs to my two great-aunts...'

Diane found herself telling the story, knowing that it mattered to this designer at least, realising that the setting for the garment she would design would influence her. When she finished the woman nodded.

'Seaside, eh? You in the Smoke for long?'

'Another couple of days.'

'Right. I'll make it for you, I work better that way. Come back day after tomorrow, I'll 'ave somefink for you then.'

'Wonderful,' Diane said. 'Will that be my first fitting? Only I open in a week and...'

'It'll be done by then.'

'Marvellous,' Diane said, uneasily aware that she seemed to be having a solo conversation, if there was such a thing. 'I don't actually know your name but if you tell me what to put I'll get a sign printed for my window.'

'Just Mona,' the woman said indifferently.

'That'll do. No address, mind. I won't be pestered.'

'Of course, if that's how you want it. Well, I'll see you the day after tomorrow, then.'

'That's it.'

Diane moved towards the door; she must leave, Mona had turned from her now not only physically but mentally, too. The way she picked up the printer and began to use it showed only too clearly that her previous work had been desultory, merely undertaken whilst her customer got her ideas sorted out.

Diane reached the door, opened it, took a step out into the hot sunshine, then turned back.

'I say, thanks ever so much, Mona.'

'Wait till you see it,' the other advised, still not looking up.

'I know it'll be special,' Diane said. 'Thanks again.'

Leaving the shop, she began to retrace her steps. She could not prevent herself from searching every face, every turned shoulder, for a trace of Tony, but she saw no one she knew for the rest of that hot afternoon.

CHAPTER SIX

Anthea caught the ten o'clock bus to Haisby, aware again of her freedom as she swung herself onto the platform and clattered up the stairs to take a front seat. Her thoughts kept playing deliciously around the money in her purse; she felt she could almost see the crisp fivers and the scatter of coins through the ugly grey and maroon plastic of her shoulder bag. Mr Parkins had advanced her what he described as a small sum but to Anthea it seemed like a limitless riches. And what a lot she intended to do with it. She could buy sandals and a skirt and blouse, she would get a book to read, a brand-new one, smelling of print and paper instead of mould. And would have lunch out and read her new book.

She remembered, of course, that the Elgoods had suggested she try to find work but decided to let herself off on this occasion. And anyway, she was still hoping that the money which seemed insufficient to Mr Parkins would be enough for someone with her humble tastes to enjoy life. She was not afraid of work but she was sure she'd never get a job, or never keep it, anyway.

She knew the bus journey well but today everything seemed different because she was in no hurry, not willing the bus to go faster so that she might escape the censure which would come her way if she did not get through all her tasks. Consequently she sat there, placid as the cows in the meadows, and planned her day. She had time now, to explore the town, time to wander round the shops, to linger in a restaurant over a meal. And when she got home she would have a nice hot bath and use the scented soap she had found in an old chest of drawers. Going to bed now was so delicious, such a treat! Before, it had been a cold wash, a scared scamper across the lino and a dive into her skinny bed where she would lie tense, sure that at any moment her father would shout for her. He nearly always had, once he became really ill, and always she had obeyed his command to 'Get in here!' Even sick unto death he had been capable of both physical and mental assault and years of practice had taught his daughter that it was always better to obey him at once.

But now! The lovely scrappy meals eaten with both elbows on the kitchen table and a book open before her, the hot bath every night, the fluffy blankets, as many as she wanted, which she had brought from the spare room to her own bed. The tin of biscuits at hand if she should wake during the night—not that she usually did, not now—and best of all the knowledge that the door would not suddenly crash wide to reveal the dreaded figure in the doorway, burning eyes fixing on hers, hands reaching out to...

The bus jerked and rumbled its way over a level crossing and Anthea dismissed her father from her mind. This was *her* day, she was free to please herself and that was precisely what she was going to do.

Presently, the bus began to enter the town environs and the cows and meadows gave way to houses and gardens. Then Anthea recognised the bus station and got, a trifle reluctantly, to her feet. Time to start living her precious day instead of just dreaming about it! She left the bus station behind and went along Queen Street, walking slowly, looking in the windows. Presently she came to a big Marks & Spencer's and went in. The wonderful food! She had been in here before, usually in search of something for her father, never for herself. Now she would go and buy something really nice for when she got home. Entranced by the bright colours and good smells she lingered along each aisle, getting almost as much pleasure from looking as she would have done from eating each item she examined.

Presently she moved to the clothing department. She examined everything here too and spent almost two hours at it, finally buying a pair of knickers so small and frilly that she found herself explaining—mendaciously—to the assistant that they were for a niece.

Armed with the knickers in a smart bag, Anthea left the store at last and stood on the pavement, jostled by passersby, blinking in the sunlight. What next? A meander down to the beach? The weather was right for it; she could buy a picnic and eat it on the sand, she could buy a swimsuit and go in the water...

Spoiled for choice, she dithered. What should she do? Oh, she must not waste this day, suppose she found she had to have a job...she might end up as companion to a wicked old man like her father...she must enjoy this day!

The clock which hung above the chemist's shop made up her mind for her. It was nearly lunchtime and she had not yet done any of the things she had set out to do. First she would find a quiet little shop where she could try on some clothes, then she would go to a bookshop and buy a book and then she would treat herself to lunch. Her mind made up, Anthea set off down Lord Street.

By two o'clock with a cotton frock in a carrier and the longed-for sandals on her feet, Anthea decided to head for her lunch. She was happy. the sandals, which had cost almost as much as the frock, were real leather, and they felt good as well as looking it.

Actually it was their being real leather which had decided Anthea. Her father always believed in buying the best, for himself at any rate, and although Anthea might have been clad in hand-me-downs, they were usually good stuff, though Albert would have made short work of frills. Once, because she had been invited to a wedding, Anthea had let Lily curl her fine, light brown hair. She had come home that evening starry-eyed, sure that this time...

The water from the hose had hit her as she entered the gate, the jet so fierce that it had knocked her straight backwards. Above the crash and swirl of the water, for he continued to play it on her as she struggled to get to her feet, she had heard his mocking laughter and the comments which had hurt more than his attack.

So she thought herself pretty with curls, did she? He'd teach her the sin of pride...not that she had anything to be proud about with her scrawny shanks and flat chest... His voice grated on but when they met again, over the tea-table, he had said, eyes gleaming with malice, 'You never could take a joke; pity you've no sense of humour. You looked such a fool, flat in the mud, whining and slipping...you'd have made a cat laugh.'

But he had never noticed her feet. Now, in the new sandals, they really were pretty. Slim feet with straight toes and little toenails like the pink shells you found on the beach at low tide. She could remember that beach from before her mother died, when they had gone down for a day sometimes. It had been just the two of them, sand in the food and warm lemonade, over-ripe tomatoes and a banana, shared. But they had been some of the happiest days of young Anthea's life and she looked forward to reliving them soon, even though she could no longer have her mother's precious companionship.

However, right here and now she was outside the shoe-shop with her shiny plastic carriers, wondering whether to visit the sea, the harbour, or the commercial part of the town.

Hunger won, so she turned back towards Lord Street. Halfway along it she spotted a

121

huge fish and chip shop but it was full to bursting and though there was a restaurant attached it would have meant sharing a table. Anthea wanted somewhere a bit quieter, somewhere she could eat without being watched.

She walked on. And reached, on the right-hand side of the road, a narrow arcade.

She looked down it and there, right at the end, was a patch of green and gold. Intrigued, she turned into the Arcade, seeing the antique shop and then, further down, a sign which said 'Sam's Place, Licensed Wine Bar and Restaurant'.

It sounded far too expensive for her, but Anthea walked past it anyway and saw that it was by no means full. There was an old couple in one corner, enthusiastically forking food into their mouths, but apart from them it was empty.

Having walked past, Anthea walked back, and saw Glenarvon Books. It was enchanting, very small, very full, with a good sort of smell and a long, thin man curled up in a chair reading devotedly. Anthea went in. There were plenty of paperbacks, but hardbacks too, some obviously new, unread. She opened one and saw it had been reduced from twelve pounds to fifty pence—incredible, she could have two or three at that price!

But they were heavy, so she selected a science fiction book by an author she admired and took it to the thin man who put a long finger in his book to keep his place and smiled at her.

'Fifty pence, please. Do you like Asimov?'

'Oh yes, very much,' Anthea said faintly. She had not bargained on conversation.

'So do I,' the man admitted cheerfully. 'But then I'd read a sauce bottle if there was nothing else.'

Anthea got out her fifty pence and handed it to him, then made for the door. But because he had been friendly she paused there, looking back. He had not returned to his book but was obviously longing to do so.

'Umm...I'm going to have lunch,' Anthea said, her voice scarcely above a whisper. 'I—I thought perhaps...the wine bar...'

'Sam's Place? I often go there; it's quiet and the food's good,' the man volunteered. 'You can read your new book whilst you eat.'

'Yes, I thought...' Anthea's nerve failed her. She smiled, ducked her head and escaped back into the Arcade. Then she walked down to the wine bar.

She was hovering in the doorway when a large woman with bright red cheeks and flowing garments pushed past her, flung open the door, and then held it for her with an impatient courtesy which Anthea found it impossible to snub by walking away.

'Come on, my woman,' the other said breezily. 'You go in, you're a customer; I'm sellin'.'

Anthea scuttled past her, head down, and found a quiet corner table where she could scarcely be seen in the shadows. She picked up the menu and began to study it whilst covertly watching the other woman. What was she selling? Fish? She smelt rather strongly. Or it could be clothes pegs or lucky heather. There was a raffishness about her, she could be a gypsy.

Even as she wondered, a figure appeared in the doorway which separated the restaurant from the kitchen. The door was propped open for ease of access and Anthea was intrigued to realise that she would be able to watch her meal being prepared. But right now a girl was coming through, smiling at the large woman. The girl was dark-haired, with beautiful teeth and large, grey-green eyes. She wore a pink and white striped overall and had a pencil stuck behind one ear.

'Morning, Mrs Evans. Can I help you?'

The big woman chuckled.

'The boot's on the other foot, dearie—can I help *you*? Do you fancy a foo free-range heggs?'

'We buy our eggs wholesale,' the girl said. 'Mind you, the boss has been trying to get free-range eggs. If you'd like to come back next week—can't spare the cash today.'

'Well now, there's a coincidence,' the fat woman said. 'I in't had no dinner yet—how about hif you give me a dinner and I give you four dozen heggs?'

'That sounds fair enough; what would you like'

The old woman smiled triumphantly and dived into her basket. She produced a stout paper bag bulging with eggs.

'There y'are, Marj, four dozen counted out,' she said. 'Now shall we say a bit of steak and kidney and veg, with a nice slice of pie for afters? And a cuppa, of course.'

'It's a deal, Mrs Evans, only you'll want the outside table, today,' Marj said, taking the bag of eggs. 'Now go and take the weight off your feet.'

The old woman shuffled out of the doorway, and by craning her neck Anthea could see her settling down at the wrought-iron table outside. She was still staring when Marj cleared her throat and Anthea realised the girl was standing by her table, pad at the ready. She felt heat blotch her face but Marj was smiling at her, seeming to notice nothing wrong.

'Can I take your order now, dear? Only don't you go offerin' me eggs or the till will look poorly!'

'Oh, no,' Anthea said, dismayed, then realised the other had been joking and laughed hastily. 'Do you often get customers like that? Is she a gypsy?'

'No, just married to a very mean smallholder who won't give her no cash but lets her sell the eggs,' Marj explained cheerfully. 'And I get her to sit outside because, well...'she lowered her voice, 'she smell of poultry and worse.'

'And do you really swop her a dinner for the eggs?'

'Why not? Don't tell the boss, but the price of the ingredients and the price of eggs probably come out about equal. Now, what would you like?'

Marj was so friendly that Anthea did not even mumble as she said that she, too, would have the steak and kidney.

'And a pot of tea would be nice,' she added shyly. 'And can I have the tea now, while you cook the rest?'

'Sure you can,' Marj said easily. She scribbled on her pad and then went back to the kitchen, to return presently with a pot of tea, a jug of milk and a china cup with roses on it. 'There you go. Chipper's on.'

126

Anthea, pouring tea, thought she had never smelt anything nicer than the scent of cooking coming from the kitchen. Cooked food was a treat because once her father could no longer eat proper meals he could see no reason why she should do so and the two of them, one in the kitchen and the other in bed upstairs, had the same invalid diet of Complan and poached white fish. No wonder I'm so thin, Anthea thought now sipping tea.

Only there had been the garden, with peas and beans, strawberries and salads. She had eaten them raw and undetected by the despot upstairs, but she only had to put a pan on the stove and the dreaded voice would shout for her to stop making his life hell, he couldn't bear the smell of food he couldn't eat, she was selfish, greedy...and it was no use telling him that it was just his fish being cooked because his sense of smell grew sharper as his ability to eat faded and he knew exactly what vegetables she was trying to cook whilst he slept.

'There. How's that?'

Whilst Anthea dreamed and drank tea Marj had cooked a whole meal and now she set the plate tenderly down in front of Anthea, obscuring the mat with the picture of London Bridge on it. Steam wafted up from the plate, tickling the palate. Anthea's mouth watered. The homemade pie was bursting with meat, rich gravy wended its way amongst golden chips, the peas and carrots were bright and fresh.

'Thank you,' Anthea said. She picked up her knife and fork and had to make herself hesitate until Marj had gone back into the kitchen. Then how she ate! Feverishly and fast, only slowing once the first edge had been taken off her appetite, so that the plate was empty before the tea had cooled in the cup.

Anthea sighed contentedly and drank the rest of her tea, then poured herself another cup. The waitress came to the doorway and raised a brow at her.

'All right was it? Want a pudding?'

'It was marvellous.' Anthea told her, her voice sounding stronger, as if the food had actually improved her self-confidence. 'Umm— the lemon meringue pie looks awfully good.'

'No sooner said than cut.' Marj picked up the enormous pie and went into the kitchen with it, returning presently with a generous slice on a pretty china plate. 'This do you?'

'Oh, yes,' Anthea said. The pie had been made by a prodigal hand, the meringue was piled up like cumulus clouds gilded by a brilliant sunset. She raised her spoon to her mouth as the door opened and the old woman's head appeared round it.

'Now orf,' she announced. 'See you next week, gal Marj.'

'Goodbye, Mrs Evans,' the waitress said. 'Go careful.'

As Mrs Evans was about to close the door another customer came past her. It was a dark, handsome young man with a frank smile. Anthea looked away quickly as he took the table in the bay, with his back to the window so that he was looking right at her. All men frightened her but handsome ones were terrifying. Not that they noticed her as a rule, thank heaven, but this one could scarcely help it, seated as he was.

Marj, however, was approaching him.

'Hello, Chris, back again! Tea and a teacake?'

'Not today. Today I'll have a beef sandwich with salad...got any horseradish?'

'Sure. Or mustard.'

'There you go again, putting words into my mouth. Can I have a touch of both or will you charge me extra?'

Marj laughed. It was the sort of laugh seldom heard in church, but it gave Anthea a lovely warm feeling, made her own lips twitch into a smile.

'Hev both, bor,' Marj said, broad Norfolk just for a moment after that glorious burst of sound. 'Anything else?'

'Yes, a pot of tea and a nice big helping of sherry trifle. All right?'

Marj had been scribbling busily on her pad, now she nodded and headed back for the kitchen.

'Fine. Shan't be a tick.'

Anthea started to eat her lemon meringue again, then sipped her cooling tea. She had taken a good look at the young man and had decided he had a dangerous face. Probably he was impatient, easily roused to anger or laughter, and his eyebrows slanted up just like his eyes did. Now, he looked across at her.

'I'm sorry, I've disturbed your peace. I like to read when I eat, too, but today I've no book.'

Anthea mumbled something, feeling hot sweat break out all over her body. Was it polite to converse with someone when you were the only two people in a restaurant? She had no idea, but she did not want to talk and she'd finished now, she might as well leave.

'Ready for the off?' the young man said. 'Want a quick cigarette before you go?'

He was holding out a packet. Anthea shook her head, mumbling to her feet. There was a bell by the kitchen door, she would ring and Marj would rescue her from this far-too-handsome man, who must have some wicked ulterior motive in addressing her at all, though she had no idea what it could be.

'Finished? What do you think of our lemon meringue? I made it, you know.'

Marj was smiling at her, looking as though she knew just how Anthea disliked making conversation and sympathised.

'Hope we haven't broke the bank,' she said next, rapidly totting up the bill. 'There you go—not too bad, eh?'

It was not too bad at all. Anthea paid, self-consciously left a fifty-pence tip and made her way out into the Arcade. She did not once let her eyes rest on the young man but kept her gaze turned away.

Now that she was out of the wine bar, though, she found she was no longer in a hurry. She was comfortably full and lazy. She peeped into the empty shop, Bonner's, then moved on to the Health Food place and looked in the window. She was hesitating near the door when a fat, hairy dog barked at her. Anthea scurried on, to the next shop, which had soaps and perfumes on display. She was fascinated by the air the Arcade gave of being a small world complete in itself, not needing the bustle of Lord Street or the beauty of the harbour nor the obvious appeal of promenade and beach.

How nice to work in that shop, Anthea thought, peering between the bottles and jars in the window of Treat Yourself and seeing a plump blonde sitting behind the counter. It would be very much easier than running up and down stairs, digging the garden, keeping the rambling old vicarage clean. Perhaps getting a job wasn't so bad, after all. Perhaps in this very Arcade someone was looking for an oldish girl or a youngish woman to sit behind a counter and sell things.

She looked in the hairdresser's next. Very nice. Little girls in short skirts bustled about, chattering like birds, waving scissors, laughing.

She had reached the end of the Arcade and was about to step into Cloister Row when someone shouted and she heard running feet. She turned, a hand fluttering to her mouth, and saw the dark young man from the restaurant. Chris.

'Excuse me...you left your book!' He was panting, slowing, holding the book out. 'I'm sorry if I scared you but it's a new book, you wouldn't want to lose it.'

Anthea forced her stiff lips into the semblance of a smile. He must think her an idiot to be so scared. But she could only manage a brief 'thank you' as she took the book from him.

'It was yours, then. I was pretty sure, but...'

'Yes. I...I bought it from Glenarvon Books.'

'Ah, I've had quite a few books from Elias myself. I'm a science fiction fan like you, you must lend me that one some time.'

Anthea felt like a stag at bay; hunted, she thought only of escape.

'I must go, I've got a bus to catch,' she muttered. 'You can have the book, if you want.'

She would have given it to him willingly, just to get rid of him, but he was backing off, shaking his head, telling her to run along now, he'd see her some time.

Anthea made for Lord Street, at a pace which was only marginally not a run and saw him, with an easy wave, going off in the opposite direction. She did have a bus to catch but not for another hour, and she did not want to spend that hour sitting in the bus station. She decided she would go back down the Arcade now he was out of sight and explore Cloister Row.

She walked slowly when she reached the cobbled way, looking up at the flats, peering into windows, reading brass plates. John O'Halloran, veterinary surgeon, Messrs Dobson & Pratt solicitors at law. A lovely green door with a big brass 3 on it, a scratched red door with a plastic 5.

She reached the end of the row and leaned against the wall, looking over it. She saw that it was seeded with all sorts, tiny ferns, a patch of pennywort, fat cushions of moss and the common toadflax which is just like miniature yellow snapdragons. It was beautiful on the beach side, nicer than the sparkling white of the Row, even.

And then she looked down and saw the beach. The big round pebbles directly below her, then the shingle ridge, then the gleaming reach of wet sand, just abandoned by the tide. The smell of it, Anthea thought, sniffing ecstatically. Oh, how she loved it! She would have liked to go down but you could not climb over the wall and drop fifteen feet, you had to walk right round, which would take time. She mustn't miss the bus.

Why not? No one was waiting. No one cared whether she was late or not!

The thought gave her a pang instead of the heady pleasure which had been hers when she remembered her freedom earlier. It was good to be free, but to have no one who cared was a mixed blessing. It was awful to realise that if she fell over this wall right now and broke her neck, it might be days before anyone realised she was missing.

But you couldn't have everything, and she no longer had to dread going home. And right here and now...she examined her purse and there was still lots of money left...she would go and treat herself to tea and cakes.

Resolutely, Anthea loped across Haisby to the bus station, queued for the ladies' toilet and then had a piece of chocolate fudge cake in a tearoom opposite her bus stand. When she was finishing she saw Mrs Saunders' daughter, Mary. Mrs Saunders had cleaned the vicarage once, and sometimes she brought Mary with her so that the two small girls could play together. Anthea got up and cantered out, clutching Mary's arm.

'Mary...it is you! Have you time for a quick cup of tea before the bus? I'll buy us one.'

Mary thought this a good idea; the two of them drank tea and chatted until the bus drew in, then they got on it and sat side by side whilst Mary told Anthea about her teenage daughter and Anthea thought how terribly lucky she was to have had such a day.

Unlocking the vicarage door later, and letting herself and Tibby into the kitchen where they would presently share the food she had bought, Anthea planned how she would have a hot bath and then take her new book to bed with her.

Oh, the luxury of it! I don't believe anyone in the world could be happier than me, Anthea thought as she and Tibby settled down to share fried herrings. I really am lucky!

CHAPTER SEVEN

Diane leaned back in her corner seat, closed her eyes and tried to relax all over, as she had been taught in Yoga. First you relaxed your toes, concentrating on making them limp and heavy, then you moved up, willing limpness in ankles, knee, hips...

Only whilst Diane was moving up her body, her treacherous toes were going stiff, and when she realised this and hastily abandoned elbows and wrists to speak sternly to her toes, those other renegade members promptly tensed up on her as well.

After four abortive attempts to get thoroughly relaxed before the train started, Diane gave up altogether, opened her eyes and looked about her. The carriage was filling up. An elderly couple were furtively eating sandwiches; a flask steamed against the window, blurring the glass, whilst sharing Diane's own table a pimply young man with a runny nose read the *Sun*.

But it was better than the next coach which was occupied by a school party. Already the sound of children singing, shrieking and, alas, swearing, reached Diane's ears every time the door opened. Still, she had always advocated mid-week travel, had always avoided Fridays until now, she should have taken her own advice. Only the truth was she could not have borne to remain in London over the weekend.

London reminded her, at every turn, of Tony. She had been mainly in that part of Town which housed the rag-trade and all the time her heart tugged away at her, urging her to telephone him, go round to the flat, do anything, so long as she ended up in his arms again.

Her heart had always been a sucker for Tony, though. It had been her head which ended their affair and it was her head, now, which stopped her from running back to the flat, using her latchkey to let herself in, and finding him.

She had owned half the flat, and when she decided not to return to London she had offered her share to Tony at whatever price an agent should set. She had half-expected a firm refusal. Instead, the agent's sum had been paid humiliatingly quickly, almost as though Tony was relieved to be rid of her.

She should have sent the key back. Perhaps she would, when she got home. It would be a sign of her new independence, her determination to forget the past. On the other hand, whilst she had the key...Diane lost herself in a daydream in which she returned to the flat, lay on the bed, fell asleep and woke to find Tony making love to her.

The train, starting with a jerk, brought her fully awake but her half-slumber had made her cross. She glared at the pimply young man and at the smart, middle-aged woman now sitting beside him. She had slept and they had looked on her sleeping face; what a damned liberty! But the faces opposite were indifferent; the young man, she could see, was too miserably involved with his head-cold to care and the woman too wrapped up in her purchases. She was peeping into a Harrods bag, smiling to herself, then turning sideways to look at her reflection in the window pane.

Conceited old bitch, Diane thought vengeful-ly, and played with the idea of surreptitiously putting her stockinged foot up the woman's skirt, making her think the spotty youth was making a pass.

Whilst chuckling to herself at the thought, Diane knew perfectly well that she would never do it and was even vaguely ashamed of having had such a low idea. And anyway, the sight of the other woman clearly gloating over a pur-chase made her think about the dress in the rack above her head.

Mona's dress. It was, as Diane had known it would be, perfect. A sun-dress made of a fine, floating cotton, it caught the attention at once with the colour—blues and golds all exquisitely blending—and the design. It was a seaside dress, the blues water and sky, the golds sand and sun, and the design was a seaside design too—shells, seaweed, birds' wings, the flash of a fin, the curl of a wave crest.

Because she had thought about her own purchase, Diane felt her animosity subsiding. When she caught the woman's eye they both smiled. After all, what woman would not want to see again the garments she had just bought? Diane found she was longing to take her own bag down from the rack, spread out the dress and rejoice in her possession of it.

Mona had wanted her to try it on and had suggested she should model it in her shop.

'It'll suit you,' she said, squinting against the lazy upward drift of smoke from her perpetual cigarette.

But Diane would not; it was too precious for that, she wanted to see it for the first time on a model in the Bonner window, not on her own too-familiar figure.

'No, but I'll buy a wax model,' she said excitedly to Mona. 'One of the really elegant ones.

They cost a bomb, but it would be worth it.'

'Thought your window was small.'

'Oh! Diane stopped short. 'It is, but surely...'

'Doesn't need a figure,' Mona said flatly. 'Just one of them wire shapes. Have it sitting dahn, takes less space. You'll know how to do it, I daresay.'

And now, sitting in the train, Diane did know how to do it. She would buy a wire shape and she would dress the window as a beach. She would use bright rugs with shells scattered over them and a picnic hamper. She would get marram grass and make it look as though it was growing, and she would have big pebbles too and some grey shingle, and her window would look superb, the dress a star.

The woman opposite put the Harrods bag down with a little sigh and delved around in a capacious brown leather handbag, pulling out a paperback novel. As she began to read Diane looked more closely at her. A square, handsome face, the skin leathering but not wrinkled. Clear blue eyes, a mouth with humour in it and sadness too. She wore a wedding ring. A practical woman with expensive clothing which she had owned, Diane's experienced eye told her, for a number of years. Diane imagined her taking her jacket off and brushing it carefully,

140

rubbing energetically at a stain on the skirt and then hanging the suit on a hanger whilst her blouse and underwear went down for washing.

What would it be like, to be old? To treasure a set of clothes because they were your best? Diane had always pitied the old and middle-aged but now saw by the contented line of the woman's mouth that there were advantages. Her fellow-passenger did not have to compete, to spend all her money on the latest fashion. Yet when she did spend how she enjoyed it! Her pleasure in the unseen garment in the Harrods bag was every bit as great as Diane's own in her unique and costly seaside dress. She would always think of it as that though it was really a Mona Mode. Mona had tacked her label into the neck because Diana had insisted, just a square of material with Mona's Modes printed, maroon on white, like a school name-tape.

Diane had been puzzled that Mona did not seem to want the adulation that was her due. She would have wanted it, had it been her, but Mona, it seemed, just wanted to be left alone. Very Greta Garbo, Diane supposed. But it was none of her business; she would make out a nice sign for her window and put it discreetly against the skirt of the seaside dress, and wait and see. Whoever buys it will want more of Mona's stuff, she found herself thinking and

141

was aware, suddenly, that she had no intention of selling the dress. She would keep it for the pleasure of owning it, not to wear, not to boast about, but simply to enjoy. When I'm old I'll get it out and look at it and it'll bring this summer right into the room with me, she told herself. When I'm old I'll show it to my children and...

The bubble burst. Her children would not be Tony's children. She became aware that her back ached, that the pimply youth's nose was running and that the children from the next carriage were bearing down on her, swearing and shouting like a crowd of football hooligans which, probably, they were.

Was I in love with him? Diane wondered drearily as the ache settled into place just below her ribs as though it had never left. Am I in love with him still? But if I'd loved him I never could have left him, he said it himself, a hundred times, and I'm sure he's right. If I'd truly loved him, the way I thought I did, I couldn't just have walked out and left him to someone else.

Not even when I found out that the someone else had been married to him for seven years and given him four children? Not even when he told me about Shelagh, the dewy-eyed bride he had left in Ireland, to bring up his children

142

and take care of the old parents? If mine had been real love it would have triumphed over that, would have insisted that he had been trapped into marriage when too young to make up his own mind. But she knew it wasn't true, so she left him.

So Tony lived in London and went home to Ireland four times a year. In the course of these visits he no doubt bonked his wife nightly, and got her pregnant. When she had enquired, in a voice thin and high with pain, whether his Shelagh was in pod again, with yet another little Cusack, he had nodded dumbly, his eyes pleading—in vain—for her understanding.

'Sure she is; she's a good Cat'olic,' he had said, his voice in his anguish at its most Irish, and for a moment she hated him. 'I've told ye, dearest Di, that what I feel for her isn't love as you and I know it but a sort of duty. She had no one, she never made a secret of how she felt about me. Having me as her man is heaven for her. 'Tis not conceited I'm being, 'tis honest with ye; she wouldn't have her life any other way.'

'And me? What about me?'

'She wouldn't grudge us; she knows I'm a normal, red-blooded man,' he had said earnestly, never seeing that he was digging himself deeper into her ill graces with every word uttered. 'She accepts that I'm two people. Here, a businessman, there a farmer, a feller that goes out in the rain in big wellies with a sack over me head, to take a look at the crops. The man I am in Ireland would bore you to tears, me darlin' girl, and the man I am here would terrify poor Shelagh into a fit.'

'Then why don't you divorce her, if you're so incompatible?' Diane blazed. 'Why not forget her and... and them?'

She had seen the look which crossed his face and had known that his real love, the steady, undying, unkillable sort, was for his Irish home, mud and all, and for his kids. She could not yet convince herself that it was also for his 'good Cat'olic', but one day, perhaps, when she was further removed from the pleasures and pains of their life together, she might be able to acknowledge that, too.

So she had left him, her job, her whole way of life. And had gone to Haisby expecting to be bored for a week or so and then to go back to London. Instead, she had found small-town life absorbing, her aunts good company, the Arcade a tiny, self-contained community which she wanted to join. And Bonner's was a challenge, a promise of fulfilment, everything she needed rolled into one. The ache of her loss would not go away, not yet, but at least there were hours together when she never thought about Tony and one day, she knew, she would begin to enjoy life once more.

Falling in love again was out of the question of course, a consummation most devoutly to be avoided. Next time, she vowed, I'll make sure that I keep my cool and my heart, too. Next time I'll enjoy the fun and the thrills of an affair but I'll make *bloody* sure I don't fall in love. That way I won't get hurt.

Opposite, the woman half got to her feet, then addressed Diane.

'I think I'll go down to the buffet car for some coffee and a sandwich; would you like something?'

'I'd love a coffee,' Diane said, realising as she spoke that it was the truth. 'A snack wouldn't come amiss, either.'

The young man cleared his throat.

'I've got a bid of a cold,' he said thickly. 'I'd like a hot drink. I'll come down with you, open doors and that.'

Diane knew from past experience that once a group of people in a train start talking it rapidly becomes a sort of mini-friendship, with everyone telling everyone else the most intimate details of their lives. The time to kill the whole thing stone dead was now; she should snub the young man and let the woman bring her back a coffee unaided. It was the only way to ensure a quiet journey. She opened her mouth to blight.

'We'll all go,' she heard herself saying cheerfully. 'Lead on, Macduff!'

When Diane woke on the Monday morning she was to open the shop, it was raining. She lay there in bed and heard the sea pounding against the harbour wall and watched the rain fall on the skylight above her and felt the first chilly foreboding slither into her mind.

She would never have known it was raining before even drawing the curtains, had she not made a lightning decision the previous evening. It was then, after supper, that the aunts had stunned her into action.

They had had a special meal to celebrate the forthcoming opening of the boutique—dressed crab and a sweet white wine. They used the lace tablecloth Diane's great-grandmother had had in her trousseau and decorated the table with a vase full of roses from Aunt Dulcie's garden.

Diane had been touched by their care and glad to show it. She enjoyed the meal, was reverent over the tablecloth, admired the roses. And then Aunt Violet had dropped her bombshell.

146

'What time do we open, dear?' she had asked anxiously, her wine glass still half raised
from the final toast. 'We want to start when
you do, naturally.'

Diane, still reeling from the shock of realising that her aunts did not know the meaning
of the phrase 'sleeping partners' had found
words on her lips before she had thought twice.

'Oh, I can manage the shop alone, easily, but
I've been meaning to ask you whether you'd
ever thought of taking paying guests? Just during the season, of course. The money would
be a help and it does seem a shame...this
lovely big place...just the three of us...'

She hardly dared look at the aunts in case
they guessed that it was just a way of keeping
them out of Bonner's, but when she did, their
eyes were shining.

'Well dear, we were very keen once, but Arthur said we had quite enough to do with the
shop, and now, with you in the big spare room,
I'm not sure...'

'I could take over one of the attics, Aunt
Dulcie,' Diane said, amazed at the speed with
which she could think under fire, so to speak.
'That would leave you the big spare room and
the single. I'm sure those rooms would let very
quickly.'

'I'd move into the other attic room,' Aunt

Dulcie said. 'That would give us two doubles and a single to let.'

'It would be too much...' Diane began and was promptly overborne by her aged relatives.

'Too much! When we've no responsibility for the shop?' Aunt Dulcie shook her head reproachfully at Diane. 'The weight of worry which has gone, dear, has made new women of us. And we've always longed to do bed and breakfast because you can charge quite a lot of money, and you meet interesting people.'

'I should find it *very* congenial,' Aunt Violet chimed in. 'I do love cooking! Imagine, we could provide real cooked breakfasts!'

'I daresay we could charge a pound a night,' Aunt Dulcie mused. 'We could join the B & B Association which Mrs Mallory runs, I've always longed to know what they talk about twice a month.'

'I think you should charge a great deal more than that,' Diane said as soon as she could get a word in edgeways. 'You have to allow for laundering sheets and so on. Then you'd like to go ahead with it? You could start first thing tomorrow.'

'I'll do a card for the window right away,' Aunt Violet said, whilst Aunt Dulcie insisted on changing her room and Diane's at once, and on making up the beds in their old rooms with clean linen.

Nothing could stop them. Notices were neatly lettered and put in the front windows behind the curtains. Indefatigably the aunts changed sheets, carried all Dulcie's possessions up to one attic room and Diane's small belongings to the other, wrote out breakfast menus, loudly derided each other's suggestions, found clean towels and laid them tenderly on every bed, and were only persuaded with difficulty not to ring Mrs Mallory right away, at midnight to discuss rates.

Diane, crawling into the narrow bed in the attic, was so tired she wondered if she would be able to sleep at all, but she need not have worried. She slept as soon as her head touched the pillow.

And now she awoke to rain pattering on the skylight above her, each drop adding to the small pond which had formed at the lower end of the pane. Last night she had not noticed the wind, either, or perhaps she was more conscious of the elements now she was so high, with only the pane of glass between her and the sky. As she watched, a seagull flapped slowly across her field of vision and vanished, grey against grey. Diane heaved a sigh and sat up. She glanced at her wristwatch; seven o'clock. The wind was moaning round the eaves and there was a big sea running. Heaven pity sailors on a day like this, she thought piously, descending the creaking attic stairs and bolting into the bathroom. It was good to get under the hot water, letting it both wake her up and massage her into movement with its hissing jets.

Dried and dressed, she sneaked quietly down into the kitchen. She did not want to wake the aunts, who must be even more exhausted than she after their exciting evening.

Aunt Violet was in the kitchen before her, however, with bacon already under the grill.

'Oh!' Diane said guiltily. 'I didn't mean to wake you...what on earth are you doing about so early?'

'Getting you some breakfast, dear,' Aunt Violet said, pouring tea. 'I heard you in the shower and I believe a hot breakfast is the best start to a day. Besides, we've a lot of clearing out to do.'

'Clearing out?' Diane said, sipping the tea. It tasted odd with toothpaste still sweetening her mouth.

'Oh...the wardrobes are still full, more or less,' Aunt Violet said wistfully. 'And there's too much truck in the attics.'

Diane, who had just about registered that her new room was crammed with boxes, bags and piles of unidentified objects, admitted that she had noticed a good deal of stuff.

'I'll have to part with it, in a good cause, of course,' Aunt Violet said now. She sounded quite cheerful in the circumstances. 'You can't expect guests to put up with stuff in their rooms.'

Murmuring agreement, Diane tucked into bacon and fried tomatoes and told herself that her chance remark had certainly changed the aunts' lives, probably for the better. They loved looking after people and would do it well and the money would be very useful indeed.

'That was delicious,' Diane said, finishing her meal and standing up. 'Oh dear, look at that rain! Could you lend me a brolly, Auntie Vi?'

'Need you really go so early? It's only half-past eight. But if you must, there's a nice rose-coloured umbrella in the hall-stand. Take that one, it will suit you.'

Diane laughed, scooped up her big bag and left Aunt Violet fussing over the washing up. She found the umbrella and fumbled with the front door, noticing that there was no sound of movement from above her. Aunt Dulcie plainly did not feel it incumbent upon her to get up and see her great-niece off.

Letting herself out into the downpour, Diane felt a bit more of her optimism draining away.

What on earth had she done? There were the aunts, both convinced that by evening they would be in the bed and breakfast business, whereas they might never get a single customer. And here was she, setting out full of such high hopes, on a day when everyone with any sense would stay indoors.

Doomed, Diane thought gloomily, putting up the rose-coloured umbrella and sloshing towards Lord Street. Doomed to fail, to disappoint people, to raise hopes which could not possibly be realised. How could she have done it to her aunts? It was because she was too selfish to endure them hanging round the shop, making her feel guilty every time someone passed without looking in. And she'd encouraged them to believe they could run a guest house when it must be clear that two maiden ladies in their seventies would never cope. They would get no customers and all their bright hopes of financial success would drain away, as Diane's own bright hopes of a life with Tony had done.

Thinking of Tony simply hurt unbearably and made Diane cross with herself for letting him enter her thoughts. Now, with rain dripping down her neck—the umbrella had a small but effective hole where the spine had rubbed its way through the material—Diane allowed herself, for one second, to hear his voice, its warmness, the touch of brogue. But just as she turned into Lord Street a passing bus took her by surprise, soaking her with a great arc of water as it thundered heedlessly through a puddle. Leaping for safety and cursing the driver was an effective way, she discovered, to stop dwelling on Tony.

Diane sloshed on, turning into the Arcade with real pleasure and greeting Archie, who was pinning back the antique shop's shutters.

'Morning, Mr Pinter...isn't it a dreadful day?'

Archie swung round and tugged off his corduroy cap, smoothing his rumpled hair flat with the palm of one hand.

'Archie, please, m'dear. Don't worry about the weather, your window is a sight for sore eyes. I'll send all my customers down just to take a look—I don't know how you did it, I take my hat off to you.'

'Thank you,' Diane said. 'I hope everyone feels the same. You like the dress? It's a designer model.'

'Thought so,' Archie nodded. 'Quality; I always spot quality. It's like antiques, it's quality which counts every time.'

'Let's hope the customers agree,' Diane said. She smiled and moved on and Archie stuck his cap back on his head and returned to his task.

Shaking her umbrella, Diane continued down the Arcade, past the still-closed shops, glancing into the kitchen of the wine bar and waving to Marj and the girls. Further along the hairdressers, Emma and Jenny, were opening up. Emma was sagging against the doorpost whilst Jenny, looking cross, was struggling with a basket of clean towels, an umbrella and the key. Diane went over to them.

'Here, let me,' she said, taking the key and turning it in the lock. 'What's the matter, Emma?'

'Hangover,' Jenny snapped. 'Been sick as a dog and now she's saying she can't work...my God, Di, we've got a list of appointments as long as your arm and she wants to go home and sleep it off!'

'Well, wouldn't it be better?' Diane hazarded.

'No it bloody wouldn't, she's a partner, not an employee! An employee can ring in sick, but a partner has to grin and bear it. Come on, Em, get inside and start work,' she added in a hectoring tone. 'It'll do you more good than moaning.'

Diane expected Emma to protest but instead she tottered unsteadily into the salon. When she reached the handbasins she began to run water and Diane was still watching when Emma began to vomit, sending her hastily out of the doorway and back towards Bonner's. As she reached it and turned her key she looked back towards Waves and to her astonishment Emma appeared in the doorway, still pale and swaying but obviously more in command, and began to sweep the step.

Shaking her head, Diane went in and closed the door behind her. She did not think she would much fancy a hungover Emma waving scissors round her ears, but perhaps Jenny would see to it that her partner stuck to washing and perming today. Not blow-waving. The thought of Emma and hot tongs put Diane's teeth on edge.

But Bonner's was lovely, now. Beautiful, calm, orderly. Diane took off her jacket and hung it over the banister, then put her umbrella up again and lodged it on the third stair. She also kicked her shoes off, though with mental reservations. She could scarcely serve customers barefoot, but did not really expect anyone much before ten.

Next, Diane turned the lights on and saw how nice the place looked in the pinkish glow. Then she switched on the wall-heater, which smelt new and rather nasty, but the odour should have gone before customers appeared.

155

Next, Diane dusted the glass-topped counter, admiring the beauty of her fashion jewellery as she did so. Nothing was expensive but the brilliant animal brooches, gaudy but effective earrings and some first-rate plated necklaces drew the eye and would enhance most of the clothing on the racks.

After that, Diane checked the till, despite knowing exactly what the float was, then pulled out her order book and put it handy. Whatever she sold must be replaced and she must know exactly what had gone or she would lose track of her stock. One day I'll have a till which does it for me, she dreamed remembering Barkworths. But until then she would have to write every item down as it went from the shop.

Promptly at nine the telephone rang. It was Sadie, ringing up from London to wish her luck. Diane described the weather conditions and her meteoric rise from first-floor double to attic and Sadie rang off, chuckling.

At ten Marj appeared, bearing a steaming cup of coffee.

'It's on the house, from Sam,' she said, putting it on the glass-topped counter. 'Fed-up, are you? This rain!'

'Fed up, worried...but thank Sam ever so much for the coffee,' Diane said ruefully. 'Is it just the weather Marj? Or is it...'

'That's the weather gal Di; we've sold three coffees and a scone,' Marj said bracingly. 'I'm off home now, they don't need me.'

Despite her words however, she lingered, turning the revolving rack, her glance approving the little touches which had taken Diane much thought and hard work.

'What do you think?' Diane said as Marj's eyes returned to the counter-top jewellery display.

'You've done wonders,' Marj said. She turned back to the rack. 'What's that fluffy pink thing?'

'Angora top,' Diane told her. 'A bit warm for summer, but nice for evenings.'

'Got it in a twelve?'

'In pink? Yes, I think so.'

'Can I try it?'

'Of course, but don't think you've got to buy something just because I'm depressed,' Diane said, only half jokingly. 'Go on, christen the changing cubicles.'

Marj laughed too, but disappeared behind the chintz curtain. There was a brief struggle and then she reappeared in the top, looking stunning.

'I say,' Diane said. 'I don't know whether it suits you or you suit it, but it looks good.'

'It's a bit of all right; but how much discount will you give me? I saw the price.'

Diane unhesitatingly took off a whopping twenty-five per cent. Marj stroked her own sleek hip approvingly.

'I'll have it. Cash, what's more, seeing as how Sam just paid me for working Saturday. Wait till Eric see it!'

She took the top off, not bothering to return to the cubicle, then put on her blouse whilst Diane carefully folded the angora top into one of her new navy and gold bags.

'You're my first customer,' Diane said as Marj handed over the money. 'Thanks ever so much Marj, and thank Sam for the coffee, if you're going back to the kitchen.'

'I am now,' Marj said, buttoning her jacket. 'Got to show them gals my new top, haven't I!'

She did like it, Diane told herself as she sipped the hot coffee. She's straight, is Marj, she'd not have bought it if she thought it was over-priced, either. She's a friend, all right, but she's a satisfied customer, too.

It was a cheering thought for a new trader, and Diane found her spirits soaring as she drained her cup.

CHAPTER EIGHT

When Mr Parkins told Anthea she might starve on the money her father had left she took it with a pinch of salt, but owing money terrified her. A Dickensian scene of bristle-chinned bailiffs marching into her home reared its ugly head as soon as the word 'debt' was mentioned, so it was no wonder that, the next time she caught the bus for Haisby, Anthea went to find work.

Two people had agreed to interview her, the owner of a boarding house on Harbour Way and the manager of Styles, the big fish and chip café on Lord Street. Anthea, sitting once more on the front seat of the bus, tried to rehearse what she should say to these prospective employers. She had been told by her friend Lily that she should blow her own trumpet a bit, but try though she might she could think of nothing to say which would seem relevant. Her ability to make one pound do the work of three would interest no one but herself and her natural talent for gardening was unlikely to impress.

At first worrying over the interviews meant she scarcely noticed the passing scene but then the bus entered Haisby and her attention was caught. How different it looked from her last trip in early May! Now all the little houses had washing fluttering on the line. Buckets and spades dangled outside every shop, rubbing shoulders with beach balls, rude postcards and shrimping nets. The holiday season had come to Haisby.

When they reached the bus station Anthea got down and examined her reflection in the nearest shop window. She wore her new summer dress, the lovely leather sandals, and a dab of face powder, a touch of lipstick. Have I overdone it, she wondered, peering anxiously at her reflection. Will they think I'm fast? At my age...and when you're applying for a job...

But it was pointless to worry. She had half an hour to reach the café and she would know, soon enough.

Anthea was a good walker, so she arrived on Lord Street with twenty minutes to spare. She walked down to Harbour Way, therefore, to check on the number of the house.

On Harbour Way the sun came out, just long enough to make the place look enchanting. The house that wanted a cleaner was Victorian red brick and not one of the cottages but even so it looked nice, a good sort of place to work.

Back on Lord Street, she walked into the chip shop part of Styles to see a group of girls chatting behind the counter and a short, fattish man in his fifties changing the writing on a menu board. He saw her and came over.

'Can I help you?' he said politely. 'If it's morning coffee, Miss, it's through that doorway...I'll get a girl to take your order.'

Such is the power of suggestion that Anthea was halfway to the door before she remembered her errand.

'I'm not a customer,' she said, her voice shaking. 'I'm...I'm Anthea Todd. I've come about a job.'

'The job? Cleaning and washing up?' The man looked doubtful. 'Well, come through to the office then, Miss Todd.'

He led her through the kitchens, which were horrid, the floors speckled with grease, into the office at the back which was pleasant enough. She followed the man in, saying 'How d'you do?' when he introduced himself as Cyril Smythe and taking the seat he indicated, as he settled himself behind the small desk.

'Well Miss Todd, I'd better ask you a few questions, hadn't I?'

Anthea smiled and blinked. This was awful, she just wished he'd say she was wrong

161

for the job at once, so she could leave!

Half an hour later Anthea emerged. She had got the job! A proper job, with proper money, and if she started at eight she could finish at one and spend some time on the beach or looking round the shops.

What should she do about Mrs Thomas, though, from *Sea View?* She had better go along for the interview—heavens, she must hurry—since she was obviously not likely to get a nice job like that!

At noon, Anthea left *Sea View* feeling on the verge of collapse. Why oh why had she never learned to say 'no' nicely? She now had two jobs, one, at Styles, which started at eight and ended at one, the other starting at two and finishing at five. It will half-kill me, Anthea thought, though it could not possibly be as hard as working for her father.

Besides, Mrs Thomas of *Sea View* was very nice, with a house far too big to cope with and only two staff to do all the cleaning and ironing and so on whilst Mrs Thomas cooked and Mr Thomas did the books and the garden.

'We're a friendly crew,' Mrs Thomas said. 'Welcome aboard, Anthea.'

Well, I've two jobs and that means two

wages, Anthea told herself, strolling along Lord Street in the windy sunshine and planning a meal at Sam's Place, a visit to the cinema and the last bus home.

Ten minutes later she was ensconced at the corner table in the wine bar, eating the best curry she'd ever tasted. Because the season was in full swing the place was no longer empty, but everyone was elderly and they all appeared supremely unconcerned with what Anthea did, or ate, or even was. Lovely, Anthea thought, tucking into her food. Two jobs, eh? Geoff would raise his brows but he'd be pleased really and Lily would say it just went to show...

The waitresses moved amongst the tables, but there was no sign of Marj. Anthea tried to peep into the kitchen but all she saw was a man with a cross face in a chef's hat, shouting at someone. It was a lovely kitchen, though, bright and shining with a modern sink unit and clean lino. Anthea told herself that she was starting at the bottom with Styles in order, one day, to be able to apply for a job at somewhere like Sam's Place. It was a lovely thought and it occupied her through the curry, the sherry trifle and the pot of tea, though a sudden stab of conscience—ought she to have eaten at the place which employed her?—got her out of her chair quite rapidly once her meal was over.

She did not see Marj when she paid, either, and was about to leave the wine bar when the door opened and the young man who had talked about books came in. He was with a girl and did not even see Anthea hovering, anxious only to escape. I've met a lot of people today, she told herself excusingly, ducking her head and keeping her gaze fixed on her feet. It's about as much as I can take. I don't want to have to meet anyone else, particularly a man.

But the man in question genuinely did not notice her. He was smiling at something the girl had said, his eyes fixed on her, so Anthea was able to slip out through the doorway, unnoticed.

Lunch had not been expensive—it had been today's special—so the cinema was still possible and some tea, too. But until then, what should she do? With delight, Anthea decided on the beach and turned her steps towards the promenade. What a day she was having—what a day!

Something very odd happened in the cinema, though. It was a Woody Allen comedy, a phenomenon new to Anthea, who laughed until tears ran down her cheeks, though she still thought the hero a splendid chap. She was sorry when the lights went up but queued for an icecream and then saw, to her astonishment, that sitting two rows in front of her was Chris, the young man she'd met in Sam's Place, and he was with a different girl.

Anthea knew it was rude to stare but she couldn't help it, and it was definitely a different girl. This one was plump and dark, the girl in the wine bar had been a delicately made child with fair hair.

Not that it mattered to Anthea whether Chris took a different girl out every hour...for all she knew it might be commonplace...perhaps one of them was his sister, she thought charitably.

Back in her seat, she was delighted to see a cartoon was the supporting feature. Laughing, gasping, cheering beneath her breath as the characters lurched from one impossible predicament to another, she forgot Chris and the girl completely. They were no longer either interesting or important.

Coming out into the twilight she might have remembered them, but she had never seen a seaside town at night before and the lights dazzled and enchanted her. She strolled along the promenade, bought a toffee apple and tried her luck at a machine which was all whirring lights and clicking, clacketing silver balls, and then had to run desperately or miss the last bus.

She made it, though. Her long legs took her

up onto the top deck and she sank into the last empty seat, glad from the bottom of her heart that the other occupant was a woman, a fat girl in tight jeans, bawling remarks over her shoulder to the couple in the seat behind.

Tired out by her day, Anthea relaxed and was dreaming out of the window, her mind miles away, when the fat girl nudged her and scrambled past, shouting to someone to ring the bell for her. And a man slid into the empty outer seat.

It was bad enough to find oneself sitting next to a man, but to have him on the outside was horrid. Anthea immediately felt trapped and squeezed so close to the winow that the metal frame dug into her arm. She did not look at the man, of course, but presently she became aware that he was looking at her. Searchingly. And then he spoke, his voice slurred.

'I know you, don't I? Who are you?'

Anthea darted a quick, horrified look at him, and it was Chris from the wine bar. Alone now, so far as she could see and staring straight at her.

'Oh...I was in the wine bar,' she said, her voice small with a shake. 'Today, at lunchtime.'

He shook his head as if to clear it, then smiled, but there was a strangeness about the smile which really did frighten Anthea. What was the matter with him? Why did he look like that? And he smelt odd too—of sherry trifle. Was he drunk?

'Wine bar...hmmm, can't remember.' He gave her a nudge, shaking his head again, reproaching not her but himself. 'I'm a little... little bit jolly, thass what I am...jus' a little bit tanked.' He turned towards her again. Anthea shrank even closer to the window. 'Whassamadder? You tanked too?'

'No,' Anthea stammered. She tried to look out, into the dark. Fortunately they were nearing the village now, she would soon get off, leave Chris behind. Unless he was staying in the village. Oh, how she hated handsome young men who felt it their duty to be nice to her!

The bus trundled on, slowing, starting, jerking until it reached her stop. Anthea half-stood, mumbling apologetically that she must get off, here.

'Your stop? Mine too,' her companion declaimed, throwing out his arms and staggering. 'This is Elverton Green, isn't it?'

He was on the wrong bus! But she dared not tell him, the driver would do that, she must get off.

Anthea floundered past him and down the stairs. She nearly bumped into the ticket

167

machine in her eagerness to disembark but at least the young man was still on the top deck, he must...

He came down in one bound, roaring a curse as parts of him hit the stairs. The driver helped him up, the young man groaned and then, to Anthea's horror, she realised that he was really getting off, at the wrong stop, in the wrong village! He'd be stranded, there was not another bus until next day!

Anthea knew now that Chris was even drunker than he appeared and that it was her duty to see he was taken care of. But instinct is stronger than duty; she flung herself into the vicarage garden and dropped like a stone into the currant bushes which grew just inside the gate. And there she lay, heart thumping, until the bus had driven off and the faltering footsteps had faded into the distance.

Had he seen her craven retreat? Would he remember where she'd gone, come hunting for her? She dared not move, fearful that he had noticed her hiding herself and was even now leaning over the gate, waiting for the inevitable moment when she was forced to appear.

She stayed in the currant bushes until she saw Tibby strolling unconcernedly up the garen path, heading for the door. Since the cat went unmolested, Anthea crawled out of her hiding place, stood up and looked wildly round. It was full dark but her eyes had long grown accustomed and she would have seen a movement immediately.

Nothing stirred. Beyond the gate the village street was deserted. Anthea made for the door, unlocked it, let herself in. Even now she was shivering, partly from her chilly sojourn amongst the currant bushes and partly because her own fear had frightened her by its intensity. Now that she was safe, she felt a fool hiding in the bushes like a child, just because Chris had been a little the worse for drink! Abandoning him in the village when everyone else was in bed!

But it was done now, and could not be undone. She fed the cat, made herself a hot drink and carried it up to bed. She drew the curtains across but first she stood for a moment, looking down into the garden. Outside all was quiet, the road empty. A frail crescent moon struggled out from behind a bank of clouds and lit up the scene. Nothing. No one. The young man had gone.

Comforted. Anthea crept into bed and cuddled down. Then she sat up and began to sip her cocoa and to remember the good things about her day. The jobs—both of them—the delicious lunch, the fun she'd had on the beach, paddling with her skirt hooked above her knees, the little waves cooling her pretty feet.

The drink finished, Anthea lay down again. And presently, slept.

Diane had dusted down and arranged her flowers in the big vase by the window. She had sold two pairs of tights to a young girl who wanted them...grr...to go with a dress she'd picked up cheap from a boutique down on the promenade.

I'm doing quite well, Diane had written to her mother earlier that morning as she waited for customers. I'm getting repeat business, always a good sign, and what's even better the more expensive stuff, which just hung around for the first few weeks, is going at last. People of discernment are becoming customers.

It was galling to acknowledge, however, that the aunts' business venture had been a success from the word go. On that very first day, when Diane had gone out with such high hopes and come home so chastened, the aunts had come beaming to the door to announce that they had already filled two of the bedrooms despite charging the very high sum which Diane had advised and since then they usually had as many people as they could cope with.

What was more, it got better. They turned

170

the biggest bedroom into a family room, put bunk-beds in the single room and were converting the third attic into another single room so that they could let Violet's bedroom to guests.

And here am I, cheering up when a girl buys tights, Diane thought sadly. Sometimes I see fewer customers in here than the aunts have sitting down to breakfast! She had had to dissuade the old ladies from doing an evening meal as well on the grounds that it would lead to visitors hanging round the house until bedtime. As it was, strangers might be met in the corridors, and the bathroom and loo were never empty. Guests left the house after breakfast and returned quite late at night, but many a time Diane, baulked of a trip to the loo or a relaxing hour in front of the telly, regretted her bright idea. On the other hand, though, the aunts were so happy and so busy that they seldom even thought about the shop, save to advise their guests to go there.

Now, with the whole day stretching before her, Diane got up and checked her window display. She had just decided that the Mona dress would only be allowed to queen it for one more week when someone outside in the Arcade caught her eye. She looked up.

A man had been walking past but seeing a

171

movement he stopped and glanced into the window. He was tall, with thick, dark hair spangled with raindrops and he wore a fawn trenchcoat and brown slacks which, combined with his height and colouring, made Diane think, for a split second, that he was someone else. Someone she knew. Before she could stop herself she had given him a friendly smile even as she realised with horror, that he was a stranger. He was a bit like Tony, like enough for her to have made eye contact brazenly, and to have smiled as to an old friend.

To her horror, what was more, the man promptly opened the door and walked in. He smiled down at her, his eyes quizzical. How could she have mistaken him for Tony? Closer inspection revealed that he did not have Tony's beauty, his face was too strongly featured and his eyes were light beneath thick and heavy brows—he looked like a gargoyle!

'Good morning,' Diane said, scrambling to her feet and wishing she had been caught in a more elegant position. 'Can I help you?'

'Good morning. Yes, I hope you can. I'm all alone in this rain-sodden town and I'm dying for a cup of coffee and someone to talk to. Would you join me in the restaurant opposite? If we sat in the window you could keep an eye on this place. I'm sure your boss won't mind.'

It was charmingly said but it was clearly a pick-up, and what was worse this chap thought her a little shop-girl happy to cheat her boss for the sake of a free coffee. Diane drew herself up.

'I beg your pardon?'

She kept her tone polite, but the frost which glittered on each word must have been almost visible. If her visitor noticed, however, he did not show it.

'I wondered if you'd care to join me for a coffee? And a cream cake too, because with a figure like yours a cream cake can only enhance the view.'

Diane the window-dresser thought she caught a patronising sneer in the words and longed to tell him to bugger off, but Diane the shop owner bit her lip. Even a man might influence who came through that door and who did not. She realised, with horror, that in future she would have to be polite to all sorts of people. It was a frightening thought.

'It's nice of you to ask me,' she said as politely as she could, 'but I'm afraid it's quite impossible. My...my boss wouldn't approve at all. Now if there's nothing else I can do for you...'

Diane turned back towards the counter, plainly dismissing the man. Once it was between them she turned towards him again, making eye contact quite deliberately now but keeping her own large orbs cool.

He met her gaze and stared, the light eyes hardening to a slight but definite antagonism.

'No, nothing,' he said evenly, his eyes growing steadily chillier. 'Sorry I asked. Good morning.'

When he had gone Diane sat down, her knees feeling shaky. What an unpleasant encounter! She had not handled it well, she knew, but the sudden realisation that he reminded her of Tony had not helped. She must put the whole episode out of her mind.

But despite the fact that he looked like a gargoyle, he was still very attractive. She wished things had been different, that she had met him in more favourable circumstances. She would probably never see the guy again, however, so she had better forget him and concentrate on her work.

Presently a customer came in, then another. And at twelve-thirty Diane put up a closed sign and made for the wine bar where she took the bay-window table so she could watch her door and ordered an omelette and a pot of tea.

Trade will improve tomorrow, if the weather's better, Diane told herself, eating Martin's light and fluffy omelette. She had wanted to advertise, but the other traders had assured her it would be throwing money away.

'In the summer your best customers will be holidaymakers,' Sam had said. 'And they don't read the local papers. Leave it till just before Christmas to advertise.'

So now she sat over her meal and wondered whether to tell Caresse that she should improve her window display. Caresse wanted to be friendly, she sometimes joined Diane over a pot of tea or a salad, but was this friendliness sufficient excuse for a little tactful criticism? Diane was plucking up her courage to stroll over to Caresse and offer a helping hand when a small, squarish woman stopped outside the boutique. She looked hard at the door, then moved along to look into the window, then moved back, a hand out towards the door.

'Sam, Mart...customer!' Diane shrieked in a very unprofessional way, leaving the restaurant at the speed of light and heading for the boutique. 'I'll pay later!'

She was just in time. The small woman was turning away just as Diane reached past her and unlocked the door.

'I'm sorry,' Diane said breathlessly, 'I was having a break...do come in.'

The woman followed her in and then one of those odd things happened. Two more customers came in, one after the other, a girl searching for fashion jewellery and a large woman wanting a dress and jacket for a wedding.

When Diane looked anxiously at her first customer, however, the woman smiled and said she was just looking, so that was all right. And what a piece of luck she chose to look then, Diane told herself jubilantly, getting out three dresses and jackets which had tactful cuts, otherwise these two might just have walked straight on by.

As it was she sold an expensive brooch and a wild silk shirt to the girl and the most exclusive of the dress and jackets to the large lady. And then she turned at last to her original customer.

'I'm so sorry...can I help you? Was it the costume jewellery which interested you?'

But even as she said it, Diane knew she was wrong. The brooch pinned to the lapel of her customer's suit sparkled with topaz and amber and was set in gold.

'I'm afraid I'm not a bona fide customer at all,' the woman said. 'Let me introduce myself. I'm Eleanor M'Quennell, and you must be Miss Bonner.'

'I'm Diane Hopgood, actually, Miss Dulcie and Miss Violet are my great-aunts,' Diane said, her curiosity thoroughly aroused. The name M'Quennell stirred a faint recollection somewhere. 'How can I help you, Mrs M'Quennell?' She had seen the old-fashioned wedding ring nearly hidden behind a solid diamond cluster.

'I'm raising money for our local hospice,' Mrs M'Quennell explained. 'And I wondered, since you're a new business, if you'd be interested in a proposition which would raise money for us and perhaps do you some good, as well. Have you got your autumn stock in yet?'

'I've got quite a lot ordered. It'll be in fairly soon now,' Diane said cautiously. She did hope this friendly woman was not about to ask her for a donation in kind because her carefully bought stock was the minimum she would need for the autumn and buying forays were difficult to manage. As she got better known, of course, the companies would send reps to her, but now she had to buy for herself.

'You have? And have you ever considered doing a fashion show?'

'What, here? Oh, it's far too small,' Diane said slowly, as light dawned and lit, for her, the entire shop in a rosy glow. 'But I suppose I could hire a venue...'

'No need,' Mrs M'Quennell said briskly. 'I live at Marlowes Hall, we've a room which would suit you, I think. If you do the show I'll organise the champagne supper. What would you charge us?'

'Nothing,' Diane said promptly. 'Not as it's for charity. But what about models? I couldn't afford to use professionals.'

'And you've not been here long enough to have made many friends; pity,' mused Mrs M'Quennell. 'However, I've got plenty of contacts, I've three sons, they probably know suitable gels.' She produced a notebook from her large shoulder bag. 'Now, dates.'

'Look, I'll nip over to Sam's Place and get some coffee and biscuits and then we can sit down and tackle what you want,' Diane said. She was really excited. A fashion show would be fun and a challenge and you never knew what business might result.

'Super idea; I'll hold the fort until you get back.'

Diane whizzed over to the restaurant and begged Martin, who was managing alone on such a quiet day, to get two coffees and some biscuits for her to take out.

'I'll bring 'em,' Martin said, cheerful for once. 'You go back Di. What's it all about?'

'A fashion show at Marlowes Hall,' Diane hissed, as though Mrs M'Quennell had ears like a lynx. 'Can't stop, but I'm terribly excited...hope it comes off!'

Diane hurried back to the shop where Mrs M'Quennell was looking along the racks, emerging with a satisfied smile.

'This stuff's summer, but it'll show well. You've got flair,' she remarked, taking the seat which Diane dragged out for her. 'Now!'

The discussion took two hours but at the end of it both Diane and Mrs M'Quennell knew exactly what they were going to do, right down to the type and number of outfits needed for a two-hour show.

'We'll do well,' Mrs M'Quennell assured the younger woman. 'Most people will come because it's for charity and because they love good clothes, and the snobby set will come because a champagne supper sounds like their sort of thing. It'll be a sell-out.'

'It sounds a lovely evening,' Diane said sincerely. 'I'm lucky to be involved.'

'I'll price the tickets high,' Mrs M'Quennell continued, studying her notebook. 'I wondered about charging separately for the fashion show and the supper, but decided against it. We'll have plenty of takers on a flat-rate basis; think what champagne costs!'

'I haven't a clue...but will you make money?'

'Good heavens, yes. The first glass of champagne and the food will be free, but we'll charge for the bar.' Mrs M'Quennell made another note. 'We'll probably take more money from the bar than anything, some people are only happy half-seas-over.'

'I'll dish out my money for the supper,' Diane said as Mrs M'Quennell stood up to leave. 'Thank you for thinking of me...what made you think of me, incidentally?'

'Something one of my sons said. He'd been past with a girlfriend, I daresay,' Mrs M'Quennell said. 'Now then, if you need to get in touch with me the telephone number's ex-directory, so don't lose my card.'

'I won't lose it, but I think we've covered most things,' Diane said, looking at the two sheets of closely written paper lying on the counter. 'Thanks again, Mrs M'Quennell.'

CHAPTER NINE

Rather to her surprise Anthea enjoyed both her jobs, though she was somewhat taken aback by the attitude in Styles. What the eye doesn't see the heart doesn't grieve over seemed to be the sum of it, and Anthea learned to turn away when a piece of battered fish skidded across the floor or cold chips were refried.

The girls were a cheerful, feckless lot and the manager was only interested in the till. Tips, which were few, were divided up with scrupulous honesty, a far cry from the way the till was treated. Anthea had uneasily seen almost every waitress tuck a fiver up her sleeve when the opportunity occurred and yet the place continued to make not just a profit but a vast profit.

Now and again the owner descended on them. He was a hard-faced man in his late fifties who put everyone's backs up by accusing them of giving food away. He hovered about all day, pouncing on teapots and lifting the lids to make sure only one tea-bag per person was being served, and that the milk in the little jugs was just insufficient for two cups of tea. He told the staff they should water down the sauces and he even scooped half-eaten food off customers' plates and sent it out again.

'What about Aids?' Elsie Brett asked. 'Oh, Mr Eagon, you din't oughter use that meat, there's a kid out there with an 'orrible cold, he's dribbled all over it!'

But Mr Eagan just muttered that you couldn't catch Aids from someone looking at your food and shovelled stuff from the rejected plates to the clean ones until he made the staff themselves look like angels in comparison.

'One of these days they're going to kill someone,' Anthea told Mollie, who worked at *Sea View* with her. Here, life was much more leisurely, though they both worked hard. But the impetus of hungry customers was not driving them on, for in the afternoons it was all preparing for the evening meal, washing, ironing and cleaning. Anthea enjoyed it and was fond of Mollie, a skinny and energetic girl of twenty who did a number of cleaning jobs during the day and spent her evenings usheretting at the cinema.

'So long as it in't you doing it, that don't matter if they kill several or a few,' Mollie said bracingly. 'As for the waitresses helping theirselves, if you ask me they're paid well below what they oughter get. You an' all, Ant.'

Anthea had never been nicknamed before but she loved it. She smiled at Mollie and ironed at a dashing rate, the tablecloths piling up beside her.

'Yes, I know. Have you ever been in Sam's Place, down the Arcade, Moll? I wish I worked there.'

'I been past,' Mollie acknowledged, zipping a curtain out of the sewing machine and reaching for the next. She was good with a needle, she told Anthea, and supplemented her income in the winter by dressmaking a bit. 'Why? Oh you go there sometimes, don't you? Nice, is it?'

'It's lovely. You can see into the kitchen and it's always spotless,' Anthea said dreamily, putting the iron down and folding a tablecloth. 'Styles is so greasy and noisy and they don't do any real cooking, you know, it's all out of packets. But in Sam's they even make the bread rolls and scones.'

'Oh, aye,' Mollie said. 'But they've got a bad-tempered chef, ha'n't they? The feller live on Harbour Way... got red hair.'

'There is a man with red hair,' Anthea acknowledged, 'but I don't think he's bad-tempered. 'I've heard him shout once or twice but he laughs, as well. There's an older man too; he seems kind.'

'Well, see if they advertise,' Mollie advised. 'Give a hand, Ant, this here curtain's too long for one to feed through.'

Anthea obediently stood her iron down again and went over to help with the curtain.

'Thanks,' Mollie said when the seam was completed. 'What you doin' tomorrer, Ant? Half-day for us.'

'I'm having my lunch at Sam's Place,' Anthea said, with the menu already planned. It would be curry if it was on or lasagne if it was not. 'And after that I might go to the beach.

183

Why? What are you doing?'

'Oh, seeing a feller,' Mollie said casually. She was a pretty thing with bubble curls, a high colour and a bold line both in chat and glances. 'What about you, gal Ant? Got someone lined up yet?'

Anthea ducked her head, feeling her cheeks go hot.

'No, I'm not interested in men. I don't know any, unless you count the young man who spoke to me in the wine bar, and that was just because he was polite, and felt sorry for me.'

'Why on earth? Ant, that's about time you stopped thinking you're no good and too old and that. Next time he talks to you, talk back! Give him a bit of encouragement. Right?'

'I don't suppose he'll ever speak to me again,' Anthea observed, wishing she hadn't mentioned Chris. 'It's just that he liked books and talking...'

'That's the best kind,' Mollie said from her wealth of experience. 'Fellers what like books and that, they're just what you're looking for. Give him a chance, Ant.'

'I don't think I want anything to do with men,' Anthea said faintly, ironing faster than ever. The last thing she wanted was for that Chris or any other man to take notice of her! She would infinitely rather be considered a dull old maid by her workmates. Oh, not Mollie, Mollie was nice, but she knew very well that the staff of Styles despised her as a confirmed spinster.

'You do as your Auntie Mollie tells you,' Mollie said. She finished the last curtain and pulled it clear of the machine, then folded it up. 'Cor, I'm worth my weight in gold to this place,' she announced. 'I'll make us a cuppa now, Ant. We deserve it!'

Because it was her half-day, Anthea stopped work at Styles at noon, to give herself time for a bit of shopping before she went in to Sam's for her lunch. She had not been again since the day she had got her jobs and hoped very much that she would see Marj. She wanted to tell her about the jobs and to suggest that, should they ever want more staff at the wine bar, she might apply.

However, she wanted something to read, so she went straight into Glenarvon Books, greeted the man in the shop like an old friend—she had been in several times to replenish her reading matter—and began to glance along the shelves. She was absorbed when a voice said in her ear: 'Still working your way through the science fiction, eh? What about that book you bought when I first met you? I'd like to borrow that one.'

She knew it was Chris and turned slowly, to smile nervously before dropping her gaze to the book in her hand.

'Oh, hello. It's...at home.'

'Never mind, that'll teach me to buy my own copies and not try bumming them off other people.' He moved along so that they were standing side by side. Anthea could tell he was keeping his eyes on her. She swallowed, wishing she did not go so red, that she could answer naturally when a man spoke to her.

'What's it to be this time, then? Asimov? Or are you going for something different? Try this one.'

He flipped a book off the shelf and held it before her. She tried to be sensible, to examine the title, make some remark, but all she could do was stare at the spine for a second and then down to the book in her own hand.

'Don't care for his stuff? He's good, really.' He smiled. 'Or is it me? Honest, Miss, I'm not a big bad wolf, just a fellow book-lover who'd liked to pass the time of day with you.'

She smiled, she couldn't help it, but stared at the lower shelves, trying to avoid his eyes.

'Am I so ugly, then? Why don't you let me walk you down to the beach, buy you an ice-cream? I'm a lonely soul and I guess you're the same. Give me a chance!'

She dared another glance at him. He was very attractive, and his last remark had touched her conscience. Give me a chance. Wasn't that what she had been saying all her life? And now people were doing just that. She must not hurt his feelings by refusing to walk along the beach!

'It...it isn't what you think. I'm not...not used to men.'

He shook his head at her, smiling still.

'You'll get used to me in no time, I promise you. Going to buy that book?'

But she was too disturbed and uneasy to buy anything. She shook her head and followed him out of the shop, jumping like a startled horse when he took her arm, but he was only steering her down the Arcade, into Cloister Row.

'Let's go and sit in the churchyard and talk about books. Do you come down the Arcade much? I can bring some books tomorrow, we can meet here if it's fine and in the wine bar if it's wet; that wouldn't worry you, would it?'

They were in the churchyard now, strolling past the long grass round the gravestones to the wilderness at the bottom, where the oldest graves were hidden by tangled trees and undergrowth. He was taller than she with a crooked, disarming smile which she supposed was charming, except that it made her feel more inadequate than ever.

'We'll sit here,' he said, when they reached a square, low tombstone under the trees. 'Let's be formal. My name's Chris Bowles.'

Anthea's manners were impeccable; she held out a hand.

'How do you do, Mr Bowles? I'm Anthea Todd.'

He took her hand and this time, astonishingly, she felt a frisson of feeling run through her, and it was not fear. It was almost pleasant, to sit in the sun with a man holding your hand. Anthea's cheeks burned but the breeze was cool on her flushed face. As Chris started to talk she began, almost imperceptibly, to relax.

She had never had a brother but he chatted as she imagined a brother would. Of little things, her life in the vicarage, how she managed now both her parents were dead, what she did with herself all week. She told him a lot about the house and garden and he told her a lot as well, about his childhood and how happy he had been then and how unhappy and lonely he often felt now. He explained that he had come to Haisby to start a youth training scheme, but was finding it hard going.

'I get very depressed when I see all the young

people needing help and yet I can't persuade them to try getting trained instead of just staying on the dole,' he said. His eyes looked wistful, Anthea thought. 'That's why I smoke a bit, to take my mind off things.'

'Does smoking help?' Anthea asked, puzzled. She thought everyone had agreed that smoking was bad for you, a dirty habit which most people despised even if they sometimes did it themselves. But Chris laughed and put an arm round her shoulders. He did not seem to notice how Anthea trembled, how she strained away from him, he just held on. And Anthea made herself relax because it was awfully rude to behave as if someone smelled nasty.

'Yes, it helps. You should smoke, Anthea, it would give you self-confidence.' He fished a cigarette out of the battered pack in his pocket and lit up. He took a couple of quick puffs and then held it out to her. 'Go on, try it,' he invited. 'You'll find you'll be treating me as an old friend in no time.'

If she refused it would look as though she thought he was unhealthy and might give her something. She took the cigarette and puffed quickly, then tried to hand it back. It was horrid, sweetish and smelly all at once, she had never understood how anyone could smoke of their own free will.

'I don't like it much,' she said excusingly. But Chris would not take her defection so easily.

'You haven't really given it a chance,' he said gently. 'You must inhale, like this...' He inhaled smoke and Anthea, watching his face, saw a most extraordinary phenomenon. As he breathed in his pupils suddenly contracted. She had never realised that this happened to smokers, and when he gave her back the cigarette she was still thinking about it and took a deep drag, carrying the smoke right into her lungs as he had shown her.

Immediately she felt very odd. She was floating, actually floating! She breathed out and he held the cigarette to her lips so she inhaled again. The floating feeling returned, and with it a conviction that Chris was her friend, a very proper person.

She smoked some more. She was no longer in the churchyard but in another place. Her mother was there, smiling, and someone was stroking her arm, pushing up her sleeve, telling her how lucky she was, that this usually cost fifty quid a shot. She felt something cold on her arm and even as a sharp pain pierced her she slid sideways, helpless, to spin in space whilst someone's mouth, the only thing she could feel in the whole of the whirling universe,

190

held her to sanity by travelling across her skin so that the terror of what was happening to her was lessened by human contact, the conviction that she was not alone. Someone else was there, someone was trying to bring her back, touching flesh with flesh. Then, though she could not feel the ground on which she lay she could feel fingers gripping her, shaking her, whilst the voice which had been so hypnotically gentle was suddenly harsh.

'Come on, come *on*! What the 'ell's the matter wiv yer?'

She felt the universe tilt and tried to open her eyes but she saw only a blur of colour, green and grey. The cold pain which had struck her arm had run, like an icy stream, through her veins and now it seemed as though it had reached her stomach. She felt herself heave, heard the suddenly angry voice saying 'What? On your feet, then,' and she heard her own voice, sobbing, pleading, and then cruel hands gripped her upper arms and the mouth which had seemed gentle was gentle no longer. Secret parts of her were pierced, invaded, and pain ripped through her so that she cried out, unable to bear it.

Her father was here, beating her, hurting her. He snarled as he breathed, like a tiger, and tore at her flesh with his teeth and with his cane. She wept and felt her bare flesh cringe as he brought a great slab of stone down on her back, and then, in a moment of brief realisation, she knew she was not being beaten by the stone but was lying on it whilst someone, or something, attacked her from above.

Presently the beating stopped. She lay crushed, unable to move, barely able to breathe. He was nearby, she dared not cry out. He had grudged her her life, now he had come back and all but taken it from her. She felt her inner self return to the broken body which lay on the tombstone but she was unable to think or see or speak, she could only lie there.

Marj had had a busy dinnertime, with Martin cooking frenziedly and Sam helping to wait on, but when it quieted down Martin went off to shop and Sam said, if she and Poppy could cope, he could really do with an hour in the garden.

She and Poppy cooked quietly for a bit and then Poppy looked pointedly at the clock and reminded Marj that when she started at seven she was supposed to leave off at three.

'Of course,' Marj said. 'You run off, love. Mart will be back soon.'

So Poppy bumped her bike up from the basement and Marj had just got the first four quiches into the oven when she heard the restaurant door go and knew she had customers. Sighing, but not too hard because she liked company, Marj got a waitress pad and went through to the restaurant.

It was Chris, the rather nice young man who was trying to help the youth of Haisby. For the first time she could remember, he had a friend with him. Marj went over to the table.

She half-recognised Chris's friend, a plain girl several years older than he. A client, she supposed, with whom he'd struck up an acquaintance.

'Hello,' Marj said, smiling at both but looking longest, naturally, at Chris. 'Can I get you something?'

Chris said they would have a pot of tea for two and teacakes, please, and Marj thought about teasing him with her preference for scones, but didn't, as he had company. She turned away from the table and returned to the kitchen, where she put two teacakes under the grill.

She was getting butter out of the fridge when there was a tap on the door. She went over and it was Chris.

'M-my friend's not well,' he said. His voice was different, the mellow tone gone. It sounded sharp, almost frightened. 'I suppose you

193

couldn't spare some water and an aspirin?'

All Marj's protective instincts were immediately aroused. She fetched the glass of water and took it through. The girl looked ghastly, and she was no girl, either, she must be in her late thirties. What on earth was handsome Chris doing with such unpromising material? This poor creature was not even attractive, she was just ill.

'Here love, try some water,' Marj said, putting the glass down on the table, the tablets beside it. The girl was sitting slumped in her seat, her head resting on her hands, her elbows splayed out across the table. Her face was sickly white.

'Thanks,' she mumbled, taking the water. Her voice was slurred and Marj, bending over her, might have thought she'd been drinking save that she could smell no alcohol.

'She's got a stomach bug,' Chris said. 'She'll be all right when she's sat quiet for a bit.' He turned to his companion. 'Take a sip of water till the tea arrives,' he said.

Obediently, the girl sipped and as Marj half turned away she stood up, choked, and vomited all over the table, the floor and her sandalled feet. She tried to apologise, but the moment she opened her mouth she simply gushed vomit once more.

'Oh God, the stupid…' Chris said crossly, but Marj would have none of it.

'What's she had?' she demanded sharply. 'She's real ill, that's no stomach bug.'

Chris looked both guilty and furtive. Marj was astonished at how a face could change in a moment.

'She's had a drop of gin,' he said. 'She's not touched alcohol before, perhaps it's that.'

The girl was shaking her head, trying to warn them; with fluttering hands she began to rise once more…and threw up again, this time with the most dreadful barking sound.

Marj ran into the kitchen, grabbed the bucket and ran hot water. She reached down a clean towel and returned to the restaurant. The young man was remonstrating with the girl, his voice now more anxious than angry. He was asking her not to do it again—as if she could help it!

Marj said as much as she began clearing up. The smell of vomit was dreadful but Marj did not have younger brothers and sisters for nothing. She cleaned up the table and floor and then began on the girl, cosseting her, telling her it could have happened to anyone, just to sit there and presently she, Marj, would fetch a taxi and get the driver to take her customer home.

When the beige skirt was as clean as she could get it, she started on the thin, nervous hands, then the under-developed legs. Marj mopped and dried, wondering all the while just what had happened to make the girl so sick. Something had been going on and Marj was sure it was something in which Chris had played a prominent part. Looking at him from time to time, when he did not know himself observed, Marj decided that Chris was not all he seemed. Fly he was, and furtive. Oh yes, he'd given that poor girl something which disagreed with her, he was a bad lot despite his looks and charm. She would have a word with her Eric...but it would do no good shouting accusations right now, she couldn't prove a thing.

Marj began washing the vomit from the girl's inner calves. Talking comfortingly as she did so, she suddenly stopped, the cloth motionless. There was blood darkening the girl's thighs, blotching between her knees, tracing a trail down her calves and puddling under the sandal instep. Was she hurt internally? Or had she simply got her monthlies without realising? But Marj tactfully mopped on, crooning placidly about small matters.

'Your poor skirt, but a good wash will fix it. And those sandals, they're good ones, the leather will clean up a treat, once they've been given a good polish they'll be like new. What pretty feet you have; wish my feet were small, like yours. My, but you'll remember today, you poor little thing...best place for you is bed, you must lie down in a darkened room and sleep it off. You see, by tomorrow you'll be fine again, just fine.'

She finished at last. The girl was clean, her skirt was beginning to dry already. She was pale still but she lay back in her chair now, exhausted but somehow more at ease. Chris looked better too, the hunted look was fading. Marj wondered whether she had imagined it, it seemed mad to suspect that he had deliberately made the girl ill. What was more, why bring her here? Why not just abandon her? There seemed no rhyme or reason in it but to Marj's sensitive nostrils the whole thing stank. She would not serve Chris again, that was certain.

'Now I'll ring for a taxi,' Marj said, getting to her feet. She turned to Chris. 'She shouldn't walk, she's been too ill.'

'No. Not a taxi. I-I've a car, I'll get her home.'

Chris was trying to sound confident but it was clear he was badly shaken by the affair. Marj overbore him easily.

'She's ill. She need a taxi. You may be her friend but a taxi's what she need. We'll get her up to Lord Street, one each side, and straight into the taxi.' Marj turned to the girl. 'What's your address, love? I have to tell the taxi where you want to go, see?'

The girl opened her eyes, winced at the light and closed them again. Marj noticed that her pupils were tiny, no bigger than pinpoints. She had not realised this happened when you were violently sick but patted the girl's shoulder reassuringly.

'I live in Little Meltan,' the girl muttered. 'Thank you...you've been so kind.'

'Think nothing of it,' Marj said robustly. 'Now sit here quiet whilst I ring for a taxi.'

She left the restaurant and returned to the kitchen to find the room full of smoke and Martin poised, aghast, in the doorway. The teacakes were cinders.

Marj ran for the taxi whilst Martin waggled the door to and fro and opened all the roof-lights to let out the smoke, then she told Martin how she had come to burn the teacakes.

'Go and take a look at her,' she said quietly, taking the grill over to the sink. 'What d'you make of it, Mart?'

Martin went through into the restaurant and returned, looking quizzical.

The place, he said, was empty. Marj rushed through, to find that he was right. The birds had flown, though someone had left two pound coins on the stained and disgusting cloth.

'The swine!' Marj raged. 'That girl was ill...real bad, Mart. She never should have walked.'

'And she was with that dark, good-looking guy who brought a couple of girls in one lunchtime, to talk about youth opportunities? We don't have many good-looking young blokes down here, I guess you must mean him. Wears an ex-Army jacket.'

'That's him, Chris something-or-other,' Marj agreed. 'What do you think he gave her?'

'I've heard the kids say he's a pusher,' Martin pronounced. 'Did she look the type to hang around amusement arcades or dance halls?'

'No...she looked like a victim, if you see what I mean.'

'Sure I do,' Martin said, rather unexpectedly, Marj thought. 'That'll be what he was after, a victim. Wouldn't care if she wasn't young, not if he thought she had some money.'

'You mean a drug pusher, don't you?' Marj said as light suddenly dawned. 'My God! I'll tell Eric as soon as I get home...If you knew that, Mart, why on earth hadn't you gone to the police?'

Martin gave a rude, derisive squawk.

'Fat lot of good that would do. I've no

evidence, it's just what the kids say.'

'And when do you hear kids talking?' Marj said sharply, wanting to deny that the police were anything but perfect yet uneasily aware that Martin had a point; the police would not act on what kids said.

'When I go dancing, or to the rollerskating rink,' Martin told her. 'I keep my ear to the ground, Marj, unlike some coppers.'

Marj sniffed and began to clean the grill. She just hoped that the poor girl got home safely, that was all.

Diane enjoyed peace and quiet on Sundays, though she could only get it now at a price. She went back to the shop. It was not an ideal place to find peace after she had spent the entire week in it, but since the advent of paying guests the house in Harbour Way was rarely empty and though, in theory, guests left the house after breakfast and did not return until evening, in practice they were in and out all day.

The aunts were happy with this, apparently, but Diane was not. On a Sunday she usually slept late, keeping her eyes determinedly shut despite the clatter. And there was Therese too, a square, beetle-browed woman who came in to clean and preached at them, according to

Aunt Dulcie, whenever they gave her half a chance. She was a practising Catholic and her religion meant a lot to her. Diane scarcely saw her during the week but on a Sunday she was much in evidence. When church finished in marched Therese, defiantly singing hymns and keeping Diane on tenterhooks in case she burst in, tipped Diane out of bed and cleaned round her. She had not yet done such a thing, though her broom often knocked and rattled against the attic door, but she ruined any chance of a real lie-in.

On this particular Sunday, Diane had stayed grimly in her room until eleven, when she had gone downstairs and had coffee with the aunts. Therese had, it appeared, been particularly uplifted by the sermon that morning. She rattled her rosary aggressively whilst Diane sipped coffee and kept breaking into snatches of a hymn about fighting the good fight and another about flinging down golden crowns, both of which had rousing tunes which Therese only remembered vaguely and words which, for the most part, had passed her by altogether. The resultant sound was not restful and Diane finished her coffee and made for the back door, glad that escape was nigh as well as the judgment which Therese had mentioned as soon as she saw Diane's strapless sundress.

'I'll be back for lunch,' she assured Aunt Violet who followed her, fluttering into the garden. 'I wouldn't miss your Sunday lunch for worlds. And I might spend some time on the beach afterwards as it's such a lovely day.'

Aunt Violet, appeased by the promise, let her go and Diane sauntered down the road, feeling content with her lot. She was selling better, and though there had been no sudden upsurge in customers those who came in usually bought and her sale goods had almost gone. The autumn stock came in daily and pleased her afresh every time she looked at it.

The weather helped, too. The sky was blue, the sun shone, and only the tiniest breeze blew. The Arcade would be pleasant and there might be other traders in. The shops closed on Sunday but everyone knew that the best time to clean, change windows, water plants, was when holidaymakers streamed past the wrought-iron gates with never a glance inside, and one was unlikely to be interrupted.

So Diane let herself in hoping for company, but she was doomed to disappointment. The frontage of Waves was still wet from a vigorous mopping, and Caresse had been in and watered her bay trees, but now the Arcade was deserted.

Diane opened her door and the heat hit her like a blow in the face. She reeled, and sud denly it did not seem such a good idea to go over to the counter and begin to leaf through magazines or try on the latest delivery of costume jewellery. She was here six days out of the seven, dammit, she would steer clear on a hot day like this!

She locked up again and knew an almost overpowering sense of release...and then the telephone rang.

Who could possibly be ringing her on a Sunday? Everyone she knew would assume that she stayed well away from the shop on her day of.

But the telephone rang on and although it was probably a wrong number, Diane returned to the shop and picked up the receiver.

'Hello? Bonner's Boutique.'

There was a muffled sort of silence and then a voice said tentatively, 'Di?'

She knew it was Tony at once. Her heartbeat speeded up and her hands went clammy so that the receiver slipped and had to be recaptured. Foolishly she found she could not speak, she could only cling to the receiver and tremble.

'Di? Don't hang up, I'm not going to upset you. Are you still there?'

A wise woman would have hung up; Diane said weakly, 'I'm here.'

'I have to talk to you. I'm...I'm not far away. When can we meet?'

'Talk away.' She could not put the phone down on him, though she was sure it would have been the best thing. 'What do you want, Tony? It's been...'

'...a long time,' he finished for her, when her voice died. 'Not my choice, Di...yours. You've taken some finding, but I must see you...tis killin' me my darlin' girl, killin' me.'

My darling girl! No one had called her that since he and she had gone their separate ways. Diane felt her knees begin to buckle and grabbed the counter for support. He's another woman's man, she reminded herself fiercely. He doesn't belong to you, you're best apart.

But the sound of him had brought it all flooding back. His voice and body were as familiar to her as her own and more loved. Oh, the joy she had known in his arms, the uncomplicated pleasure his mere presence had given her until she found out about Shelagh! Would it hurt so much to have one little meeting? She could feel, in anticipation, the adrenalin coursing through her veins, the sheer physical pleasure that just seeing him would bring. Damn the pain of it, people were meant to know pain as well as pleasure and all she'd known for months had been emptiness.

'Di, my darlin' girl? Hold the line, would you?'

She began to protest, to explain, but she heard his receiver clatter down and all at once, without knowing how she knew, she sensed his nearness. She put her own phone down and walked like a zombie out of the shop, along the Arcade, and up Lord Street.

He was walking towards her, not smiling but lit from within by the same joy which lit Diane as she gazed at him. He had found her and she was glad, even though the pain would return when he left her, the pleasure of this moment would be worth every pang, every lonely sob tonight.

She had not meant to run into his arms but that was what she did. They stood in Lord Street, kissing, scarcely noticing when they were jostled by a group of teenagers in kiss-me-quick hats.

He released her at last, though he kept hold of her hand. His face was flushed and his eyes shone with tears. Diane squeezed his fingers; he had always been emotional, easily stirred. It was the Irish in him, he used to say when he could not hide his feelings.

'Where can we go? Not the beach...your shop?'

Diane nodded, remembering the unlocked

door, the Arcade with its padlock ignored, swinging on the end of its chain. She would have to go back, put things right, so why not take him there, just for a few minutes?

She knew it would be wrong of her to take him into the shop, of course. If they were alone, who knew what might happen? The longing for him which she had thought submerged, almost drowned, had surfaced so strongly at the sight and feel of him that it was next to indecent. Her whole body, awakened after its long, un-wanted sleep, was crying out for him and he, she guessed, would be feeling just the same. So they would lock the shop and walk on the beach or have a meal in a noisy restaurant. But she would show him round Bonner's.

She unlocked the door. They stepped inside. She shut the door behind them and after only the slightest hesitation, locked it.

Across the quiet, sunlit shop they looked at one another, his eyes locking with hers, a faint question in their depths.

Diane sighed and walked into his arms. Her head sank onto his chest and her hands moved caressingly up and down his broad, muscled back. She was home. She had been away a long time, but now she was home. The long voyage was over, the harbour waited. When he began to kiss her, his lips moving from her mouth to her throat, from her throat to her breasts, she knew what would happen. She had tried to break free and it had proved impossible. Later they would talk, decide what to do, but now they must have their moment.

CHAPTER TEN

On Monday morning Diane woke feeling wonderful. Her whole body was awake and alive, when she moved strength and health flowed through her veins, making her tinglingly aware of every inch of her skin surface.

Making love to Tony had been like a rebirth, she mused now, lying in her narrow bed and letting her mind play, once more, over the scene in the shop. How they had loved! On the counter, behind it, in the middle of the floor, in the changing cubicles...they had spent the whole afternoon exploring each other, making certain that neither had changed.

Tony was a marvellous lover. He had always been able to awaken Diane's desire so that their coming together had been a wonderful thing, a blast on the trumpets of eternity, and even now, alone, she could make herself yearn just by bringing to mind the way he had aroused her.

When they were sated with love they talked, and Tony had explained why he had followed her.

'I was like a different feller,' he said lazily, his hand caressing the curve of her hip. 'No use to anyone wit'out you. No use to Shelagh, even.'

Diane stiffened; she could not help it. But Tony was determined to go on with his explanation, though he turned his head and kissed her cheek.

'Me poor darlin',' he said tenderly. 'Listen, will you?'

He explained. He had meant to live a wholesome, honest life with no more love apart from the marital sort. But he had missed Diane so, been so miserable without her, that he had taken early leave and gone home.

' 'Twas different, and Shelagh sensed it,' he admitted. 'I wanted to make love yet I'd no fire in me belly for her; it was you I wanted, me darlin' girl. I tried, but 'twas a poor performance, a shadow of what I'd achieved before.'

'You mean...you *couldn't*?' Diane asked incredulously. 'Oh, Tony, don't say you couldn't because I can't believe it.'

'Nor you should, for I could, but any fool who'd known me before would have realised my heart wasn't in it. No fire, like I said. So after three days—and nights, of course—Shelagh faced me with it. Said I'd fallen out of love with her. And I was so unhappy, me darlin' girl, that I told her the truth before I thought. No, I said, quite the opposite. Because I loved Shelagh true I'd stopped seeing a girl who'd meant a lot to me. And Di, darlin', Shelagh said she'd sooner share me than lose me altogether. ''She's taking nothing from me nor the littl'uns,'' Shelagh said. ''She's giving you happiness, so go back to her.'' I started searching for you from that moment on.'

And Diane, who had been so certain that to cheat on a wife was wrong, to give only half your love was wrong, had said drowsily that she supposed she understood. But all she had thought about had been that she would not have to live without Tony ever again, that he could come down here at weekends and make love to her, that they could buy a little place here...

But then, dressed and sober, they had walked up the Arcade, let themselves out into Lord Street, and Tony had dropped his bombshell.

'When'll you be moving back, then?' he had asked. 'To the flat, I mean.'

And she had known the whole afternoon had been a gigantic mistake, because Tony had no intention of coming down here to see her, putting himself out. He wanted his live-in lover back, to satisfy his desires between the trips back home to Ireland. And she had looked at his dark and beautiful face and been sure that he had never told his wife, that she had never suggested her husband went back to his mistress, that the whole thing had been a lie, hastily cobbled together to get her back.

'I'm not moving back,' Diane had said, infusing lightness into her voice. 'You'll have to come down to me, darling.'

He had argued, pleaded, even tried bullying a little. She had listened, nodded, sympathised, and said no. Over and over, until he had to hurry back to the station to catch his train, she had said no in every way known to man—or woman—and Tony had refused to believe her adamant, insisted that she would come to her senses, give their love a second chance.

He did not understand her passionate feeling for Bonner's; that it was her brain-child and could not be lightly abandoned. He knew she had grown fond of the aunts, that was very laudable, but a small shop, when she could have the whole of Barkworths, to play with? It was impossible that she could throw that away for a poky little boutique tucked away down a dark alley!

She knew his spite came from his disappointment, a very real disappointment, so she tried not to be hurt by it, but of course she was. They parted with his insistence ringing in her ears that, should she change her mind, she should get in touch, and she had gone home to her quiet attic room and her single bed.

So why, after such a day, had she woken all a-tingle on this not particularly bright Monday morning? Diane stretched luxuriously and decided, shamelessly, that she felt great because she had used her body for the purpose for which it was intended. In other words she had made love and it was a simple physical well-being which might well have followed a vigorous game of tennis or a session in the sea.

And the dark depression which had haunted her for so long? Where had that gone? Would it return, presently, to turn the dull and drizzly day as dull and drizzly as it really was? But she thought not. She had believed she was pining for lost love, but now she suspected that she had been pining for sex, after months and months of having it on tap, so to speak. And having discovered that, perhaps she would also discover that there were guys who could do it as well as Tony or perhaps even better.

She would not fall in love again, though. But neither would she do without a man for months. Why should she? She still loved Tony in her own peculiar way but that love had faded a lot since they parted. What had not faded had been desire, which he had so adequately gratified, but she would never again confuse desire with love. In future, she would see that her desire was satisfied without the hassle and confusion of falling in love. I'll write to Tony, she decided, because she realised that, as she stood on the station waving him off, she had probably looked pretty lost and alone. She must make it clear to him that his old magic had only worked in certain ways; in others it had left her cold.

Will I continue the affair with him? she asked herself, taking off her nightie and getting into the shower. But she knew she would not. Her first feeling, that it was wrong of him to cheat on his wife and wrong of her to let him, had been right. There were millions of unattached men around. She would find herself one of them.

Anthea woke on the Monday morning and lay in the grey dawn-light trying to will herself back to sleep. But it would not work any more than it had worked yesterday or the day before that. Just because you ached in every limb that did not mean you could go to sleep and stay that way. You woke when your body had rested long enough and that was the time when the thoughts crowded in and the time you tried your hardest to remember just what had happened to you the previous Friday.

She could still remember almost nothing, however, save for the pain and the fear. They crept out to meet her like a clammy fog whenever she tried to force her flinching mind to tell her just what had happened after she sat down on the gravestone and began to smoke that cigarette. She had inhaled smoke, there had been a weird floating sensation, and then pain had piled on pain, sickness had overcome her, and after that all was a tilting, foggy confusion until she had come to herself to find she had been bundled like a rag doll into the garden of the old vicarage. She was lying amongst currant bushes and the rain was falling on her and even above the howling of the wind she had heard her own cracked and exhausted sobbing.

She thought that she had been there a long time; the rain had soaked her, the grumbles and mutters of thunder had frightened her, but she had not moved until she was sick again—she knew it was again because she could smell stale vomit—and as she finished throwing up she became aware of a raging thirst. She knew she must quench it or die so she struggled to her feet and lurched to the back door. She had no handbag, no coat, but the spare key was under a flower-pot in the coalshed. She managed to find it, use it, lock herself in. Then she had collapsed on the kitchen floor, too weak at first even to crawl to the sink for some water.

The storm was full force now as well, filling the house with sound. Upstairs a window banged, terrifying her, but at least it galvanised her into action. She must have a drink, even if someone was creeping down the stairs to get her this very second.

She drank and then wanted to pee but at first was too frightened to leave the kitchen. Then she thought someone tried the handle of the back door. Certainly it moved, but the wind was really violent so it could, she told herself have been the storm.

Nevertheless, fear got her upstairs. She shuddered into the spare room and latched the swinging window. She dared not let him find her, bring back the whirling madness which had plunged her into nightmare...was it today, or days ago? She had no idea, she only knew she could take no more. If he came for her she would kill herself sooner than return with him to hell.

She went into the lavatory and locked the door. It had a tiny high window and for the first time she felt less immediately threatened. It was good to relieve herself, but then she was sick again, her head whirling giddily, so that she sat back on the seat rather than fall in the restricted space.

She sat there a long time, trying to listen. She heard the thunder grumble closer until it seemed to be right overhead. Lightning flashed and the beating of her heart reverberated around her empty head, her emptier body.

She thought she could hear something, even through the storm. Someone was trying windows, knocking on doors, threatening to kill her if she did not let him in. She had no idea who it could be but it was someone evil.

Presently the orchestrated roar of the storm lessened and Anthea first dozed and then slept. She woke, listened... the thunder was grumbling off into the distance now, like a lion leaving its prey...and then slept again. Next time she woke it was grey and quiet. Looking through the window she could see the trees, leaves hanging almost motionless, and smell the freshness of rainwashed earth. The new day had begun.

She unlocked the lavatory door and scuttled across the landing to her bedroom. She climbed between the sheets, dirty, bruised and bleeding, and pulled the blankets over her head. Sleep hit her like a mallet; she drowned in it gladly, welcoming its dark oblivion.

She must have slept all of Saturday without waking again and most of Sunday, though she had forced herself to go downstairs at one point to get a drink and something to eat. Down there, she remembered the intruder she had imagined and looked, shrinkingly, for signs of entry. It was a big, old-fashioned house and surprisingly difficult of access she knew, having been locked out a couple of times. She searched thoroughly once she started, going from the bleak, stone-sinked scullery right through to the big living room.

There was nothing, no sign of an intruder. She must have imagined the whole thing, but something had happened to her, something dreadful, she had not imagined that.

She even paused for a moment at the door which led down into the cellars. Fear came like a miasma from the cellars for it was down there that father had imprisoned her for sins too bad, it seemed, for a beating to be sufficient punishment. There was no electric light down there, nothing but coal and huge, scuttling spiders. She had not been in the cellars since her father's death and was glad she would not need

216

coal now, in summer. In any case the cellar door was bolted with a big iron bolt which needed all her strength to draw back. Small chance of anyone being able to get in through the cellars! Upstairs was safe enough; being an old house the drainpipes were half-rotten, anyone trying to climb them would be lucky to escape with broken legs. And anyway the conviction grew, as she went from room to room, that she was safe. The storm was over, the sweet new day begun and the malignant spirit which had seemed to haunt the house during the thunder claps and lightning flashes had been laid to rest with dawning.

So she fetched food—bread and jam and tea—and carried it and her radio back to the bedroom. She ate and drank, heard a news flash, knew it was Sunday and slept again.

But now, waking, knowing it was Monday, she had hard work convincing herself that she must get out of bed, feed the cat and go to work. Of course you must, she told herself, or you'll lose your job and then what'll you do? Now you must forget it, because it's over, she instructed herself, forget it like you did when Father...

She looked at her wristwatch. It said six o'clock and she was wide awake, she might as well get up even if she decided not to go to work today. She found it impossible to imagine herself a normal person, chatting to Julie, who usually shared the early shift with her. Anthea knew she was a different woman from the one who had cleaned up on Friday morning, a lifetime ago.

By six-thirty she was washed and dressed. She got cat-food, put it in Tibby's saucer and opened the back door. It scared her to do that, but there was no one there, only a ground mist swirling and the fresh smell of the currant bushes as Tibby knocked against them in his hungry rush for the back door.

The cat ate, however, with a scrambling eagerness which was only half-explained by the fact that he had been ignored all weekend, then darted out into the garden again. He looked wild-eyed and Anthea went after him and was relieved when he wound round her legs and stood on tiptoe to be fussed, purring like a tractor as he did so.

Presently she told herself that she would go out even if she only went to the village shops. She had eaten her meagre supply of food and God knew what had happened to the shopping she had been bringing home on Friday. She supposed she would never see it again but fortunately she had some money in an old honey jar on the kitchen dresser. She would use that.

She went back into the house and had to fight an urge to go back to bed and pretend she was ill. Instead she locked the back door, took her money in her old brown purse and went through to the hall to unlock the front door. She stepped into the porch. The misty morning was giving way to what might become a sunny day. She stood in the porch for a moment, then stepped out, onto the garden path. Her heart immediately started going like a trip-hammer. She knew she should pull herself together and go to work, be with people. How on earth was she going to walk down the path and then along the village street, though? I can't do it, she thought desperately. It's no use knowing I must, I simply can't.

The bus saved her. It rumbled round the corner and the driver, who had been taking her to work each morning for weeks, spotted her hovering. He pulled up and opened the door.

'Git a move on, gal,' he ordered her, not unkindly. 'We're early this morning, hop you aboard!'

Even in her misery, Anthea could not just ignore the bus driver. Without a coat or cardigan, with her purse clutched in her hand, she lolloped across the pavement and onto the bus. All the time her heart beat like a drum but then she was on the bus and sinking into a seat.

The bus filled up gradually and drew nearer to Haisby. Anthea realised that she did not want to get off, but when they reached her stop a number of people were queueing to alight, amongst them Mrs Rutherford and her daughter Ella. They were not friends of Anthea's but today they were her salvation. As Mrs Rutherford drew level with Anthea's seat she tapped the other woman's shoulder.

'Come along, Anthea, we've reached your stop, just you hop off before me.'

Anthea found herself being herded down the aisle and then abandoned on the pavement whilst the bus—her refuge—bowled on. She felt horribly vulnerable, a snail torn from its shell, standing there whilst early workers hurried past, but presently her courage began to return and she made her way along Lord Street to Styles.

The door was open, and Julie was brushing the floor. Anthea slipped inside and went into the back for her overall. If she worked hard and kept quiet perhaps everything would be all right.

When Anthea left Styles at one it was for the last time. Mr Smythe had been very nice about it and had given her two weeks wages in lieu of notice, but he had been determined. He could not employ a woman who dropped whatever she was holding when a man spoke to her, nor one who cringed away when he walked past.

'I've never struck a woman in my life,' Mr Smythe had said, his eyes blinking. 'But if anyone were to see the way you behave, Miss Todd...'

It had been easier to apologise, take the money and go, but Anthea crept along to *Sea View* with a heavy heart. No doubt they would take one look at her—she was bruised all over—and tell her that she could not stay there, either, and then what would she do? She might as well walk into the sea and not stop until she was drowned, because she would never apply for another job, not if she lived to be a hundred.

But as soon as she walked into *Sea View* everything changed. Mollie took one look at her, pushed her into a chair and put the kettle on.

'Who hit you? What happened?' she demanded, sugaring Anthea's cup with a prodigal hand; 'Oh, someome oughter be horsewhipped, that they should!'

'I can't remember,' Anthea said haltingly. She could still only recall crawling up to the house, letting herself in, and getting to bed.

Liz came into the kitchen, having finished

221

the upstairs cleaning. Now, Liz looked at Anthea's bruised face, eyes widening.

'My word,' she said slowly. 'Who done that, Ant? Not that lovely feller I saw you with, Friday? Coming out of the bookshop, you were.'

It was like opening a familiar door and finding a black pit full of writhing monsters right under your unsuspecting sole. Anthea shuddered, and right in front of them all she put her head in her hands to shut out the memories which Liz's words had woken from their uneasy sleep.

Chris! His name was Chris and he had beaten her until she was black and blue, then abandoned her beneath the currant bushes, throwing her down like a rag doll, indifferent to her fate once she was off his hands.

'Anthea?' Mollie's voice was a shocked whisper. 'What's up, my woman? Don't cry like that!'

But Anthea could not answer, could only give great, painful sobs that nearly tore her heart in two. She had been free, fear and her father banished to the grave together. And Chris—hated name—had released them again to torture her. Somewhere in the churchyard her father had found her and had treated her as he had done so often before. She knew that he had

222

done it as Chris, that it had been Chris's body which assaulted her, yet the spirit which had led him had been her father's.

Mrs Thomas was kind once Mollie had spoken to her. She put Anthea in a taxi and sent her round to the surgery where a young doctor, forewarned, saw her and Mollie together, Anthea clutching Mollie like a drowning man.

He prescribed a tranquilliser and a few days off work and then told Mollie that her friend shouldn't be left alone in the house, so Mollie rang her mum and told her Anthea was coming to stay and then took Anthea back to *Sea View*.

'Mum doesn't mind at all,' she assured her friend. 'She's always glad to have friends stay. We'll come in to work together, Mrs Thomas say you can just sit for a day or so, and when you're better I'll come home with you to settle you in. Are you still worried, Ant, even though the doctor told you that chap won't dare come back?'

'He will come back; he'll come back and kill me,' Anthea said, her voice dull with despair. 'Why shouldn't he?'

'What, after what he did? Ant, he gave you heroin, that's why the cigarette was so odd and made you float away, like. He wanted you to

223

want more only it made you ill and that frightened him, so he knocked you about because you'd scared him and then shoved you into your garden and ran. The doctor's seeing the police for you, telling them the guy's a drug pusher. We'll never see him round here again you may be sure!'

Mrs Thomas had put Anthea to bed when Mollie brought her back from the surgery. Now, Anthea pushed back the covers and put a long, thin leg cautiously out. Mollie saw that the insides of her friend's thighs were blue with bruises. She cleared her throat uneasily.

'Um...Ant, old dear, can you tell me what he did to you, that Chris?'

'He beat me, like my father did,' Anthea said huskily. 'Can I really stay with you, Moll? Oh, you're the best friend anyone ever had.'

'Oh, a beating,' Mollie said, much relieved. 'That's all right then. Yes, of course you can stay with us and if you're coming downstairs for a bit you can give me a hand in the kitchen.'

'For a week, or two weeks, can I stay? We could both watch, see if he comes back to town. If he doesn't then I shan't be afraid to go home,' Anthea said eagerly, clattering down the stairs.

'Two weeks, three, that'll suit us,' Mollie said easily, secure in the knowledge that her

224

easy-going mother and half-a-dozen assorted brothers and sisters would scarcely notice quiet old Anthea. 'You won't mind being a bit cramped, I daresay?'

Anthea thought of being surrounded by people, with Mollie there all the time, and a big smile spread across her face.

'Mind? It'll be wonderful!'

Sam, early-birding it again, noticed as he walked along Cloister Row that the leaves on the tall limes around the churchyard were beginning to turn gold. Autumn would not be long arriving, which was both good and bad. The colours were brilliant, the weather unusually lovely, with a frail, here-today-gone-tomorrow beauty which always touched Sam's heart, but the fallen leaves choked the gutters and the holiday-makers, like swallows, returned to other climes leaving Haisby to solve its own problems—and fill its own restaurants—which meant a tightening of belts all round and sour looks in the pubs when business was discussed.

On the other hand, Sam consoled himself, as the weather got colder office and factory workers grew more reluctant to venture out for a meal, so the sandwich business thrived, the girls coming in with their cream leather shoulder bags bulging with money.

The beach was a joy again as well. No more fighting for a square inch every time the sun shone, now you could find miles of deserted sand and the sea, warmer now than at any other time of year, seemed to beckon enticingly.

Martin was beginning to settle down too, as Sam had hoped he would. Oh, the lad still yearned for the fleshpots of the big hotels, but at least he wasn't for ever getting at the staff, either chasing them with intent to fondle or making their lives a misery. He was more even-tempered at home, too. He didn't grumble about Sam's cooking and often helped out.

At first Sam had only to look at Martin to be reminded of the man on the desert island who has just heard about sharks. He stands wistfully on the sand, longing to swim off but scared he'll end up as someone's dinner. Now Martin was that same man enjoying his sojourn on the island instead of resenting it, considering Sam not a gaoler but a benefactor. Of course he cast wistful looks at the sea now and then, but he was building a raft. When he set sail again he would do so safely, with a fair chance of reaching the further shore.

Some of it was me, Sam told himself now, but an awful lot is Marj. Odd how all the things Martin hated in other people he tolerated in Marj—the frankness, the determination to do it her way, the impish sense of humour. Even her flat chest went uninsulted, which said a lot.

The trouble will come, Sam thought dolefully, when Martin makes his move and Marj repels his advances. She's got her steady feller, Eric, she isn't likely to throw him over for a red-haired chef with an uncertain temper and an even more uncertain career.

Still, it hadn't happened yet and until it did, peace reigned. Sam looked over the wall to the beach below. The gale had whipped the sea into a frenzy and as he watched, the sun, beginning to emerge from the water, sent an arrow of brilliance across the turbulent sea, turning the dawn-coloured sand to gold.

It was bloody beautiful! Sam stared with all his eyes and wondered whether he and Martin could have a day out some time. How nice it would be if we could take Marj with us, Sam thought, to keep Martin happy. And someone else, so I wasn't a gooseberry. But who? Since his marriage had failed Sam had steered clear of women. Joanne had been ambitious and she'd had quite a strong sex drive. Sam wasn't ambitious, he liked a quiet life, and his sex drive was more like a sex putt, short and gentle, take it or leave it. In fact he'd left it now for...he closed his eyes to calculate, opening them on the brilliant sunrise...Good God, eight

227

years, and he wouldn't be bothered if it went another eight. Sex was something everyone was supposed to do well by instinct but he had Joanne's word for it that he was the exception. So why push your luck? Why not just go for long walks, swim, grow vegetables and prize roses, instead of all that banging and bonking?

Despite the howling gale, Sam heard footsteps pattering along the cobbles and turned as Poppy hurried up beside him.

'Sam, I come early...can I have a word? I feel awful mean...only it's my whole future, you see.'

'Fire ahead,' Sam said. It did not sound like a complaint and Martin hadn't been too bad with Poppy recently.

'It's Emma, in Waves. Oh, Sam, they need an apprentice to start in a week. And Emma said...'

'She said if you applied, you'd get it,' Sam said cheerfully, but with a sinking heart. Youth training girls were hard to find and harder to train into usefulness.

'Yes. So you see, I've been ever so happy, but...'

'You go for it,' Sam advised. 'I'll tell Martin when you give in your notice.'

'Well actually, Sam...'

'Go on, surprise me,' Sam said heavily.

'You've already told Emma you'll start next week.'

'Yes. She was going to advertise, see, and...'

'All right, I understand. You'll only be with us until Friday then?'

'I would,' Poppy said eagerly, 'but you owe me some holiday, Sam. I might as well take it from tomorrow.'

They were standing side by side, looking over the wall. Sam thought fleetingly of giving a loud despairing cry and jumping...what a fool he'd feel, though, if he broke both legs and left his neck intact! And anyway, they would manage, they always did. He could get Marj to put in more hours, stick an advert in the local paper...

'We'll manage,' Sam said. 'Come on, Poppy, we'd best get the sandwiches started.'

With the fashion show getting near, Diane found herself busier than she had ever been. Mrs M'Quennell had sent six models and Diane had asked Marj to help out, and with herself that made up the eight which she and Mrs M'Quennell had decided were necessary.

They were all different types, too, which was a help, though there were six size twelve and only two fourteens. But Mrs M'Quennell—or her sons—had chosen carefully. Two blondes, one golden and the other platinum, two redheads, one almost ginger and the other chestnut. Two with brown hair, one with bubble curls and the other with a long plait of beige-coloured hair. Diane and Marj were the darkest, counting as black for fashion purposes.

Diane had asked the girls to come in to choose the clothes they wanted to model, carefully putting away the choices as they made them. She was excited now and even Marj admitted to the odd tingle when she thought about parading up and down the long gallery at the hall, wearing lovely clothes.

Rather to Diane's surprise everyone in the Arcade was going to attend the event. They whistled over the cost but promptly shelled out. They were all determined to see Marj and Diane on the catwalk, particularly when Marj let slip that she had modelled semi-professionally in a big store a few years back. Even the aunts had bought tickets, partly to support their niece but also out of curiosity. Therese had promised to lodger-sit, though Diane doubted that they would have many customers by the time the show was staged.

For holidaymakers, to Diane's guilty relief, were becoming thin on the ground. However, the aunts had discovered a whole new race of beings called 'commercials', and were laying their lures, so the house would not be empty for long.

'When the pantomime comes, we'll get theatricals,' Aunt Dulcie had remarked that very morning, and Diane had braced herself for an even odder variety of people than holidaymakers and commercials. Theatricals would call the aunts 'darling', and come in at midnight, very noisily, and insist on late calls every morning as well as hogging the bathroom before and after every show.

'We've got a name for value, you know,' Aunt Violet said when Diane murmured that the theatricals were presumably happy with their usual arrangements. 'Our breakfasts are very popular and we've decided to do evening meals in winter. It's either that or see all our commercials go over to Mrs Robertson.'

They could not bear that, Diane knew. Mrs Robertson with her gnomes in the garden, her pottery flight of duck in the hall and her much-vaunted teamaking facilities in every room brought out the worst in the aunts.

'She doesn't say her sheets aren't laundered after each guest, nor that she buys bacon bits,' Aunt Dulcie had been heard to mutter vindictively, gazing balefully, at the neon signs and the seductive notice announcing, 'Cheapest and best!' which made the street look, according to the aunts, very common indeed.

But today, when she left for work, the aunts were temporarily reconciled to Mrs Robertson, for their rival had tried to get a ticket for the fashion show, and failed! So she applied to the aunts, she who had marched past them, nose in air, muttering about old women horning in on her business. She had asked them to put in a good word for her!

'Can you get her a ticket, dear?' Aunt Violet asked anxiously. 'She's dreadful, but she *is* an associate.'

'It's proving terribly popular,' Diane admitted. 'But we're having more printed; I'll do my best.'

Autumn had arrived, Diane noticed as she walked along Lord Street, though the young chestnut trees in their little wire cages were still hanging on to their golden leaves despite the wind, and a few small conkers lay on the pavement. She slowed as she approached the entrance to the Arcade. Archie was struggling with his shutters, fighting the wind which wanted to blow them closed as soon as he unlatched them. Diane grabbed one from him and pulled it back, then pinned it in place. Archie shouted his thanks and dealt with the remaining one, then moved, with Diane, into the comparative shelter of the covered way.

'Phew! The wild wind doth blow,' Archie remarked, peering out into the gale-racked street. 'It's sheltered down here, though.'

Diane agreed, moving down towards Bonner's and seeing her green and gold sign swinging violently. Perhaps it would be better to take it in. The wind seemed to have veered round even in the short time she had been out and was now blowing directly down the Arcade, shrieking and moaning as though the covered way were a wind-tunnel especially invented to try out the power of the elements.

'I hate a wind,' Sam called across to her as she unlocked. 'You should see my runner beans...they're flat, half of 'em.'

Diane, fighting hair out of her eyes and mouth, said it was a shame and hurried into the shop. It looked welcoming, the autumn stock with its deeper shades and sturdier materials warmer and more permanent-looking than her summer stock had been.

She was booking up when the door shot open and Sam fell in, a hefty box in his arms.

'Delivery, Di,' he said, standing the box down. 'Postman brought it.' He stood back, dusting his hands. 'Not more stuff for the fashion show?'

'Probably,' Diane said. 'The trouble is, I should sell quite a lot after the show, but how can I replace it? Unless I let the aunts take over for a day or so I'm stuck here...I could close, I suppose, but I don't want to do that whilst I'm building up trade.'

'You want a stand-in,' Sam said, pushing both fists into the small of his back. 'Why not put an advert in the window? It's a good time of year for temporary staff with the holiday season finished. Go on, I'm trying to get a temp. to take Poppy's place.'

'Poppy? I didn't know she was leaving.'

'She's not going far,' Sam said, and told the story of Poppy's chance to become a hairdresser. Diane could see that it caused a problem for Sam.

'Tell you what, why don't we all advertise for a stand-in?' she said, struck by a brainwave. 'I could do with someone a couple of days some weeks, just a day others, and you could take on someone to do the cooking instead of Poppy, and Archie might like someone on a Thursday so he could go to the sales. Even Caresse could take time off if there was someone she could trust to take over. Between us we could employ a worker full time.'

'We could try,' Sam said. Diane could see the idea cheered him immensely. 'It might work, because no one wants just a few hours each week, it's always easier to fill full-time vacancies.'

'Grand,' Diane said. The idea of some freedom was exciting, it could mean buying trips to London, the odd morning off, a day in bed when you had a stinking cold...it opened up endless possibilities. 'I'll do a notice, shall I, and we'll put it in the window of the restaurant and on my door. What about Archie's window? It's the best in some ways.'

'No, let's just use ours for the time being,' Sam decided, having thought about it. 'After all, some of Archie's stock is worth thousands, he'd want someone trustworthy.'

'So do I,' Diane said, alarmed at the thought of being ripped off by some slinky lady. 'Oh well, we can but try.'

CHAPTER ELEVEN

Despite Anthea's longing for company, she found that staying with Mollie Evans had its disadvantages. She had become, without knowing it, the sort of person who liked a space around her and Mollie's family invaded everyone's space all the time.

For the first week this did not seem a disadvantage but during the second week she found that Mrs Evans wanted to talk, and Anthea knew so little about the sort of things Mrs Evans talked about that she was embarrassed by her lack.

She did not watch television because they had never had a set, she went to the cinema, but rarely. She knew nothing about men and Mrs Evans' frankness horrified her, particularly because there did not seem to be a Mr Evans yet Mollie's mother could scarcely have produced her children without some outside assistance. Anthea might not know much but she was not entirely ignorant!

Then there was Mrs Mullins, Mrs Evans' dearest friend. Mrs Mullins suffered from insatiable curiosity. One session with her and Anthea felt like a wrung-out dishcloth. She felt she could not bear to be caught and mangled again by Mrs Mullins, so she began to leave the house early in the morning and to wander about the streets, learning a good deal about the town and its occupants and a good deal about herself.

She was not a coward, for a start. She was facing up to the fact that she might meet Chris Bowles round any corner, and although she suspected that if she did so she would simply fall to the ground in a faint, at least she no longer let the fear put her off the town.

Then there was work. Anthea had always worked hard and found her enforced inactivity irksome. Two or three times she walked past Styles wondering whether she dared go in and ask for her job back, but the truth was she had not enjoyed working there and was put off even further by a chance meeting with Elsie one morning.

'Don't you come back there, gal Anthea,' Elsie said fervently. 'We've got a plague of rats. The health people shut us down twice one week and yesterday a big gingery one ran across my foot when I was using the chipper.'

So that put the lid on Styles, because Anthea did not fancy becoming intimate with rats.

She had remembered being taken into the Arcade and going into the wine bar that fateful Friday. She could even remember being ill there, but it was all hazy, nightmarish. It put her off the Arcade at first, but then she saw Marj washing down the paving quite early one morning, and Marj looked so pretty and her whistle was so piercingly sweet, her smile so frank, that Anthea decided she jolly well would walk down there and scotch that particular fear once and for all.

The first thing she noticed was a card pinned inside the door of the boutique. She stopped to read it, idle and more relaxed that she had been in days.

'Wanted, reliable person to stand in for traders in this Arcade,' she read. 'Hours and salary negotiable.'

A job! And in this very Arcade where she had longed to work! But she'd be no good at it, she'd better forget it. Besides, she'd only had cleaning and catering experience. She could not possibly stand behind the counter in a posh shop like Bonner's Boutique.

She turned to the restaurant...and there was the same notice, in their window. She put her hand tentatively on the door knob and the door opened; an elderly lady came out, smiled at Anthea and held the door wide. Anthea went in, sat down and rehearsed what she would say when Marj came out. 'I see you've got a staff vacancy...I wonder if you could tell me what hours you'll want...I noticed the card in your window...'

Marj came out. She passed a menu and smiled and all Anthea's precarious courage fled.

'Oh, coffee, please,' she said. 'And...and a scone.'

She drank her coffee and ate her scone and left without a word about the advertisement. I am a coward after all, she reproached herself

238

as she went up to *Sea View* to start her half-day's work.

So Mrs Thomas, telling her very kindly indeed that she was laying all her summer staff off as from the following week, came as an even harder blow.

'I'm sorry, Anthea,' kind Mrs Thomas said, her eyes pleading for understanding. 'But in the winter I almost close down, I don't do commercials you see, I'm just holidays. All the other girls knew...I didn't realise you thought it was permanent.'

'I didn't,' Anthea lied, 'but I thought it would be for a few weeks longer. Never mind, Mrs Thomas, I expect I'll get another job easily enough.'

She had known all along, of course, that she would have to get another job, because she could scarcely survive on the money Mrs Thomas paid her. But she had always put off actually thinking about it, because she managed, didn't she? Meals were often provided in catering and the garden at the vicarage had done her proud. It was the intangibles like rates and something called an insurance stamp which haunted her. And next year she would have to plant seeds and presently she would want manure to fertilise the soil.

The roof leaked, too. She didn't mind the

damp but Mr Parkins said it would cost thousands to put right. Was there a law which said you could not have a leaking roof? She was never ill, but there had been food poisoning scares. Suppose she got listeria or salmonella and was unable to work for weeks? In a proper, full-time job, Mollie had explained, the firm paid you even if you were sick, but part-timers were expected to live on air when they were ill.

So when she and Mollie finished work that afternoon the two of them made first for the Arcade, armed with pencil and paper, intending to sit in the wine bar and to write a list of the things Anthea was good at.

The job would be gone, of course. Anthea knew that and would not have glanced at the wine bar window, but Mollie gravitated to Bonner's like a moth to a flame.

'Ooh, look at that dress,' she sighed, wistfulness in every syllable, 'In't that beautiful?'

Anthea looked—and there was the card, still in exactly the same place. She touched Mollie's arm, pointing.

'Look, Moll. Wouldn't that be marvellous?'

Mollie turned and read the card, then she opened the boutique door and towed her friend inside. She barely let the girl behind the

240

counter get out her standard, 'Good afternoon; can I help you?' before she was in
full spate.

'Oh, yes..you've a card in your window, you
want a replacement person for the Arcade,'
Mollie said breathlessly. 'We were wondering...'

'Actually, we're looking for someone a bit
older than you,' the other girl said. 'It's quite
a responsible job and though I'm sure...'

'That in't me,' Mollie said. 'That's my
friend, Anthea here. Is she old enough?'

The girl turned to look at Anthea; she had
clearly scarcely noticed her before, concentrating completely on Mollie, who was doing
the talking. But now a big smile spread over
her face. She was delighted, Anthea saw.

'You? It's actually you who wants the job?
Well, if that isn't the weirdest thing!' She
turned to Mollie, her eyes sparkling. 'You see,
your friend here came and read the card this
morning and then went into the restaurant.
Marj and I agreed that she was just the sort of
person we're looking for, but she only wanted
a coffee—we were really disappointed.'

'Oh,' Anthea said feebly. 'Me? I mean...you
thought I could do it?'

'I don't see why not,' the girl said. She
held out her hand. 'I'm Diane Hopgood and

your name is...?'

'She's Anthea Todd,' Mollie said impatiently when Anthea just stared. 'Go on, Ant, tell her a bit about yourself. Tell you what, I'll go over to that caff opposite and have a pot of tea; you join me when you're through here.'

Left alone, Anthea was forced at least to answer questions and presently she realised, with great surprise, that she was enjoying herself. Diane had laughed over her being sacked from dirty Styles, commiserated over the job with Mrs Thomas folding, and then pointed out that she would need references, even from a clergyman's daughter.

'Mrs Thomas would give me one,' Anthea said timidly. 'And the Reverend Elgood. Probably Mr Parkins, my solicitor, would too.'

'Can I ring them right now?' Diane said. 'Once we've got that cleared up then we can talk about hours, salary and so on. You see, the present plan is that I'd have you one day a week, sometimes two, Sam would have you to help out with the cooking, and that you'd fill in at Treat Yourself and for Archie's antiques. I've spoken to them and they've agreed that if we get the right person they'll all come in so you get a proper salary with your stamp paid and everything.'

'Shall I go over and see Mollie?' Anthea said

242

tactfully. 'I've written the telephone numbers down.'

She went and sat in the window table, on pins, until Diane put her head round the door.

'They would all trust you with their lives, money and favourite dog,' she said joyfully. 'Can you come back now, Anthea...we use first names in the Arcade...and we'll settle the final details.'

'I'll have to go home tomorrow,' Anthea said as she and Mollie made their way to the Evans' house. 'Isn't Diane awfully nice, Moll? She said to buy a cheap, simple skirt and blouse, and I wondered if perhaps some of my winter things would do? I've got a couple of good tweed skirts that Mrs Hedges from the post office found up for me, if I bought a couple of new blouses...'

'Or nearly new,' Mollie reminded her briskly. 'They have some decent stuff, Ant, at the Nearly New. That's good enough for work, even in Bonner's.'

Anthea, saying she would take a look, then, did not bother to explain to Mollie that Diane had been explicit about clothing.

'To sell anything you need to be neatly dressed,' she had explained. 'However, to start with just come in looking tidy and with your hair

243

tied back and we'll go on from there.'

Anthea had looked down at the faded beige skirt which had been a good buy in early summer, and at the white blouse which was no longer all that white. Even the sandals were suffering from too much wear—and why on earth hadn't she listened to Mollie and bought clothing instead of chocolate bars to pander to her insatiable appetite for the sweet things she had never been allowed when her father was alive? Still, she did have some money saved up. She would get some things before Monday, when she started the new job.

'So you mean it? You'll go home tomorrow to stay? Or is this just a visit?'

How Anthea would have loved to back down, to say that it was just a visit! But she knew she could not stay away for ever, and Mollie was eager to accompany her and be a house-guest for a while. After all, Chris Bowles had never got into her home and he did seem to have left the neighbourhood, so why should she be frightened of going home to the old vicarage?

'No, not just for a visit, I'm going to stay this time,' she said firmly. 'You'll come with me, won't you, Moll? For a week or so?'

'I can't wait,' Mollie said joyfully. 'A week or so in the country, with no Mum telling me what I oughter do and no kids to drive me mad...that's my idea of heaven, old Ant!'

'Martin, you can't say I lecture you, or go on all the time,' Sam said when he'd had a word with a jubilant Diane. 'But I'm going to do both now, so you'd better sit down and listen.'

The two men were in the kitchen, Martin cooking in a desultory fashion and Sam clearing up after him. Now, Martin dug his hands deeper into the bread dough he was beating up and scowled. He hated being talked to, Sam knew, but this was a must.

'Listening? Right. Now look, Diane's just interviewed this girl...'

Sam told Martin the whole story as he, Diane and Marj had pieced it together. About the mugging and about Anthea's life with her father, though they only heard a much-edited version, handed on to them by the present incumbent of the parish.

'The father was a harsh parent and a difficult man,' the Reverend Elgood had said. 'We're very fond of Anthea, she's a good, hard-working person and so honest it's almost embarrassing. She's sensitive though and needs careful handling.'

Diane had passed this on verbatim to Sam, since the wine bar and the boutique would clearly be Anthea's main employers, and Sam

245

was immediately determined that Martin should know he would have to mind his manners in front of her.

'She's a lady, Mart,' Sam said earnestly. 'I won't have her upset by your language, nor your shouting. Do you understand?'

'Me, shout?' Martin said, clearly affronted. 'And swear? Sam, when did you last hear me use foul language?'

'Five minutes ago, when you called it the buggering bread,' Sam said promptly. 'And you shouted at Poppy when she came into the kitchen half an hour ago to get herself a can of Coke.'

'She doesn't work here any more, she's got no right to walk in here bold as brass,' Martin said sullenly. 'And I wouldn't call it buggering bread except that it rhymes.'

'It's alliteration,' Sam said patiently. 'Unfortunately alliteration's no excuse. Suppose you'd been frying fish?'

'I wouldn't have called it buggering...Oh, I see what you mean,' Martin said. He sniggered. 'Everyone swears these days...didn't you say she'd worked in Styles?'

'Oh yes, of course, she'll not take offence over language, then,' Sam said, very relieved. He had heard Cyril Smythe in full swing when something had annoyed him; the only word he

246

steered clear of at such times was moderation. 'But the shouting, Mart...you won't shout at her, will you?'

'Not unless she's a bloody fool and drives me wild,' Martin said simply, rolling his dough into a ball and cramming it into a greased loaf tin to prove. 'Everyone shouts when they're driven to it. Lor, Marj shouts all the time and you never tell her off!'

He sounded thoroughly aggrieved and Sam hastened to explain.

'Marj shouts *lovingly*, if you see what I mean. You shout crossly. It isn't just the volume, it's the feeling behind it.'

'Oh damn it to hell!' Martin shouted. He reached behind himself and untied his apron strings. 'I've got no poppy-seed left for the beefburger buns, I'll have to nip out, Sam. Hold the fort, will you?'

Sam, shaking his head, watched his nephew rush out of the kitchen and down the Arcade. How could you reason with Martin, who was always so sure he was right? Well, he had best mind his manners, that was all, because Sam knew that Poppy might easily have stuck to catering had it not been for Martin. This time I won't have it, Sam decided fiercely. If Martin starts on Anthea it'll be he who's searching for a new job. He had had a brief interview with

Anthea and had liked her immensely and what was more with Archie, Caresse and Diane all employing her as well, it would look absolutely dreadful if she refused to come into the wine bar for fear of Martin's temper.

Presently, Martin returned with the poppy-seed. He was full of the joys of spring, whistling to himself as he began to turn the rest of the dough into buns, painting the tops, putting them on the greased baking tray, telling Sam he was going to the fashion show just so he could kid Marj about her modelling.

Perhaps it will be all right, Sam told himself without much hope. Perhaps Martin will take to her, or perhaps she'll not mind his yells. Anyway, it did seem as though Martin was improving a bit. They would have to wait and see.

As soon as she had recovered sufficiently to think straight, Anthea had rung Geoff Elwood and explained about the attack and told him she was staying with a friend for a few days. Geoff had undertaken to feed Tibby and keep an eye on the place but when she rang and explained about the job he was glad to hear she would return.

'If you need us, just run down the road and ring,' he said. The telephone was one of the many modern conveniences that the old vicarage did not have, but luckily, there was a public box just by the bus stop, so it was not a great matter to make a phone call.

So on a fine Saturday in October, she and Mollie walked up the front path towards the old, red-brick vicarage set in its jewel of a garden, and Anthea found that what with companionship and sunshine, her fears seemed foolish. The house had seemed sinister when she compared it with Mollie's little home, but the reality was very different. All week she had been sick with fear that she would be too afraid to go through the front door, but something had changed since the last time she had been in the house. Either her self-confidence had improved or her love of the house was stronger than her fear of the man who had abused her. Whatever the reason, as soon as she walked into the house she knew she was safe.

'It's odd,' she said to Mollie as they ate their supper at the big kitchen table. 'But I feel quite happy and comfortable now. I don't feel as though there was someone lurking behind every door, I just feel the house is mine and will take care of me.'

'Yes, but you didn't oughter to live here alone, Ant,' Mollie said. It must be awful to heat in winter and you'll rattle round like a pea in an empty pod. What you want is somewhere small enough to manage alone, which don't cost the earth to heat. And what about the garden? That'll all grow over, if you don't spend all your spare time in it.'

'I love gardening,' Anthea told her. 'And the house is all right now I know it isn't haunted.'

'Haunted?' Mollie looked uneasily round the big kitchen. 'Oh, heck, ghosts?'

'Not ghosts, exactly. You see, my father... well, he didn't like me, he beat me even when I was quite...whilst he was alive I was afraid all the time. Even when he was dying I was scared. And there were things he said...but I don't want to talk about it. When Chris hit me there was a bad feeling in the house but now it's quite gone. So I'll stay here until I decide whether I want to move or not. I won't be pushed out by fear.'

'I'm glad you feel like that but I wouldn't stay here alone for a fortune,' Mollie said frankly. 'It'll be fun with the two of us, though.' She put her coffee cup down and stood up. 'Well? You going to give me the tour, then?'

Anthea enjoyed the next half hour. She and Mollie toured the whole house. They viewed the scullery which had never been used in Anthea's time, the pantries—there were three—and the study. Mollie thought the parlour was cosy and was impressed by the size and faded grandeur of the sitting room. Back in the hall again, she pointed to a door at the foot of the stairs and asked what was inside.

'It's the cellars,' Anthea said with a shudder. 'My father shut me down there when he was really furious. I was terrified. Even now…' she moved quickly past the cellar door and back into the friendly warmth of the kitchen. The cellars still had the power to make her flesh creep.

'And where do I sleep tonight?' Mollie asked, when the tour was finishing up in the orchard, where Anthea picked windfalls for dessert. 'Fancy having rooms and rooms to choose from!'

'There may be lots of rooms, but we're a bit short of blankets, so I thought we'd share the double bed in the pink room,' Anthea suggested. 'After all, we've been sharing your single bed for ages, but if you'd rather have a room of your own we'll just take half the blankets each.'

'No fear,' Mollie said. 'I in't never slept on my own and I don't intend starting now. That'll be a rare old giggle in that great old room, just you and me…I'll feel like a queen!'

Mollie fitted in well with life at the vicarage. Each day the two girls left in the misty autumn morning to catch the bus and got down on Lord Street, for Mollie had a job there now, in a flower shop.

Anthea worked for Diane for the first week so that she had the job, the till and the stock-lists sorted out in her mind, and found there was little beyond her capabilities. She would work for the others one by one, with the owner standing by, and in a month, Diane calculated, she should be standing in for someone every day.

And then, one sunny Saturday, Anthea had a heavy post. The long brown envelopes thudded onto the hall floor and she very nearly didn't bother to open them because she and Mollie were planning to strip the orchard. The cider people paid a good price for windfalls and the rest would go into the loft to be stored for the coming winter.

However, Mollie went and fetched the letters and returned to the kitchen, where the two of them sat in their pyjamas crunching their way through brown toast and marmalade.

The first letter was a rates demand with a note pointing out that, due to his illness, the Reverend Todd had not yet paid last year's rates. They would be obliged if the estate would please send them a cheque.

Silently, Anthea opened the next letter. It

252

was a bill from the electricity board. Same story. Another from the coalman, also pointing out that he would be grateful if now that the Reverend Todd was dead, someone would kindly pay the money owing.

'What'll you do?' Mollie said, awed by the sums her friend would need.

'Ring Mr Parkins; what's in that other envelope? Oh, dear God, when did Father last pay an account?'

It was a tax bill; Father had not paid tax, either. Interest is owing, the tax man said ominously, on unpaid tax from five years back.

Anthea put the letters down on the table, propping them up with the marmalade jar, and heaved a sigh.

'Well, I couldn't pay that lot if I lived to be a hundred and worked every day of my life,' she said cheerfully. 'The apple money was to buy me some clothes—it won't even dent this lot!'

'Jesus wept! What'll you do, Ant?'

'Ring Mr Parkins, like I said. And then probably sell the house.'

Presently Anthea went down to the phone box and rang the solicitor. She found him at his home and explained about the bills.

'I imagine your father compounded with his creditors, through his doctor perhaps,

253

promising payment of all debts from his estate when he was gone,' Mr Parkins said drily. 'Not a sensible thing to do, nor a kind thing, but...'

'Quite,' Anthea said, almost crisply. 'What do I do? Pay off the bills little by little, from my earnings?'

'You won't sell?'

Anthea thought of the happiness she had known for the last few days, but it would have to end soon, anyway, when Mollie went home.

'I'll sell,' she said, so quietly that Mr Parkins had to ask her to repeat the remark. 'Yes. I'll sell. Only could you see to it for me, do you think? I'm afraid I'd be awfully easy to cheat.'

If Mr Parkins agreed with her he was far too polite to say so, but he said he would deal with the sale.

'When winter comes you won't have any difficulty in getting a flat in Haisby,' he said. 'And then, if you'll allow me, I'll have repairs put in hand for you...nothing much, just a lick of paint, doors rehung and so forth. It's a valuable property, you see, and with all that land there's no knowing what it might fetch.'

Anthea agreed she would find somewhere in the next few weeks, Mr Parkins said he would send a builder round and they parted on their usual good terms, two polite, rather old-fashioned people who respected each other,

Anthea thought wryly. Did she have more in common with dry Mr Parkins than with her dear Mollie?

But Mollie completely understood Anthea's mixed feelings when it came to the house.

'It's lovely in lots of ways and not so good in others,' she agreed. 'Tibby won't come indoors though, will she? She eats her food and then bolts out again. Perhaps you're a bit like that yourself...you do love the garden, don't you, Ant? I think you'll be just as happy in any house.'

It was true, Anthea thought. They were having an Indian summer, she had spent hours in the garden, and she was not at all prepared for winter. However, she had had half a ton of coal delivered, just in case she should have to spend the winter in the house, and Mr Parkins paid the bills, promising he would pay himself back out of the estate, when it sold.

She was getting on so well with Diane, too. At first she had dogged the younger girl's footsteps, copying the way Diane treated customers, running up and down stairs, rushing here and there at Diane's bequest. For now, with the fashion show only three days away, Diane was employing Anthea full-time apart from a half-day with Caresse and another with Archie just to be fair. Sam and Martin put Marj onto full-time and brought Sue in to waitress, for business was still pretty brisk and they had agreed to wait to get their 'share' of Anthea until after the show was over.

'Oh, lor', here comes Sarah,' Diane said, as a girl paused to glance in the window. 'Be a pet, Ant, and go upstairs for the brown velvet two-piece. I had to have it shortened so Sarah's coming in to try it on.'

Sarah was one of the models, the platinum blonde. Anthea fetched down the two-piece, stroking the material as she cantered down the stairs. It would look wonderful on Sarah, matching the girl's big, velvety-brown eyes.

It never occurred to Anthea to wonder whether it would look equally good on herself. She knew it could never do the things for her that it would presently do for Sarah. But she also knew that it was the sort of outfit that nine out of ten women would covet.

Slowly, falteringly, Anthea's natural good taste was stirring. Stunted by years of neglect but not yet entirely dead, it was telling her that it knew a good thing when it saw one. Diane could have told her that this was just another way of describing flair, but as yet she had had no opportunity to realise Anthea's potential.

And Anthea was too busy building her new life to care.

'She's awfully shy; we'll never get her to wait on without going bright red and mumbling,' Marj told Sam at the end of Anthea's first session in the restaurant. 'But Martin seems to get along with her.'

Sam and Marj exchanged heartfelt glances; one nightmare receded, though you could never be sure with Martin. He was a chap who blew hot and cold, Sam remembered. But it was a good start.

'She can cook,' Martin remarked, when asked what he thought of Anthea. 'She's a natural, got a light touch. Doesn't *know* anything, of course, but she's very teachable.'

The other girls liked her, too. Sandy said she used ingredients sensibly so that a tub of grated cheese, in Anthea's hands, lasted as long as it did in Sandy's own. Alice said she might never make a waitress but she was quiet and accurate at totting up a bill, and Sam himself liked the way she washed her hands before each task, splashing right up to the elbows without being asked. He also liked her soft voice and her eagerness to please, though he had to hide irritation when she cringed because he or Martin had walked by. Dammit, neither he nor Martin were into hitting women so why must she behave as if they might?

257

He knew the answer though, so tried not to let it get him down. And poor old Archie, that perfect gent, also admitted that at first he was worried that she blinked and ducked if he stood too close to her.

'But she's learning,' he told Sam tolerantly. 'Girl's shy, got no self-confidence, but it'll come. Real little lady, our Anthea.'

On the afternoon of the fashion show Diane, who had remained cool so far, succumbed to nerves.

She shouted at Helen, easily the most obliging of the models, for dropping a hat-box and Helen, edgy herself, burst into tears. Jenny from Waves, following close on Helen's heels with a huge tray of equipment, cannoned into the other girl, trod on the hat-box and dropped her own contribution all over the paving. Jenny swore colourfully, Helen wept and Sam, who was driving the mini-bus for them, tried to soothe the weeper and quieten the swearer, attempting to undo the harm caused by Diane's brief spate of temper.

'I'm sorry,' Diane said as they began to load the bus with their stuff. 'I wasn't nervous, but now my teeth are chattering with terror. Suppose it's a real mess? Suppose the timing's out and the music doesn't fit and the compère goes bananas and doesn't follow the script?'

'Shut up, Di,' Sam muttered. 'Do you want to have everyone in tears? It's a good job women never have to fight a war, models are like soldiers, they have to know enough and no more. Buck them up, encourage them, tell them dirty jokes if all else fails, but don't let them dwell on things which may never happen.'

'You're right,' Diane said, going round to take the front seat beside him whilst the models squeaked in the back. 'At least Marj is calm, but I wish I'd never agreed to model three out-fits myself. Having to go out there under all those lights...'

'Shut up!' Sam hissed. 'Did you ever hear the one about the bishop and the actress when they went fishing?'

Diane said no, she hadn't, and didn't hear a word of Sam's subsequent story. The respon-sibility! They had sold hundreds of tickets, the supper and champagne would be first-class, but the show was what most people had paid their money to see. Suppose they thought the clothes too way-out, too Londony? Suppose they had come expecting to see the sort of thing they saw each month in *Vogue*? Little silk dresses for seven hundred quid were not to be found on Diane's racks, nor sporty tweeds for nearly twice that price.

All the way to the hall Diane worried, but once there she took the attitude she always adopted in the dentist's chair. All you could do was suffer in silence and, when it was over, be very polite to the dentist because in six months' time you'd be there again, no matter how hard you prayed to God for 'flu.

At least this is a one-off, Diane told herself as she got out of the mini-bus. I'll never do it again, never never never!

'Well, Diane, you've done a first-class job; aren't you pleased with yourself?'

Diane smiled graciously at Tufton M'Quennell, her hostess's youngest son, the one who farmed the estate for her. He was a serious, dark-haired man in his late twenties, unmarried, hard-working, and he seemed to have taken an instant liking to Diane. He had been down to the shop in the Arcade two or three times and had twice taken Diane over to Sam's for coffee and a chat.

'Hello, Tufton, I'm glad you enjoyed it,' Diane said, feeling much better now that the show was finished and the supper—the fun part—was still to come. 'What a lot of people, I scarcely know any of them!'

For the place was humming with yuppy

young men and their elegant girlfriends. You could pick out what Mrs M'Quennell called the county, all right, with their wonderfully well-cut clothes and hand-made shoes, but the younger people were more daring. Lots of designer jeans, fabulous silk shirts, Italian shoes which cost the earth and looked it. Or the opposite, the deliberately scruffy look with hair spiked and skin cosseted and eyes which slid scornfully over anyone not earning fifty thousand a year.

Diane knew there were two more M'Quennell boys, Rory and Ashwell, but had never met them. In fact, as she had just said, she knew very few people here apart from the Arcadians and one or two customers.

'I'll introduce you,' Tufton said eagerly. 'Meet my brother Ashwell for a start. He's in the Army and engaged, but his fiancée's in Germany right now.'

Ashwell was tall, his hair mid-brown, his whole expression and cast of countenance determined, so that the chin which, on Tufton was merely firm was, on Ashwell, decisive. His eyes flickered approvingly over Diane.

'Hi. Nice to see old Tuf with the belle of the ball,' he said genially. 'Ma says you're to bring her to supper, Tuf, as soon as she's changed.'

Diane, still in ice-blue taffeta, gave a guilty squeak.

'Oh heavens, I forgot, I really must go, I promised...'

'Wait a mo,' Tufton said as Ashwell moved away. 'You've not met Rory yet—you must meet him, the only really successful M'Quennell—he's something in the city as they say.'

'Well, I'd love to, but...'

The long gallery was still crowded, though people were beginning to head for the supper room but even so, Diane saw someone she knew. Heavens, what rotten luck, it was the fellow she had christened the Arcade Ogler, the ugly one who had tried to pick her up that morning weeks and weeks ago! What was worse, he was heading straight for them, looking not at her but at her companion. A nasty suspicion gripped Diane; tall, dark, ugly as a gargoyle but with a certain presence and a great deal of self-confidence...could it possibly be...?

It was, of course.

'Well, if it isn't Tufton,' the Arcade Ogler said affably. 'And clutching a shapely wench, to boot.' Diane looked up at him, prepared to be cool, but he was looking at Tufton, the pale eyes warm, a lock of hair flopping over his brow.

'This is Diane Hopgood, who organised the

262

show,' Tufton said, a proprietorial hand on Diane's waist. 'Diane, my brother Rory.'

'How do you do?' Diane said. She held out a hand, very cool and correct, her eyes steady on the eldest M'Quennell's face.

'Hello,' Rory said, ignoring her hand, his tone indifferent to the point of rudeness. She saw that he was not looking at her but past her, actually staring at someone else! Diane boiled. 'Awfully good show; my felicitations. Known my brother long?'

'Not long,' Diane said guardedly.

'I see. Tuf, do you know that incredibly sexy poppet with the pink hair and holey trousers? She was sitting opposite me at tea. I want to know her better.'

Tufton laughed. 'Pink hair and torn trousers? That'll be Letty Dunlop. Fancy her?'

'I fancy anyone who'll sit in m'mother's drawing room airing her fanny,' Rory drawled whilst Diane stared coldly into space and Tufton choked on a laugh. 'Lead me to her, dear boy.'

'All right; you don't mind, Di?'

Diane was conscious of a great number of emotions all churning about in her insides, but none of them was indifference to Letty Dunlop meeting the Arcade Ogler. He had not needed an introduction to a shop-girl, he just propositioned her, let him do the same to high-born, fanny-airing Letty. But she could scarcely say so!

'No, of course I don't mind. I'm going to get the girls to the changing room now. See you later.'

'The girls are in the West wing,' he said, speaking without being spoken to. 'Down the long corridor, second door on the right.'

'I know where the changing room is, I've got to tell the models,' Diane snapped, moving away faster.

Rory raised his voice infuriatingly, the drawl even more obvious.

'All right, no need to get your knickers in a twist. Most of the models cut their teeth on my old coral and bells and know their way round here blindfolded. You're the only stranger in these parts.'

It cut, of course. Diane kept on, grimly ignoring him though her cheeks flew twin red flags. The hateful pig! If she ever saw him again—and pray God it was in a dark alley—she would knee him in the groin and hope she unmanned him for good.

However, it would not do to show her feelings and anyway she was soon too busy to do more than simmer when she thought about Rory bloody M'Quennell. She found Helen,

264

the little red-head, almost in tears because everyone else had disappeared to change and she had no idea which way they'd gone.

So much for clever bloody Rory, Diane thought vengefully, taking Helen's arm. If she had indeed cut her teeth at the hall she had forgotten the layout since!

The two of them were heading across the gallery when another red-head accosted them. She was small, with short curls clustered about her head, greeny-blue eyes and a great many freckles. She looked like a friendly puppy, eager for a pat.

'Miss Hopgood? Could I possibly have a word? Press.'

Diane was about to enquire what she should press when she realised that this child was waving a notebook at her and meant to intimate that she was a reporter. They come younger and younger, she thought, bemused, whilst indicating that she would be happy to give the other a moment of her time.

'Hooray...shall I walk along beside you? I'm Ceri Allen of the *Chronicle*. I wonder if you'd mind telling me names and so on, and who modelled what? I'm not very well up on good clothes, I don't have the language, I'd probably describe the thing you're wearing as a blue silk frock. If I could interview you it'll be much

265

better publicity for your lovely shop.'

'I've got a list,' Diane said, laughing. 'Would that help? I'll tell you lots tomorrow if you can pop down to the boutique. Any write-up is nice, but a good one would be super.'

'Grand,' Ceri Allen said decidedly. 'I say, do you think I can have some supper, or is that ticket-holders only? I'm actually starving.'

'Hang about until the rush is over and they'll be delighted to feed the Press,' Diane advised. 'You know where Bonner's is, I hope?'

It was not a foolish question, as she had learned to her cost. Dozens of Haisby inhabitants seemed almost proud to admit they had never been down the Arcade. But this particular young lady nodded at once.

'Yes, of course I do. Actually, I'm about to start flat-sharing on Cloister Row. I often walk past Bonner's; when I'm rich I'll buy lots of your stock.'

There could be no greater compliment, Diane thought delightedly, making a firm appointment to have coffee with Ceri next morning.

This meeting of twin souls, however, was interrupted by Jenny, who rushed up to them eagerly.

'Hi, Di...Ceri...Helen,' she said. 'Will you need me any more Di? I've met the handsomest young man and he wants to take me to supper...will that be okay?'

All Diane's vague discontent came rushing back. Even Jenny had found a man, all she, Diane, had done was lose Tufton to the vile Arcade Ogler.

'Good God, Jen, I'm not your keeper,' she said crossly. 'Do what you like.'

'Oh!' Jenny said blankly. 'Sorry...as you're organising...'

'I'm the one who should apologise,' Diane said remorsefully. 'I'm tired and strung-up. You go off and have supper with your fellow, Helen and I want to change. Bye, Ceri, see you tomorrow.'

'You were talking to Rory earlier,' Helen remarked as the two of them headed once more for the West wing. 'He's awfully nice, he does something awfully high-powered in the city, I believe.'

'He looks it,' Diane agreed limpidly. She was visualising a road-drill as she spoke—awfully high-powered.

'Though Tufton's nice,' Helen added hastily. 'He's awfully nice. Serious, too.'

'Mm hmm,' Diane said. Nice, she thought crossly, described Tufton exactly.

'I like that girl...Ceri Allen,' Helen ventured next, as they found the West wing and began to traverse the long corridor. 'She's got red hair, too. Did you think she was pretty?'

Diane looked speculatively at Helen, who was very pretty and very silly, too.

'Pretty? Not really. But lively and attractive...she's that all right.'

'Like Marj,' Helen said despondently. 'Everyone was talking about Marj, saying how marvellous she was. It isn't fair to compare her with us though, she's professional. Or was.'

'Yes, she was. And she was good,' Diane agreed, pausing in front of the door behind which the models were changing. 'I expect she made the rest of us look pretty amateur, but I don't think it matters.'

Diane had been delighted with Marj, who had stalked along the cat-walk, lending that undoubted touch of authenticity to the whole show, whilst her face became the haughty mask which most professional models wear.

'My boyfriend said he wanted to meet her,' Helen moaned. 'Isn't it *awful*, Di, to feel really jealous of a girl who works in a *kitchen*, when you're in public relations and earning masses of lovely money, like I am!'

'It's just human,' Diane said comfortingly, pushing the door open. 'Don't worry about it, Helen.'

Inside the room the models were sprawled

on chairs in their undies. Eyeing the fabulous breasts of Susan, the long tanned legs of Amanda and the sylph-like slenderness of Sarah, Diane wondered why Helen wasted her jealousy on Marj. These girls were the pick of the bunch and would probably become her customers.

'Thanks, girls, you were marvellous,' Diane said now. 'Where's Marj?'

'Here,' Marj called, emerging from behind a rack of clothes. She was fully dressed in a cream linen suit with black shoes and jet beads round her neck. Diane knew that the suit was cheap and the shoes and beads plastic but Marj made her clothes look a million dollars.

'Well, pleased with yourself, gal?' Marj grinned at Diane and strolled across the room, still using her exaggerated model's walk. 'Reckon it couldn't have gone better, and it was a bit of fun and all.'

'It was fun, but isn't it hard work?' Susan said, putting on a cobwebby black stocking. 'And the clothes are scrummy, Di. I adored the things I modelled and Mummy said she'd definitely buy me the blue grosgrain for a pressie...I'm getting Sarah's brown velvet for myself, though.'

'I'm terribly tempted by the lilac wool dress with the lace collar,' Helen said wistfully.

Diane forbore to tell her that she would look washed out in it. 'I did enjoy myself, awfully, Di. Will you do another?'

'I might do one in the spring,' Diane said brightly. Nothing had been further from her thoughts than another fashion show but after this evening only a fool would have failed to see the advantages. 'If I do, are you on as models again?'

There was a chorus of agreement; they had all enjoyed themselves, apparently.

'And did you see Rory?' one of the girls said. 'Isn't he the most gorgeous thing? Wish he came home more often.'

'He's awfully nice,' Helen said pensively. 'Not as kind as my boyfriend, but awfully nice. Not like some of those awful hooray henries.'

'That's because he isn't a hooray henry, he's a stockbroker,' Sarah observed, putting on lipstick.

'They'll be handing round the champers out there,' Amanda reminded them. 'Don't hang around, girls, whilst all the best men get snapped up, get a move on!'

They began to hurry but Marj strolled to the door and opened it, then turned in the doorway.

'That's no use you hurrin', mawthers, I'll be down there hours ahead of you, snappin'

up the fellers so fast there'll be none left.
Cheerio!'

Her blackbird's shout of laughter rang out
above their outraged cries as she closed the door
behind her.

CHAPTER TWELVE

The day after the fashion show, Rory M'Quennell came down the Arcade. He did not glance
into Bonner's, though Diane was all set to ignore him had he done so, and this really in-
furiated her. To be prepared to snub someone
and then to be snubbed by them was really un-
fair, done specially to annoy no doubt.

What was worse, he went to see Marj. Diane
saw him tap on the kitchen door and then go
in and so he must be after Marj.

Diane frowned to herself. What did he think
he was doing, visiting Marj? She was a lovely
person but scarcely the sort of girl to grace the
Ogler's Porsche.

You bitch, Diane thought, surprised at
herself, you're a rotten little snob.

'Yes, Mrs Deane, the dark red's a better colour for you. You've got a delicate complexion

271

and blue drains it.'

Quack quack quack went Mrs Deane from the changing cubicle and Diane continued to peer across the Arcade into the kitchen, though she could see little apart from shadows. The tallest shadow would be Rory, she supposed.

When the phone rang she snatched it up and had great difficulty in keeping her voice warm and friendly.

'Bonner's Boutique; can I help you?' she cooed through clenched teeth. Damn Rory-Arcade-Ogler-M'Quennell, cutting up her peace!

'Hello, me darlin' girl.'

The voice on the other end of the phone was distorted by distance, yet she would have known it anywhere. Diane forgot her customer, Marj, even the Arcade Ogler.

'Tony! Well, this is a surprise.'

'Ah Di, me love, don't be like that. Mustn't you have known I couldn't hold out, that I'd come runnin'? I must see you; can I come down?'

'Today?' Diane's whole body was remembering, with pleasure, what Tony's presence might mean. She had given Anthea a day off after the hectic business of the show, so she could easily arrange to shut for a few hours...but then her eye caught a movement as the cubicle curtains fluttered and her conscience smote her. No going back, remember? 'I'm sorry, Tony, not today. I'm busy.'

'Come on, love, you wouldn't hurt me by refusin' to see me, and me all of a ferment to come to you?'

'Ha! Even the thought of your fermenting doesn't make me automatically free to see you whenever you choose to turn up. Where are you, anyway?'

Last time he had rung from down the road; this time she thought he was further off. The blarney was a bit too stage-Irish, he wasn't as sure of himself as he was pretending.

'I'm in Norwich, at a sales conference. Very nice, sure, but the moment I set foot in the county I was thinkin' of you every moment.'

'Really? And if you'd been in London you wouldn't have given me a thought? Thanks!'

'No, you eejit, haven't I t'ought of you every wakin' moment for weeks?' His voice deepened. 'Say you'll see me for five minutes!'

The curtain of the changing cubicle had stopped rustling but Mrs Deane had not emerged. Doubtless she was riveted by the one-sided conversation. Diane tried to make her tone impersonal.

'All right. Can you get here by six?'

'Six! Sure an' isn't that hours away...

couldn't you make it earlier, I dare not miss the last train to London.'

'Goodbye, Tony,' Diane started and heard his voice change its tone with some satisfaction; that would learn him!

'No...wait! Don't ring off, six will be fine...Where?'

'On Lord Street, outside the Arcade. See you, Tony.'

She put the receiver down and seconds later Mrs Deane emerged, the red dress held out.

'I'll take it, dear. My Harry will be right pleased with it, we saw one like it at the fashion show.'

Diane began to fold the dress, congratulating Mrs Deane on her choice. She was ushering her customer out when she saw the kitchen door opposite opening. Slowly, Rory was emerging with a tray in his hands. Marj darted past him and opened the door which Diane had just shut behind Mrs Deane.

'Visitor for you,' she said, giving Di a roguish glance. 'Coffee and butter-cakes for two.'

Rory came through the doorway and put the tray down on the counter. He smiled down at Diane with just enough triumph to annoy her all over again.

'There! If the mountain won't come to

Mohammed…Do you take sugar?'

This man is the son of my most influential customer, Diane reminded herself. I cannot afford to antagonise Mrs M'Quennell. Indeed, it might have been the Arcade Ogler who had first suggested that his mother might approach the boutique about the fashion show.

'No, thank you,' Diane said primly. She sank onto her chair, pointing wordlessly to the one on the customer's side of the counter, upholstered with cream and gold stripes.

'She's offering me a seat,' Rory said in tones of wonderment. 'Fancy, she isn't quite the dragon I'd imagined.'

'What can I do for you?' Diane said as he sat. 'Is it something about last night?'

'In a way. Mother was delighted and has made over five thousand quid for the hospice.'

'Marvellous,' Diane said sincerely. She sipped her coffee. 'Do tell her it's done me a lot of good as well, would you? Heaps of people who saw the show have been in.'

'Pretty, witty Letty will be in as well, later,' Rory said smoothly. 'I told her to buy jeans without holes and said you'd the best supply in town.'

Diane's hackles rose almost perceptibly, she felt sure, but a glance at Rory showed him to be examining, with apparent interest, the

275

display of costume jewellery in the case nearest him.

'Thanks for the recommendation,' she said dryly. 'May I try a butter-cake?'

'Sure.' Rory stood up and offered her the plate, then took one himself and bit into it. He spoke rather thickly. 'These are nice, but what a surly bugger that chef is; glared at me every time I spoke to the girl.'

'He glares at everyone,' Diane assured him. 'He glares at me from time to time, but he's okay really. We're a happy little lot in the Arcade.'

'Good. Do you frequent Reynards, the Health Club on Lord Street?'

'I'm a member,' Diane admitted. It was a good little club and she had already made use of her membership several times, enjoying the pool, the sauna and the steam room.

'I'm not a member,' Rory said. 'I'm not here often enough to make it worthwhile, but if you wanted to take me as your guest we could take the plunge together, this evening.'

Diane stared at him. The previous evening he had snubbed her effectively by referring to her as 'the only stranger in these parts'. He must know dozens of members!

'Reynards? This evening?'

'Or, if you'd prefer it, we could get into my

car and whizz over to Norwich to the theatre, or a nightclub, have a meal, whatever you'd enjoy.'

He was looking straight at her, the light eyes sparkling, and Diane could see very well why the girls thought he was the most attractive of the M'Quennell boys. But...she was seeing Tony, later.

'Oh I'm sorry, tonight's out. I've got a previous appointment.'

'Oh, well, at least I tried. Never mind, eh? Some other time.'

He was on his feet, the smile gone, the eyes cool once more. Diane got to her feet as well, glad that she could show him she was no pushover, that she had a decent social life without any help from him. But he had picked up the tray with their empty cups and was heading for the doorway.

'Nice having coffee with you,' he said over his shoulder. 'See you!'

'See you,' Diane echoed. She wished she had explained that her previous appointment was not a polite fiction but he had given her no opportunity and anyway, Rory M'Quennell was a ship that passed in the night, he was nothing to her. Tony had been, quite simply, her life. For old times' sake if nothing else, she would see Tony this evening.

But the gargoyle face and the light eyes stayed in her mind for the rest of the day. What would it be like to be kissed by the Arcade Ogler? Would he take the ghastly Letty out tonight and persuade her to remove what was left of her trousers? Not that she'd need much persuading. Diane told herself bitterly. Pink hair indeed!

As the days drew shorter, Anthea began to look forward to selling the house. Mollie had been right; the cold which she had never noticed when she had no real comparison bit into her now, when she entered the house after a day in a warm shop or wine bar.

'It's awful,' she told Elspeth one evening, when the vicar's wife had called to see how she was getting on. 'When I was here day and night I never really noticed the cold and anyway, we had a fire going in the kitchen all the time. But now I sit down here with the oven on and the door open, and then I freeze in bed, even with a couple of hotties. It's the draughts; they cut across the room like knives.'

'Mr Parkins told Geoff he'd advised you to get a flat,' Elspeth said. 'He'd like to have some repairs done, apparently.'

'He did, but now he's seen how few people actually want the old place he's changing his mind,' Anthea said despondently. 'Builders, now—they're very keen. But of course they want planning permission to build on the garden and that takes time, so I'm still here, waiting.'

'Would you like to stay with us?' Elspeth asked, in a tone which Anthea recognised at once as Christian Resigned. 'I'm sure we could fit you in somewhere.'

She was expecting another baby and her figure fluttered with smocks, scarves and floating panels. But her expression was clear enough—kindness overlying resignation.

'I couldn't possibly, but it's good of you to ask,' Anthea said politely. 'I have to be in work by seven when I'm making sandwiches and that means catching the first bus. I always open up whichever shop I'm in before nine, as well.'

'I see...you're a different person, Anthea dear, now you work,' Elspeth said. 'You've got self-confidence. It's done you a power of good, earning your own living.'

'I think it has,' Anthea acknowledged. 'I'm fatter, too, though I've always loved my food.'

'Yes, your face has filled out; you look really pretty,' Elspeth said generously.

Anthea laughed. 'It's sweet of you to say so, Elspeth, but I am healthier, and very much happier. That's about all I can claim.'

'You dress so well,' Elspeth said, her eyes approving Anthea's green wool dress with the chocolate-coloured belt and matching shoes. 'I'd call you elegant.'

'I've learned a lot from Di, and she lets me have things at cost because it advertises her stock.'

'Lucky you.' Elspeth moved nearer the stove and shivered. 'Surely if you moved out into lodgings you'd be better off? Think of the heating bills you'd save, and the travelling expenses. I'm sure Mr Parkins would agree, if you put it to him like that.'

'It's an idea,' Anthea said longingly. She had enjoyed the journey in summer but now that the evenings were drawing in it was a penance. She was often so tired she could scarcely relish her supper and even reading in bed was a limited pleasure when your fingers and nose froze. 'I could have a word with Di—her aunts let rooms.'

'You do that. I'd like to think of you settled. January and February can be dreadful— remember the year the snow melted in the night and then the flood water turned to ice and all the gates were frozen shut?'

They discussed past dreadful winters for a bit and then Elspeth remembered she had been despatched to invite Anthea to spend Christmas

280

day with them.

'Thank you so much, but I'll see where I am by then,' Anthea said diplomatically. She had no intention of spending the holiday with the Elgoods and no intention, either, of letting them see how she would hate it. The children were sweet but out of hand and Elspeth, though possibly a saint, was not a good cook. Anyway, she might have to work; Sam and Martin were doing a Christmas dinner and it sounded as though it would be good fun.

'Well, all right, we'll leave it for now,' Elspeth said. She sipped her coffee and helped herself, absently, to another slice of cake. 'So bad for my figure, but I do love your apple cake. Tell me, what will you do about Bonfire Night?'

'I'm going to the beach bonfire in Haisby,' Anthea said quickly. 'I'm staying with friends afterwards.'

'That sounds lovely; I must remember to warn everybody to keep their pets shut up...Oh by the way, you know your Tibby's gone over to the enemy?'

Anthea laughed. Tibby did not appreciate an absentee owner and a house where her fur was blown backwards by draughts.

'Yes, but I'm happy for her. Mrs Kershawe

told me she'd adopted her, poor thing! I tried to persuade her that Tibby really wasn't starved or neglected, but I don't think she took much notice. Actually, Tibs deserted me in her heart ages ago—remember that storm? I was ill and probably Tibby felt let down but at any rate she took a dislike to the house around then and never came in for more than a few minutes after that. She'd rush in, gulp down her food and make herself scarce. I'm sure she's much happier with Mrs Kershawe, and butchers always eat lots of meat, so she'll get better food, too.'

'Cats are cold creatures,' Elspeth, a dog-lover, remarked as she put on her warm tweed coat. 'Well dear, you're invited for Christmas if you want to come. Take care of yourself and pop round some time when you've got a moment; you'll always be welcome.'

Anthea saw her guest out and returned to the kitchen. Elspeth had just given her the final nudge in a direction she had been meaning to take for weeks. She would ring Mr Parkins on Monday morning and tell him she would have to move out for the winter, and she would start looking for lodgings. She was sorry for the house, it had been a good place once, when her mother had been alive, but it had known more tears than laughter of recent years.

And if I sell you, maybe other families will be happy here, Anthea told the house as she moved around the kitchen. The decay's partly my fault. I meant to light fires in the main living rooms every weekend but I was always too busy and too tired. Fires might discourage the mould from growing any further up the walls. But her horror of the cellars was still a very real thing. If Mollie had been here...but she was not so the fires went unlit and the supply of briquettes, which Anthea used for the range, shrank and was replenished each month in the old bicycle shed by the back door.

Thinking of fires made her remember that she had not yet damped down the range and made it up for the night. She kept a bucket of dust handy to sprinkle over the briquettes and then she closed the air-vents right down and the fire stayed in all night. I'll have a hot bath later, Anthea promised herself. Some of her happiest moments had been spent in that big, oddly-shaped bath, with a legitimate reason for locking the door and knowing herself safe, for a while at least, from the Reverend Todd. And now she had scented soap, good talc, a thick bath towel—Friday nights were wonderful.

Piling on some more briquettes and then sprinkling the dust was easily done, but Anthea knew she should refill the hod with fuel otherwise, tomorrow morning, she would have to venture outside whilst still warm from bed.

'You'll catch your death,' her mother would have warned, so now Anthea slung her old brown duffel round her shoulders, put on her wellies, and prepared to meet the chill.

She opened the back door and it was not only cold, it was raining. Damn! But the duffel had a hood, so she pulled it up and sallied forth. A quick shuffle—the boots were several sizes too big—across the paved yard and then she was in the pitch dark of the bicycle shed, bending down and fumbling for the shovel which always leaned just here, picking it up and pushing it into the pile of briquettes.

She was about to put the first load into the hod when she heard a peculiar sound, a sort of whistling roar. It faded, then came again. Anthea's hair stood up on the back of her neck. She stayed very still, peering round. Was it an animal? Or a sound carried from the village by some freak weather condition?

Even as she stared her eyes, gradually becoming used to the dark, saw a thicker blackness in one corner of the shed, and her ears recognised the sound. Someone was snoring. Someone was curled up on the musty piles of church jumble which she had meant to burn when she had time.

Heart thumping, Anthea stole forward. Poor chap, should she wake him, tell him to move out? Or might it be a dangerous thing to do? Suppose he was a drunk? A drunk could get violent, she knew. Perhaps she ought to go down the road to the box and dial 999.

But first she filled the hod with fuel, putting off making a decision, and as she turned to leave the shed the snoring stopped.

'Whazzat? Oozair?'

A deep voice, sounding either drugged with sleep or drink, she could not tell which. Anthea stared at the figure, which was sitting up and staring back.

'This is my shed,' she said quietly, though her voice shook a little. 'What are you doing here?'

'Oh...I'm only sleeping, missus,' the voice, now that its owner was fully awake, was a plaintive whine. 'Thass a turble night out there; you wou'nt want a chap to be under an 'edge on a night like this yur, would you? Not a kind lady like you?'

Anthea could see that he was dark-haired and quite young, but somehow she knew he was harmless. Also he was sober, his voice slurred with sleep but still perfectly under control.

'You can stay here until morning,' she said calmly. 'But then you must be on your way.

This isn't a suitable place for anyone to sleep.'

He gave a rusty chuckle.

'Don't I know it! But thanks, missus.'

He was snoring again before she reached the door and though she hurried into the kitchen and locked the door behind her she did not find the thought of the poor tramp in the shed frightening. I have no money and no possessions, she told herself as she climbed into bed. Nothing, in fact, that anyone would want.

She was almost asleep when two thoughts occurred to her. The first was that she had felt only a healthy fear of a stranger when she had first seen the man in the shed. It had never crossed her mind that it might be Chris Bowles. He had had enough malignancy to abuse her just for the sake of it, so his return was not that impossible. But it seemed to her that he had gone completely, as her father had gone, so she never wasted a thought on him any more.

The second thought was that compared to the man in the shed she was rich as Croesus. A house, a fire, food in the pantry and a warm bed; what more could she—or he—ask for? Perhaps she really should have rung the police. But she did nothing, snug in her bed. Drowsily she checked her nightly precautions in her mind. Doors locked, windows snicked, bolts shot. Satisfied, she soon slept.

When Diane had first thought of getting Anthea to work for the Arcade traders as a whole she drew a blank with Lana and Barry, who were doing abysmally badly, and got a satisfactory response from Archie. But Caresse had been difficult as only Caresse could be. She had been sitting in her shop eating marshmallows and jumped when Diane came in, hastily stuffing the sweets into the drawer nearest her. She was too late, however; Diane had already seen the big puffballs, to say nothing of the moustache of icing sugar around Caresse's mouth.

'Morning, Caresse; I was wondering if you'd be interested in a stand-in...'

Diane knew her spiel by heart and Caresse's eyes brightened when she came to the nub of her story. Anthea had been working for the boutique for a week and Diane knew Caresse had envied her the ability to go off now and then. As they all knew, it was not easy to get someone who could be trusted to run a small shop just for a day or so each week.

Caresse, however, was not going to rush into anything.

'Anthea?' she said doubtfully, pretending to blow her nose so that she could wipe away any traces of marshmallow. 'Now that'll be the tall

287

woman I've seen in and out of your place, lately. So she's not full-time with you, then?'

'No, of course not. I did explain,' Diane said patiently, knowing full well that Caresse was just playing for time whilst she thought the thing through and decided whether the adoring Ronald would agree to her employing staff.

'Mm...well, I suppose she'd suit some people, but she isn't very *glamorous*, is she, darling?'

'Why do you say that?'

'Well, Di, this is a *very* glamorous business; I often say to Ronnie, it's myself I'm selling as well as my product. Even if my customers don't realise it, they look at me, then at the product, they're considering, and they think it'll make them look like *me*, you see, so then they buy.' Caresse gave a tinkling laugh. 'But if you don't mind my saying so, Di, that wouldn't apply with Anthea. She's extremely plain and so *knobbly*, somehow.' She stroked her own rounded breasts, covered in mohair today. 'I can't imagine people queueing up to buy from her, I'm afraid.'

'So you think people buy my clothes because they hope to look like me? But Caresse, when you bought that two-piece I'm sure...'

'Don't carry it to absurd lengths, love,' Caresse said hurriedly. She did not want to

288

hear a comparison between Diane's long-legged figure and her own plump person, Diane knew. 'Anyway, I didn't say it applied to clothes, just beauty aids. I can't see Anthea selling my sort of stuff, that's all.'

'Well, I'm sorry I troubled you,' Diane said, moving towards the door. 'Can't stop, Caresse, got a busy afternoon.'

'Wait...I'm, not saying no, precisely...'

'It doesn't matter, don't worry, Caresse,' Diane said, crossing her fingers behind her back. 'Archie's giving her a full day, Sam wants her for two and I could use her for three, so if you aren't interested...'

'It was lovely of you to think of me,' Caresse said breathlessly. 'Of *course* I'll have her for a day, we have quiet days. Put me down for a Wednesday, nine until five.'

Diane made the right noises and hurried back to her shop, reflecting that for someone who seldom came in before ten o'clock and often left by three, Caresse had a nerve to insist on nine till five from Anthea. But it was typical of Caresse.

So now, Anthea was full-time in the Arcade. Diane knew she was not happy with Caresse, who never missed an opportunity to try to prove, to her own satisfaction, that Anthea could not sell beauty aids, but it had meant that Diane and Anthea between them had been able to dress the window of Treat Yourself so that even Caresse had been heard to say that Anthea was quite gifted in that department.

The Arcade is on the up-and-up, Diane told herself now, looking down the brightly-lit covered way. Christmas was coming, there would be all sorts of fun—a tree which they would all help to decorate, holly and mistletoe over the windows and doors, paperchains, fairy-lights, you name it, the Arcade would have it. But right now, Diane was on her way to see the quietest trader of all. Miss Turner, the tailoress.

The trouble was, as Diane got more customers, so she began to realise that she needed someone for alterations. Just to change hemlines, to put in darts, to move a button a couple of inches. When she said this to Mrs M'Quennell, who had popped in for a little chat and fallen in love with a jade green skirt which was at least six inches too long, Mrs M'Quennell, placidly paying for the suit by cheque, had said that Diane should pop along to Miss Turner, who also worked in the Arcade.

'Best tailoress in Haisby,' she stated. 'I always go there if I need something special. She's marvellous, and perhaps she would like the work, though she seems to have half my generation at least popping in and out. She could do it magnificently.'

Once it would have been hard to find a moment but now Diane simply went over to Sam's where Anthea and Martin were apparently cooking together in perfect amity, and 'borrowed' Anthea for half an hour whilst she went prospecting.

The maroon door had a sign on it which said, 'Please come in', so Diane complied. Inside, there was a smallish room divided in two by a long counter. Behind the counter sat Miss Turner, wheelchair-bound but working away at an industrial sewing machine as if her life depended on it. She finished her seam as Diane entered, then turned and beamed. She was a very small, skinny woman with thin grey hair parted in the middle and screwed into a tiny, hard bun on the back of her neck. She had a little button of a face with eyes magnified by a large pair of tortoiseshell-rimmed spectacles and she wore a smart grey suit with a lemon-coloured blouse beneath it.

'Good afternoon,' she said cheerfully. 'Cold out?' She had a London accent and her movements, as she zipped one lot of material out of the machine, tied ends, snipped them off and cast the garment into a large basket standing nearby, were quick and neat. She reminded

Diane of a Beatrix Potter mouse working away busily. She almost expected her to snip the thread with her teeth and was quite disappointed when Miss Turner produced scissors.

'Yes, it is cold,' Diane admitted. 'Um…Miss Turner, I was telling Mrs M'Quennell that I didn't have anyone to do alterations and she suggested that you might be able to help. I'm Diane Hopgood, by the way, I've got the shop…'

'Bonner's Boutique,' Miss Turner said, seizing another length of material and feeding it into the clattering maw of her machine. 'Ah, Nell's a good woman, never forgets her friends. I made her wedding dress, you know,' she added. 'Been in and out ever since, has Nell.'

'I never think of Mrs M'Quennell as Nell, but of course it's short for Eleanor, isn't it,' Diane mused, leaning on the counter and gazing curiously at the only finished garment in sight. 'I say, did you have to alter that?'

'That was a maternity dress with a high neck and a multitude of tiny pleats. It must have been hell to alter, Diane thought. If Miss Turner was up to shortening that…

'No, that's one I made,' Miss Turner said. She finished the next seam and dropped the material into the basket. 'I make more'n I alter, one way and another. Now, you was

292

asking about alterations....'

Miss Turner touched something and her wheelchair purred into life. She shot back from the machine in the neatest three-point turn Diane had ever seen and came round the counter. All along one side of the room, Diane now realised, clothing hung on rails. Miss Turner came to rest neatly alongside a rail, picked up a stick with a hook on the end and selected a couple of garments, hooking them down neatly and throwing them onto the counter.

'See them? One was Miss Hebditch's best suit, only she'd got bigger and the suit jest hadn't.' Miss Turner's face was split by an engaging, long-toothed grin. 'So I let out the darts and put a piece of the hem in as an extra panel where it won't notice, under the arms.'

Diane picked up the suit jacket. It had been enlarged with great care and expertise.

'And this is a feller's trousers, took in round the waist,' Miss Turner said. 'See? Now I put the darts where I did and shortened the waist-band because...'

Her talk became technical and Diane just nodded and smiled, the smile broadening as she saw again the care which had been employed.

'If you do my alterations even half as well

as you've done these, everyone will be delighted,' Diane said when Miss Turner stopped talking. 'I'll bring the stuff up to you if it's standard, but if someone wants a fitting can I send them up here?'

'You better had,' Miss Turner acknowledged. 'I've a room in the back...we live at the back in a nice little flat, me and Percy. I take my ladies through there to be measured. Want to have a look? You can meet my Percy at the same time.'

Diane was demurring when Miss Turner zipped her chair in a big circle, disappearing through what Diane now realised was a curtained opening. Her voice came back to Diane, slightly muffled. 'Come through, Miss Bonner.'

Diane followed her. Percy proved to be a handsome Amazonian parrot with a raucous laugh and a number of catch-phrases which, Miss Turner said proudly, he had learned from the telly.

'Ever so quick he is,' she confided, 'learns anything he hears if he likes the sound of it. He used to love *Dixon of Dock Green*, really missed it when it went off.'

'He must be quite old,' Diane said respectfully. She had a vision of her parents as young lovers, watching *Dixon of Dock Green*.

'Oh, he is. To my knowledge he's thirty and since he wasn't no egg when I got him, I suppose he's quite a bit older than that. My friend was a sailor and brought him back from the Indies. Of course, that was before I was tied to this thing,' she added, thumping the arm of the wheelchair with the heel of her hand.

'And now it's just you and Percy?' Diane tried to make her voice light. 'Don't you get lonely?'

'What, with the telly and all my ladies coming to see how I'm getting on with the bits and bobs? No jolly fear,' Miss Turner said decidedly. 'Mind, I miss car rides. Used to love going out in a car, I did. And I miss men, a bit. You don't get many men in here, they send their womenfolk in when they split their trousers and mostly they go for readymades in the tailoring line. But now and then I goes for a spin in me wheelchair, up into town, along the promenade, round all the amusement arcades. Then I buys a bag of chips for me lunch and a fizzy drink and I look at the sea and remember...oh, all sorts. It's good, remembering. Because I wasn't always stuck, do you see?'

'No, of course you weren't,' Diane said. 'I can drive, though I don't run a car right now, but if I were to hire one you could show me round the district, perhaps.'

'It's very kind of you,' Miss Turner said, suddenly formal. 'But I'm sure you've got better things to do than go hiring cars and I do very nicely with me ladies and Percy and the telly.'

'I really wouldn't mind...' Diane began, and was put firmly in her place.

'It's not a matter of *minding*, dear. The nights are drawing in and I've that many orders for Christmas that I dare not shift from the machine until Christmas Eve, and then there's the orders for New Year parties. No, you pop in from time to time and we'll have a lovely talk, but I won't be beholden, not when I'm so busy.'

Diane left, feeling that she had been careless of the old lady's pride, yet still happy that Miss Turner had agreed to do her alterations. And when she confided in Sam that she felt she'd gone too far in offering Miss Turner a car ride, Sam soon cheered her up.

'Miss Turner, with the maroon door? Do you know, I thought she was a figment of someone's imagination,' he said. 'We've been here over a year now and we've none of us set eyes on her. What's she like?'

'Little and thin and lonely and proud,' Diane said sorrowfully. 'She's confined to a wheelchair you see, but when I offered a car ride she gave me the brush-off. I thought I was help-ing, but...'

'Oh, is *that* Miss Turner? She comes in sometimes for a coffee,' Sam said. 'Chirpy little soul, isn't she? Well, I shouldn't think you hurt her feelings, Di, she strikes me as very down to earth. If she said she was too busy that'll be just what she meant, nothing more. Why were you going to see her, anyway?'

'I need someone to do alterations,' Diane ex-plained. 'She's a marvellous worker and she's agreed to help out, so I'm delighted about that.'

'So you should be. What's her flat like? I've often wondered.'

'The shop's quite small but the room at the back, where she measures customers, is pretty large. There's the parrot in a huge old wicker cage, a couple of chairs and not much else. I didn't see her living quarters.'

'I expect you will, in time,' Sam said com-fortably. 'Want a coffee? How about a bit of Martin's banana gateau? It's marked down as it doesn't keep well.'

Diane had been in the kitchen leaning against the fridge but now she straightened guiltily.

'Heavens, Sam, I forgot I'd borrowed Ant off you. I'll send her back right away...and I'll pay for two coffees and two gateaux and

Ant can eat hers whilst she's working.'

'It's all right, Martin's finished the cooking. Now he's down in the cellars, doing something to the wine. We aren't staying open this evening so we'll be off home soon.'

'Okay, and thanks, Sam,' Diane said gratefully. 'Can I take the coffee and cakes back with me?'

Sam made her up a tray and Diane paid, then went back to the shop with it, Sam hovering to open the boutique door. Anthea was selling a customer a beautiful smoke-grey sweater and some imitation pearls to go with it.

'You'll look like a duchess,' she was saying as Diane entered the shop. 'Pearls always look so *good*, somehow, even though they aren't real.'

The customer paid and at last the two of them were alone.

'Miss Turner's a gem, and she's agreed to do the alterations,' Diane said triumphantly. 'So that's settled.'

'Good. Di, I was wondering...'

'Fire ahead,' Diane said as Anthea hesitated. 'Do you want a day off to do some shopping?'

'It's not that. I had a word with Mr Parkins at the begining of the week about moving into

Haisby. When the snow starts I'll be lucky to get in every day, you know how it is.'

'No, I don't,' Diane said honestly. Her knowledge of Norfolk winters was confined to old stories of her mother's skating exploits. 'Are they worse than the London sort?'

'I believe so,' Anthea admitted.

'But I thought you'd decided not to buy until you'd sold?' Diane said, remembering past conversations. 'Have you seen something really nice?'

'No, but Di, do you think your aunts would like a lodger, just until I do sell? Mr Parkins says the estate will pay.'

Diane's face cleared; as soon as Anthea mentioned hard winters all sorts of horrors had reared their heads. She knew very well who would get the blame if Anthea failed to turn up on a Caresse day, for instance!

'The aunts would love a lodger,' she said eagerly. 'They'll give you a special price of course, because you'll be a long-stay, and it would be fun to have you living in Harbour Way. But does this mean I can't come over to your place for my holly and mistletoe?'

'No, indeed. In fact I'm planning a big ''Cheerio'' party,' Anthea said, bright-eyed. 'I'm going to ask *everyone*. We'll have lunch, then go out for the greenery, then have high tea. It'll be my Christmas present to the Arcadians.'

'I'll do the invitations for you,' Diane offered. 'What about the cooking?'

'I'll do most of it, but Martin and Marj both said they'd help, if I'd buy the ingredients,' Anthea assured her. 'And my friend Mollie's going to help me decorate and light the fires and prepare. I'm really looking forward to it.'

CHAPTER THIRTEEN

'You wouldn't think I'd enjoy making mincepies after making them all day yesterday, at Sam's,' Anthea said, rolling out pastry. 'But actually, I love it.'

Anthea and Mollie were in the kitchen at the old vicarage, Mollie perched on a stool watching, Anthea vigorously cooking. The room blazed with heat, for later the guests would arrive and be greeted with mincepies and coffee before they set off to cut greenery. Every room had a fire in the grate, though Anthea suspected most people would congregate in the kitchen, where they would serve the food.

'How many are coming?' Mollie asked now,

starting to spoon mincemeat into the pastry cases as Anthea cut them out. 'Isn't it cold? There are great long icicles hanging down from the shed roof.'

'Yes, I know. Water collects where the gutter's blocked,' Anthea said vaguely, wielding the cutter. 'I don't think more than fifty people will come, but a lot who said they would probably won't after all.'

'Di said you'd asked the poofs who run the Health Club,' Mollie said rather disapprovingly.

'Elf and Andrew? Why not? They're ever so nice. They eat at Sam's often and pop in to see Di, as well.'

'What about Ceri whatsername, the newshound? And the little blonde nurse?'

'They share a flat in Cloister Row. Ceri did a piece about the boutique...they're nice too, Moll.'

'Hmm. Good thing Di told you to say it was a bring-a-bottle party, or you'd be bankrupt.'

'I wouldn't, because I'm only providing coffee,' Anthea said stoutly. 'Just remember, Mollie, that this is my first party and don't try to tell me I can't afford it because it looks as though I jolly well can...did I tell you Mr Parkins has been offered a fabulous sum for the vicarage by a builder who's got planning

301

permission for houses on the garden?'

'Only ten times,' Mollie said affectionately. 'Don't count chickens, old Ant. There's many a slip...'

The partygoers came in groups and in ones and twos. They crowded into the kitchen and wolfed pies and drank coffee. Elf and Andrew turned up first. Andrew was stocky and brown-haired and looked absolutely normal to Anthea but Elf, who was slight, curly-haired and blue-eyed, with the elfish looks which had earned him his nickname, had a good deal of rather feminine charm.

Sam and Martin came, armed with bottles and with food, too. Marj came with her Eric, a hefty young man with a fresh complexion and dark hair. Elias from the bookshop brought his teacher wife, and all the staff from Waves came, faces bright with excitement.

Everyone came. Anthea's original idea of a lunch-party had been abandoned when Diane pointed out that it would mean almost no one could come from the Arcade, so it had turned into an evening do instead. They would cut holly by the light of bicycle torches and lanterns, though when at last they were all fortified by mincepies and coffee, plus nips from assorted bottles, it was seen that the moon was full and the sky clear.

'It's a lovely night,' Diane said, as Anthea led them through the back garden and out of the back gate. She had brought Tufton, who might not be God's gift to women, but who was smitten with her. The Arcade Ogler had presumably left Haisby the day Tony had come visiting, so Diane imagined he had gone back to London. If he's home for Christmas I hope he comes round to ask me out and finds Tufton in the shop, she thought now, taking Tufton's hand as they passed into the narrow lane. It would have been muddy but the sharp frost put a stop to that; the ruts were difficult to walk on but at least one's feet did not sink in.

'It's only a ten-minute walk,' Anthea called encouragingly from the van. She strode ahead, boots planted firmly with each step, the bobble hat which crowned her head rakishly tilted. 'Just up this hill and into the copse and we'll start work.'

Diane smiled to herself as the unwieldy group spread out. Caresse squeaked, 'Isn't this *fun*, Ronnie?' and Ronnie rumbled something about fresh air and the size of the stars. It made Diane look up and Ronnie was right, the stars looked huge tonight, each one seeming to sizzle along in space, heading right for them.

'The mistletoe's in our old orchard,' Anthea

was explaining breathlessly. 'I thought we'd cut that last because it's easy, with the step-ladder. But the holly will take some getting because the berries are always at the top of the tree.'

Tufton put his arm round Diane.

'Here, old girl, when it comes to the top of the tree, I'll give you a lift,' he said in her ear. 'Nice, light little thing you are—no problem.'

Diane thought how Tony would have loved this evening, with the moonlight and the sparkling stars and the cold air like wine. He was a countryman at heart, she had always known it, he would have revelled in this expedition.

Oh Tony, Tony! But any day now he'd be off to Ireland, to his Shelagh and the kids, to a real family Christmas. And would he think of Diane, stuck down here with the aunts? Would he hell! Diane pulled Tufton's head down to her level and kissed his mouth.

'I say!' Tufton exclaimed. 'Oh, Di, I say!'

'Here Sam, you hold the branch...no, if I hold it and you cut...'

'I've got the shears,' Sam said. 'Hold it *low*, Ant, don't waggle it miles above my head!'

'I'm trying...oh, frost keeps falling on my face...do hurry!'

The party had reached the copse and spread out even further. Now, Sam and Anthea struggled over their tree, which not only had the best berries, but which was feet taller than any other holly in the wood. Anthea was tall but weak, Sam was about the same height but strong, and between them they had managed to force down a prince of a branch—nay, a king! It was a wonderful branch with berries the size of cherries.

Now, Anthea put her full weight on it and Sam stood on tiptoe and between them they managed to cut most of the branch until the ground was littered with perfect boughs and they were scratched, glowing and proud.

Presently, laden, the two of them made their way back to the lane, meeting many other couples similarly bound. Mollie joined them, with a walking holly-tree which turned out to be Eric. Marj had disappeared, he said airily, before he had cut nearly enough, and then Mollie had wandered by...

'Why should Marj disappear?' Anthea asked Sam, but found herself shushed. Sam thought he knew why Marj had disappeared, but he did not want trouble and Eric was an aggressive young man. Marj, Sam knew, was probably just being kind.

'She'll turn up,' he said soothingly to

Anthea. 'She's probably back in the kitchen already.'

As it happens, he was more or less right. Marj was not actually in the kitchen but in the butler's pantry where all the bottles had been stacked. She had gone in there with Martin to check that the red wine was breathing, white wine cooling and beer just standing neatly in rows.

How she came to find herself locked in Martin's arms she could not have said but, having got there, she was not at all eager to break free. Warmly, they cuddled and mumbled and in Martin's case at least, pawed hopefully at anything which looked as though it might undo.

Presently they descended to the floor, and found it hard. So Martin stood up, lifted Marj, and carried her into the nearest room with a couch. He dropped her on the cushions and fell on top of her so rapidly that she had little chance of doing more than express slight doubts as to the wisdom of their actions...'Oh Mart, should we...shouldn't we...oh, Mart!'

Many hours of plundering large ladies had prepared Martin for all sorts of obstacles, but he found on this occasion his fingers were all thumbs, that his heart kept beating loudly and that he was anxious not to hurt her. This was a phenomenon which had certainly never occurred before—Martin was always too anxious to get his end away to give a toss whether he caused someone else pain in the process—and it held him up. But Marj was making appreciative noises and suddenly he found he wanted to kiss her almost more than he wanted to get inside that bloody stupid tight sweater. His lips met hers and he saw stars and heard violins and his hands just wanted to hold her, lovingly, not lecherously.

It was all very strange; Martin kissed on and then, with a wriggle, Marj was suddenly curled up on his lap and his fingers found the warm flesh of her tummy. They moved up, finding an obstacle he recognised at once from previous peregrinations...he continued to kiss, and his hand thrust aside the little cotton bra...aaah, at last!

He had forgotten how tiny her breasts must be and for a moment, finding one cupped neatly in the palm of his hand, he felt cheated. But then he moved his hand and felt the nipple harden into a response, her small, apple-shaped breast seeming to thrust itself against his fingers as though asking to be stroked, squeezed...

Martin was only conscious of the woman in his arms, her warm suppleness, her response.

And then she was pushing him away, laughing when he moaned her name and tried to get back to the lovely cosy position he had just un-willingly, vacated.

'Come on, old Mart,' Marj said bracingly. 'The others are back, I can hear Eric's voice. You go through, I'll just nip up to the bathroom and make meself respectable.'

'You are respectable,' Martin whimpered, trying to get his arms round her again. 'Oh, oh...Marj, I must...'

'Not now,' Marj said. She took his face be-tween her hands and shook her head at him, her nose inches from his own. 'Eric's twice your size, sonny-Jim. If he finds out we've been cuddling there'll be hell to pay and I don't want to spoil his evening. See you in a mo.'

'What about my evening?' Martin wailed, getting to his feet and noticing with astonish-ment that he was fully dressed even unto his duffel coat. 'What about spoiling my evening?'

'Your evening? I've made your evening, you duzzy fule!' Marj said and her delighted shout of laughter tumbled down the stairs towards him as she climbed up them.

And Martin, stumbling back towards the kit-chen with his arms full of bottles, realised she was dead right. She had made his evening! It was weird, because though he was fond of her, thought her a real friend, the sort of colleague everyone wants, he had not had the slightest idea that he would find her sexually attractive. I mean how could I, he reasoned with himself, setting the wine out on the table. How could I find a skinny, dark-haired woman attractive? She's flat-chested! Not a melon to her name, not even a lot of bum, she's got a boy's bum really. She isn't my type, not for bonking, she isn't. I should have made a dead-set for Caresse, or for someone with class.

But he had not. What was more, he could have. Everyone was in a Christmas mood, a *giving* mood. Caresse had ditched Ronald and come back to the house earlier, he could easily have suggested that he and Caresse check the wine instead of he and Marj.

You're slipping, he thought crossly now, going back to the pantry for more wine. And there, descending the stairs with her hair brushed out into a soft halo, with her eyes bright as stars and her kissable mouth smiling, was Marj.

It's just Marj, the girl you see every day at work, the girl who lives with a copper and has the loudest laugh in the world, Martin reminded himself desperately. It's only old Marj!

But his unreliable heart gave a great big thump and he knew it didn't matter whether she had lemons or melons. She was...oh hell, she was what he wanted!

He stood right at the foot of the stairs and smiled up at her and she swept past him, just giving his cheek a light caress as she went.

'Eric, where've you been?' she demanded querulously, and her eyes were fixed on someone over Martin's shoulder, someone a good deal taller than Martin. 'I've been looking for you all over—give us a kiss!'

'And she's in love with a boneheaded copper,' Martin said viciously to himself, going back to the pantry for more bottles. He picked one up, wrenched the cork out, tossed it aside and lifted the bottle to his lips.

When he threw the bottle into the bin five minutes later it no longer seemed quite so important that his love—yes his love—was not only indifferent to him but in love with someone else. He would woo her and win her... hick...as soon...jus' as soon as he had the time.

Martin returned unsteadily to the kitchen. He was smiling blissfully, his intentions towards Marj firm in his mind. She was a li'l darlin', that Marj. His Marj. A real gem. Prettiesgirlinnaworl'.

Martin collapsed onto a hard chair, soft as a feather bed in his bemused state, and smiled and smiled.

'It was the best party ever,' Mollie said, smiling at Anthea across the breakfast table. 'No one would ever know it was your first, Ant, you was just like a society hostess, everyone seemed special. Want some more toast?'

'No thanks, I'm full,' Anthea said. She and Mollie were finishing breakfast, though it was past noon. 'I'm going to bag up all the leftovers and share them out between me and your mum. I won't be here long enough to eat all those pies and things.'

'You move into Harbour Way in a few days, of course. Tell you what, Ant, why don't you leave here with me tomorrow morning and stay with us until you're due to move in with Di? I'll help you pack.'

'That would be lovely,' Anthea said gratefully. 'There isn't much clearing up to do here and if you're sure your mother won't mind me staying we'll go up now and dress and pack. Tell you what, tonight will be our last night, so we'll light a fire in the bedroom. As a treat.'

'All right,' Mollie said. 'I'll have another bit of toast if there's some left. The food went down well last night, didn't it? Never seen people eat like it.'

'Picking holly's hungry work,' Anthea observed. 'I've finished, so I'll go and lay the fire in our room.'

'I'll come too, I can eat as I work,' Mollie said. The two girls went upstairs, Anthea with kindling and coal. When the fire was laid and lit, they began the onerous task of getting all Anthea's possessions out of the old-fashioned wardrobe and chest of drawers and putting them into black bin-bags.

'There isn't much,' Anthea said at last, having filled a bag. 'A lot of this isn't even fit for a jumble sale.'

'I'll have that soft Viyella stuff for dusters,' Mollie said practically. 'Oh damn, look at the fire!'

Their lovely fire was little more than glowing ash.

'We'll fill a couple of buckets so that we can keep it going all day and all night as well,' Anthea said as they hurried down the stairs. They had reached the hall by now and Anthea bent to pick up the bucket which stood by the cellar door. 'Goodness, I'm going to have to eat less, it was hard work bending to shovel coal for the party-fires.'

'You aren't fat,' Mollie said. 'You unlock and make sure the torch is okay whilst I fetch the other bucket.'

'Hurry up, then,' Anthea said, unbolting the cellar door. She shone the torch; it looked pale and comfortless in the sunny hall, but gleamed gold when she turned it on the cellar's depths. The stairs were steep but whitewashed so it was light enough to see where you trod. Anthea began to descend, keeping a wary eye out for spiders or rats, but saw neither. At the bottom she only had to take a couple of steps and there was the coal, a huge heap of it.

The shovel the girls had used the previous day leaned against the wall. Anthea picked it up and began to dig. She had half-filled her bucket before she heard, faintly, Mollie's footsteps coming back across the hall.

'I'm using the old chicken bucket,' Mollie called as she reached the head of the cellar steps. 'I'm just coming...'

A gurgling scream came from the cellar, bringing goose pimples out all over Mollie, causing the hair on her head to start upright. She dropped the bucket, fortunately only on the top step where it stayed, rocking.

'Ant? What is it? Have you seen a rat? Ant!'

She leaned through the doorway, trying to see into the dark. Anthea was backing across the cellar, away from the coal. Every stiff, stumbling backwards step spoke of a terror so great that Mollie was rooted to the spot.

'Ant! What's the matter? What happened?'

Anthea had reached the bottom step. She was

coming up towards Mollie, still backwards, but now she reached out a long, coal-daubed hand and pointed.

'Loo-ook, loo-ook,' she moaned. Her voice was not her own, it was higher, shriller, with panic crisping it. 'Loo-ook!'

Mollie crept down the steps until she was on the same one as Anthea and followed her pointing finger. There on the floor by the coal lay the torch where her friend had dropped it. And illuminated by the light, flung out, fingers still half-curled, lay a hand.

Neither girl knew how they got up the rest of the stairs and back into the hall. Mollie remembered slamming and bolting the door to the cellar and putting her arms round Anthea.

'It can't be what it looked like,' she kept insisting. 'It's old rubbish—a glove, that's it! One of them plastic gloves people wear to pick up coal, that's got left down there. We'll look tomorrow, Ant, but it's only an old glove.'

'He's under the coal,' Anthea whimpered. 'Under the coal! He's been here all the time, Moll, lying under that coal. That's why Tibby wouldn't live here any more, she knew. Cats know things like that. He must have come in at night, thinking he could get me by sneaking up the cellar steps and into the house.

314

Only the cellar door was bolted and he couldn't get in...' she clutched Mollie's arm '...and he couldn't get out, either, because the chute's awfully steep. And he died there, walled up, alive!'

The last word was a shriek. Mollie grabbed her friend and shook her, then slapped her face hard. Then she put her arm round Anthea's shoulders and led her out of the hall and into the kitchen.

There, she poured milk into a cup, added a generous tot of rum and a dash of hot water, then watched as Anthea sipped, choked, and finally drained the cup.

'Better?'

'Yes.,..no!' Anthea caught Mollie's hand in a convulsive grip. 'You think I'm mad but I *knew* it, that he was there, under the coal. That night...I heard bumping, a lot of noise. I knew he was trying to get in, he was very cunning, he would have thought of the coal chute into the cellars as soon as he saw the trap-door. I heard banging...but the thunder was making such a din...he must have been crashing his fists on the door to try to make me let him out. But I was ill, Moll, from all the stuff he'd given me, I didn't know, didn't understand...so he died in that horrible way!'

'If it really was a...what we thought, then it'll

315

be some old tramp,' Mollie said uneasily. 'If it is that Chris fellow, Ant, you'd better forget you ever knew him. You didn't have nothing to do with his death, he got in there and got killed and that's the truth.'

'I must find out,' Anthea said looking wildly about her. 'I'll have to go down there again; I must know if it's him...I'm sure it's him!'

She turned and before Mollie could stop her she had hurried out of the kitchen and across the hall. Mollie, in hot pursuit, saw her swing back the heavy door, take a step—and disappear. Horrified, Mollie heard her friend's body thumping from step to step as she crashed down into the cellar.

'Ant!' The torch still lay by the coal, but now against its light Mollie could see her friend's body, suddenly small and crumpled. She ran down the stairs intent on reaching Anthea and getting her out of that incriminating cellar. She would drag her upstairs and call a doctor at once!

However, Anthea came round seconds after Mollie arrived in the cellar and proved to have a lot of bruises and possibly a broken arm. The two girls staggered up the steps and Mollie rang the doctor, who arranged for an ambulance to take Anthea to the hospital for x-rays. Mollie had time to remind Anthea that she must say she had fallen down the house-stairs and not the cellar ones before the ambulance men came in and carried her off.

When she had the house to herself once more, Mollie locked the doors, got the big lantern from the shed, and unbolted the cellar door, stealing down the stairs with a thumping heart.

Ten minutes later she came up the stairs again. She was white, and once she gagged and put a hand to her mouth. Then she went into the kitchen and put the kettle on. A nice cup of tea might not take away the memory of what she had found under the coal, but it would make her feel a bit better, might even help her to decide what to do.

She had not known the man but he was youngish, with thick, dark hair. He wore an Army combat jacket, blue jeans and black lace-up shoes.

The kettle boiled and Mollie made tea. As she drank she racked her brains. What to do? What to do?

'Well, Ant, Sister say you've no broken bones but they're keeping you in overnight for observation, because you were concussed.' Mollie, who had breezed up the ward with her eyes fixed on her friend and a big smile on her face, sat down on the coverlet and leaned close. 'Here you are, nightie, washing things, all nice and ready for you.'

It had taken Mollie a lot of hard thinking to solve the problem of the cellar but now all she needed was a quiet word with Anthea. Her initial feeling, when she saw that her friend was in a small ward with only four beds, had been dismay, until she noticed that the other inmates were all very old. Then she touched Anthea's arm and the two heads got close.

'Ant, you haven't said anything, have you? Only that you fell?'

'I told them you'd given me rum and milk to keep out the cold and I fell downstairs,' Anthea said, her pale face breaking into a smile.

'That's great. Look, I checked the cellar.'

Anthea's smile disappeared and Mollie could see horror dawning once more in the mild eyes.

'Don't worry, but I had to make sure. I think you're right and it was the guy who beat you up. But I doubt he's recognisable. So I've worked out a plan. Sister wants to keep you here for a couple of days and you'll be staying with me when you come out. I rang your Mr Parkins and he says the deal's been completed and you'd have had to move out soon anyway, because the builder's going to knock it down.'

'Knock it down? Oh, yes,' Anthea said fervently. 'And I'll have money to buy a little place of my own.'

'Yes. But Ant, you could just walk out and let the buyer flatten the place.'

Mollie paused hopefully, to see Anthea's head shaking, her expression managing to be both timid and mulish.

'No, it wouldn't be the right thing to do. We must tell the police.'

'All right, I thought that was how you'd feel so I worked out a plan. When you go back to your house to pick up some stuff we'll "discover" the body then, and ring the police. We'll say the guy must have broken in whilst you were in hospital.'

'He's under the coal I had delivered in October,' Anthea said with a shudder. 'They'll know he's been there at least that long.'

'Yes, I forgot. But he's a stranger, a tramp, right? We'll say he must have broken in whilst you were staying with me in September and let it go at that. It's the truth, more or less.'

'There was a tramp actually, quite a young fellow,' Anthea said, remembering. 'He was asleep in the bike shed. But it isn't him down there, it's...it's that other one. I've never seen him since the day he attacked me and besides, I think I've known he was dead because I

319

wasn't scared that he'd come back, not after that night. It was the way I felt after my father died, that he'd gone completely.'

'Okay. But you'll play it my way, Ant? Please?'

'Of course. But goodness knows how I'll get through two days here,' Anthea said, shifting uncomfortably on the hard mattress. 'I'm starving hungry and all they've given me is a teeny little bit of toast and some tea.'

Mollie laughed.

'I can tell you're better when you start thinking about food,' she said. 'Now I'll go and explain to Di that you're in hospital and won't be at work for a few days. I'll come and see you again tomorrow.'

In a way, Anthea's being in hospital did Mollie a good turn; she found herself with a temporary job which might well last over the Christmas period. She helped out at the wine bar, waitressing mostly, she stood in for Caresse and for Archie, and Diane was really glad of her help in the boutique, for with the approach of the festive season the shops were busy from morning till night.

Because of this, Mollie decided to do Anthea a good turn, too. She would 'discover' the body herself, going back to the old vicarage

320

ostensibly to get some more stuff for her friend. She would go in full daylight of course, on a Wednesday afternoon when she was not wanted in the Arcade. Thus Anthea would be protected from her own pointless honesty and the mad desire to confess to being involved, for Mollie was well aware that if asked straight out whether she had known the dead man, Anthea would not be able to lie.

On the bus, however, joggling towards Little Meltan, it did occur to Mollie that though she had a first-rate excuse for her visit—collecting Anthea's coat and boots for her release from hospital next day—it might be slightly harder to get anyone to believe that she had had to visit the cellar in order to light a fire for her short stay.

However, the moment she entered the vicarage she realised that a fire would be necessary to air Anthea's thick wool coat. You could almost see the damp rising, surfaces were dulled by it, even the mirror on the hall wall showed a blurred reflection as she passed.

As much to comfort herself as for its light she clicked the hall switch down. She was halfway up the flight and telling herself that she would get the clothing together before she visited the cellar when there was an enormous crash followed by a scream which rivalled the one Anthea had given on making her own discovery a few days before.

Heart thumping deafeningly, Mollie rushed down the stairs, pausing a few feet across the hallway. The noise was coming from the cellar! Awful pictures flashed across her mind from a surfeit of horror films on the telly. He had come alive! A ghastly, rotting figure, he was even now thundering on the door, seeking revenge!

Someone was certainly thundering on the door and a voice could now be made out, its notes cracking with terror.

'Lemme out, lemme out...oh, my Gawd, I never done it, I never seen anything like it...lemme out!'

The door shuddered beneath the blows but the bolts were strong. Whoever was on the other side of the door would have to stay there until Mollie decided to open up. Unless, of course, it really was a ghost. But a ghost would have appeared through the door and wouldn't have banged or shouted.

Mollie put her mouth close to the door.

'Shut up! I can't let you out for a moment, I've lost the key,' she lied. 'Hang on whilst I fetch help.'

'What? Wiv *that* down there in the dark, a-grinnin' at me? Oh, my Gawd, my Gawd...'

Mollie left him wailing and ran out of the house, down the path and onto the road. She could see the new vicarage from here and headed towards it, but luckily her hatless, coatless rush did not go unnoticed. A small mini drew up beside her.

'You all right, Miss? That's a cold old day to be a-runnin' round with no coat.'

A country bobby, red-faced, cheerful, squeezed behind the wheel of his little car.

'Oh, officer, there's a feller in the cellar of my friend's house...she's coming out of hospital tomorrow so I was just...'

'Hop in,' the policeman said. 'Which house would that be? I'll sort 'im out for you, Miss.'

'The old vicarage,' Mollie panted. She climbed into the passenger seat and collapsed, her breath steaming on the chilly air. 'I don't know how he got into the cellars but he's banging and screeching...he scared me stiff, I said I'd go for help because I'd lost the key but it's only bolted really...I just wanted someone with me.'

'He's bin coal stealin', I daresay,' the policeman said comfortably. 'That's a popular sport, this time o' year. Usually they nips in and out and no one any the wiser. I reckon the chute musta broke so he can't git out.'

'I don't know,' Mollie said as the car screeched to a halt outside the gate. The door still stood open and the two of them walked up the path and into the house. Mollie pointed to the cellar door. 'He's down there,' she said.

The sound of her voice galvanised the trapped one into action once more and he shouted, following this with a series of blows to the stout wooden door.

'Stop that!' the policeman said sharply. 'Who's that down there?'

There was a pause whilst the trapped one obviously considered the wisdom or otherwise of giving his name.

'What's that matter who I am?' he said sullenly at last. 'Let me out or I'll hev this bloody door flat! Hev you any idea what's down here under that coal?'

'No, and nor should you have if it's under the coal,' the policeman said reproachfully. 'That sound remarkable like Dickie Roberts to me.'

'Oh! Is that you, Fred?'

'That's me.' The policeman began to heave at the big old bolts. 'This here door in't often used,' he observed to Mollie and then, to the prisoner, 'stand back, lad.'

The door opened inwards, showing the terrified, coal-streaked face and bulging blue eyes of a man in his twenties, thin and agile, wearing dirty grey gym shoes on his feet and a filthy boiler suit. He bolted out of the cellar as soon as the door opened but Fred caught his arm.

'Come on, Dickie, you were trespassing with intent to steal coal, but you scared the wits outer this young woman! Why all the racket, eh? Why din't you just take some coal and go?'

'I came down the chute, didn't I?' Dickie said sulkily. 'I meant to leave the lid up but it fell down. Made that way, I reckon; the old vicar was that mean...and then, when I saw 'im under the coal I dropped my torch and it broke and I couldn't see no light 'cept under that door, there.' He pointed to the cellar door behind him. 'I'd hev gone up that chute like lightning do I could see it, I'd hev forced the trap up, but all I thought was to get away from...' he jerked a thumb towards the cellar steps.

'Why? What did you think you saw?' The policeman peered into the dark. 'In't there no light down there, no electric?'

'I don't think so,' Mollie said, 'Anthea keeps a torch in the drawer of the kitchen dresser, though. Shall I fetch it?'

Fred agreed so she ran out and came back in time to hear Dickie describing, in lurid detail, what he had dug out of the coal.

'...a feller's *head*, that was...can you wonder

I shruck out? All black an' mouldy with staring eyes...wait till you see it, that's all.'
Dickie's shudder was genuine.

'Here's the torch,' Mollie said, pushing it
into Fred's hand. 'Do you want me to go with
you?'

'No, Dickie and me'll go together,' the
policeman said. Dickie began to protest that
he would sooner die, but the officer of the law
would have none of it.

'You're under arrest, my lad,' he pointed
out. 'I aren't leavin' you up here whilst I go
down there.' He turned to Mollie. 'On second
thoughts, Miss, would you care to hold the
torch for me? I'll need both hands for Dickie
by the looks of it.'

So the three of them crept down the cellar
steps with Mollie shining the torch ahead of
her, prepared to show horror and shock at what
the beam would presently illuminate.

She did not have to act; the sight which met
her eyes was made worse by the fact that Dickie
had clearly not even seen the hand but had attacked the pile of coal from a different angle
and had virtually had the head on his shovel
before he realised just what he was digging out
of the glistening lumps. No wonder he had
shrieked and fled!

'Yes,' Fred said, after a pause during which

Dickie moaned and Mollie held the torch steady but kept her face averted. 'Yes, he's dead all right. Been so some while, I'd say.' He spoke into that little box clipped to his top pocket which had squawked and rumbled away once or twice, unheeded until now. 'This is 492, I'm at the old vicarage in Little Meltan; there's a body in the cellar here, been dead a while. Can you send someone out, please?'

'They came and showed me a photograph,' Anthea said next day. 'It could have been anyone, but it was him.'

'Did you say so?' Mollie was sitting on Anthea's hospital bed but now Anthea was sitting on it as well. 'You didn't say so did you, Ant?'

'Yes, I did. I said it looked like a man called Chris Bowles who came down the Arcade sometimes. But I'm afraid they probably thought I was—well, remarking on a resemblance rather than identifying him. Only at least they've got a name, now.' She looked piteously at Mollie. 'How could I let some poor woman go on hoping he's alive when he's dead, Moll? Or let someone who's scared of him go on being scared?'

'So the police hadn't been informed that Chris Bowles was missing?' Mollie said thoughtfully. 'That say a lot, that do. I reckon if you disappear and aren't missed, then the world's a better place. Now we'll forget him. I brought you some brochures from the house-agents, so you can start thinking about buying again.'

'That'll be fun,' Anthea said. She was fully dressed and ready to go. 'It's straight to Harbour Way, then? I'm really looking forward to staying there and going back to work! Oh, I'm so glad it's over, Moll, and no one any the worse!'

CHAPTER FOURTEEN

The sea in winter. Sometimes calm and silver, as though iced over by the frost which gripped the land. Or blue even, beneath a clear winter sky. But today it was all grey and white, broken up into waves which dashed in every direction, driven by a fitful and gusty wind which at times blew sand and spume up onto the promenade and then, all in a moment, reversed itself and blew them back into the angry waves.

I've never lived by the sea before so I never knew what I was missing, Diane mused, walking back towards the town. I love it, yet nonetheless there's a part of me that misses the big city, dirt, impersonality and all.

Christmas had come and gone with parties, kisses and presents. The Arcade had opened until ten every Thursday and Friday evening and everyone had done good business, in fact by Christmas Eve Diane had been down to a suede suit so expensive that she was sure it would never sell and a cerise model gown which made most people look ridiculous. She had sold them both on that afternoon and gone into Sam's in a state of euphoria with a thousand pounds in the till and wall to wall smiles, to find the restaurant crammed, the staff rushed off their feet, and Martin making what looked like yards of pancakes whilst Marj fried chips in the chipper, poached eggs in the pan, and hotted up beans in the microwave.

They had all mucked in then. Diane had waited on and enjoyed it, with Anthea cooking alongside Sam and Marj and Mollie rushing back and forth whilst Martin continued to produce perfect pancakes finer than lace which the customers ate joyously.

It was as she rushed across the restaurant with a plateful of pancakes that Diane saw the Arcade Ogler again. He was peering in through her window as though hoping to see her inside.

Ha! Diane thought triumphantly, well, he can jolly well wait until I'm through here. But he hadn't. He'd gone, and she'd had two brandies with Sam and Martin and wished everyone a merry Christmas and then reeled home to the aunts with a frightful headache and gone early to bed.

So now, with the holiday over, Diane went into her empty shop and sat on the counter swinging her legs and wondering what she should do about the January sale.

She would have to have a sale, of course. Sam told her that it deferred the suicide months for everyone, did a sale, and she had promised blithely that her sale would be the best yet. Well, so it would, but the only way to get good clothes quickly would be to rush up to London whilst the warehouses were putting out their own winter stock at minuscule prices.

What was more, she told herself now, battling against the wind, I need something special for my spring window, another Mona dress. Whilst I'm in town I can call on her, she's bound to have just what I want. And she would see Tony. Just meet for a chat, nothing more. Tufton had turned out to be worthy but unbearably boring so that her last meeting with Tony, which had ended almost in a quarrel, had seemed amusing by comparison.

Poor Tony! He missed her terribly, swore he would never love anyone the way he loved her, but he had been unable to resist what she thought of as cheap jibes, so they had parted ruffled. He had gone back to Ireland for the holiday but would be in London again by now.

It would take some arranging, her trip. But she would beg Anthea's services for the whole week which would mean visiting the others when the shops opened again after the holiday.

'First you foist her on me, then you drag her off,' Caresse grumbled when she was asked to give up Anthea the following week. 'She's an odd girl but she has her uses—did you see her window? I was quite cross actually, because the window's my *thing*, but Ronnie thinks it's good so I let it stand.'

'It's a super window,' Diane said, looking down on it from above. 'Unusual. I like the loofahs.' She did not admit that the idea behind the display had been her own for it would only annoy Caresse. 'Where did she get all the bits and pieces in the background?'

Caresse shrugged and bit into a peach. She was trying to lose a bit of weight but since she seemed to think that eating peaches as well as marshmallows constituted a diet, Diane did not think much of her chances of success.

331

'God knows. She said something about ordering the loofahs from a salesman and she found the pumice stones round the back, but how she managed to make the whole thing look like an aquarium full of tropical fish I don't know. Still, it amused her.'

Diane gritted her teeth; she could not argue, Caresse would neither forgive nor forget. After a pause, Diane said cautiously, 'Well? If you have Ant for two days this week, can I have her for your day next week?'

'I suppose so. I usually re-do my window each week...' Diane blinked at this blatant lie, '...but as we're so quiet I'll leave it until after your sale. Kiddies like the fish scene, I must say.'

Despite herself, Caresse sounded pleased. And so she should, Diane thought, considering what a superb display if was. Anthea's wasted on us, she thought guiltily now, she listens to what you say, carries the idea in her mind's eye and manages to produce just what you saw in your head. That is a rare gift.

'Thanks very much, Caresse; how's Ronnie?'

'He's buggered off to Paris,' Caresse said, tightlipped. 'I wanted to go too, but he said I mustn't leave the shop!'

'How unkind,' Diane said feebly. 'Why not?

You could have had Anthea or Mollie for a few days.'

'Yes, I told him that, and he just said the business couldn't afford it. And need money, Di, he does *not*, he's stinking rich.'

'And if you remind him I bet he says he didn't get stinking rich by backing losers,' Diane said shrewdly.

'How did you know? That's amazing!'

'Yes, well,' Diane said. She opened the door and slid into the Arcade. 'Got to go, Caresse, but thanks very much.'

Walking up the Arcade towards Archie's, Diane guessed that a shrewd businessman like Ronnie would have begun to realise he'd picked a bad'un in Treat Yourself and Caresse. She was all talk and no do, but she had probably spun him some yarn about previous experience and natural ability which had fooled his dazzled eyes. Not so dazzled now, evidently, if he was refusing his pink sugar-lady a trip to Paris!

It would be bad if Treat Yourself went, though. Diane decided she would nag Caresse, get her to pull her socks up, then reached the antique shop and opened the door. Archie was snoozing behind the counter, head resting on an old cushion. He woke as she entered though and came to all of a piece, as a soldier should. His eyes opened and he seemed at once entirely awake, not snatching his feet off the counter or trying to pretend he had not been asleep, as some would have done.

'Hel-*lo*, young Diane; caught me napping,' he observed, standing up in a lithe fashion which belied his seventy years. 'What can I do for you?'

Her errand was soon explained and Archie was happy to let Anthea go for his day next week.

'She's an odd gal,' he said, picking up a duster and rubbing a Georgian teapot. 'Quiet, but very pleasant. Got a real feel for old stuff, too. Seen her stroking things sometimes, you can see she loves 'em. People buy from someone quiet.'

The next on Diane's list was Sam's. Anthea was there and knowing Diane's errand, made herself scarce, saying she had to put the shopping away and clumping off down the cellar stairs with Mollie.

Martin stopped making bread and leaned on the long dresser which ran the breadth of the kitchen. Sam was doing the books upstairs, he said, if Diane wanted a special word.

'It's more with you, Mart, really,' Diane said. 'I want to steal Anthea off you next week, so I can go to London. Will it be terribly inconvenient? I'll be back Friday afternoon, so it'll just be for the five weekdays. And you can have her tomorrow as well as today this week.'

'That'll be all right, then,' Martin said easily. 'She does a lot of cooking for the delivery business you know, and she never stops working. Pity she won't wait on but she's certainly first-rate at cakes and pastry, nearly as good as me. Yes, we'll manage next week.'

Diane thanked him and hurried back to the boutique. It was always quiet between Christmas and the start of the sales so she settled down behind her counter to cash up, book up and then go home. When she was ready to leave she actually played with the idea of ringing Tufton. She did not feel like being talked at by the aunts all evening. On the other hand she was off to London next week, and the thought of the aunts, alone all day, made her sorry she had even considered defection. Besides, Anthea would be there, sharing the task of being talked at. She would go home.

She was glad when she walked into the hall to be met by a bright-eyed Aunt Violet.

'We had a telephone call from London for you, dear, not five minutes ago. He tried the shop but just missed you, and he said would you call back.'

Diane thanked her and went to the phone. It was Tony—who else would ring her from

London?—and besides, several times they had remarked on a sort of telepathy which meant that if one was thinking of the other, the other would get in touch. So it stood to reason that it would be Tony ringing now, conjured up by her thoughts, her mixed and muddled desires.

As she dialled she was amused to see Aunt Violet making her way slowly towards the kitchen and Aunt Dulcie mounting the stairs at a snail's pace. Poor dears, they did love to know!

'Hello, Di.'

He had known it would be she; but that was nothing but commonsense. He had asked her to ring back, hadn't he? Yet she was unwillingly impressed.

'Tony, my aunt said you'd rung.'

'That's it. I was wonderin', me darlin' girl, whether you'd be comin' to Town for the warehouse sales?'

More telepathy? Or more commonsense?

'Umm...yes, probably.'

'Next week?'

'I think so. From Tuesday through until Friday.'

'Wonderful.' The old magic was almost at work. Almost, but not quite. A cool, detached part of Diane's mind was standing back saying suspiciously. 'What's he plotting?' Tony never did anything which, in the end, wasn't to his advantage.

'Why, Tony? Are you buying too?'

He laughed. Barkworths did not buy in for the January sales; they had huge warehouses to store stuff in.

'No. Darlin' Di, 'tis lonely for you I am. Can we meet?'

'I don't know, I'm going to be pretty busy.'

'You'll have plenty of time in the evenings.' When she did not immediately answer he said anxiously, 'You're comin' alone, aren't you?'

'Yes, I am. But I've been going out with someone else, sometimes.'

'Me too,' Tony said mournfully. 'Me, too.'

Diane felt mean rage engulf her. Him too? What did he mean? He was a married man, he had no right to take another mistress? She had kept out of his life because he was married, and he knew she was right. She forgot the still-open kitchen door and Aunt Dulcie hovering. All she could think of was the pain she had suffered during their months apart.

'Tony Cusack, can you look me in the face and tell me...'

'Darlin' girl, I'm not lookin' you in the face, but I'm hopin' to do so before I take a step we may both regret. I'll meet your train. What time does it get in?'

'Nine-thirty,' Diane snapped and put the phone down. How dared he? How could he? She would tell him what she thought of him, she would say she and Tufton were lovers... oh, how could he?

'Everything all right, dear?'

Aunt Violet popped out of the kitchen, a wooden spoon in one hand. Curiosity glowed from her.

'Yes, fine. My boss from Barkworths wants to see me whilst I'm in Town. He's meeting my train.'

'Yes, the nine-thirty,' Aunt Violet said. 'You sounded very *cross* dear. Don't you like him?'

'Not much,' Diane said, and made an amazing discovery. She did not like Tony much. She had loved him, sometimes she thought she loved him still, she certainly lusted after him, but she did not really like him. It occurred to her for the first time that love and liking should go hand in hand, that she should have liked Tony and not simply adored him.

But it was supper and Anthea was coming downstairs. Diane rushed up them, to change. Soul-searching must come later.

Diane got into the taxi, so cold and angry that she could hardly think straight. The driver shot back his little window and stared at her and she

338

realised she had simply leapt into his cab and had not yet given him her destination.

The address of the flat was on her mind, of course, which was why she snapped it out, but as soon as she said it she regretted it. Tony had stood her up, so what? She should simply go to her hotel, get into bed, and forget him. Still, she had given the driver the address and it wasn't far from her hotel. She would walk the rest of the way. She wondered what sort of an excuse he would offer for leaving her hanging about on an icy platform in the depths of January. It had better be good!

She got out of the taxi and looked up at the flat for a long time, but although she had her key she turned away. She knew that if she went in now she'd find Tony in bed with some... some trollop. No, she would go to her hotel.

She was very tired, too. She found the hotel and booked in, then went to her room and got into bed.

It was a long while before she slept.

At ten next morning she was at the flats. He'll be at work and so will *she* be, she told herself, climbing the stairs. It's not nosiness exactly, it's just that I want to know what happened to him yesterday, she said to her conscience, putting her key in the lock. He had not changed the Yale; her key opened it easily.

She stood in the hall, rooted to the spot for several moments by memories and by the great rush of painful nostalgia which attacked her as soon as the door swung open. It was...the same! Honey-blonde carpet, the japanned table they had picked up in the Portobello Road, the old Jacobean chair with its carved back and big, square seat, the cushion still indented by the last sitter.

No flowers. But Diane's still-life which she had painted in Art school. Tony must have kept it because it went with the decor, there could be no other reason.

So the hall was unchanged: what about the living room? Diane opened the cream-painted door cautiously, as though it might bite, but it just hid...

Chaos. Cups on the mantelpiece, plates balanced on occasional tables. Crusts on plates, drink in cups, dregs in glasses. She crossed to the kitchen, which opened off the living room. More chaos. Dirty crockery everywhere, unwashed clothes in heaps, the cooker layered in stale food.

The window panes were filthy, the plants dead, the sink itself so rimed and grimed with grease that she shuddered. The washing machine was pulled out as if for action but someone had given up on it halfway and the little window showed mouldy from washing which had been left to its own devices for weeks.

She's a slut, Diane thought. A slut! But she knew she was hitting out at a phantom because no woman would have let such a state of affairs happen, or not the sort of woman Tony would choose. Was he ill? Had he let the flat to someone else? Even a wild party would not have had such a result.

Diane left the kitchen and walked across to the bedroom, then stopped. This more than any other room in the flat, was their room. It was in here...if this room was like the others...

Diane opened the door and went in.

He lay on the bed, smoking. He had what looked like a three-day growth of beard and his face was hollow, grey-skinned. He did not look round when the door opened but continued to stare up at the spiral of smoke which curled towards the ceiling. Only her shocked whisper brought his head round.

'Tony! Dear God, what's happened?'

He stared. The cigarette dropped from the corner of his mouth, on the point of falling onto the sheet.

'Di? Oh Di, me darlin' girl, what...where...?'

'You said you'd meet me last night...what's happened, Tony? Are you ill? Why aren't you at work?'

He sat up and rubbed his eyes, then pinched out the glowing cigarette and flung the stub to the floor; Diane winced.

'Last night? Oh, but 'tis tonight I'm meetin' you, my heart's love! By tonight I would've... Dear God, 'tis a fine mess I'm in.'

He lurched to his feet and crossed the room, pulling her into his arms. He smelt of sweat and dirty socks and when he kissed her his mouth felt unsure, his skin painfully bristly. But he was Tony and it was still magic to be in his arms, nothing would change that. Nevertheless she kept the embrace short, pushing him away quickly.

'It was last night, so I came round and used my key...I just wanted to look at the place, see what...I wish I hadn't, Tony! What's happened. Is it drink?'

Tony shook his head, clinging to her. He squeezed her convulsively; she could feel the tremble running through him.

'I stink—you mean, but 'tis not the drink, me darlin' girl, as well you should know. I cant live wit'out you, Di, and that's the truth.' He steered her towards the door which led to their bathroom. 'Come and talk to me whilst I clean up, me darlin'...'

They reached the bathroom and she saw he was in tears. Crying. A grown man. Great sobs shook him whilst he tried to explain, but all he could do was cry like a five-year-old.

Diane sat him on the bathroom stool and applied a wetted flannel to his eyes and washed the dirt from his face. Then she put her arms round him and laid her soft cheek against his bristly one.

'We'll work it out,' she crooned, smoothing his hair away from his hot forehead. 'We'll work it out, me darlin' boy.'

Three hours later, with Tony and the flat both clean once more, Diane made a decision. She took him to a quiet little restaurant they knew and talked to him, putting her own feelings into perspective and making him see what he was doing to them both.

'We're both having a hard time, Tony, building a life for ourselves without the other, but we'll only succeed if we're whole-hearted about it. I've been a fool, telling myself that you were a part of my past, but all the time I've been waiting for the moment when it got too hard and I let myself collapse back into being your lover again. You've been the same, telling yourself that it was just Shelagh and you now, against the world, but you haven't done the obvious thing. You haven't brought her over to London or gone back to Ireland for good, and that's the only way, my love, because you aren't the sort of guy who can manage alone. You need someone to share your life with, whether you call her your wife or mistress... Do you see?'

'And the answer wouldn't be for you to come back to me?'

Diane laughed but shook her head chidingly.

'Indeed it would not! Shelagh's your real love, her and the kids. You've got to get them over here, or you'll have to go back to them, but you aren't made for celibacy and separation. And you aren't too good at casual affairs, I take it?'

'That I'm not. It's either yourself or Shelagh and perhaps I've known it all along but didn't like to admit it. Shameful, it seemed, to need a woman like that.'

'Well, it's not,' Diane said robustly. 'If you were to ask Shelagh, she'd probably tell you it was her duty to be with her man as well as her pleasure. What's it to be? Bring Shelagh to London or go back and be a farmer, like your Da?'

He stared at her across the table but she did

344

not think he saw her; he was seeing the farm-yard, the rolling green acres of his native land, his kids coming shouting in at the gate after school. Could he ask them to give it up, live in the big city? Or would he become that other Tony, the one with a sack round his shoulders and big wellies on his feet, tramping his land, nurturing his stock?

But Diane knew it did not matter what he did. Whichever way he chose he could be hap-py, and though he was no longer necessary to her happiness, she wanted his life to be good. She had realised, all in a moment, the truth of what she had just told Tony. That because he was there, waiting, she had not bothered with other relationships, had thought in the confus-ed way one does, that the separation and pain would be what she had to pay for the joys of illicit love when she returned to Tony once more. And she knew now that her love for Tony, which had been real and honest, had also been rose-tinted first-love, which was wearing thin as life took her in hand. And Tony must have been in love with the idea of having two women when the usual ration was one. The idea of a greedy little boy with a lollipop in either hand hurt, but was at least honest. It was hard to reduce what they had shared to this, to put tabs on emotions, tidying them away into yesterday's files, a temporary foolishness of youth. But it was safer, too.

Now, Tony sighed.

'Me darlin' girl...I'll do as you say. Sure and I don't know which way we'll jump, me and Shelagh, but we'll jump together. Is that it? Is that what you're wantin' me to do?'

'It's what you've got to do,' Diane said. She leaned forward and over the table their lips met in a gentle farewell kiss. 'I'll miss you, Tony, but you're doing the right thing. Be happy.'

Tony's hand cupped her chin for a moment, then rubbed along her jawbone in a caress she remembered well.

'We'll not be meetin' again.'

'No. Unless it's by chance, I suppose.'

Tony shook his head, his eyes dark.

'No indeed. We'll say goodbye now, for you'll not be wantin' to come back to the flat.'

Diane looked at him through a blur of tears, though she would not let them fall. He had made his decision, chosen which way his life would go, and she was no longer a part of it. She saw that he had grown up at last, that he was now in truth a married man with four children. He would no longer need her to take care of him because now, for the first time, he would be taking care of his family.

Tony stood up. He looked very tall and dark,

very handsome. Diane stood up too, but he shook his head at her, motioning her back to her seat. She knew he was near tears and did not want to shame himself by weeping.

'Goodbye, me darlin' girl,' he whispered, then turned on his heel so quickly that she doubted if he heard her murmured goodbye.

Diane stayed in her seat, wet-eyed but content, and watched him leave her for the last time.

On her last full day, Diane decided to visit Mona's Modes again. Despite the harrowing parting with Tony she had done well in the sales, and felt a lightness of spirit which she had not known for many months. It was as though Tony had been a physical weight, holding her down. She had loved him, but his very existence had prevented her from seriously considering other relationships, and now she was free from the shackles of their combined past, she would stop being a fool and start going forward instead of marking time.

But I shan't fall in love again, she told herself as she reached the corner of Mona's alley. Not twice I won't. Next time I'll enjoy all the good things without believing that anything's for ever.

She walked on and there was the little shop.

She pushed the door open and entered.

Immediately she saw things had changed. The place was clean and tidy, the floor covered in smart tiles. It smelt of air freshener instead of tobacco.

Whilst Diane was staring the door at the back opened and a woman came through. For a moment she thought it was Mona but then she realised that this was a younger person, though she had Mona's thinness and huge, black-rimmed eyes.

'Can I 'elp you?'

'I've come to see Mona about a design. She did one for me back in the summer, and...'

'I'm 'er daughter. What was you thinkin' of?'

'Something striking, for a very small window. Your mother had all the ideas to tell you the truth, I just went along with whatever she suggested.'

The girl sighed.

'That's the trouble, I ain't me mum, for all I look like 'er. Oh, I can print and make up from a pattern, but the shape of a dress...I can't *invent*, you see. Only me mum does that and she's ill.'

'Ill?'

'Yes, in 'ospital. Look, I've got some of 'er

designs, some she did to a pattern before she was took. I'll show 'em to you.'

Half an hour later, Diane realised just what Mona's daughter meant. In the folder of designs she produced half a dozen had been converted to paper patterns and only these could she make up. She was not capable of the leap of imagination which would turn the more dramatic designs into practical garments. And nor am I, Diane told herself, turning away from the spread sheets.

'All right, then if you make up that one...' she pointed, '...in cornflower blue cotton. If you bill it cash on delivery that should be all right. And now, can you tell me which hospital your mother's in? I'd really like to see her, to tell her what a difference her design made to my business. Is she well enough for that, do you think?'

The kohl-rimmed eyes met Diane's, then their bright glance fell away.

'She's very ill,' the other woman said. 'But she'd like to see you. I'll jot the address down.'

The hospital was small and slummy on the out-side. Inside, it smelled of that combination of surgical spirit, ether and cabbage which many people find hard to take.

Diane was one of them. Holding her nose would have been rude as well as hard—she was carrying roses and some good chocolates—but she tried to breathe as little as possible as she hurried along the corridors, searching for Nelson ward.

Presently she reached it; double doors, grimed with use, led her into a long room with beds on both sides and narrow windows looking out onto more brick walls with narrow windows. But the room was bright with strip lighting whilst every available surface was crowded with flowers.

'Yes, dear? Can I help you?'

A small nurse with a restful face spoke to Diane as she hovered.

'Oh yes, I'm looking for somone called Mona, I don't actually know her last name.'

It was enough for the nurse, however.

'That'll be Mona Leverett. She may be sleeping, she's very ill, you know. But if you'd like to sit by the bed she's due for another injection in thirty minutes or so, she usually wakes about now.'

Diane followed the nurse's small figure down to the third bed from the end. Mona, unmistakably Mona, lay on her back, propped up by pillows. Her nose, sharp as a blackbird's beak stood out from the shrunken face. Her mouth was half-open defenceless. She snored a little.

The nurse indicated a chair and Diane took it. As she waited she watched the woman in the bed.

Mona had been thin before but it had been, Diane thought a healthy thinness, the result of tremendous nervous energy. Now she was skeletal, the hands on the sheet so frail that they seemed transparent, each vein standing out, like a relief map. It was strange to see signs of the old Mona on this white and emaciated stranger—the fringe of hair discoloured by nicotine, the heavy eyelids, darkened now by pain and weariness instead of by eye-shadow.

When Mona moved Diane was unprepared for it and jumped; it was like seeing a corpse suddenly recover. But she pinned a smile into place. She was visiting the sick to cheer, not depress.

'Yes? Can I help you?'

It was so unexpected here, yet it was what Mona must have said a thousand times, when she looked up in the shop and saw someone standing there. Diane smiled and held out the flowers and chocolates.

'These are for you. I don't suppose you remember me...'

'I do; you're the gal what 'ad me seaside

dress. Did it go well, eh?'

'It was sensational,' Diane said. 'It's done me no end of good.'

'Oh, ah. I been waitin' for you to come back, knew you would. You'll be wantin' suffink for your spring window now, I dessay?'

'Well,' Diane said, taken aback, her own needs completely forgotten.

'Course you does. Got suffink for you, an' all.' Mona picked up a pile of papers lying beside her bed. 'My gal ain't interested in these; says they're too difficult to make up!' She laughed, then coughed. Diane, horrified, saw blood speckle her lip. She looked round wildly for the nurse but Mona was continuing obliviously.

'They're all I got, me designs. Strange, ain't it, I only met you twice but I knew you'd come back. So I done these for you special. You'll get 'em made up?' It was a plea.

'I could give them to your daughter,' Diane began, but was fiercely interrupted.

'Nah! Poor gel, she can't face 'em, too difficult see?' Her voice, which had been faint, was growing fainter yet, blurring. 'You can get 'em made up...these ones, they *matter*, see?'

'But they're valuable...' Diane started, and was interrupted this time by the nurse.

'My, you're chatty today, Mona! Nice to see

352

a friend, I see you've give her some of them drawings...you're a kind person, dear. Now I'll just give you your injection and then you can chat for a bit longer. How's that?'

Mona said nothing but she turned her head on the pillow and the great, haunted eyes met Diane's and, for a moment, locked. If there was a message in their depths Diane knew she understood it. The drawings would go on, though Mona would not. Nevertheless, she was handing Diane a problem; she was no seamstress. She could appeal to Barkworths, who knew everyone and everything, but they had no expertise save in the selling game. Should she try a top designer? Such people were notoriously indifferent to anyone's designs save their own.

The curtains swished back whilst Diane was still wondering what to do for the best. The nurse smiled encouragingly at her and then said loudly, as though Mona were deaf: 'Right you are then, love, here's your friend back.'

Mona's eyes were softer now and her lips drooped. Whatever the injection had contained it had robbed Mona of much of her small supply of energy. A painkiller of some sort, Diane supposed.

'Mona? Are you sure you want to give me these designs? They must be worth a lot of money…Wouldn't you rather your daughter had them?'

The round, fleshless head on the thin neck wobbled into a negative.

'Nah! She's got…'undreds. Won't do…a fing wiv 'em.' She sighed and her head rolled sideways into a more comfortable position. 'You'll put 'em…in a winder, wiv…me name on.'

The nurse arrived just as Diane was saying in the calmest voice she could manage that she was very grateful and would personally put the finished garments in her window with Mona's name in large letters nearby.

'All serene?' the nurse said, her voice so low that Diane had to strain to catch it. 'She'll sleep now. When she next wakes, she'll be glad of them flowers.'

'Nurse, is it all right to take the designs?' Diane said uncertainly. 'They're really valuable, you know.'

The nurse looked at her indulgently, as though she was sweet but definitely simple.

'Valuable? Oh no, love, they aren't valuable, we chuck most of 'em away, they're only scribbles. As for taking 'em, she give 'em you, I heard her say. Now you just go off whilst she's asleep.'

Diane looked at the sheets in her hand. Fine,

354

clear lines slashed across the paper, each one a unique and beautiful design. How could the nurse think they were worthless?

'They aren't scribbles,' Diane said gently. 'But you're right, probably they're only valuable to me. Tell me, does she sleep a lot, now?'

'That's right. They do, at her stage. It won't be long, now. It could be two hours or two days. Possibly even two weeks, if she wants to hang on for some reason, but it's likelier to be days. Poor dear!'

She was a good girl but she did not mean it; they were all alike to her, the dying. She nursed them and was kind to them, gave them their painkilling injections and watched them slip away, some quickly and easily, others fighting for life, weeping to see it go. But she could not feel for them; it would have burnt her out, Diane supposed.

They reached the double doors at the end of the ward. Diane had given the nurse the flowers but now realised she was still clutching the chocolates. She held them out wordlessly, a question, unformed, all but on her lips.

'Oh no, dear, she won't eat again,' the nurse said, very kindly. 'You'd best keep 'em.'

'No. Give them to someone else...from Mona,' Diane said, thrusting the box into the

355

nurse's hands. And then, with only one quick, backward glance at the still figure on the bed, she left.

Something odd happened to Diane on her way back to the station. She had been marching along the road, determined to save money by walking, when in the crowd ahead of her she spotted a familiar head...Tony must have come to find her!

She told herself that she was cross with him but hurried, nevertheless, to catch him up. And when she did so, and glanced sideways at him, it was not Tony, it was Rory M'Quennell.

And the odd thing, the really peculiar thing, was that her heart gave an excited little hop, as though it had been longing to see old gargoyle-features for months and was daring to be pleased because he was here.

She dealt firmly with her heart, after that. She got into a different carriage and stayed in her seat, though it would have been far nicer to have gone along to the buffet for a cup of British Rail coffee.

He was a professional fascinator, she told herself scornfully, remembering his pursuit of horrid little Letty. He was conceited—he hadn't believed her when she told him she had a previous engagement, and anyway she hadn't wanted to go out with him at all. She could have walked past him with complete indifference, in fact.

But she did not put it to the test. She stayed in her seat and did not even visit the loo, with the result that when the train pulled into Norwich Thorpe she was dying for a wee. Even so she waited until nearly everyone else had got out, then scooted for the toilets, and because she had been so desperate spent ages glued to the seat and missed her connection to Haisby which meant she was not even on the same train as Rory when she finally left the station.

She would not have admitted it even to herself, but the last leg of the journey was dead boring.

For days and days, after her trip to London, Diane worried about the designs. She rang her friend Sadie at Barkworths, but Sadie could only suggest that Diane approach the big designer houses and when she did so, just what she had feared happened; they were only interested in designs which had originated with one of their own people.

'Smaller houses might steal the ideas, which is why I won't approach them,' Diane explained to Anthea, as the two of them sipped coffee in the window of Sam's Place, eyes fixed on the boutique in case a customer should appear. 'I've tried and tried to work out a pattern for myself but I'm not clever enough. Oh Ant, what shall I do?'

She had told Anthea all about her London trip, leaving out the bits about Tony. Now, Anthea sat up straighter, putting her coffee cup carefully down on the table before her.

'I suppose you've thought about Miss Turner? She made those uniforms for Waves, you know. Couldn't she help?'

'She's a dressmaker, not a designer,' Diane said patiently. 'She's probably not even as good as Mona's daughter.'

'Yes, I see what you mean, but someone told me Miss Turner made wedding dresses to her own design.'

'That's possible. What's so hard, Ant, is making up a garment to someone else's design, because when you design something yourself you know all about the sides and the back, but someone else's design is a mystery, if you see what I mean.'

'I think I do,' Anthea said doubtfully. 'Oh, a customer. I'll go, shall I?'

She hurried out, leaving Diane to finish up her coffee, pay, and then return crossly to the boutique.

She had promised to do something practical

with the designs and so far, all she had done was make a number of abortive telephone calls and waste hours of her time in trying to sketch, from the front views which were all Mona had done, how the back and sides would probably look and how the effect was to be achieved.

What was more, good though Anthea was and much though Diane enjoyed her company at home, Anthea was house-hunting. At first Diane had revelled in the house details, the little plans, the poring over ordnance survey maps, for Anthea wanted a country house, but as time went on she grew so envious that she quite hoped Anthea would soon move out. Oh, to have a place of her own, free from other people! Not the aunts. They were delightful, only a real beast would resent them, but the lodgers! Commercials are loud-voiced, they are big eaters, they change the television channel without consulting anyone else, they hog the bathroom, smoke in the dining room and make passes at anything under the age of forty. And the aunts were doing so well with commercials! They usually had a full dining room now, and Anthea's friend Mollie came in every evening to help cook the meal. She was a nice little soul, but she and Anthea chattered away in the kitchen and the commercials hogged the living room and Diane was often forced to take refuge in her attic at an unnaturally early hour, just so that she didn't forget she was a lady and clip someone across the ear!

Sometimes Diane went to the Health Club and sat and talked to Ceri, the reporter from the *Chronicle*. Sometimes she talked to Elf or Andrew, and they shared the worry of how to survive until summer came round again. Tonight, she remembered was Mollie's night off which meant that Therese would be in, rattling her beads and singing her hymns and making pointed remarks about the ungodly, which meant anyone who didn't attend Therese's church so far as Diane could make out.

It crossed Diane's mind that she could ring Tufton and get him to take her out for a meal, but she decided against it. It wasn't fair to lead him on.

So when she and Anthea shut up shop and Anthea set off eagerly for Harbour Way, Diane lingered, getting the books up to date, then going over to chat to Sam and Martin, who had a birthday party in the functions room later.

Finally though, she had to go home. She marched along, bent nearly doubt to keep as much of her as possible shielded from the wind, and reached Harbour Way when the evening meal was long over.

Diane approached the front door—and heard, above the roar of wind and waves, the voice of Barty Mewiss. Of all the commercials she knew, Diane hated Barty the worst, with his vulgar laugh, his fund of filthy jokes and his hearty, aren't-I-wonderful approach. Could she stand Barty, tonight? But it was awfully cold and wild out here.

From inside the house, Barty laughed again. Diane's reaction was simple and instant. She turned away from the house and into the storm.

She had her thick camelhair coat on and her boots, but she turned her collar up and tried, tortoiselike, to shrink inside it. The wind was fierce now she was facing into it and the tumultuous sea, visible even in the darkness, hurled its phosphorescent wavetops towards the land. When she reached the promenade she walked along it for a while, then stopped and stared out to sea. A wild night! God have mercy on all sailors.

Diane sighed sharply. She had rung the hospital this morning, only to be told that Mona had died peacefully a couple of hours earlier. Fear no more the frown o' the great, Thou art past the tyrant's stroke; your poor thin, painracked body has gone but will your spirit live on in your work? Will you get your last wish, Mona the unsung genius? If I have

361

my way you will, Diane vowed. If I have my way your memory will know the fame you despised during your lifetime.

But the wind and waves were too strong for pleasure now and Diane made her way homewards. She slipped into the house, put her nose round the kitchen door to assure the aunts she was home, and then went to her attic. From here, as the wind whined and the ships bounded on the bosom of the deep, Diane could imagine Mona's soul, which no longer feared the elements, reminding her...the designs are important to me. Help me, through them!

In bed at last, Diane lay on her back and looked up at the storm clouds racing overhead, at the occasional spattering of rain as it fell on the overhead window-light. There was a gull on the ridge of the roof, she could just see its tail feathers. It was clinging on with all its strength, the stupid creature, but every now and then it disappeared, only to reappear again a few minutes later. Bloody but unbowed, Diane concluded. Gulls! What an idiot that bird must be, to choose to perch on a roof-ridge on a night when the wind could tear a great ship from its moorings, let alone a little bird from an exposed roof-top.

It took her a long time to get to sleep and just before she nodded off she saw the gull's tail feathers come back into the window-light. He had nearly gone that time, but had managed to recover.

She slept at last, only to dream of Tony, of shipwrecks and disasters of gulls and racing storm clouds. When she woke at two a.m, however, the wind no longer howled and it was raining almost gently. Diane was aware, fleetingly, of an almost overpowering sense of melancholy and loss, and when she touched her cheeks they were wet with tears, yet she could not recall the dream which must have affected her so strongly.

The gull had gone. She thought that this had some deep significance but when she tried to work out what it was she fell asleep again and, this time, slept soundly till morning.

CHAPTER FIFTEEN

Weight had never bothered Anthea one way or the other, but now she saw she was eating too much. Looking at herself sideways Anthea could see a nice fat bust, which was lovely, but the fact was that she, who had always been a size twelve, had blossomed into a fourteen and was now burgeoning into a sixteen.

And Diane was so slim! Not skinny, like I was, Anthea thought, struggling to fasten her skirt. And the aunts had grown used to Diane refusing to eat, so they piled Anthea's plate instead.

I must learn to say no, Anthea told herself now, slipping her feet into her good walking shoes. She checked her appearance in the mirror once more before leaving the room. Good thing I'm tall, she concluded, because I still don't look fat, just sturdier. But I'm jolly well cutting down on these huge meals. I'll diet tomorrow. Not today, because Martin's doing hotpot today. But tomorrow I'll diet.

Only was it worth it? she mused, descending the stairs. What was the point in cutting down on the aunts' lovely meals when presently she would be in her own home, able to eat nothing but salads if she wished?

There was bacon, egg and fried tomatoes for breakfast. And coffee and toast.

I'll diet tomorrow, Anthea concluded, unfolding her napkin.

Later, in the shop, Anthea did a stock-take with Di and forgot to eat any lunch, which was good. And then Di came in with cakes, which was bad. At three, Di suggested Anthea might like to nip round to the estate agents because when Di had walked past earlier she'd seen a new property in the window. Anthea went, and came back with details of a place called Cuttens Cottage out at Cocklebank which sounded perfect.

'They all do,' Diane said rather gloomily, when consulted. 'If you'll hold the fort for a bit, Ant, I'll go and see Miss Turner.'

'Why don't you close, then you won't have to pay me,' Anthea suggested. 'What's more, I could go over to give Sam and Mart a hand; they've got a big buffet on the trading estate tomorrow.'

'You're a gem,' Diane said thankfully. 'I don't grudge your wages but I know Sam would be glad of some help. If you're late I'll tell the aunts to pop something in the oven.'

'If I'm late Sam will feed me,' Anthea assured her. 'Off you go, Di, and good luck with the designs.'

Diane, who was already at the door, looked back, eyebrows climbing.

'Whatever makes you think I'm taking the designs? Can't you see I'm taking Mrs Harvey's slacks for alteration?'

'Intuition...and the papers under the slacks are rustling,' Anthea said, smiling. 'Good luck, Di!'

365

Diane had visited Miss Turner several times now and was, she hoped, a welcome visitor. At any rate as she went into the shop Miss Turner abandoned her work and turned to beam.

'Hello, Diane, dear,' she said cheerfully. 'Got some work for me?'

'A bit. And a puzzle too, Miss Turner. Can you spare a minute?'

'I certainly can. We'll have a cup of tea.' Miss Turner spun her wheelchair and disappeared through the curtain, Diane following as a matter of course. Miss Turner rocketed across the back room and into the kitchen and by the time Diane joined her, having stopped to exchange small-talk with Percy, she was already filling the kettle.

'Fetch Percy through for me, love,' she coaxed above the gush of the water. 'Hang his cage on that hook; I'll finish for the day, now.'

Diane obeyed, carrying the wicker cage and its colourful occupant through and admiring Miss Turner's expertise with the kettle as the older woman flicked the switch with the aid of a short stick.

'Special tap, with an extension so's I can reach from me chair,' she said chattily. 'Electric kettles are a boon if you're handicapped.

Not that I think of meself as being handicapped, because you learn to live with it.'

'You manage marvellously,' Diane said as Miss Turner got cups out, whizzed across the floor to fetch milk from the fridge and then produced teabags and an enamel teapot. 'Was this place specially designed for you?'

'Not really. It's all on one floor but the rest I did bit by bit, and ended up well satisfied. As you see I don't bother with doors, I keep the place well heated instead.'

Diane had noticed the warmth; she was glad she had not bothered to put a coat on to run down the Arcade.

'It's very neat,' she said now, as the kettle boiled and Miss Turner knocked the switch off with her stick and made the tea.

'Yes, it's neat. Central, too, which is a blessing. Sit down, dear, you make me nervous towering over me. Here's your tea; now how can I help you?'

Diane took the cup and sat down. The room was a living-kitchen with a smoothly boarded floor and two red velvet-covered chairs. But it was cosy, with lots of pot plants, a couple of occasional tables, some prints on the walls and a very large television set in one corner.

'That's a colour telly,' Miss Turner said proudly, following the direction of Diane's

367

gaze. 'It's wonderful! I got a video once, but I sent it back; I like me pals, not fillums. You know, the ones that's on every week, two or three times a week, some of 'em. The soaps, the announcers, that lovely blonde girl—what's her name, Anneka Rice, that's it—and old Terry. He's favourite, old Terry, as my young man used to say. What's that on your lap?'

Diane had left the alteration on the counter in the shop but now she got up and handed the sheets of paper to her companion.

'They're designs. Tell me what you think.'

Miss Turner examined the sketches carefully. Diane had only brought four, but they were typical in that they were all striking and unusual as well as apparently impossible to make up.

Miss Turner reached the last one, subjected it to the same intense scrutiny as the others, then laid them all in her lap and looked across at Diane.

'Well! That's original thought, that is. Who done 'em?'

'Not me. Someone I met in London…she gave them to me just before she died. Wanted me to get them made up and put them in my window. Only I'm no dressmaker.'

Miss Turner nodded thoughtfully. She picked up one of the sketches again and stared

368

down at it.

'Hmm. What material, I wonder? I'd favour voile for this one, but it would depend who's to wear it—these designs were for perfect figures, you realised that, of course? You'd want long legs, a long neck—wouldn't do for some of my customers!'

'I think they were designed for models,' Diane said. She was afraid of breaking into Miss Turner's train of thought. This was the first time the designs had been discussed on a practical level by someone who made it sound as though she could actually make them up. But probably when it came to the crunch Miss Turner, too, would admit that without more specific drawings no one could possibly work on the designs before her.

'Now this one...' Miss Turner brandished a drawing that Diane particularly loved. '...this one will need a brilliant colour, with something paler and softer for the scarf. It's near the face, see, so you won't want it too bright, not fair on the skin. Which of them was you wanting, dear?'

'Any...all...' Diane stammered meaninglessly. 'Can you make one of them up, then?'

'I can do 'em all,' Miss Turner said cheerfully. 'Got no side or back views? Never mind, I'll get it just the same.' She tapped the topmost sketch. 'This woman knew what she wanted. I'll just follow her lead.'

'And you can actually make them all?'

'We-ell…it's a quiet time of year, there's my regular ladies, but they won't be wanting much till the weather warms up.'

Diane realised that Miss Turner was not mulling over the possibility of actually creating the garments, but whether or not she could spare the time to do the work.

'Be like old times,' Miss Turner said. 'Before all this…' she tapped the wheelchair significantly, '…I worked as a designer in a London fashion house, you know, got to make up all sorts.'

'Golly! What's that thing about entertaining angels unawares? You are a marvel, Miss Turner,' Diane said sincerely. 'Don't you miss the excitement of working in London? Why didn't you stay, wheelchair or no wheelchair?'

'Oh, I could have,' Miss Turner said. She smiled up at Diane, amusement in every line of her small, expressive face. 'But it ain't all it's cracked up to be, fame and fortune. You gets as tired of it as you get of anything after a while. I come down here to marry, but Jackie was killed and for a bit I was just numb, like. When I was meself though, I realised I was happy here; didn't want to go back to the rat-race. And here I am, and aren't you glad?'

Diane laughed and so did Miss Turner.

'Glad? It's just about the best thing that ever happened to Haisby, I reckon,' Diane said. 'You and I will make a wonderful team. I'll credit you with the making when I put the designs in my window.'

'Can't be bad,' Miss Turner said prosaically. 'When do you want 'em by?'

'If you could make up the one you're looking at now first, April or May will be fine for the rest. Is that possible?'

'Don't see why not. Tell you what, you go round the shops and get sample snips of material and bring it here. I get trade discount, see. What about a figured brocade? Or a wild silk?'

'You'd better pick the material, I think,' Diane said. 'You'll know best what will suit the design.'

'If we went together,' Miss Turner suggested, 'we could have a good old poke round and a nice argue, then and there. You free tomorrer, any time?'

'Sure. How about eleven in the morning? The light will be good for colours.'

'Right-ho. Pick me up at ten to the hour and we'll go orf,' Miss Turner said beaming. 'I've seen a rare pretty figured brocade in Bonds which would do us a treat, been longing to make it up ever since I first set eyes on it. But I daresay you'll not want to go up the city? You'd have Holt in mind, or Aylsham, I daresay?'

Diane knew a cue when she heard one.

'I'd love a day in Norwich,' she said and found, to her astonishment, that it was true. 'We'll get a taxi there, have a nice bite of lunch and then examine every bit of material in the city.'

'Oh ah,' Miss Turner said contentedly, putting her wheelchair into motion as Diane got up to leave. 'I do love a day's shopping.'

Diane reached the door, said her goodbyes and was halfway through it when Miss Turner said something which caused Diane's heart to miss a beat.

'It'll cost you,' Miss Turner said.

By the time February arrived, Diane could see the truth of Sam's bitter remarks about the starving months. It began to snow before January was through but by February the weather was so bad that almost no one bothered to come down the Arcade.

Thanks to Sam, however, at least she had expected a lean time and had put money aside for it. And one dark day, with the glass roof of the

Arcade sagging dangerously under the weight of the snow, she noticed that the Health Food shop had not been opened. She mentioned the fact to Sam, who shrugged, standing in the doorway keeping his hands warm round a mug of coffee.

'Done a moonlight,' he said briefly. 'Poor buggers, they couldn't pay the rent, you see. They didn't have a backer or any capital and once the place started to slide there wasn't a damn thing they could do about it, except disappear. Hadn't you noticed how low their stock was getting?'

'Yes, but it seemed sensible, with so few buyers about,' Diane admitted. 'So they were preparing to go? Why couldn't they have said, Sam? Why run away in the night?'

'Because their shop isn't owned like ours,' Sam explained patiently. 'They're only lease-holders. And if you move out and tell the landlord you're broke, he'll still expect your rent. Unless you go far enough to lose him, of course.'

'Caresse is lease-hold,' Diane said thought-fully. 'But she's got Ronnie.'

'Sure. Though how much longer he'll go on letting her run the place into the ground no one can be certain. Still, Caresse said Ron gave her two years and she's got another eight months to go.'

'How are you managing?' Diane asked curiously. 'Thank God you warned me, Sam... when does it get better?'

'At Easter; earlier if the snow clears,' Sam said. 'As for us, we're lucky. The delivery business booms when the snow's down because people don't want to struggle out to the shops. But even the hairdressers suffer in weather like this and once Reynards closes...'

'Closes? Oh no, not the club!'

Diane loved the club, spending at least half Sunday there and nipping in most evenings, too. With no steady boyfriend and not much to do in the shop the club had kept her sane. But Sam laughed at her, shaking his head.

'Don't be so literal, Di! Reynards always closes for a month, so Elf and Andrew can have a holiday and drain the pool and so on.'

'My God—a month! Oh Sam, whatever shall I do? I'll have to get a feller!'

'Try jogging,' Sam said unkindly. 'It's a lot easier on the emotions than sex. Besides, didn't you have that M'Quinnell bloke at one time? The one with the silly name?'

'Who, Tufton? Well, we did go out a few times but he was so boring I just had to stop seeing him. Where do Haisby girls go to pick up men?'

'Police canteen,' Marj said, emerging like a jack-in-the-box from the kitchen, her face a delicate shade of puce. 'Phew, it's hot in there, Martin's using two ovens and I'm cooking pies in the other two and we've got the grill roaring away and the chipper's on full bore...when I got up this morning and saw it had snowed again I never thought I'd be too hot by dinner-time!'

'If your meat pies burn I shan't rescue them,' Martin said sourly, popping out between Sam and Marj and putting a proprietorial hand on Marj's shoulder. 'Ever been sledging, Marj?'

'Yes, millions of times. With Eric.' Marj said crisply. 'Oh, I do love it! I make Eric pull me and the sledge to the top of the hill, then we both roar down. Oh, that's great, two on a sledge.'

'Bet you tip it up,' Sam observed. Marj nodded vigorously, her big eyes shining.

'Sure we do—all the more fun, scrabbling round in the snow and laughing and shrieking. I do love sledging.'

'I'll take you on Sunday, if you like,' Martin said. He put his face against Marj's hot cheek. 'Say yes, just give me a chance for a change.'

'Eric's on days...I could, I suppose,' Marj said, looking thoughtful. 'On the other hand

I don't want to stop you taking some lovely young thing out...how about askin' old Di here? I heard her a-moanin' because Reynards is shut.'

'I'd sooner take a boa constrictor,' Martin said cordially. Never one to mince words, he had fallen out with Di over a customer.

'Good, because I'd sooner go out with one,' Diane assured him. 'I'd rather go sledging with a mad gorilla than you, Mart. Reckon I'd be a lot safer.'

'I can see you'd be attracted by a mad gorilla,' Martin said. 'It would need a mad gorilla to risk taking you out, icicle-pants.'

'Better than furnace Y-fronts.'

'Is that my nickname?' Martin looked complacent. 'It says it all; Martin's hot stuff.' He flexed an unlikely-looking bicep. 'Well, Marj? Are you going to show this...this gorilla-lover that you're willing to stoke my boiler?'

Diane went off into a shriek of laughter which rivalled Marj's and Sam, grinning, told them to stop acting like kids and get on with their work. Martin pulled Marj as close as he could, plonked a kiss on the side of her neck, got his face slapped—lightly, Diane saw with regret—and returned to the heat of the kitchen. Diane waited until she heard over doors open and anxious cries from the lips of the cooks and then moved nearer to Sam.

'What is it with those two, Sam? Who's interested in whom? Marj slaps him down and then capitulates and they go off together and then they come back and she's with Eric again.'

'Martin's growing up and Marj knows it,' Sam said. 'They're good for each other. Well, Marj is good for Mart, anyway. What is it with you two, come to that? Why did you and Mart quarrel?'

'When a customer who spends a fortune in the boutique is unwise enough to bend down in a bikini, so that her rear end pokes through the cubicle curtains, she doesn't expect a skinny chef to bellow out, ''You don't get many of them to the pound,'' does she, Sam? I could have killed Martin and I told him so when she'd left...never to return, I might add. I know it sounds funny now, but it wasn't at the time and until Mrs McIntyre comes in again I won't see the joke, or forgive Martin.'

'It was awful,' Sam admitted, though with a grin lurking. 'Did he apologise?'

'Who, Martin? Are we talking about the same guy? Of course he didn't. But actually we enjoy insulting each other so I shouldn't worry about it. Oh, whatever shall I do on Sunday, with Reynards shut?'

'You'll be sweet to the aunts, praise their
377

Sunday lunch, doze in front of the telly and go for a nice walk before tea,' Sam said. 'Be like the rest of us, Di!'

By Sunday it was snowing again. Tiny flakes, the sort that lay and continue to lay until there are very big drifts. Diane had a cooked breakfast and felt bloated but she managed to slip Anthea—who anyone would have thought was usually only fed once a week—half her bacon and the second piece of fried bread.

After breakfast Anthea did her room, washed her hair, darned her tights (in this day and age? thought Diane; if the day comes when I darn tights may I be struck down!) and then went into the kitchen to help the aunts with lunch.

Diane mooched. She also tidied her bedroom and wrote to her mother and put her hand out towards the phone twice, because it would be a wrong act to ring Tony. She had managed to part from him painlessly, well fairly painlessly, and had no intention of getting embroiled all over again. Even if he was still in London, which he probably wasn't.

She watched the snow, too, as it whirled and gusted, and thought how vile it was and wished—almost—that there was a Martin in her life who could whisk her up into the hills and take her sledging.

After lunch, roast lamb followed by blackcurrant tart, Anthea dressed in her warmest clothing and went off to call for Mollie to go house-hunting. Mad, Diane thought crossly, and wished she could go with them. She knew they would welcome her, but the old adage about two being company was particularly true with Anthea, who always tried too hard to see that no one felt left out.

'There's a nice quiz on television,' Aunt Dulcie murmured, as Anthea opened the back door and slipped out, causing a flurry of snow to whirl in and dance round the tiles before melting gracelessly into puddles. 'Shall the three of us watch it, dear, or would you rather see sport?'

'Oh, didn't I say? I'm going out...going to meet...umm...Ceri, the girl from the paper. We're having tea out. I don't know what time I'll be in, but not late.'

'Try to keep warm,' Auntie Violet said anxiously as she watched Diane struggling into her camelhair coat, her furlined boots and thick sheepskin gloves. 'You won't be in for tea, then? There's chocolate torte...but if you're out to tea...'

Her voice trailed plaintively off. Aunt Violet

loved feeding people and Sundays were always quiet.

'I'll have a piece of the torte with my bed-time drink,' Diane said. She dropped a kiss on her aunt's soft cheek. 'Don't worry, Auntie Vi, I won't be late.'

Diane went out quickly, shutting the door after her with a near-slam. Leaving the house behind, she turned right and walked briskly, aware of possible watchers. If you listened to the aunts the entire population of Harbour Way spent their days with their faces pressed close to their net curtains. She did not want it reported to her aunts that their niece had sauntered along aimlessly.

On Lord Street though, the wind was quite strong enough to make her hesitate. The snow had stopped for a moment but what was the point in a good long walk on the beach, she would only get chilled to the bone? She might as well go into the shop, turn on her heater, and write letters.

Diane turned her footsteps towards the Arcade, but when she reached the gates she realised she had not brought her handbag with the keys, but only her green leather purse. So it was either go back to the aunts or go on the beach.

The beach won the day. How could she go

back to the aunts when she had told them she was meeting Ceri? So Diane continued down Lord Street, turned right and then right again and was on the promenade. Or at least, she told herself as she slogged across it, she supposed she was on the promenade; she could see nothing but her own boots, left right, left right, as she fought the gale.

But of course it was the promenade and presently she reached the edge of it and jumped down onto the sand, turning left this time. There were snowflakes on the wind again, icy kisses on the skin, a momentary veil of intricate, formless lace across the eye.

Presently, however, Diane discovered that she was almost enjoying herself. She began to feel warm and to know that her blood was circulating fast, bringing colour to her cheeks, making her body aware of its excellent health and strength.

She strode on and began to notice things; little shells half embedded in the wet sand, the way the gulls stood, back to wind, shoulders hunched, like bad-tempered old men weathering a storm. Blow all men, I can enjoy myself perfectly well alone, she thought, even on a day like this!

But then she fell to thinking how nice it would have been had Tony been striding along beside her, if the walk could have ended in tea and toast closely followed by bed, warm blankets, tangled limbs, the intimate caresses of a lover who knows how to please. A shiver coursed pleasurably all over Diane, starting in her stomach and descending like an arrow to the heart of the matter and making her realise, with some dismay, that she needed to spend a penny...go to the loo...have a pee.

Naturally at this point she was at the far end of the beach with no public toilets for miles and very few dwellings. The beach was flat and pebbly too, with not a discreet dune in sight, and it was at least half a mile to the next beach café, which might or might not be open.

Could I piddle on the pebbles? Diane wondered doubtfully, looking about her. Well of course she could, but past experience told her that the moment she lowered her jeans someone would appear, probably with an elderly relative in tow. Sod's law, she believed it was called.

The maddening thing was that until she had put it into words, the urge to wee had not been overpowering, but now, of course, it was all she could think of. Where, when, how? She slogged on, because there was no point in standing about trying to visualise the coast ahead. How long, dear Lord, how long before she reached that beach café?

She arrived at last and it was shut. But it was almost on the sand, and it was a substantial building. Would it be awfully sinful to squat down beside it and wee on the cracked concrete where, in summer, string bags of coloured balls and racks of postcards lured holidaymakers up off the beach?

Diane looked along the shore; miles and miles of wet, wind-blown sand looked back at her. If she went on she would have to resign herself to a long and increasingly painful walk before she saw another building half so suitable. And she knew full well she would not use the pebbles, not blatantly, like that.

So the café it would have to be. Diane walked round it slowly, examining both it and the surrounding environs. It was perfect, with no houses near enough for the occupants to spy on her, the big car park empty save for a rubbish drum on its side rolling hollowly with the wind, and the deserted road.

Diane went round to the front of the café again. Here she was sheltered from view, save for that of someone approaching from the storm -tossed sea. A boat full of cheering sailors, perhaps? Or a submarine suddenly surfacing...? But these prospects seemed remote enough to make the risk worthwhile.

Diane began to struggle out of her jeans. She got them down, lowered her frilly pants, somehow cleared them by a very unusual crouch and at long last, let go. The relief! The only disadvantage was that it seemed to go on for ever. Diane squatted there and waited for the flood to turn to a trickle, and then she thought it must have stopped and began to get up, to discover she was still going. Only a hasty crouch saved her from wet boots at best and wet knickers at worst.

But it did finish, and Diane managed to stand upright, though her knees squeaked protestingly, having presumably got almost fond of being bent double. She heaved her pants into place and had her jeans halfway up her calves when she felt something warm and wet touch the back of her knee. Heavens, she was not still going, was she?

Diane looked down over her shoulder. A slit-eyed bull terrier stood there, sniffing at her leg with a naked pink nose. When it saw her looking it grinned, lolling a tongue, wagging a thin, almost hairless tail. It looked like an outsize Chinese white mouse. It also looked strong, ruthless and potentially violent. Diane stopped pulling her jeans up. Suppose it did not wish her to make sudden movements! She had never owned a dog and bull terriers had a strange reputation. Weren't they the ones whose teeth were so situated that once bitten, you were there for good? They couldn't let go even if they wanted to, which they usually didn't?

'Hello, old boy,' Diane said in what she hoped was a firm sort of voice. 'Bugger off, there's a good dog. Di wants to put her trousers back on.'

The dog seemed to think this was a good idea. He came closer and jumped up playfully, as if to assist. Diane would have backed but she was hobbled by her jeans and anyway if she backed the dog might assume she was scared—which she was—and she knew one should never show fear to a dog.

'Good boy,' Diane said encouragingly, therefore. 'Here...' she looked about her and saw a round pebble cast up from the shore. The very thing, if she could reach it! She shuffled towards it and the dog, immediately divining her attention, lowered its front half to the ground but left its bottom waggling in the air and barked encouragingly, pushing the pebble with its wet, wide-nostrilled nose.

'Oh, hell,' Diane said crossly. Would it snatch at her hand if she tried to pick the pebble up? Would it bite her boot if she kicked the wreched stone? Or would it continue to stare hopefully from her to the pebble and back again, its bum ridiculously hoisted aloft, whilst she gave one last huge heave at her jeans?

The problem was never solved. Whilst she was still thinking about it a voice from behind her said, with more than a hint of tongue in cheek, 'I appreciate you playing with my dog, but don't you think you ought to dress, first?'

The voice was sickeningly familiar.

Diane turned slowly, glad that her camelhair coat was full-length. It was, of course, the person she least wanted to catch her in her present predicament.

It was Rory, the Arcade Ogler.

'I'm very sorry Monster caught you with your...I mean caught you at a bad moment,' Rory said ten minutes later, when he and his dog were allowed, by a furious Diane, to emerge from behind the closed café. 'He's only a pup, he's got absolutely no direction. But surely you aren't still blaming us, are you? I haven't trained him to find knickerless females, you know.'

'I was *not* knickerless,' Diane shouted. 'It was just...I'd walked an awfully long way...'

'I know, I know. You fancied some air,' Rory said soothingly. Diane choked on a laugh which made things worse because her best course clearly lay in remaining angry. 'Don't think you're alone, the old wind on my cheeks is one reason why...'

'I don't think that's funny,' Diane mumbled. 'The fact is, well, I was taken short, and...'

'I saw,' Rory said mildly. Diane, conscious of the lake-sized proof of her erstwhile occupation, wished she had kept her mouth shut.

'Yes. Well why don't you and your dog bugger off and let me continue my walk? I haven't got all day, you know.'

'But we're walking too; why can't we walk with you? Monster isn't a monster, you know.'

Diane giggled without meaning to do so. Then she looked suspiciously at Rory. He was wearing a sheepskin coat, a striped scarf, and his trousers were tucked into wellies; black ones. Diane was just grateful they were not green.

'Where did you spring from, anyway? I was absolutely alone and then you and that...that animal appeared from nowhere.'

'We came along the shore,' Rory said. 'Minding our own business, of course. We saw you walking round and round the café and wondered what you were doing, but then we lost sight of you because Monster left the beach in pursuit of a gull which seemed slower than the rest, and I had to follow because he's only a puppy, and when we had made each other see reason we were right behind the café so we walked alongside it, came round the corner, and there you were.'

'Oh,' Diane said doubtfully. 'So you're just out for a walk, like me?'

It would have been rude to ask which way he was walking and then do the opposite but Diane was tempted. She looked into his light grey eyes though, and decided against it. He was a M'Quennell and his mother was a good customer as well as a friend. She, poor woman, could not be blamed for having borne the Arcade Ogler. What was more Rory was being relatively polite to her right now and she found she did not want to rouse his antagonism again.

'That's right. Let's get moving, shall we? No point in hanging about here catching our deaths.'

They moved off, side by side, Monster dashing ahead, dashing back, leaping at gulls, storming down the beach to the very edge of the water before retreating, sheepishly, from the advancing waves.

'How far do you want to walk?' Rory said at last, when it was clear that Diane did not intend to make conversation. 'I ask because my car's parked about half a mile further on. If you can keep going that long I'll treat you to tea and then run you home.' He looked sideways at her through the steadily whirling flakes. 'Because you're pretty wet; all three of us are.'

'I can manage another half mile.' Diane said, trying to sound grateful and not grudging. She had walked at least three miles from Haisby by now and found she had no real urge to walk three miles back, especially if going on another half mile meant a lift. And tea. But it would not do to admit this to her companion, who was quite conceited enough already, in her opinion.

'Good. Best foot forward then.' To Diane's annoyance he put his arm round her shoulders. 'Shall I give you some help?'

'No thanks,' Diane said coolly. 'I'm pretty fit, actually.'

'I'm sure.'

They strode on for a while in silence and then Diane began to feel that it was her turn to talk. It was a pity that her mind turned straight to what it did.

'The last time I saw you was at the fashion show. Did you find your pink-haired lady?'

Rory chuckled. 'Indeed I did. A real little sport, young Letty. Game for anything.'

'So I understand,' Diane said. 'Are you still seeing her?'

'Which bit? Oh, you mean am I still taking her out; yes and no.'

'What does that mean?' Diane tried to make

389

it light but it still sounded rather unfriendly. 'Either you are or you aren't.'

'Does it matter? To you, I mean. I thought you were supremely uninterested in me and my carryings-on.'

'So I am,' Diane said hastily. What on earth had made her ask him a question like that? 'Sorry, I was just making conversation. Tell me about Monster; how old he is and where you got him and so on.'

Rory looked down at her; he was, she acknowledged, very attractive in an ugly sort of way, even with a gale blowing his hair all over the place.

'He's ten months old and I've had him sixteen weeks. He was chucked out by someone who thought he wanted a bull terrier and speedily decided he didn't, so I took him on. Actually, I brought him home intending to hand him over to Tufton because London's no place for him, but Tuf isn't too keen, he prefers gun dogs, so I'm going to try to persuade Monster that he can wait for me in the car without eating the steering wheel or the brake and sit by my desk without raising his leg all over my files and my secretary. He's got such looks and charm, though, that I'm sure the staff will fall over themselves to do things for him.

Diane looked at the squat, bulging, bow-legged figure gambolling heavily ahead of them and snorted.

'You can't fool me! He may have a beautiful nature—may—but that's the end of it, he's ugly as sin. He's an albino as well, isn't he?'

'No he isn't,' Rory said, sounding affronted. 'He doesn't have pink eyes. He's a fine specimen, old Monster, Kennel Club registered, the lot. Can't you see what a grand fellow he is?'

Diane shook her head.

'No. Actually I think he's rather horrid, all that pink. His nose is pink and his eyes are pink-rimmed, even his private parts are pink.'

'So are mine,' Rory pointed out, making Diane snort into her coat collar again. She kept laying herself open for ripostes like that, what had come over her?

'I daresay,' she said coolly, however, trying to keep her face straight. 'But you don't run about on the beach...' She stopped, realising that to finish the remark would end in her discomfiture.

'Woggling them? How do you know I don't?' Rory put his arm round her and pulled her close and Diane was about to give a sharp cry and attack him for his daring when he released her and she realised he had merely turned her from her steady tramp along the beach up towards a car park which she could just see beyond the dunes. 'There's my car, and the hotel. See?'

Diane saw, through the snow, a pleasant building with four round turrets, each with a gold weathercock topping it. On a day like this all four were twirling so fast they were little more than a blur, but even so it made a pretty picture against the snow.

'There's a nice lounge open to non-residents …but if we were to become residents, of course, we could go to our room and relax in a hot bath and order a full dinner to be served up there.'

Diane walked on pretending she hadn't heard.

'You aren't tempted? Pity. I'm sure Monster would join me in a foam-bath at the drop of a knicker, but then I'm not inviting him.'

'I trust you aren't inviting me, either,' Diane said severely. She could not understand why he was being so nice to her, so natural, when before he had behaved like a pig.

'Me? Invite my brother Tufton's girl to join me in a bubble-bath? Perish the thought! You are still Tufton's girl I take it?'

'I never was,' Diane said frankly. 'We go about a bit, though we haven't done so for a long while, but we were never more than friends.'

'Really? That isn't what Tufton says.'

'Then Tufton lies,' Diane said testily. 'Your brother is a nice guy, but he's only kissed me twice. Look, I didn't press my question about Letty, so you can bloody well mind your own business about me and Tufton.'

She made to move on but Rory caught her arm, stopping her short. He turned her to face him and now the light eyes were steady on hers, the mouth no longer smiling.

'Di? Cards on the table. I haven't seen Letty since before Christmas.'

'Snap,' Diane said after some thought. 'Now what?'

'Now I hug you,' Rory said exuberantly but Diane, as soon as he let her go, set off at a sharp trot for the hotel, calling back over her shoulder.

'I told you I was fit; I can almost certainly outrun you, so I shouldn't bother to chase me if I were you.'

'Ah, but could you outrun Monster? Now that I do take leave to doubt. Despite his funny little legs he's got a terrific turn of speed. Want to try him? I'll hang on to his collar and give you a fifty-yard start and I bet he'll still catch you up before you reach the hotel.'

'Don't bother,' Diane said, slowing. She was still not too sure of Monster's good intentions but had had the opportunity of studying his excellent teeth. 'I'll be generous and let you and Monster go first, if you like.'

They reached the foyer in a group and Rory pushed her inside ahead of him. Monster needed no invitation, which was as well, since no one spoke, but pranced across the hall and into a lounge, flinging himself down in front of the open fire with the air of one who owns the entire establishment and doesn't mind boasting about it. Diane longed to follow his example for now that she was inside she became conscious of soaking clothes, rat-tailed hair and a blue complexion. Which was annoying since Rory was wet but immaculate still.

'Let's get you out of that coat,' Rory said, helping her off with it and then heaving her boots off, too. He draped her things over a radiator and then turned and surveyed her, shaking his head.

'Dear me, those jeans are soaked. There's nothing much we can do about them, though, unless you'd like to book in?'

Odd how she could tell, now, that he was joking. In the Arcade his jokes had seemed pointed, his invitations insulting.

'I'll live with wet knees, thanks,' Diane said

primly. 'Where's that tea you promised me?'

Monster watched them seat themselves comfortably close on a big, chintz covered sofa, then gave a huge yawn, got up and wandered over to Rory, nudging his fingers, demanding affection. Rory rang the bell, then slung a casual arm round Diane's shoulders. This time she let it stay.

'Isn't this cosy?' he demanded. 'Just us and our little lad waiting for tea...I don't think toast will do, I want cakes as well. And crumpets. Sardines on toast, perhaps? Or poached eggs. How do you like your steak cooked?'

'Just tea and toast would be fine,' Diane said, but with watering mouth. She was starving after all that exercise!

'Aw, shucks, ma'am, Monster and me's growing fellers. You wouldn't grudge us a grub-stake? It's on the house...well, on me, anyway.'

A motherly woman came in presently, clucked over their wet things and went out again, to return after a short interval pushing a trolley set with a noble tea which included most of the food Rory had suggested, though not the steak. But there was a big blue and white teapot, two cups and lots of milk and sugar.

'You be mother,' Rory said, pushing the teapot towards Diane. 'Then we'll see who can eat the most.'

'Monster will if you don't look out,' Diane said warningly. The bull terrier's nose was already pressed lovingly against a crumpet.

'Oh, well. One down and five to go,' Rory said, handing the dog the object of its desire. 'Come on, Di, eat up or I'll announce Monster the winner here and now and call the competition off.'

An hour later the three of them left the hotel, now warm and relatively dry.

'Into the car and off we go,' Rory said, pushing Monster into the back, where a wire grid stopped him from joining his betters in the front seats. 'I really enjoyed that; thanks for joining me, Diane.'

He sounded serious for once and Diane, equally seriously, said: 'Thanks for inviting me, Rory. It was a splendid tea; we did have fun, didn't we?'

He nodded, handing her into the passenger seat and going round to get behind the wheel.

'Helped to pass a snowy Sunday very pleasantly. Now I'll take you home and then Monster and I will have to make tracks.'

'For London?' Diane said, her heart sinking a little. Just when she had discovered he was not the beast she had thought him he intended to leave her life once more. How typical of her luck just lately!

'Yes, London for a couple of weeks, then I'll come down to leave Monster with my mother and go off to New York,' he said casually, starting the engine. 'Still, I'll be back by Easter.'

'That will be nice for you,' Diane said politely. He might mean nothing to her, but she did see him now as friend and not foe. 'You can pop into the boutique when you get back and I'll take you out for a meal to say thanks for that tea.'

'I might do that. Unless you and Tufton get back together, of course.'

'I can't get back together with someone I've never been with,' Diane reminded him crisply. 'Tufton's nice, but...'

'Precisely. But...' Rory said dreamily. He drove in silence after that until they reached Harbour Way and then he drew up outside the house and made a long arm, pulling her across the seat until she was half on the handbrake and could feel Monster's hot breath through the grille.

'You enjoyed being with me and I enjoyed being with you,' he said, manoeuvring her with a wicked neatness which showed he was no stranger to lovemaking in a sports car. 'Now let's see if we enjoy the same sort of kisses.'

Twenty minutes later Diane got out of the car, waved as Rory drove off, and hurried into the house. She was astonished at the strength of desire his kisses had awoken in her, she had enjoyed every moment of their tangled embrace, had forgotten the brake, the possibility of interested observers, everything, in fact, but the feel of his mouth on hers and the sensitive movements of his hands.

He would be a good lover; she knew it with the sort of certainty which told her that he would have been right for her, as well. He had known just what would please her, and she found to her astonishment that she was comparing him with Tony—to Tony's detriment. And this, she reminded herself, in a small sports car with no elbow room, heavy winter clothing on, and a noisy bull terrier trying to get your attention through a metal grille.

Rory M'Quennell, in short, was worth further investigation. Damn his wretched work taking him to London, Diane thought rebelliously, hurrying up the stairs and into the bathroom. She would take a hot shower to get rid of the last traces of her walk.

Presently, under the water, she began to feel happier, less tense. He would be coming back in a couple of weeks, to leave Monster with his mother. And she intended to enjoy relationships with men in future and give no more thought to permanence or falling in love.

It would be fun to have an affair with Rory. Even the thought made desire tingle all over Diane. An affair! After months and months of celibacy she was actually contemplating an affair! She felt like rushing out of the shower and dashing naked down the road to let him have his way with her! Oh, Diane, she mourned, shocked at herself, have you no pride?

It appeared she had very little, for throughout the evening the only thought that crossed and recrossed her mind was: how can I wait two whole weeks before seeing him again?

Yesterday hate, today lust, Diane thought, just before she fell asleep, and was shocked anew by her reaction. But shocked or not, it was the way she felt. Whatever Rory's faults or attributes, he had finally made her think of something—someone—other than Tony, and that had to be good.

CHAPTER SIXTEEN

The cottage at Cocklebank had turned out to be just what Anthea had dreamed of. It was on a very remote part of the coast and they saw it for the first time in deep snow, but even so, Anthea took one look at it and knew she'd found her dream-house.

Not that it was much from the outside. A long, low building with a motheaten thatched roof, cob walls from which the whitewash was flaking, and a little porch. It would have won no prizes in *Good Housekeeping*.

But because it was a fisherman's cottage it faced straight out to sea, separated from it by the salt-marshes, with a channel coming straight up to within a couple of dozen feet of the front hedge. I could keep a boat, Anthea told herself. And the garden at the back was big, though the agent admitted there almost nothing in it, because the Cuttens, who had owned it, had been in their nineties and did not care for gardening.

Inside, there was a tiny front hall, a big living room and a big kitchen. The ceilings were low and threaded with black beams, the floors were quarry-tiled save for the living room, which was pitch pine. The pine floor was not level, it heaved as though it belonged to a ship at sea, and the walls were covered with the beastliest paper Anthea had ever seen, but she loved it anyway.

Upstairs, there were two big bedrooms and one which had been converted into a bathroom. That is to say, it had a bath standing on its four little iron feet in the middle of the floor, a handbasin up against one wall and another floor made of wide pine planks which rose and fell like the waves of the seas. In one corner, looking a little self-conscious, was a flush lavatory. It must have been taken from an old house somewhere, Anthea thought, because the china was blue and white and the seat was red mahogany and beautifully warm to sit on.

The bedrooms were just large and bare, one with a view of the sea, the other of the snowy landscape beyond the garden.

But it was the kitchen which decided Anthea that she would live here come what may. It was an old room which had scarcely changed at all through the years. It had an old-fashioned range for cooking and heating and a wall-oven which could be lit if you needed it. One window overlooked the side of the cottage and another, with a low sink in front of it, framed the back garden.

But what chiefly charmed Anthea was the well. It looked like a round-topped table at first glance, then you saw that the 'table' had a stone base. And if you pulled back the wooden lid you looked down, down, down into darkness. The well was brick-lined and little ferns grew in the crevices and a fresh breeze blew up into their faces. Mollie drew back, alarmed, but Anthea loved it. It was perfect, her own source of fresh water, though she would not need to use it for the cottage was on the mains.

'I love the well but you don't, do you?' Anthea said shrewdly as Mollie stared. 'Does it scare you?'

'No...yes! It's like having a secret passage opening into your living room. You wouldn't know what might come up it.'

'It isn't like that at all. You couldn't climb up it, it just leads to water,' Anthea assured her. 'Anyway, there are latches which you'd keep closed, just in case someone picked up the lid and fell down by accident. I think it's a lovely thing to have in your kitchen.'

'It doesn't remind you at all of the cellar at your old house?'

Anthea's stomach gave a great, terrified heave. It did it quite often lately if something upset her. But it was just the mention of the cellar that had done it, not any resemblance between it and the well. The cellar was hateful, the well was delightful, it was as simple as that.

That evening, back at the house on Harbour Way, she told the aunts and Diane that she would be moving out quite soon and then sat in front of the fire, mulling over her plans for her new home. I'll have a cat, or perhaps a dog, she planned busily. I shan't be lonely, not with the marshes so close, and the sea, but a cat or a dog would be nice. There's a bus service a mile away. I can walk that each day, and I'll get some of the furniture I liked from the vicarage, Mr Parkins said I might, and put that into the cottage and buy more if I need it.

She had put an offer in and knew that it would be accepted because the agent had made no bones about it. The place was not everyone's cup of tea, he said with wild understatement, and the executors of the estate were eager to sell. Anthea, with the money from the sale of the old house, was eager to buy, so the formalities would not take long.

But Anthea had been happy with the Bonners and even her longing for her new home could not blind her to the fact that, in a way, she would be losing some good friends by her move. The old ladies were dears, and marvellous cooks. Violet and Dulcie used recipes which were strange to Anthea and put before 'our girls' all sorts of delicacies which Anthea had never tasted before. Seafood was often on the menu, and Aunt Violet's halibut in shrimp and walnut sauce had to be tasted to be believed. Anthea had spent an instructive Sunday afternoon in the kitchen learning how to cook it and had passed her knowledge on to Martin who had been uncharacteristically grateful.

Another bonus from living at the Bonners was the new intimacy which grew up between Anthea and Diane. Diane was beautiful and talented and Anthea knew that she herself was ugly and dull but even so, they became friendlier than they could have done when meeting only in the boutique. Sharing meals, waiting for the other to vacate the bathroom, walking on the beach, their intimacy grew and strengthened until it became a friendship which both valued.

And Anthea, for the first time in her life, realised that beauty and talent do not necessarily make for happiness. Diane had lots of friends and a thriving business, yet she was not happy. She hankered first for a married man she had once known in London and then for someone else who was also, it appeared unavailable.

She enjoyed the shop but often told Anthea that she missed the bustle of London, and she was kind to the aunts but found them difficult, sometimes even boring.

Yet here I am, plain as a pikestaff, with a precarious hold on a very odd sort of job, no visible means of support other than my salary and the money for the house which Mr Parkins has put in trust, yet I'm happy as a king, Anthea told herself. I'd love to have lots of friends but I've only got Mollie, who's an awful lot younger than me, and Di, who's my boss. My stomach heaves when things go wrong, I eat too much so I'm bursting out of my nice clothes ...but I'm so happy I sing all the time and have a job not to walk around grinning like an idiot.

Spring was making tentative efforts to get established by the time Anthea could really call the cottage her own and a March wind was shaking the last of the snow off the branches of the trees. Diane, told her friend would move the following weekend, immediately announced that she would hire a van and drive Anthea and all her goods and chattels over to Cocklebank.

'I haven't driven for months, it'll be fun for me to take you over. When's the furniture from your old house being delivered?'

'When I'm in,' Anthea said, pleased and

scared both at once and feeling the palms of her hands damp with excitement.

'Oh. What about the bed?'

'That's coming first, before the rest. Mr Parkins said he'd arrange for Mr Stockley at the garage to bring it over.'

'Mr Stockley? What garage?'

'Right up on the main road there's a garage. It's quite close to the bus stop and Mr Stockley runs a hire-car, so he said if it was too rough in winter to get down to the cottage on foot, he'd run me. Isn't that kind? And he's got a big van, too, so he's fetching the bed. I'm having the big double from the spare room.' Anthea added. 'It's wonderfully comfortable. And I'm having all the linen, blankets and sheets and things, I mean. Not curtains, they're mostly old and rotten.'

'I see. And how's the rest of the stuff getting there? Not all with Mr Stockley, surely?'

'No, I'm having a real removal van because of the sideboard and the big dining table and the grandfather clock. But they aren't essentials, so they'll come down the following weekend, once I've got a bit of carpet down and some curtains up. Oh Di, I'm so excited!'

'I'm glad…and I'm longing to see the place. Tell you what, I'll bring a picnic lunch and we'll spend the whole day rearranging everything. Pity it's on a Sunday but that's one of the disadvantages of being in business.'

'I don't mind,' Anthea assured her. 'I'd thought about getting a cat or a dog, but I think I'll have my work cut out just managing the cottage, at first, so I'll live alone for a bit.'

By the time Anthea waved Diane off, the cottage was looking quite presentable and Anthea was warmed, not only by her first fire, but by Diane's admiration, for her friend thought the cottage was wonderful and envied her everything, especially the well.

'A well in your very own kitchen,' Diane marvelled, peering into the echoing darkness. 'How romantic!'

'Ow-ow-ow...tic-tic-tic...' echoed the well and both girls laughed.

'Ha-ha-ha-ha-ha...' giggled the well, making them laugh more.

'It's a real feature,' Diane said, when they had lowered the lid again and latched it with the big, swinging metal clasps. 'You won't have to lug water up though, will you? I didn't see a bucket.'

'No, I'm on mains water,' Anthea assured her. 'But the water's beautifully clear; I lowered a bucket on a rope one day last week, to show Mr Parkins, and its fine. What do you think of my fireplace?'

On a previous visit she and Mr Stockley had torn down the modern mantelpiece and shelves and ripped and burrowed into a layer of loose and flaking plaster and found a very large, slate-framed fireplace. So now Anthea had a wide hearth with a basket grate piled with brightly burning logs.

'The fireplace is wonderful,' Diane said. 'It's the sort of cottage anyone would love to own.'

And Anthea, dreaming of her life here, loved Diane all the more for her unstinting praise.

Over the next couple of weeks, the cottage gradually filled up with the right sort of things. Anthea had no carpets downstairs and no curtains, either, but she had the old walnut piano her mother had played on when she was alive. She had no smart three-piece suite but the chesterfield and one armchair from the living room at her old home, and an oil painting of her great-great-grandfather in his regimentals and a water-colour of her great-great-great grandmother, clearly a Regency belle, in a thin gown with a high waist, looking pensively at the perfect rose in her hand. Mr Parkins wanted to get the pictures insured; he said they were worth a lot of money but Anthea had no intention of selling them and less of paying out vast sums to insure them, so she simply said vaguely that she would see to it and put the matter out of her head.

So no carpets, no nice modern cooker or fridge. But a big double bed in each of the bedrooms, a number of faded Turkey rugs scattered about to keep your toes warm, and two old but good dressing tables, one in mahogany with a red velvet-covered stool, the other in cherry wood with the stool upholstered in faded green brocade.

What more could one ask? Anthea wanted nothing else. When she had waved Diane off she went down to the creek in her wellies to see what she could find. She found thick black mud which, in summer, would squelch between exploring toes; after the mud, hard sand and then water, with shells seen dimly through its greenness. Weed further out, toing and froing with each wave, and beside the creek the marsh, stretching out to the horizon, beckoning, tempting with promises of the seas beyond.

At the head of the creek there were a couple of boats stranded above the mud, on the long shingle bank. We'll have a boat, Anthea planned, and then wondered why she had said 'we' without a second thought. But it didn't matter. There was time, now, for everything.

'Have you seen that M'Quennell chap, the dark

one with the interesting face?' Anthea asked a few days later, as she and Diane sat over their lunch. 'I know you said something about him being in New York, but I seem to remember you said he'd be home by Easter.'

'He writes,' Diane said lightly. 'He'll be home quite soon. Why, Ant? What makes you ask?'

'Because he's important to you, isn't he?' Anthea said, highly daring. 'You were so happy, Di, when he was last down, you were all lit up like a Hallowe'en lantern.'

'You're daft,' Diane said, laughing. 'If you tell me I look like a turnip again I'll sack you!'

'You can bring him to the cottage if you like,' Anthea said. She had never asked a man into her home save for Mr Stockley and Mr Parkins and they scarcely counted.

Diane laughed again.

'My dear Ant, I've only been out with the bloke a couple of times,' she said. 'He may not even come down the Arcade to see me.'

'He'll be round,' Anthea said positively, and felt a little stab of envy. 'There's someone in this world for everyone, Di, and I get the feeling that Rory M'Quennell is for you.'

Diane only laughed again but Anthea, turning away, completed the sentence in her own

410

head. 'There's someone in this world for every-one, Di...except for me. I'm different. I'll always be alone.'

'Spring, spring, spring,' Marj carolled, flicking a feather duster over the picture rail in the restaurant. 'Oh what a beautiful morning...'

'Shut up,' Martin shouted from the kitchen. 'It's not a beautiful morning, not when you make that bloody awful din.'

'Shan't,' Marj called back, and shrieked with parrot-like laughter. 'Go to hell, Martin Samuels. I can sing if I want.'

Martin was in a mood. The trouble was he was suffering for the first time in his life, from Love instead of Lust, and he wasn't happy. Before, he grumbled to Marj, he had always known where he stood, which was as near as possible to someone with big boobs, but now all he knew was that he wanted Marj and was confused and miserable by his apparent inability to get her and his obstinate lack of desire for anyone else.

'You've turned me into a wimp,' he had snarled at her the previous day when they were sharing a sandwich and a can of Coke. 'I was happy with what I could get, before. Now I'm not happy at all.'

'Old Grab-and-Go Martin, you were then,'

Marj said, giggling. 'All I've done is make you grow up, Mart, and realise that there's more to life than shows of temper and women who will or won't. Tell you what, you're a much nicer person, honest. I mean, take Anthea; she's still with us and they were taking bets, up and down the Arcade, that you'd drive her into giving notice in the first week.'

Now, Marj was considering whether to start singing again and give Martin hell if she objected, when a customer came in, which put a stop to the songs and the feather-dustering in one fell swoop. Marj slung her duster into the kitchen, picked up a menu, and approached the customer.

'Would you like the menu?' she asked politely, handing it to him. 'We don't serve lunches for another thirty minutes or so, but if you're hungry, the all-day breakfast is on all day.'

The customer grinned. He was a dark-haired man with light eyes and a face so ugly that it was in fact extremely attractive. Marj knew she had seen him before but couldn't put a name to him.

'I'd love your all-day breakfast, but actually all I dare have is two cups of coffee and two scones,' the man said. 'And I don't want to have them in here. Could you bring them over to the boutique?'

Light dawned. So that was where she had seen him! He was one of the M'Quennell's and he had come to see Di.

'Course. You go now and I'll bring the tray presently,' Marj said robustly. 'Di's on decaf now; shall I make it two?'

'No fear; I need caffeine,' the man said positively. 'But bring her the decaf by all means. And don't forget the scones, with lots of butter.'

Marj went back into the kitchen to find Martin peering round the edge of the till, trying to see who she had been talking to.

'It was one of Di's fellers,' Marj told him, taking pity on the look of puzzled uncertainty which Martin cast at her. 'Goodness, Mart, did you think it was Eric?'

At the hated name a frown etched itself on Martin's brow. He looked hurt and puzzled, like a sick monkey, and suddenly Marj was ashamed of herself. She teased him and taunted him and let him go so far and no further...What was the matter with her, for God's sake? She had never been a tease, had always despised such women, and she was not in love with Eric, their affair had gone flat despite what she led Martin to believe. Why didn't she give the poor bugger a chance?

He's dead plain though, Marj thought to

413

herself now, glancing across at Martin's freckly face and greenish eyes. He's thin, too, no Mr Universe. Yet on the rare occasions when she had let him kiss her, give her a hug, he had shown a puppylike warmth and a degree of ardour which had surprised her.

'Tell you what, Mart...' Marj was beginning when Sam emerged from the cellars, a large ham cradled in his arms like his first-born.

'Mart, give me a hand,' Sam ordered. 'Don't forget, you two, that we've an in-house eighteenth on tonight. Marj, Sandy's up to her neck in grated onion down there, go and give her a hand before she cries her eyes out, there's a good girl.'

Another chance missed, Marj told herself sarcastically. What were you going to do, then? Throw the poor dog a bone? But she stomped down the cellar stairs a lot less graciously than usual...and had to run up them two at a time to tell Sam she was awfully sorry, she had taken an order for coffees and scones and had completely forgotten to deliver them.

Anthea was in the boutique when she became aware that she was feeling odd. She had been late getting up that morning, had had to run the best part of a mile to catch her bus, and the resultant stitch had plagued her for most

414

of the journey, but then it had faded. Only now it was back again...curse curse...and the pie and chips which Marj had just delivered no longer appealed.

'Not eating, Ant?' Di was at her most cheerful and Anthea knew why. Rory had been down to the shop several times and she knew Di had been out with him and was enjoying his friendship. 'I never thought to see you turn down food.'

'I've got a pain,' Anthea said. 'I thought it was just a stitch, but it can't be. I feel quite sick.'

Presently Anthea had to grab the key and make a run for it down to the toilets by the church, where she vomited. After that she felt better for a bit, then the pain started again.

'Di, I'm sorry but I feel really bad,' she gasped when Di came back after her own lunch. 'I think it may be food poisoning, I've been ever so sick.'

'Look, I'll call you a taxi,' Diane said. 'You can go to casualty if you like, only perhaps you'd be best in your own bed if you're going to be ill.'

'I'll be all right on the bus,' Anthea protested. 'But if you don't mind I think I'll leave now and catch the four-thirty. The pain's gone, more or less, but I'd like to get home.'

Diane agreed, rather reluctantly but Anthea was feeling much better and strode out confidently. Halfway to the bus station, however, she could feel the pain approaching, a faint niggle in the small of her back gradually increasing until it was like an electric drill. It seemed to last a century, though it could only have been two or three minutes, but then it ebbed and Anthea hurried onwards, secure in the knowledge that it would leave her alone now, perhaps for an hour.

She was right. The pain disappeared and she caught the bus, reached the cottage, and made up the Raeburn. She put the kettle on and made herself a cup of tea, then ate a cheese and pickle sandwich, and then, on her way upstairs to run the bath, the pain returned.

Hotter, stronger, really getting into its stride, it bored through Anthea from back to front. She sat on the stairs as it roared in like the tide of the flood, then ebbed with awful slowness, and when it had gone she tugged up her jumper, for so violent had it been that she could scarcely believe it had left no mark.

But her round, smooth stomach looked just as usual. I'm all right, Anthea thought, rearranging her clothing and getting up. The pain was the cheese and pickle sandwich, what an idiot I am, I really should have waited until I'd had the bath, if I get into the hot water that sandwich will bring the pain back, sure as eggs is eggs!

She got into the water, however, and lay back, happily relaxed. Lovely Friday, with the whole weekend to look forward to!

She was just planning her evening meal when the pain started again and this time there was an urgency about it which really frightened her. She wanted to scramble out of the water, meet it on even terms. Something urged her to crouch, arms round knees, the better to tackle it, but it was too late. She had scarcely moved when it was upon her.

It came down on her like a horse galloping, and stayed longer. When it finally ebbed she was exhausted and frightened. She was ill, far from friends, not on the telephone—what should she do? It was a quarter of a mile to the nearest neighbour, if she could reach them they would get a doctor, but could she reach them?

Towel-girt, she got to the kitchen and was beginning to dry herself when the pain came again. She was unaware of dropping her towel but she must have done for when it ebbed she was crouching naked, on the floor between the Raeburn and the well, and all of a sudden she was no longer frightened, she was angry.

How dared this pain attack her when she was alone! She would show it! The next time it came she would push and push and push it right out of her body...how *dare* it invade her here, in her own home, where she was so safe and happy?

She squatted on the towel to keep her feet warm and when the pain came again she began to push, and she knew she was doing the right thing because the pain itself told her so. Push, push, it seemed to cry; there's something not right, something I need to expel, you must push it right out of your body and then you'll be fine!

After the third pain she thought she had won; hot water deluged her feet, soaking the towel. She leaned back, exhausted but happy. She must have had a bladder obstruction and moved it with her pushing and the water which had been giving her such terrible pain had rushed out.

But then the pain came again; push *harder*, it screamed at her, tearing at her back with red-hot tiger claws. Push harder, you stupid bitch, don't you know you've got to push and heave and fight the pain out of you, until it falls to the floor with a plop?

She was pushing as hard as she could though, and the pain had changed, it was just a sort of prod now, telling her that she must push, must not give up even when she grew tired and long-ed for nothing so much as a quiet snooze. It drove her into a crouching position, with her hands gripping the lid of the well, and she groaned and grunted and pushed...pushed... pushed...and the thing was too big, impossibly big, she would never do it, never get it out, she would be nothing but a huge scarlet pushing pain for the rest of her life...the rest of her life...

The pain came again, but she scarcely need-ed its reminder; her whole life was bound up in the need to expel whatever it was from her body. And she was winning, she knew she was, she could feel it...She gave an enormous, grun-ting heave, felt her body split in two like a chestnut husk when the nut is ripe...and sank back onto her haunches, knees in the air, hands releasing the well-cover. She had done it! The urge to push, the pain, had all left her in peace, Softly, she lolled back, then glanced down, be-tween her knees.

Blood! A lot of blood and a big fat pink *thing*, blood-streaked. Anthea stared at it. It was a baby! A baby which had been growing inside her all these months! Ugh! It had somehow managed to sneak its way in and had just fought and choked and forced its way out!

It was dead, of course. She sat up and saw, for the first time, the blood-boltered kitchen and knew a hot wave of shame, though as God was her witness she had done nothing wrong, nothing which should have called this beastliness down upon her. She would put the baby and all the beastly blood and the fat, baglike thing which had slithered from between her thighs as she sat up, into the dustbin and forget them.

No. Not the dustbin. Dustmen collect dustbins.

Anthea stared wildly round the kitchen. The shame of it, if she had to tell people that she, an unmarried woman, had given birth to a baby! Then her eyes fell on the well. She picked the baby up by one leg whilst she heaved up the lid.

The well would do! It might have been made for the disposal of sinful things. She would throw the whole lot down the well, all of it, even the bloodied towel, and never think of it again. She would be innocent once more, unsullied.

The lid came up sweetly and Anthea dangled the pink, bloody, botchy thing—she could scarcely think of it as a baby—over that long, dark drop.

Afterwards she thought she must have been a little mad, yet perhaps God has His own way of bringing us to acceptance. As the baby swung over the well it gave a squawk and a mew, like a cat, and opened its eyes.

It was not dead! The shock frightened Anthea so much that she jolly nearly dropped it, which would most certainly have killed it, but instead, she and the upside-down baby stared at each other.

It was like meeting a friend. It was better. It was like Christmas morning when you are four, or winning first prize in the egg and spoon race, or the quiet certainty of being loved.

Anthea gathered the baby back into her arms and turned away from the well. She scooped the bloodied towel from the floor, then changed her mind and limped over to the sink. With one hand, for the other was fully occupied with baby, she fished a clean tea-towel out of the drawer and began the dab to small face.

Presently it occurred to Anthea that one should bathe a newborn child. Still awkwardly, with one hand because she could not bring herself to put the baby down, she ran warm water into her red washing-up bowl. Then she dunked the baby in, splashing water gently over it, humming her favourite tune to it as she did so.

When it was clean she dried it carefully on another tea-towel. The baby, it seemed, had liked the water; at least it mewed again on finding itself suddeny ashore. Poor baby! Anthea held it close to her bare breast and the baby nuzzled at her, found the nipple, sucked for a second and then just snuggled up.

'I'll call you April, because you were born in April,' Anthea told the baby. 'All the time I've lived in this house I've been waiting for someone to arrive; it was you!'

She was delighted to discover this and even the baby, soundly sleeping after its long ordeal, pouted its lips in a muttersome way as though it approved of her, had been waiting for her, too.

Anthea sat down in front of the Raeburn, then realised how she must look—naked, bloodstained, with the baby in one arm.

'I really should have another bath,' she told the baby's sleeping and indifferent face. 'I don't like to put you down, but I suppose I must. I'll put you in our bed.'

The baby mewed again when she put it into the cold bed but it soon warmed up as she piled blankets on. It slept very nicely, she thought. It didn't have many eyelashes and it had an odd little button nose with white dots on the end, but otherwise it was definitely nice.

She put her face close to the baby's face and it was softer than silk and warmer than flower petals. She lifted one of its hands—such long-fingered hands, such tiny, teeny nails! It was still attached to the bag-thing, which seemed a pity. She remembered that she had heard somewhere that you should tie the cord in two places and snip between them. Or was that with puppies? But even if it was, it probably applied equally to human young.

So Anthea bathed, put on her nightdress and returned to the bedroom. She pulled back the covers but the baby did not like this at all and curled up its little legs and mewed protestingly.

'Come along, kitten,' Anthea said. 'You're right, it is jolly cold here, so we'll do your cord-thing in the kitchen. And I'll make us a cup of tea and a sandwich because it's been hard work and we're hungry.'

While she was dealing with the cord. Anthea noticed that the baby had a sack and a little pipe-thing between its legs. She rolled it over and stared. Then she smiled. Then giggled.

'You're a boy, April,' she informed the baby. 'I can't call a boy April!'

The baby did not like being uncurled and mewed again.

'Silly kitten,' Anthea said. 'You're a baby person, not a baby cat. You're a baby boy!'

The baby boy mewed again as Anthea cut the cord. If something goes wrong I'll run to the neighbours in my dressing gown, she decided, but inside her some calm, steady part of her was saying it was all right, the baby was fine, she had cut the cord beautifully.

'There! Wrap you up,' Anthea said, suiting action to words. 'Now, kit...hey, that *is* a boy's name! Right, from now on you are Kit Todd. Master Kit Todd.'

Master Kit Todd burped. Anthea picked up the blanket-wrapped bundle and carried it over to her favourite kitchen chair. Then she held a bit of bread soaked in milk near its mouth but the baby—Kit—did not seem interested. So Anthea lay him on the chair and went into the pantry and ate everything in sight. Then she made and drank tea and then she and the baby went off upstairs to the little bedroom with the floor wavy as the sea and the big double bed with its brass knobs shining and slept like logs until dawn broke.

CHAPTER SEVENTEEN

'Di, I wonder if you could spare a minute? I'm worried.'

Diane looked up enquiringly as Sam's usually smiling face appeared round her door.

'Sure. I'm only pricing stock,' she said. 'What's up?'

'It's Anthea. She's so good, always on time, usually early, in fact. But she hasn't shown up and she knew Martin was going to look at cars this afternoon. I can't understand it...was she all right on Friday?'

'No, she had a stomach ache,' Diane said, belatedly remembering. 'Oh lord, poor old thing, suppose it was food poisoning? She's not on the phone...I'll shut the shop and go over, or do you think we ought to phone the police?'

But Sam was reassuring.

'Anthea's sensible,' he said. 'I'll get Marj to run over to make sure she's all right, though. We aren't busy and I got Mollie to come in.'

'Thanks, Sam,' Diane said gratefully. 'I would like to get this new stock priced today.'

Back in the kitchen, Sam told the staff what Diane had said.

'So I thought I'd ask you to go over, Marj my dear, and see if she's all right,' he said. 'You can catch a bus and then get that taxi fellow to run you to the cottage; the wine bar will pay. Would you like to go as soon as you've finished those dinners?'

'I'll take her,' Martin volunteered. 'I've more or less made up my mind to buy that Ford Cortina I was telling you about but I've not taken it for a test-drive yet. The bloke in the garage won't mind if I run out to Cocklebank. Would that help, Marj?'

Sam watched apprehensively as Marj tossed her dark hair and looked challengingly at Martin. There had been a lot of tension between the two of them lately and it worried Sam. Oh, they were always sparring, insulting each other, but once there had been a warmth about it. Now it was as though Martin felt he had suffered enough, and he was becoming downright brusque with Marj. And of course the more Martin snapped the less easy-going Marj became, even spending a whole afternoon in tight-lipped silence because Martin had criticised her apple cake. It was not like either of them and it was beginning to worry Sam. Martin had been getting so reasonable, too, so thoroughly

426

pleasant to live and work with. Really, Sam thought now, if he's going back to being a swine again, thinking of nothing but his own pleasures and giving the rest of us hell, I can't stand it. I don't know that I should, either. Perhaps the more you let Martin get away with the more unbearable he becomes.

But now, Marj smiled and put her hands behind her to untie her apron.

'Thanks, Martin,' she said pleasantly. 'I'd like you to run me over to Cocklebank if you're sure the garage won't mind.'

Martin smiled too; the smile lit his plain, knobbly face and gave it a good deal of charm. Sam hoped Marj noticed. Poor Martin really needed something to put him back in Marj's good books, perhaps if they got on well this afternoon...

But Sam, beginning to make a ham salad, did not hold out much hope.

'Nice to see sunshine,' Marj said rather stiltedly as she and Martin walked along Lord Street. 'I always think April sunshine's special.'

'Yes, it's lovely,' Martin said. 'The garage is the one off Queen's Square. When we get there, let me do the talking.'

'Please yourself,' Marj said huffily, and could have bitten her tongue out. The trouble was

427

that she had behaved like a fool and was blaming Martin for it. She had told Eric it was over between them.

She still didn't know quite why she had done it, except that she truly felt their affair was over, stale and sad compared with the excitement of their first two years. Eric had said he was upset but she'd had the feeling that he had noticed the decline in their relationship as well as she.

And then she had seen him with a girl. A girl at least three years younger than Marj, with fair hair and expensive clothes and a soft laugh. She was a small girl too. Marj was used to being five foot eight but she had always secretly longed to be six inches shorter, to have men take care of her. And because of the small girl she had been horrid to Martin, blaming him for her dissatisfaction with Eric and thus for Eric turning to small girls for comfort.

Yet you don't want Eric, she reminded herself now, because without looking she knew Martin had turned away from her. If you don't want Eric, why snub Martin?

But she didn't know why she did things. She didn't want to be nasty to Martin, she wanted to be very nice indeed to him, but for some reason it just wasn't happening. Having kept Martin at arm's length for so long it seemed to have become an irreversible habit, a thing she would go on doing for the rest of her life unless something occurred to break the spell which bound her.

'Here we are,' Martin said quietly. 'Do you want to wait outside or come in?'

She wanted to go with him.

'I'll stay outside.'

'Please yourself,' Martin said, in bitter parody of her own words, and disappeared into the showroom.

'It's a nice car,' Marj said as the Ford Cortina roared out of Haisby by the coast road. 'Are you really going to buy it?'

Martin shrugged.

'I was. It'll mean a big bite out of my savings, though.'

'Yes, but you could get about a bit more, go to Norwich for an evening out,' Marj suggested. 'Eric and I used to go dancing, to the theatre, all sorts.'

'Used to?'

Marj felt her cheeks grow hot. She hadn't told anyone that she had moved out of Eric's place, nor that she suspected a blonde had moved in. She realised with some surprise, that it was simply not important to her. Even Eric's lovemaking, or lack of it, wasn't important. He had no imagination and was selfish with it,

Marj told herself. Besides, she had suspected him of two-timing her even before the little blonde, and hadn't cared enough to make an issue of it. What on earth was the matter with her? A year ago she would have given Eric his marching orders, raised the roof, probably wept for a week. Yet now she hadn't even bothered to tell Sandy and had certainly not told Martin.

Yet you blamed him? she asked herself incredulously. You blamed Martin because you lost Eric? No, it wasn't that. She blamed Martin, she supposed, for not knowing by some sort of instinct that the affair with Eric was over and that Marj was...well, free.

'Used to go dancing?' Martin said again. The thin, freckly hands gripping the wheel were white-knuckled suddenly. 'What do you mean?'

'That we don't any more,' Marj said. 'Not for ages, anyway.'

'Why not?'

Tell him, tell him, Marj's inner self urged. Tell him you're sick of Eric and you've moved out. But some imp of perversity refused to let it be that easy.

'Oh, no reason. Eric does shifts.'

'Yes, I forgot.'

They drove on. Marj looked around her. The countryside was beautiful even now, with more buds than bursting leaves, more bare plough than fields misting with crops, so what would it be like later, once the trees and grass really got going?

'Only a month to bluebells,' Martin said, when she voiced the thought. 'We ought to...' He stopped.

It was Marj's turn.

'We ought to what?'

'Have a staff outing,' Martin said shortly. 'A picnic or something. I'll talk to Sam.'

After that there was silence until they reached the cottage and then Martin drew the car into the lay-by beside the hedge and the two of them sat and stared at the small dwelling.

'Is it the one?' Martin said presently. 'If so, shouldn't you go and do your wonderful-Marj-come-to-save-you bit?'

'I'm not wonderful,' Marj said crossly, getting out of the car. 'But at least I care.'

She slammed the car door rather harder than she should have but Martin, getting out of the driver's side and also slamming the door, did not seem to notice. He came round the car and the two of them walked slowly up the garden path. There was a thread of smoke coming out of the chimney and Marj had the feeling that the house was occupied, yet no one answered her knock.

431

'Better go in,' Martin said. 'If she's ill...' he sounded concerned and for the first time for days and days, Marj realised, he had addressed her without note of rancour in his voice. Clutching this, she agreed that they should go in and opened the door, though slowly, as though she expected to find Anthea in a compromising position on the other side.

Instead, there was the tiny hall. She and Martin looked up the stairs but by mutual consent by-passed them and opened the only other door, walking into a long room with a few nice pieces of furniture scattered about and a piano against one wall. The fire was laid but not lit. Marj was about to turn round and leave the room again when Martin laid a hand on her shoulder.

'Listen.'

Someone, somewhere, was singing. It was less like singing, perhaps, than a drowsy and pleasant buzz, a bit like a bee's song and a bit like a cat's purr but most of all like someone humming a lullaby.

'It's coming from the next room,' Martin murmured. 'That door over there.'

Marj walked across the room, tapped on the door and opened it. Martin was at her shoulder and they both stared through the doorway.

The room was a kitchen, with beams and a

sloping low window. There was a smell of baking bread and the floor, which was of red quarry tiles, had rag rugs scattered across it. A round object like a table stood in the middle of the room with a basket of linen on it and in the easy chair by the open stove sat Anthea. Her blouse was open and she held a small, shawl-wrapped object in the crook of her arm. The object had a head of soft black hair and was clearly being breast-fed.

'Oh, Ant!'

Marj had not meant to sound shocked but that was how it came out. Anthea looked up, blinked, then smiled with genuine welcome.

'Marj, Mart, how nice of you to come over! Did you knock? I didn't hear but I couldn't have come to the door, not when he's feeding.'

'F-f-f-feeding?' Marj stammered. She felt totally at a loss, foolish beyond belief, even angry, to have been put in this position.

Martin, however, took it in his stride. He moved across the room and stood so that he was looking down into the baby's face. Anthea's breast was largely obscured by the child and by her blouse but to Marj's surprise she made no attempt to hide herself away from Martin but simply looked down again at the child's small face.

'He's a nice little chap,' Martin said. Easily,

433

as though finding Anthea breast-feeding a baby had come as no surprise to him. 'What do you call him, Ant?'

'He's Kitson Todd, but I call him Kit,' Anthea said. 'You can hold him later, if you like.'

'Is...is he *yours*?' Marj chipped in. It was, she realised a bloody silly question since it was as plain as the nose on the baby's face to whom he belonged.

'Yes, he's mine. He's very nice, really he is, though you can't see much of him right now.'

'How old is he?' Martin asked craftily. Anthea smiled up at him.

'Four days. He arrived on Friday, then there was Saturday and Sunday, today's Monday. That's four days,' Anthea said, removing the child from her breast with a pop like a cork being heaved from a bottle and lying him over her shoulder. She pushed her breast back into her bra without any false modesty and stood up. 'He likes me to walk up and down whilst I bring his wind up,' she explained. 'It's astonishing what a lot I've learned in the past few days. The doctor sent this nurse-woman in to talk to me, and she explained. Babies swallow air, though how they do it when they're drinking from you I can't imagine. I've got a book which helps too,' she added.

'You had him...gave birth to him, didn't

434

you, Ant?' Marj persisted. She knew it must be so, but her mind simply couldn't accept that such a thing could have happened and none of them any the wiser. 'Who's...who's...'

Martin gripped her arm; too tightly. She tried to jerk it free and found herself unable to do so.

'My dear Marj, Anthea has told you the baby's hers, and she's clearly doing a very nice job of bringing him up. I shall give him a little present for being born, I think.' Martin delved into his pocket and produced a ten-pound note. 'Buy lots of nappies,' he advised Anthea, grinning. 'That's for Kitson...but I'll be coming back in a day or so with something from all the staff, and that'll be for you as well.'

'Oh, but...Ant, Sam asked us to come, just to see if you were all right and...'

Once again, Martin's fingers bit into Marj's soft upper arm.

'She's fine. Do you know about grants and things, Ant, which you can get until a baby's several months old? Because you won't want to come back to work quite yet, will you?'

'When I come back, I'll bring him with me,' Anthea said. 'It was awfully kind of you to give Kit some money, I've got to buy some muslin nappies, I don't think the disposable sort agree with his little bottom, so I'll use the money for that. And of course I've got some money from the sale of the old vicarage in my bank account. But I won't let you down, Mart, I'll be back to work as soon as I can.'

'Is there anything we can do, Ant?' Marj said as Martin steered her back towards the door. 'I feel so guilty, I can't even give Kit any money, because I've only got about tenpence in my purse. But I'll bring him something nice next time I come over.'

'I've got a car, now,' Martin said over his shoulder. 'If you need a lift any time, Anthea, don't hesitate to give us a ring.'

Back in the car, the two of them sat very still, staring back at the cottage. Why isn't it me with that baby, Marj thought suddenly. I never even knew I wanted one, wanted to settle down, but now that I've seen what Anthea's got, oh, I'm envious.

'Better get back,' Martin was saying prosaically now. 'I didn't tell the chap from the garage that I was keeping the car for hours, I don't want him reporting it stolen or anything.'

'You shouldn't have told Ant you had bought it,' Marj said, 'You aren't going to, are you?'

'Yes I am. I've got a feeling I'm going to need a car.'

'Oh.' Marj said feebly. She was still in a state of shock over the baby and now Martin was being odd...he had been awfully good with Anthea, she realised now, much better than she. It had been she who stammered and stuttered and asked all the wrong questions and Martin who was calm and sensible and spared Anthea's feelings. What was wrong with the world? It had suddenly turned upside down!

When Martin put his arm around her it was as much of a shock as seeing Anthea with the baby had been. But a nice shock. Her mind told her firmly to pull away, to keep him at a distance, but unfortunately her body did not agree and cuddled into the curve of his arm in an annoyingly submissive fashion. You'll give him the wrong idea, her mind said coldly, but another part of her was stating defiantly that it was *not* the wrong idea, it was the right one, and furthermore it was an idea which her body had been keen to see implemented.

'These seats recline,' Martin said presently. He had done no more than cuddle Marj, reassuring her with his arms that she was all right, that her reaction to Anthea's baby had been a natural, if unfortunate, one.

'Do they?' Marj said.

'I'll show you.'

He managed to work the button without letting go of her and all of a sudden there they were, with lots of space to play around in, both flat on their backs.

But not for long, Martin scooped Marj up and started being very masterful and forceful and Marj, who was used to keeping Martin at bay and bossing him about and seeing him look sad and greedy and hopeful, clutched and kissed and murmured and enjoyed every minute of the foreplay which Martin apparently insisted on and which Eric, it seemed had never heard of.

Once, it crossed her mind that though this lay-by was overlooked only by the sea, with the hedge between it and Anthea's cottage both thick and high enough to hide the car, it was still no place to do what they were doing. Suppose...

She voiced the thought aloud and Martin, who had managed awfully neatly to get most of Marj's clothing off without her noticing, kissed her in a warm and wicked way until her protests blended into little cries and murmurs of desire which Martin clearly thought far more appropriate.

Presently, when Marj felt she had definitely reached the point of no return and was about to surrender herself completely to Martin's expert and arousing caresses, they stopped. Martin pulled himself away from her, sat up and caught her by the shoulders, looking deep

438

into her eyes.

'Marj? Is this what you want?'

'Yes,' Marj said baldly and urgently. 'Yes, yes, yes! Now!'

'Here and now?'

'Oh, *yes*,' Marj squeaked, reaching for him, trying to pull him close once more. 'Oh, oh, Mart!'

'But what about Eric?'

Marj stopped tugging at him and sat back. She let her eyelids droop and a slow smile spread across her face.

'Eric? Who's he?'

And Martin, with a triumphant cry, caught her tightly in his arms and covered her face with kisses.

Much later, they drove to a deserted bit of beach and walked and talked. Marj said she realised the father of Anthea's baby must have been that awful drug-pusher who had beaten Anthea up that summer night last year, and did Martin think it would spoil the relationship between mother and son when Anthea realised. Martin shook his head.

'No. I'm positive that to Anthea, the child is all hers. She conceived it, carried it, gave birth to it, nurtured it. She'll never think of that Bowles bloke as having anything to do with

Kit, and nor he has, if you think about it in the right sort of way.'

'You're probably right. You seem to know an awful lot about such things, Mart.'

She was looking at him as she spoke, wondering why she had ever thought him plain and gawky. He was strong, handsome, wonderfully good at lovemaking, generous, intelligent...

She saw the shadow cross his face, too.

'Yes. Learned the hard way, didn't I? My mum left, buggered off with some feller and left me and Dad to cope as best we could. What hurt was I knew she couldn't even have liked me, far less loved me, or she would have taken me with her. Aunts and that, Dad's pals, they thought I was a nuisance, held Dad back. Love's dead important, Marj. When I have kids each one of 'em will know he or she's the best-loved person in the world, I'll make sure of that.'

'So you're going to have a family, eh? Who's the lucky girl?'

'You are,' Martin said serenely. He turned his face, for she was within a couple of inches of his height, and kissed her temple, his mouth gentle. 'You can fight it if you must, Marj, just so long as we both know you'll give in, in the end.'

'Then there isn't much point in fighting,'

Marj murmured. Her heart was beating so loudly that she glanced down at her breast to see if it showed. How odd that she had despised Martin and been so keen to keep clear of him when she knew, now, that he was right for her, that she'd want him for always and not just for a couple of years. 'When shall we tell them?'

'Tonight; I want to get the wedding arranged quickly, so we can move into a place of our own. But we'll have the wedding first; not like most people.'

'And you'll stay with Sam?'

'For a while. It's taken me a long time to realise that Sam's good through and through, but I've done it at last. He was dead good to me when I was a kid, it was always me who pushed him back, but now I've accepted him I'm certainly not going to let him down.'

'Nor me,' Marj murmured. 'I wonder what Diane will say when we tell her about Ant and the baby?'

'She'll be surprised, of course, but she won't be thrown. You know that ugly bloke who's been taking her out?'

'Rory M'Quennell?'

'Is that his name? Well, I wouldn't be surprised if they make a go of it, and if they do Di won't stay in the Arcade, she'll go back to

London. Don't know what'll happen to Bonner's then.'

'Oh dear, more changes,' Marj said, but she was not really thinking about the boutique or the Arcade. Her mind was far too full of Martin.

Rory M'Quennell hunted slowly but thoroughly. His past might be littered with lovely girls—well, it was—but he knew he'd met the only person he'd ever want on a permanent basis. And of course it had to be a career girl with a place of her own and two old aunts dependent upon the income she brought in.

That Diane was giddily in love he had no doubt, that she would simply give in to his blandishments and let him whisk her off to his London flat he doubted very much. She had gone through a lot to get the boutique off the ground and now, with her second summer starting, she was able to see her own startling success. He had started by gently suggesting, had then stayed away for a week or two so that she would miss him not only physically but mentally too, had taken her off to Scotland for a weekend, plied her with everything she most enjoyed, and she still shook her beautiful stubborn head whenever he suggested that the time was ripe for her to move in with him.

He wanted a family; babies to brighten his mother's eyes, for so far none of her sons had married. He told Diane she would make a wonderful mother and Diane, nursing Kit when Anthea was busy, nodded and agreed that she too, would like a family one day and suggested that they might have a relationship where they slept together at weekends and parted during the week.

'What about New York?' he demanded. 'Last time I was there for a couple of months, next time it'll be for six, after that it might be two years. I don't want to leave you behind for that length of time.'

She was not afraid of London but seemed in some way to be afraid of permanence. She kept saying she loved him, proving it too, but then shying away from the marriage he had in mind. She was delighted that he did not want to live with her because he had lived with other women and this was different, but she still did not want to leave Haisby and the aunts and the boutique.

They had slept together, of course. It was not the easiest thing to arrange in a small place like Haisby and the aunts were so old-fashioned that it would probably hurt them deeply to know that sometimes on Sundays he and Diane had booked into a shabby little hotel along the coast and spent most of the day in bed. At first, Rory had thought he could persaude her to anything, in bed. She loved it so, was full of delight, approving of innovations, laughing at him and with him, splashing into the bath on top of him, sending waves of water onto the floor, laughing...they always seemed to be laughing.

But she would not agree to marriage. Her mind, which was so elastic in most ways, was firm as steel on this one point. Marriage was a commitment and commitments, it seemed, hurt. He knew she had had a boyfriend who had left her—or had she left him?—Rory had had heaps of girlfriends, some of whom had moved on before he was ready to let them go, and it hadn't affected him like this.

And then they went to Bath.

'Rory's got business down there,' Diane told the aunts. 'We're staying with friends of his, the Millers, at Apple Tree Cottage.'

They were indeed staying at Apple Tree Cottage, and it was certainly owned by the Millers, but the family were in America and had merely lent their home to Rory.

'You'll love it,' Rory told her as they drove down through the burgeoning summer lanes. 'It's the sort of place everyone dreams of owning. But the Millers are practical people, so it's been modernised most delightfully and is wonderfully easy to run.'

'Which is as well, since I'll be running it for the next couple of days,' Diane said drily. 'I hope I make as good a job of it as Anthea will make of Bonner's.'

Rory laughed; Diane admired Anthea's ability in the shop but was, he thought, just the tiniest bit jealous that she had also managed to cope with the baby, bringing the little boy in with her each morning, taking him home each night, and never letting her adored child interfere with the efficient and sensible way she coped with the business.

She was just the same in the wine bar, where Kit lay in his pram outside the kitchen door when Anthea considered the atmosphere in the room to be unhealthily warm, and inside when it was cooler. And Archie was, as he put it, quite made up by the little chap, finding him an old coral and bells to teethe on—not that Kit showed any signs of teeth yet—insisting that Anthea accept a solid silver pusher and spoon, an antique high chair, which he brought up to date at his own expense, and various miniature objects which he saw in the sales room and could not resist.

Rory, an amused observer, found himself

almost as fascinated as Diane was over the various goings-on in the Arcade. They were a nice friendly lot, but they did get into some complicated situations! Look at Marj and Martin, at each other's throats for the best part of a year and now suddenly billing and cooing, planning their June wedding, whilst Sam stared doubtfully from one to the other, plainly waiting for the bubble to burst.

The sun was sinking as Rory brought the car to a halt outside Apple Tree Cottage. He climbed out, found the key where Geoff Miller always hid it and unlocked the front door. He grinned at Diane and held the door wide.

'Welcome,' he said lightly, but he knew that his expression of loving lechery would be immediately interpreted correctly by his love. A whole weekend!

Diane had almost longed for this weekend, but now that it had actually arrived, now that they were inside the cottage, she found that she was feeling quite nervous. She and Ron had made love in hotel rooms on Sunday afternoon, they had had that weekend in Scotland in a huge hotel, masquerading as Mr and Mrs Hopgood since the M'Quennell name was a bit too well known in the area he had chosen. There had been other occasions of course; crammed un-

446

comfortably into the back seat of the car, down on the sands, between the dunes, in a hayfield...but, delightful though it had been, they had always been that bit on edge, aware of the risks, never quite alone.

But now...a real bed, Diane saw, not a hotel bed. The room had a sloping ceiling, an old-fashioned wash stand and the huge old bed, invitingly spread with fresh white sheets. The carpet was thick and soft, there was a door leading off to an en suite bathroom, but even so it was patently a room full of loving use, not a transitory hotel one.

Downstairs there was a model kitchen with—bless the Millers—a note inviting them to help themselves to anything in fridge or freezer. The living room was a dream out of a shiny magazine and through the french windows they could see a wonderful garden complete with lily pond.

Diane cheated at suppertime and cooked two pre-frozen meals but Rory was on his best behaviour and congratulated her on her house-keeping. They drank apple wine with their meal, and then had cocoa and biscuits before going to bed.

Bed was wonderful. The best, Diane sighed when they finally decided to go to sleep. Tomorrow Rory would have to attend a meeting in Bath, his reason for borrowing the cottage at all, but Diane planned to get up and potter round, making a light lunch for them both. In the afternoon they would go for a long country walk before driving into Bath for dinner.

A totally relaxing country weekend, Diane thought luxuriously. And Rory had said he wouldn't nag her about getting married. He might think about it—she was sure he did—but he would not keep on. Not this weekend.

Even Monster had been left behind. Diane was quite fond of Monster now but objected to his presence when delicious intimacies were planned, so Rory had left the dog in Norfolk.

No cold nose poking into bed in the morning, Diane reminded herself drowsily just before she fell asleep. Oh, this is the life!

The best-laid plans of mice and men usually go awry but Diane found herself next morning getting up to wave Rory off and then pottering in her hostess's exquisite kitchen. Rory had refused breakfast but gulped orange juice and gobbled a slice of buttered toast. Now Diane, who never normally ate breakfast, poured juice for herself, cooked one solitary brown egg, buttered bread, made coffee and carried her meal into the living room.

As she finished the egg and reached for her coffee cup, Diane took a newspaper off the low table. It was weeks old and must have been saved for the picture on page one, which showed the village through which they had driven the previous evening. It was a 'good' paper, not light entertainment, with text taking preference over photographs. Diane, who rarely had time to read a newspaper and did not care for television when shared with the aunts' guests, turned to the inner pages. Goodness, it just showed how out of touch she was becoming, there had been one of those awful disasters, one of the Irish ferries had hit another in a storm a few weeks back. Her eyes roving incuriously over the recriminations, survivors' stories, Diane remembered the storm. She had watched a seagull struggling to remain on the roof-ridge...she had pitied anyone out on such a night...reading on she saw a list of the dead.

Her eyes went to the name at once, but it was a coincidence, of course. Anthony Terence Cusack, father of five, the youngest only a few months old, left a widow, Shelagh...

Diane's eyes closed of their own volition. An icy numbness swept through her, with shock, hovering batlike. It could not be Tony, he could not have died like that, not Tony, so vital so full of life! One moment warm and safe on the ship, the next struggling in black water, trying to swim, choking as the detritus of collision bounced around him, forcing his winter-clad body lower in the waves. Then the relentless tug of the deeps, sucking him down whilst he fought to stay on the surface, then fought to get back to the surface, knocked and battered by the sea until there was no more hope, no memory to sweeten the struggle with promises of safety. The water had invaded his lungs, the heart's steady tick would falter and stop, snatching the coloured world which he had so loved from his grasp, tossing his patient little wife, his beloved children, into the unsure hands of others. His last thoughts would have been of them, torn from him.

It was useless to deny the truth of what she had read. She knew now that he had died, could even remember, vaguely, the nightmares of that wild night six, eight weeks ago.

Diane opened her eyes and picked up the newspaper again. Her body cringed deeper into the soft sofa cushions, tears filled her eyes and welled over, drowning her cheeks, but she read on. There had been heroism that night and she knew Tony would have done his best before the darkness took him, knew that Shelagh and the children would be brave too, because Tony would never have loved a cowardly little fool, though it had pleased her, once, to tell herself that this was so.

Oh, Tony, Fear no more the heat o' the sun, Nor the furious winter's rages! I loved you true, Tony, in my fashion...I'd have given anything to have spared you that.

Snatches of songs, poems, chased each other through her head; a litany to death. He will not grow old as those who are left grow old ...to throw away the dearest thing he owned as 'twere a careless trifle...the minstrel boy to the war had gone, in the ranks of death you'll find him...when he died little children cried in the streets...

The tears dried at last, the sobs turned to hiccups. Diane got up off the sofa, she felt strangely peaceful, as though she had been forgiven for some long-ago sin and had wept for her part in it. She went upstairs to the bathroom and ran a bath; she got into the water and lay back.

Tony was dead and she mourned him, perhaps she would always mourn him, because he had been her first love. It had been Tony who had taken her young, untried body and taught it that love is a beautiful thing. But she could not mourn him as his wife could because, she, Diane, no longer loved him, had in truth loved him as her first lover, not as the one man in her life.

My life with Tony was over months ago, she reminded herself. It's right to cry for him but not for what you had together, because you ended it for the right reasons, not the wrong ones. Choosing is what matters and it's Shelagh I must feel sorry for now. She's lost a lovely feller in Tony, and now she must turn round and learn to live without him not from choice but from necessity.

She thought about Rory. God, she was lucky! He was the best thing that had happened to her, and he was mortal! Just suppose it had been he aboard that ferry? Suppose the airliner taking him to New York in a few months' time crashed? Suppose she lost Rory, she who had never really had him? Oh, she'd been to bed with him, they were lovers, but she had no true claim any more than she had had with Tony. No one had told her Tony was dead because their relationship had been first clandestine and was now over.

So, if Rory dies, you're content not to know until you read it in the paper are you? her mind asked her. Just to keep your independence, to prevent yourself from ever again knowing the pain of a broken relationship, you're prepared to keep Rory dangling to stay in Haisby whilst he goes off all over the world without you? You're prepared, in short, to lose him. To see another woman grieving when…if…

'We'll get married!' Diane said it aloud, sitting bolt upright in the cooling water suddenly seeing her own stupidity, her cowardice. To deny happiness in case of pain was both stupid and cowardly and she had always thought of herself as intelligent and brave. She would marry Rory just as soon as she could and after that they would start a family. Hostages to fortune all round. Diane thought defiantly, pulling the plug with her toes and scrambling out of the water. Life is meant to be lived, not agonised over.

Wrapped in the towel, she made her way into the bedroom and plucked her pink cotton dress and a pair of sandals out of her case, then returned to the bathroom to dress in the warm, steamy air. She had got the dress on, and one sandal, when she heard Rory's car draw up outside. She abandoned everything and flew down the stairs, dot and carry one, getting the door open before he was right out of the car.

'Rory! Did you have a good meeting? Let's get married,' she gabbled. 'Oh, I haven't cooked lunch yet, are you early or what?'

Rory crossed the gravel in a couple of strides, lifted her off her feet and kissed her cheeks, the tip of her nose and then, luxuriously, her mouth. When the kiss was over he stood her

453

down on the hall parquet and smiled at her.

'What a welcome! What brought this sudden urge to marry on, when you've been pretty cool about the idea before?'

Diane's mouth was opening to tell him, to pour it all out, when commonsense prevailed. She was doing the right thing for the right reason, but it was scarcely a reason which Rory could appreciate.

'I missed you,' she said simply, resting her cheek on his chest. 'Oh Rory, I did miss you!'

Rory turned her in his arms and guided her over to the foot of the stairs.

'You are my very darling girl,' he said. 'Yes, let's get married, and I'll take you to lunch at the Christopher to celebrate. When you've put some knickers on, of course!'

CHAPTER EIGHTEEN

'What a fabulous summer this has been,' Anthea said, as she and Mollie strolled along the beach, with Kit snoozing in a sling across his mother's breast. 'I never guessed when I took the job as relief in the boutique that I'd end up as full-time manageress there! Thank heaven Sam volunteered to do the books though. I'd never have managed that in a million years.'

'I never thought I'd end up sharing a house with you, out here in Cocklebank, or working in Bonner's three days a week,' Mollie said, smiling at her friend. 'Two weddings in as many months, an' all—they'll be calling the Arcade the Marriage Mart at this rate!'

'Which wedding did you like best?' Anthea asked. 'Di's was fabulous, of course, with the party in the grounds of Marlowes Hall, but somehow I liked Marj and Mart's best, they were so happy.'

'And they're staying in Haisby, not going off like Di and Rory,' Mollie said. 'How did the aunts take it when Di told them you'd take over the boutique whilst she went back to London?'

'Very well. I think they'd always expected it so they weren't really surprised, and they were over the moon that she was marrying Rory. Aunt Dulcie spent ages trying to work out her relationship to Mrs M'Quennell and hardly worried at all about the boutique. Though Di's still doing the buying, which is an enormous help.'

'Does Di mind? Doing the buying, I mean.'

'Not her, she said it suited her very well.

She's working part-time in Barkworths although she doesn't need to, because Rory's awfully rich.'

'Lucky old Di,' Mollie said, without any sign of jealousy, however. 'Do you think we ought to turn back, Ant? It's long past Kit's bedtime.'

'He doesn't have a bedtime, not unless I want him to,' Anthea said dreamily. She gazed out across the marshes, misty lavender, green, brown, towards the blue line of the sea on the horizon. 'Still, perhaps you're right, he'll need feeding and changing soon, won't you, poppet?'

'Poppet' worked his mouth and clenched and unclenched his small fists but gave no other sign that he had heard. Mollie laughed.

'I'm surprised he isn't fat, the way you spoil him! Ant, you know when you were in Sam's this morning?'

Anthea did two morning's cooking at Sam's Place in return for Sam doing the Bonner books. It worked well, but Anthea did wonder how they would manage at Christmas, when everyone was far too busy to keep books up to date during the daytime.

'Yes? What happened? Did someone else try to buy Mona's dress?'

Both girls laughed. It was a familiar dilemma

that as soon as a Mona dress appeared in the Bonner window someone would try to buy it. Diane had decreed that the special dresses would go to London after a month, where they fetched what she called embarrassingly large sums, the money split equally between Miss Turner, who had made them up, and Mona's daughter.

'No, it wasn't that,' Mollie said now. 'It's Lana and Barry's shop. The lease has been sold, guess who's coming in?'

'Jeweller? Travel agent? Card shop?'

'Wrong, wrong, wrong. That's hand-made chocolates! Mr Bender told me this afternoon after the lease had been signed by the new people. They're a family business, the mum makes the chocs in a confectionery kitchen about ten miles outside the town and the young people sell 'em. What do you think?'

Anthea stopped to consider and Kit woke and gave a hungry mumble. Immediately Anthea unslung him and cuddled him, kissing the petal-soft cheek, pushing her face into his neck so that he gurgled and dribbled, his face lit up from within by perfect happiness.

'Think? It's marvellous news,' she said. 'It'll do the Arcade a power of good. Wait till I tell Sam!'

'Everyone will be pleased,' Mollie said. 'It's

457

always the same, every new trader brings different folk down the Arcade, and each person who discover us tells someone else. Why, by Christmas they'll be queueing up for our clothes, and the new chocolates...'

'And Archie's antiques, and Elias's books...'

'And Waves' haircuts and Miss Turner's dressmaking...'

Giggling, the two girls made their way back to Cuttens Cottage where they both began their own evening tasks. Anthea unbuttoned and glued the eager Kit to her breast and Mollie put the kettle on and started to cut bread for the sandwiches she and Anthea ate each night before bed.

Presently, with the baby fed and the sandwiches ready, Anthea began bathing and nightgowning the small, milky Kit, occasionally taking a bite of her sandwich as she did so.

'Marriage is a wonderful institution,' she observed. 'Martin's really different, he's nice to us all, as if he liked each and every one of us very much. Marj always was nice but she's got softer, somehow, and she has such a tender look in her eyes when they rest on Martin...it's lovely to see them together.'

'I hope I find someone, some day,' Mollie said wistfully. 'Did you know I went out with

Marj's Eric a few times? But he wasn't right for me.'

'I once said to Di that there was someone special in the world for everyone,' Anthea observed. 'It's true, too. There'll be someone in the world for you, Moll. You just have to wait and he'll appear and whisk you away from me.'

'Sometimes I wouldn't mind, but then again I reckon I'm pretty dam' lucky just livin' here with you and Kit and bein' happy in my work,' Mollie said. 'Still, I'd like to get hitched one day.' She stood up, stretching and yawning. 'I'm off now. Want me to take your drink up?'

'Please.'

Mollie went ahead up the stairs, Anthea close behind with Kit dozing already. At their bedroom doors they parted, Anthea to lay Kit gently in his cot and start getting ready for bed.

As she undressed and put on her nightie, Anthea remembered the stab of envy she had felt the day she had told Diane that there was someone in the world for everyone. Now, she looked at Kit's pink fist curled up on the pillow, at the soft down of his hair. Someone for everyone. Someone, even for Anthea Todd, spinster of this parish. Mollie would marry and go, everyone would move on, change, find love, happiness, a partner. Yet she, Anthea, would never be alone again.

Just the two of us, she thought, looking down at Kit as he slumbered. Always the two of us. Once a part of me, now wonderfully separate, yet still a part. In her mind she watched him down the years, saw him toddle, walk, run. He would go to school, bring home his friends, meet a girl. One day, he would fall in love.

With my body, I thee worship. With all my wordly goods I thee endow.

There were other loves than the sort Di and Marj had found, perhaps there were greater loves. Anthea knew she never could, never would, love a man. But the baby in the cot would be a man one day, and she would love him until she died.

All this talk of love, she thought, climbing into bed. So love came full circle, in the end. Through Kit she would know love, and when in his turn he met the right girl, when they had babies, then Anthea would love them...all of them.

She was on the very edge of sleep now, thoughts comfortably blurring, body warm, mind gently rocking. Dear God, thank you for Kit, and my home, and my job. Dear God, I don't deserve such happiness, such riches. God bless Mollie and Sam...God bless Mummy and Daddy...

And Anthea Todd slept in her big old bed, as Kit slept in his cot.